A Deadly Game

28 November

For Camille —

This doesn't exist without you. Which is why it's impossible to thank you enough

Gary

A DEADLY GAME

Gary M. Lepper

 · 2016

Copyright © 2016 by Gary M. Lepper.
All rights reserved.

No part of this book may be reproduced or used
in any form or by any means without prior written
permission of the author, excepting brief quotes
used in connection with reviews.

This is a work of fiction—the characters, locations,
and actions described herein are imaginary and any resemblance
to actual people (living or dead), places (e.g., whatever may
be the executive offices of the San Francisco Giants),
and events is purely coincidental.

Cover design: Dave Johnson
Printed in the United States of America.
First printed November 2016.

ISBN: 978-0-578-18699-3

PHOSPHENES
Walnut Creek, California

www.garymlepper.com

Library of Congress Cataloging-in-Publication Data
has been applied for.

1 2 3 4 5

For my granddad, David A. Kenmuir,
the only hero in my life

Chapter 1

Early autumn, City of Denver

HE FLINCHED WHEN A SUDDEN AND JAGGED burst of light flashed in front of him. Then he counted—one, one thousand ... two, one thousand ... three, one thousand ... four, one thousand—before a deep boom overtook the light. Symbolic, he thought. The thunder's getting closer and so am I.

He looked at his reflection in the huge 12th-floor window of his office. The classic embodiment of a leader, he thought: 43 years old, suit custom-tailored to his lean six feet, clean shaven, dark hair trimmed above his ears (rock 'n' roll bands be damned). What he considered his best feature wasn't visible: a slight limp that he'd explain, with modest reluctance, as the result of a wound in his left thigh, where he'd been bayoneted during hand-to-hand combat with a Vietcong soldier. Not quite true, but close enough: during the war, yes, but the result of slipping in muck during a monsoon and being impaled on a tent peg.

When he returned from Vietnam, he became executive vice-president of his father's computer hardware business. Five years later, a cerebral aneurysm soundlessly killed his sleeping father and transformed the business into *his* business.

He'd always known he had the decisive, shrewd, and prescient intellect of a leader. Unfortunately, those same characteristics had been resented all his life—which was why he'd been thwarted in running for student offices in high school and college, as his classmates always had chosen others' popularity over his competence, and why his Army career had stalled, as his intimidated contemporaries and even commanders had deprived him of deserved opportunities and promotions. Now, finally, he was in command.

. .

AS EXPECTED, THE BUSINESS THRIVED under his leadership. Until about three years ago, when it started to decline. Granted, it'd been undramatic: a piece here, a piece there, but slow and steady, like hunks of soil eroding off a riverbank. He'd been stunned and puzzled—until he realized that he was the victim, not the cause.

Two destructive influences, both totally out of his control and not at all his fault, had converged on him. First were the slob Californians: unshaven, dressing in rumpled sport shirts and Levis as if they worked on a loading dock or a construction site, and having no sense of propriety. Second were the insufferable Asians: America had spent millions to develop new technologies, only to give them away so gook countries could exploit *American* markets, for god's sake. No home-grown business like his could compete with their cheap labor and government subsidies.

Looking back on it, he wished he'd surrendered to one of the attempts to take over his business. One major battle and one crisis, and it would've been over. Instead, he'd beaten them back. Ironically, it'd all been a waste of time and so damn much money, since the modernized plant—humming with new equipment and systems that now manufactured products faster and cheaper than ever—still wasn't rapid enough to keep pace with what seemed to be weekly technological changes or cheap enough to yield sufficient profits. Consequently, his business was enduring the commercial equivalent of death by a thousand cuts: a product here, a service here, a customer there. Worse, the handwriting on the company wall was spelling his own name as well; if it went down, so would he.

About two years ago, he'd begun agonizing over how to rescue himself. His first impulse had been a high-risk, large-dividend investment of some kind, but he'd backed off when his research revealed that such an investment, by its very nature, also implied a high risk of failure. He'd imagined a lucrative drug sale—but he had no notion how to acquire any drugs, let alone in sufficient volume. Plus, drug trafficking was just plain dangerous.

As one idea after another succumbed to some insurmountable flaw, his desperation began to deteriorate into panic. Then, a little over a year ago, "The Plan" revealed itself. It was magical: one moment there was no solution, and the next moment there it was, vivid and brilliant.

He examined and refined it so it conformed to sound business principles. It had no flaws; it couldn't fail. By next October, a little less than a year away, he'd be free to do whatever he wanted. Screw the hippies and the gooks and his whiney employees.

He turned away from the storm raging outside the panoramic window and went to what had been his father's desk. He moved aside the plastic holder that protected a baseball signed by Stan "the Man" Musial, his favorite player, and reached for the cell phone whose number was known to only one person. He called that person.

When his call was answered, he said, "Hello, how are you?" He regarded a polite greeting as proper behavior for a patrician such as himself. He would've said "Good morning" but, for all he knew, maybe it was afternoon or evening where he was calling.

The man who'd identified himself only as "Mr. Jones" replied merely, "Good." He was boorish and plebian.

The businessman said, "Let's do it. It's a go."

Mr. Jones asked, "Anything changed?"

"No. It's just as I told you before. However, I can't emphasize enough how critical the timing is."

"Yeah, you can. How about you? You remember that the total payment's due by mid-December?

"Yes, I do. It'll be there. Other than that, do you need anything further from me?"

"Nope. That'll do it."

"How will I know when you've started?"

"Buy a newspaper."

Mr. Jones (whose true name was Emilio Colonna) hung up with no farewell and immediately dialed another number. When that call was answered, he said, "I just spoke with the customer who wants multiple purchases. He's ready to go."

"Glad to hear it. He understands that he pays up front?"

"He does and he will."

"Excellent. How many?"

"He's not sure. Two after the turn of the year, and he'll let me know about the others."

"Good. Can you set up the first two, or do you need me to become involved?"

"No, I'll do it. Besides, I've already made some preliminary arrangements for the first one." Colonna delayed half a second and then wondered, "You sure you want to go ahead with this? Not too late to back out. Tell this customer to go fuck himself."

"No. Won't be doing that. Much, much too profitable. And it's the very type of service that we went into business for." He paused, but when Colonna said nothing, he continued. "You're still not on board with this, are you?"

Colonna considered just saying he was and being done with it. Instead, he said, "Not really. There's a reason why these people are avoided. Which makes sense, because there's an inexhaustible supply of others who carry no heat and never get noticed beyond the back pages."

The man on the other end wanted to lighten the conversation. He'd been over this topic many times, too many times, and had no desire to do so again. "Mixing your metaphors. Heat. Pages." He forced a chuckle.

Colonna wasn't amused or placated. "Fuck meta-whatever. Say it however you fucking want, but it comes out the same. A lot of risk."

"And a lot of reward. Because the ordinary, routine service is already being provided by others. Which is why ours will have—already has, let me remind you—such a valuable market. Yes, it's riskier, but we'll minimize that by not over-selling. And, like I just said, the money's extremely good."

"I know, but . . . "

The man interrupted. "Listen to me, Poison"—Colonna's nickname was the result not only of being deadly, but also of having a face that, when he crossed his arms close to his chin, looked like the label on a bottle of rat killer—"You know I value you. If I didn't, I wouldn't have chosen you in the first place. But I have no intention of going over this again. If you're not in then, frankly, you're out. What's it going to be?"

For Colonna, the two warning signals might have been airhorn blasts. First was the use of his nickname. The man was religious about security and never, but never, said anything that might reveal anything personal or specific. That he just did meant that his short fuse was burning too close. Second was the tacit reminder that they weren't equals. For him to be allowed to state his opinion was one thing—hell, he was often *asked* his opinion—but pushing it was quite another. Besides, he was very mindful that he could become another "purchase," any time the man wanted. No, this was a time to shut up and backtrack: "Hey, I'm just sayin'. What the hell, I understand who makes the final decisions. And you know I'm with you. Always have been."

The man on the end of the line was satisfied. In truth, he hadn't *not* been. However, it never hurt to occasionally remind even the most loyal subordinate who was in charge of whom. "I know. Change of topic . . . I read where that bad boy young actor Nate Randall got the bejesus kicked out of him in some after-hours bar brawl."

On the other end of the line, Poison's smile was toxic. "I read the same thing. Hard to say what really happened, though. There being no witnesses."

"The producer whose trophy wife young Nate was schtupping must be pleased."

"Tickled fuckin' pink."

"And the wayward wife herself?"

"Quite a scandal. Found naked, unconscious and wrapped only in a sheet on the lawn of their children's school. She should be a model of loyalty hereafter."

The man said, "See? The Beatles were wrong. Money *can* buy you love."

Poison sneered at the phone and thought, Beatles? What the fuck?

The man asked, "We square now?"

Colonna took a deep breath, exhaled in a form of relief and said, "Oh, yeah. Always were, far as I'm concerned." Then he added, "When the customer pays, we go."

Chapter 2

Late February, City of Phoenix

BRENT BRITTAIN, THE SEATTLE MARINERS' vacuum-cleaner first baseman and the previous season's American League batting champion, awoke at 6:00 a.m., as always, whether at home or in this rented condominium near the Mariners' spring training camp. These few weeks of desert solitude were cleansing him emotionally; they'd be the last time he'd be alone, undistracted and unwatched, for the next six months.

He put on cut-off sweat shorts and a Washington State T-shirt with a faded, snarling cougar. His lower legs and forearms were finally losing the angry red of fresh sunburn, while his torso and upper arms remained as white as powdered sugar. Standing on the rear patio, with his hands on his hips, he began twisting from side to side.

He could see two early-bird golfers on the fourth tee. Probably "snowbird" fugitives from the salted roads and single-digit temperatures up north. Possibly one would be a nonbeliever who'd later rummage for an errant golf ball beyond a "Beware of Rattlesnakes" sign and learn that a golf sock is a target for an irritated rattler, not a barrier.

Now stretched and limber, Brittain went inside. He laced worn Army combat boots over heavy socks, pulled scarred leather chaps over his shorts, and zipped up an abused leather jacket. In the garage, his Honda CR500 dirt bike responded to its kick-starter and began rumbling like a discontented leopard. It vibrated impatiently, as if it knew only a few rides remained before spring training began.

Brittain drove up Pima Road and casually waved at a police car at the corner of Bell Road and then to another by Dynamite Boulevard. The officers knew when the famous rider and the bike with the Mariners' trident *M* painted on both sides of the gas tank would be coming. It was like spitting sunflower seeds in the dugout: Brittain didn't stray from his habits, ever.

He turned off the paved road at the usual place, paused to tighten the strap on his helmet, and lowered the heavily pitted Plexiglas visor. Like a dog circling to find the ideal spot before lying down, he squirmed on the seat until he was perfectly comfortable. He revved the powerful engine in neutral and then snapped it into gear, launching himself into the desert.

What appeared to be desert trails were only narrow vestiges of animal wanderings. As their routes had adjusted to slight shifts in the sandy terrain, so did Brittain's. Hunched over, he leaned to the side to preserve as much speed as possible around each sharp uphill turn. Pebbles and desert debris ricocheted off his jacket and chaps; it was like driving through buckshot.

He stopped, as always, near the top of Pinnacle Peak. He idled the bike next to a huge saguaro cactus, his favorite, that had a bulky arm extending out from each side; if cacti had a baseball team, he imagined this would be its power hitter. Phoenix was clearly spread out before him on this morning.

A Deadly Game

Behind him, the mountain was proud and silent. Great day for a ballgame, he thought.

He moved the bike gently forward. As soon as he tilted it downward, he gunned it—and began his wild return to the highway four miles below. The downhill ride was fun and fast, with exciting hairpin turns. Cut them, swing them wide, accelerate or decelerate, take them cleanly or in a skid. One of his favorite turns, shaped like a paper clip, loomed ahead. He loved careening into the curve as fast as possible, feeling the rear wheel fishtail in the loose dirt before braking at the last second to stabilize, a marriage of speed and balance.

As usual, he braked and leaned into the sharp curve as soon as the wheel began to fishtail. Nothing happened. He didn't panic, but merely released the brake lever and then squeezed it more firmly. Again nothing. His third squeeze was as tight as possible, but the wheels still didn't react. But *he* did, since he realized that, at this extraordinary speed, he wouldn't be able to hold the bike through the sharp downward turn that was essential in the radical curve at the top of the paper clip. He'd have to lay down the bike. But where?

In that same nanosecond, the bike preempted his decision. It catapulted off the path and aimed itself directly at a rock outcropping. When it struck the huge rocks, it pinwheeled into the air and ejected Brittain on the first flip. Both, equally twisted and broken, would be discovered in the boulder-strewn ravine during the search later that afternoon.

Baseball mourned the death of one of its youngest and most talented stars, and commentators remarked on the propensity of young athletes for high speeds and risky adventures. Parents extracted oaths from their children never to ride motorcycles. Cynics said he got what he asked for.

Because Brittain's death was so easy to explain, no one questioned whether the dirt bike's brake fluid was among the other fluids that had vanished into the thirsty sand.

Later the same week, City of Tulsa

THE WINTER ACHILLES SIMON THOUGHT would never end was almost over. He'd fly to Florida in a few days and report to the Chicago White Sox spring training camp. Sportswriters were already touting him as a preseason favorite for Rookie of the Year. Jimbo Barber, so long a fixture in center field, would have to find a comfortable place on the bench.

Simon guarded his knees like a surgeon protects his fingers. A damaged knee would make the thrust of his first step tentative and weak, and his speed would vanish along with his nickname, Blaze. Worried about the concussive force of each stride even on relatively smooth asphalt, he only ran on grass or dirt, despite his conditioning coach warning him to worry more about twisting or breaking an ankle on such notoriously uneven surfaces. "Thousands of people run on paved jogging paths. Wanna guess how many end up sprawled on the ground with a broken knee? A total of none. That's how many."

Simon listened dutifully but didn't change. Besides, his destiny didn't have asphalt: either it had grass in centerfield, the glory position, the fabled home of Mantle and Mays, which he covered in a blur, or it had dirt on the base paths, where he stole bases like a runaway burglar. He'd tried running on the dirt track at the local high school, but it'd been incredibly boring and made him feel as if he were listing to the left, like a boat taking on water. So he ran in the large park near his apartment.

When he reached the hilly portion of the park, he turned onto one of his favorite routes, an isolated dirt trail that meandered through the trees, where he could be alone with his dreams and the rhythm of his muscles. As the slope became steeper, he bent his head slightly downward and tilted his shoulders forward. His jog then became a sprint and the sprint a sort of reverie. To anyone watching, he was merely a man running up a hill. But in his imagination, thousands of shouting fans were standing to watch him nip the inside corner of third base and race toward home, again to score the winning run in the bottom of the ninth.

Nearly at the top of the hill, he noticed a large tree limb had fallen across the trail. It was an inconsequential obstacle that he could pass over with the ease of an Olympic hurdler. The Asics Alliance on his left foot thrust forward, ready to land securely on the other side of the limb, with the right to follow an instant later.

However, his left leg was able to complete only half of its stride because his left foot snagged a nearly invisible strand of wire stretched four inches above the surface of the trail. He became like a toddler whose body had tilted too far ahead for his legs to keep pace.

As he fell forward, his hands and arms instantly snapped out to break his fall. They supported him in an impromptu push-up, so that only his palms, the outside edge of his right knee, and the tips of his shoes contacted the dirt surface. The moment his hands and arms accommodated his weight, he'd draw his knees into a squat, poised to spring back into a standing position almost before his brain registered that he'd even touched the ground.

He wasn't given a chance to spring anywhere—because two men had burst from their hiding places in the bushes on opposite sides of the trail as soon as he'd started to fall. And, just as his hands and arms were accommodating his weight, the heavier man fell across his back and collapsed his chest onto the dirt. The smaller man simultaneously grabbed his right foot and twisted it sharply, exposing the outside of his ankle.

Reacting instinctively into a sort of reverse bench press, Simon began to lift the more than two hundred pounds draped across his back. It should've been easy, but it wasn't—because he couldn't get any leverage on the ground with his right foot which, for some reason, was twisted and immovable.

As the heavier man felt Simon pushing him slowly but inexorably upward, he looked sideways at the smaller man. His expression spoke for him: *What're you fucking doing back there?* The smaller man answered by slamming a mallet against Blaze's ankle. The bone shattered only a couple seconds before a second blow pulverized it.

Simon screamed and groped for the searing pain in his devastated ankle. He couldn't reach it because he was now flattened by the weight pressing on his back. A coarse voice, thick with the smell of old cigarettes, said, "Fuck you, nigger. This park's for whites only," as the smaller man cut the wire from the tree on the other side of the trail. The two assailants then disappeared into the forested shadows.

Many editorials reviled such racial prejudice. Others reminded readers that the legacy of Robinson and Doby was not yet fulfilled. Angry and embittered, Blaze watched the baseball season go on without him.

Chapter 3

Wednesday evening, April 17, City of Walnut Creek

D<small>AVID</small> K<small>ENMUIR</small> <small>PLAYED</small> <small>FOR</small> <small>THE</small> "Enchantment Lingerie" team in the men's over-thirty softball league, a safe haven for aging athletes who might not yet be over the hill, but certainly were peering over the top. The league let them pretend they still could do what they used to do without a bunch of twenty-somethings showing them that they really couldn't.

The incongruous team name was due to the willingness of a player's wife to have her business pay for the uniforms (thankfully without pastel colors or lace trim) and equipment in exchange for naming rights. Over time, the name had redeemed itself through abundant notoriety and much humor.

Kenmuir, the second baseman, instantly realized that the groundball coming at him was nothing but trouble. A fast skimmer zipping over the dirt infield like a hovercraft was bad enough, but it also was to his right. Unless he could flip it to the shortstop to force out the runner from first for the last out, the runner on third would score easily and end the tie. As he pivoted and lunged for the speeding ball, he felt as if he were moving in slow motion.

He twisted his left hand into a backhand position and extended his arm toward the ball. Almost there. He needed only another inch, maybe less. But the sharp pain in the back of his left shoulder told him the shrapnel scar tissue had refused to stretch further. Worse, he couldn't move his glove any lower. Still as if in slow motion, he watched the ball roll under his glove and taunt him by grazing the webbing as it passed by. He didn't see the runner on third score what ultimately was the winning run.

An early evening game like this one always was followed by dinner at the spacious Leaning Tower of Pizza, with its separate room for arcade games, a beer-wine bar as long as a bowling lane, and indestructible wooden furniture. It was ideal for the families of Enchanted's roster of friends that had changed very little over the years. Kenmuir, his best friend John Trauber, and several others were lawyers; the rest were CPAs and business executives. They'd played together for so long that even their wives and children knew each other well; most also had known Mary Kenmuir before the divorce.

Kenmuir parked his navy-blue Audi 5000 in the restaurant parking lot, but delayed going inside. Sure, ground-ball base hits were common and most didn't matter. But this one did—and he considered himself responsible for it and thus for the loss as well. He was supposed to make the difference, to never again fail the group. *That's* why it mattered to him, "only a game" or not.

He closed the car door and thought, fucking crybaby, snap out of it. He loved these gatherings. The loud and familiar company was a substitute for the family he didn't have. Father to none, but unofficially "Uncle Dave" to many. Would it ever be otherwise? Not likely.

A Deadly Game

He barely got inside before John Trauber was beside him. "How're you, man?"

Kenmuir chuckled falsely. "Not bad for someone who can't field a routine ground ball, I guess."

"Fuck the ground ball. I'm talking about your shoulder, LT, the scar tissue."

Then-Sergeant Trauber (aka "Lizard" due to his ability to move soundlessly in the jungle) had been part of the special combat unit commanded by then-Lieutenant ("LT") Kenmuir in Vietnam. The North Vietnamese had overrun the unit after an ambitious captain denied Kenmuir's plea for withdrawal. Trauber was alive only because a wounded Kenmuir had killed the enemy soldier who was about to shoot Trauber a second time. As the unit's sole survivors, he and his LT were bonded in a way that could never be duplicated.

Nowadays, Trauber would sometimes talk about his experiences "in-country." Kenmuir never would. He'd been the commanding officer and he blamed himself for not keeping his men alive. He always would; it meant nothing that neither Trauber nor anyone else did.

Trauber reacted to Kenmuir's what-the-hell-are-you-talking-about look by saying, "Spare me, loo-ootenant, sir. I play centerfield, remember. I saw you wince. You can go bluff someone else."

Kenmuir shrugged. "Yeah, well, sometimes when I stretch too far all that puckered skin gets pissed off." He nodded his head in self-disgust. "Still should've had it." He smiled. "Why else be blessed with the reflexes of a panther?"

"You're always too hard on yourself, LT." Trauber grinned. "Though I did forget about the panther part." He tilted his head toward the pizza parlor. "Enough. Let's go inside. I'll buy."

Kenmuir held out his hands and seemed aghast. "Damn. I must truly be pitiful. *You're* going to buy?"

"I am, sir. Come on."

About a half-hour or so later, when he was waiting for an opening at one of the two pool tables, Kenmuir was approached by Len Sellers, their third baseman. "I've been told to fetch you, Dave old boy. My wife brought her friend Karen to the game. She wants you to meet her."

This happened regularly. For most of the wives, Kenmuir, the bachelor, was an empty base waiting to be stolen. Better for everyone to get him married off; no more a potential distraction or uncomfortable anomaly.

After all, what wasn't to like? Prosperous lawyer. Good sense of humor. Nearly 6' (the "missing" half-inch always had been damned annoying). Solidly built, thanks to cooperative genes and an aggressive daily regimen of sit-ups and push-ups. Not handsome enough to turn heads, but good-looking in a way that grew on you and marred only by a three-inch or so reddish-brown scar on his jaw just below his right ear (the cause of which he always explained flippantly and never genuinely). Hair fashionably long, with slivers of grey that irked him, but he'd cut it all off before he'd dye it. Clean shaven ever since his one attempt at a moustache grew out blonde on either side with a dark brown center and made him resemble Hitler, at least at a distance.

A Deadly Game

No, the wives—and even Kenmuir's male friends, as it happened—didn't understand his persistent bachelorhood. Not that there wasn't plenty of speculation.

Karen, the friend, was objectively attractive, but not in a way that attracted Kenmuir. They shared some *loud* small talk over the restaurant's bedlam: superficial biographies, a few laughs, and some references to the Sellers family which, after all, was what they had in common. He was pleasant and so was she. A very likeable woman and a potential friend, but *not* a date.

Such encounters were monitored by Ginny Trauber, who knew Kenmuir had saved her husband's life and reciprocated by protecting his, like the big sister he'd never had. Even from the other side of the room, she recognized Kenmuir's strained expression and thought, time's up. She told her younger daughter, "See Uncle Dave over there? Go tell him that Daddy needs to see him." In fact, she had no idea where her husband was.

Thus summoned, Dave expressed how good it was to see Pris Sellers: "Always makes my heart beat a little faster." And how he'd enjoyed meeting Karen: "Be sure to come again, so we can talk longer."

As he walked back toward the bar with his empty wine glass, he glanced at Ginny in the distance and mouthed "Thanks." She cupped her fingers and pointed them toward her chest with an apparently baffled look of *Me? What'd I do?*

He found Trauber and said, "I'm out of here, Lizard."

"Okay. But I know you, man. You're going to chew on that damn ground ball until tomorrow. Don't. You miss one, you catch one."

Kenmuir smiled ruefully. "Yeah, I'll keep that in mind."

That same evening, City of San Francisco

CANDLESTICK PARK, THE "STICK," WAS HOME to the San Francisco Giants. It was located on a picturesque site at the end of a small peninsula and bordered on two sides by the fabled San Francisco Bay. Visitors were charmed by the small whitecaps bouncing on the surface of the bay, while seagulls swooped overhead and sea lions barked on the rocky shore.

Less than two hours earlier, as before any San Francisco Giants' night game, the one road from the Bayshore Freeway was full of traffic. Arriving fans included visitors from Atlanta or Houston or any other warm National League city, who'd spent a pleasant day strolling through the city in shirtsleeves, riding the cable cars, wandering through Ghirardelli Square, and having lunch at Fisherman's Wharf. For their evening at the ballpark, they took the precaution of throwing on a sweater or perhaps a light jacket as protection against the cool but refreshing breeze that picked up in the late afternoon.

Then the sun went down.

By the fourth inning, the visitors had no feeling in their hands or feet. They'd happily pay any price for earmuffs or a ski parka. If they left early, all the sooner they could have the car heater blasting.

Regardless of when the fans actually left, all were long gone by the time "Hammering" Hank Jackson, the Giants' all-star left fielder, began his leisurely drive home to the City of Alameda, the quaint island on the other side of the bay near Oakland. He'd played well that night. A pure hitter, reminiscent of Rod Carew, his only struggle was with fly balls that were pushed every which-way by the Stick's swirling winds. While outfielders in other ballparks could camp under a fly ball and let it come to them, Jackson had to wander around, first a step this way, then a step that way. He didn't so much catch fly balls as intercept them before they hit the ground.

Jackson had a small sandwich from the post-game snack table but, as he neared his home, he craved something sweet. Maybe a candy bar. So he pulled into a 7-Eleven before he crossed the estuary into Alameda. He drove to the far end of the parking lot, partly because he scrupulously avoided exposing his immaculate black Cadillac Fleetwood Brougham coupe to any scratches and partly because the big car needed extra room in the surprisingly crowded lot.

The store's interior was bright and busy. Jackson plucked a Three Musketeers bar, his favorite, from the candy rack—to his credit, he didn't take two—and stood in line behind a burly man with a carton of Bud and an elderly Asian man with a small container of orange juice and a package of pork rinds. Neither they nor any of the other patrons scattered around the store paid any attention to him.

Back outside, he strolled into the parking lot. When he entered the empty aisle between the two rows of parking spaces, he heard tires squeal directly behind him. Reacting solely to the sound—because there were no impending headlights—he instinctively leaped sideways. Good thing, because the car came so close that it actually grazed his hand.

Further down the aisle, the Asian man was easing his Ford Fairlane out of a Compact Only space. Because he had virtually no room to maneuver, he was moving as slowly as a closing drawbridge and concentrating on his sides, not his rear. After all, if a car were coming, he'd see its headlights.

Smash.

The unlit car jerked so quickly into reverse that it burned through several hundred miles of tire tread. Just as quickly, it swerved forward and tried to squeeze between the Fairlane and the rear of a parked Pontiac Firebird. As the Pontiac's rear bumper was gouging a furrow down the unlit car's driver's side, an Oakland police officer came out of the store, holding his evening snack of Dolly Madison powdered sugar "Gems" and a Dr. Pepper. Like Jackson, he was able to see part of the license plate; when those two parts were joined later, they produced a full reading.

The car sped out of the parking lot and into the night, still with its lights off.

Chapter 4

Monday, April 22, City of San Francisco

Lawrence R. Lange III, Kenmuir's former fraternity brother at Stanford and the administrative vice president of the San Francisco Giants, had called that morning: "Could you come over here, roomie? I can't get away, but I also can't wait. Shitty drive for you, I know, but I'll owe you one."

For Kenmuir, the answer was a no-brainer: "Sure. Just tell me what time." If your friend needed help, you helped. He'd learn the reason later.

Taking advantage of the unusually light noon traffic westbound over the Bay Bridge and his Audi 5000's responsive accelerator, Kenmuir made the hour drive to Candlestick Park in forty-five minutes. Not his record, but very good time nonetheless.

For years, Kenmuir had urged a complete redecoration of the Giants' executive offices—or at least a plush carpet and a couple of cushy chairs. "That's why lawyers drive fancy cars, roomie. Who wants a lawyer who can afford only a Plymouth or a Dodge? Same with a major league baseball team. Unimpressive reception room, sixth-place team. Luxurious reception room, pennant winner. Simple."

The Giants' receptionist, Rhonda—no last name, just like Charlemagne or Attila—was as impressive as the reception area was not. Her Afro was only slightly smaller than the Kingdome and her dresses might originally have been bedspreads.

She glared at Kenmuir the moment he entered the room. For no known reason, she'd never liked him. When her gaze shifted from his face to his feet, Kenmuir stopped. He'd learned long ago that somewhere between the door and her desk was an invisible, but nonetheless distinct, line that created a no-man's land, much like the distance between the exterior wire fence and the single strand wire border on the interior of a prison camp. Step over the line and you're history.

Instead of offering any greeting, she merely activated the intercom as her eyes remained fixed on Kenmuir. With a voice that had the menacing rumble of a wary cat warning away an intruder, she said, "Mr. Lange, Mr. Kenmuir's here to see you."

Lange must've been waiting impatiently, because he appeared immediately. He was immaculate as always: glistening Bass Weejun loafers, starched white Gant shirt, unrumpled except where the sleeves were rolled up by two turns, and foulard tie. To the world, he looked fully composed; to Kenmuir, he was plainly agitated. In his office, he began describing the Wednesday night incident with Hank Jackson before Kenmuir could sit. "It was no accident, Dave. It was intentional."

Didn't sound that way to Kenmuir. "It's possible, I guess, but not likely. The world's full of assholes who act like assholes. That's their job."

"No fucking way. No headlights, and the only pedestrian in the parking lot just *happens* to be Jackson, and the car guns right at him? What're the odds? A zillion to one?" He began to pace around his office, nervously flipping a baseball from one hand to the other.

Kenmuir grinned. "A zillion?"

Lange shook his head and half smiled. "Okay. Maybe less than a zillion. But that's not all. It gets worse. Turns out the Jetta—which is what it was, by the way—was stolen. No surprise there, I suppose, but it was stolen right here at the Stick, for chrissake! Which has to mean that the asshole waited and then followed Jackson right from here. Still think it might just have been an accident?"

Kenmuir held up his hands in surrender. "Sometimes shit just happens. That said, I'll admit that I'm starting to agree with you."

"And that's not all."

Kenmuir suspected what was coming next, "Oakland PD found the car?"

"Exactly. Two days later, abandoned by the curb in some low-rent neighborhood."

Kenmuir realized that he was increasingly becoming more interested in whether Lange would drop the ball than in what he had to say. Consequently, when Lange passed near enough, he reached out and snagged the ball. "Stop it."

Lange hugged himself to confine his hands. "Sorry. I'll sit." He sat in the other guest chair and swiveled it toward Kenmuir. "It'd be bad enough if he were a utility player." He stood up and resumed pacing, "But no. This is an all-star who plays every day and is always in great shape. Raised in Oakland, still lives near there. Great local fan base. Plus, we have a huge investment to protect."

"Gotcha. Has OPD produced a report on the stolen Jetta yet?"

Lange snatched several stapled pages from the top of his desk. He said nothing as he thrust them toward Kenmuir, who read as Lange kept pacing. Kenmuir then patted the pages against the top of his thighs and dropped his eyes. "Strange."

"No shit."

Kenmuir looked back up. "No, not just in general. Specifically, the report describes the Jetta as parked at the curb at almost a 45° angle. *That's* what's odd. Who the hell parks like that?"

"Someone in a hurry?"

"No doubt. But any driver's instinct is to pull parallel with the curb. I'd understand if he'd even run up over the curb. But at a diagonal? Nah. And, as you say, that's not all. In addition to a long scrape down the driver's side, consistent with what Jackson and the cop saw at the 7-Eleven, the right rear quarter-panel is badly smashed in. Where'd that come from?"

"Maybe the car later hit something else?"

"Or something hit it. Because the Jetta's owner claims it didn't have so much as a ding on it. But if it happened in transit, you'd expect that someone would've reported it. Plus, no neighbors told OPD that they saw or heard anything." Kenmuir shrugged. "Though that's hardly surprising. First, it was late. Midnight, give or take. Second, I know that neighborhood from back when I was on patrol. Its residents see nothing, hear nothing, know nothing."

Lange sat on the front edge of his desk. "Here's what really worries me." He straightened his already-straight tie. "What you probably don't know is that Jackson's got a helluva quick temper. Basically a good guy, but he can blow real fast."

"You're afraid that his temper's pissed off somebody?"

"Right. Which makes me worry that there's more to come. And that's why I need you to find out what really happened."

Kenmuir hadn't understood Lange's sense of urgency or his insistence on an eye-to-eye meeting. Now the other shoe had dropped. Big shoe.

Kenmuir cocked his head and looked at his friend with a combination of amusement and disbelief. "Find out what *really* happened? I can do that. Want me to read the report out loud? Because that's as good as it's going to get." Kenmuir put his hands on the arms of the chair, leaned forward and pretended to be ready to stand up. "Good to see you, roomie. I'll send my bill tomorrow."

"I'm serious, Dave."

Kenmuir leaned back. "I know you are. Which means you need a detective, not a lawyer."

"You *were* a detective."

"Right. Were. As in 'used to be' and 'not any more.' One hell of a difference between investigating crime as a cop back when I was a pup and taking depositions as a lawyer in my sunset years"

Lange rebelled. "Sunset years? You maybe. Not me." In fact, both Lange and Kenmuir were three years from their 40th birthdays. "Besides, this is your kind of project. Oakland PD's stymied and too busy and you've acknowledged there're too many odd circumstances."

"Of course OPD's stymied. Driver's not even described, let alone identified. And, unless the driver's a total idiot, he wore gloves, so there won't be any prints. There's nowhere for OPD to go. And I can't change any of that, so ditto for detective Kenmuir, crime buster emeritus."

"I understand, but I need someone else who knows what he's doing to look at everything for *me*. Someone who won't blab to the press to get some publicity." Lange crossed his arms over his chest. "If there truly is nothing more and you end up agreeing that it's a dead end . . . well, then I'll be satisfied." He frowned. "Not happy, but satisfied."

Kenmuir said nothing. He'd rushed half way around the bay because Lange needed his help. He'd assumed it was some special legal work, like a contract or maybe a discreet negotiation. Nothing like this—which, the more he thought about it, the more enthused he was; he missed investigations.

"All right, but I'll have to get an outfit."

"Outfit?"

"Absolutely. Can't be a detective without proper detective accessories: thin-lapel suit, short-brim hat. Didn't you watch *Peter Gunn* as a kid?"

"Very cool guy. You, on the other hand . . ." Lange turned, picked up an envelope from his desk, and faced Kenmuir. "Here's your very own copy of the police report. If Jackson's on the wrong side of someone, I'd rather pay a few thousand than lose $2.3 million. As quickly and quietly as possible."

Kenmuir slipped the envelope into his coat pocket and tossed the ball back to Lange.

Chapter 5

Tuesday evening, April 23, City of Oakland

SHORTLY AFTER 6 P.M., KENMUIR PARKED across from where the Jetta had been found. He'd chosen the time deliberately. Most residents would be home, either because they'd been there all day or because they'd just gotten home from work. And, thanks to daylight savings time, they'd be able to clearly see the nonthreatening man in a suit.

He stepped out of his car and looked slowly around. It had been a decade or so since he'd last been here, a young cop on routine patrol . . .

He'd been expected to go to law school after Vietnam; after all, his brains and mouth seemed to equal lawyer. Back to Stanford, everyone had presumed. But he'd needed time to tend to his own wounds—and he'd dreaded the prospect of sitting still in a classroom or explaining to naïve, idealistic classmates, only three months out of college, how many babies he hadn't killed or why fighting in the war wasn't the same as endorsing it.

So he'd joined OPD, where virtually all the younger cops had been in-country and didn't need to be told about babies or buddies. Promoted into the Detective Bureau shortly after his fifth anniversary, he'd been paired with Sergeant Dan Franklin, who became a combination of mentor, favorite uncle, and big brother.

One morning, he was stranded in the Alameda County District Attorney's office while waiting to testify in a criminal trial. Easy duty, smoking cigarettes and bullshitting with deputy DAs and cops from other departments. Shortly before lunch he was told to return to the Detective Bureau. Right now. Strange—but it was the nature of the law enforcement business to be strange.

All sound stopped the moment he walked in the door: every typewriter, every telephone call, every private conversation. He started to talk, but Sergeant Lewis cut him off: "Dave . . . Danny's been killed."

Every muscle in Kenmuir's body stiffened.

"There was a call for backup. Danny was nearby and he responded."

"No he didn't. No way. He wouldn't do that." Dave's eyes started watering from both grief and anger. "I'm his goddamn partner. He doesn't respond to shit if I'm not backing him."

"He responded because that's his job, Dave. He covered the back of a house. Asshole came running out the back door and started shooting. Caught Danny in the head. It was one chance in a thousand."

"What the hell does *that* matter? Make it a million. Odds don't count when you're the one. He should've waited for me." He could hardly breathe. *First my unit in 'Nam and now my partner. When does it end?*

Two days after Danny's funeral, Detective David Kenmuir resigned from the department. Two more years of going to law school at night would be too grueling, he explained. His fellow officers said they understood; they also understood the real reason, but said nothing.

Kenmuir blinked away his memories and returned to the present.

The neighborhood hadn't changed. Most houses were rentals, worn and plain, and most had single-car garages converted long ago into an extra room or storage shed. The residents still parked their older-model cars by the curbs or in their driveways—though some had now migrated onto their front yards.

Where the Jetta had been dropped off was the same as hundreds of other strips of street throughout the city: a battered curb blackened by years of smudges from rubbing tires and an aged concrete gutter, extensively cracked and chipped. However, there was an anomaly: a relatively-fresh black arc began at about one-third of the width of the adjacent driveway—where a heavily-used GMC pickup truck was parked, about ten yards up from the street—and extended some seven feet toward the center of the street. Odd configuration and location, but also irrelevant, Kenmuir thought, since a car being towed doesn't leave *any* skid mark.

Kenmuir's subsequent house-by-house canvass produced nothing. Sometimes the door was answered, sometimes not. Sometimes the occupant spoke English, sometimes not. Sometimes the occupant was polite, sometimes not.

One Hispanic woman, who spoke in single words and gestures rather than sentences, managed to acknowledge that, yes, she'd seen the car down the street parked "like at the market." In addition, she "was hearing" it was pushed that way, though she didn't know who "was being doing that" or how.

No other resident had a similar memory, but one thought the GMC truck owner was "some kind of cop"—*a cop?*—who worked strange hours and slept during much of the day. He was big, wasn't very friendly, and didn't like to answer his door. If Kenmuir wanted to talk with him, he'd have to keep knocking; "but watch out, 'cause he'll be pissed off."

Kenmuir was willing to take that chance. He pressed GMC's man's doorbell button and heard no interior sound, so he pressed it a couple more times. Silence. He knocked courteously. It was the proverbial tomb. So much for courtesy. He pounded loudly.

That brought a result. The door was answered by a very large boy: leonine head, nose obviously broken more than once in the past, broad shoulders, large potbelly, heavy legs. He didn't look as if he'd been sleeping. Unless maybe he slept standing up.

"Yeah? Whadda you want?" Not welcoming, but not forbidding, either.

As with the other residents, Kenmuir explained that he was "helping the police"—which wasn't quite true, but who'd challenge him?—about the abandoned car parked by the curb last Wednesday night.

"Why the hell bother?"

"Well, sir, because it was a stolen car, and we have to follow up. I understand that you're a police officer, so you understand."

The man gave out a derisive laugh. More of a snort, really. "Fucking neighbors. Uniform and badge equal cop and not immigration. That's all they care about. Nah, I'm only a security guard down at the mall."

Not brothers-in-arms, but perhaps cousins. Kenmuir hoped that would make him cooperative. "Did the police interview you about the car?"

"Nope. No one's asked me shit. On the other hand, they could've been here, and I wouldn't know it 'cause I work graveyard and sleep during the day." He shifted his weight, but didn't move. Clearly no invitation to come inside was forthcoming. "Hell, I only heard you 'cause you pounded with some battering ram. That and I'm getting ready to go out." He reached for the edge of the door as if ready to close it. "Even if they had, I got nothing to say anyway."

So much for the cooperative-cousin theory. Kenmuir kept talking, trying to stop the door from closing. "Did you at least notice the car at any time? It was a green Jetta."

"'Course I did. How could I miss it? It was right in front of my fucking driveway."

"That's what the police report says. Right by your driveway."

"No. Not *by* my driveway. I wouldn't have given a shit about that." He waved his arm in a semicircular motion. "Look around you. Everyone parks in the fucking street. But this cocksucker parks *in front of* my driveway. Blocks a quarter of it. Maybe more. Fucking jerk."

Odd that the police report didn't make that clear. The difference between 'by' and 'in front of' is significant. "When did you first see the car?"

"As soon as the motherfucker pulled up. I was getting in my truck. Going to work."

Paydirt. "So what'd you do? I mean, you must've been surprised."

"Surprised!? Fuck that. I was pissed. How was I supposed to get out? So I yell at the motherfucker as soon as he climbs out of the ... what ... you said Jetta? 'Move your fucking car!' He stopped for a sec. Probably didn't expect anyone to be around at that time of night. Close to midnight, 'cause that's when I have to be at work. Midnight.

"He looks over his shoulder and sticks up his arm and gives me the finger. Motherfucker. Then takes off. Doesn't walk. Doesn't run. Somewhere in between. So I leap in my truck. Block my driveway and flip me off? Fuck him. I'll hurt his fucking ass."

Kenmuir had no doubt the big man could do just that—and probably had many times.

"So I keep my eye on him. It's dark, but not *that* dark. Besides, he doesn't go far."

"Can you describe him?"

"Not really. White guy is all. Too dark to see any detail." He tilted his head and twisted his lips. "Not quite true. He had long hair. Light colored. Blonde? And his forearms were dark. Too dark for such a pale guy. Lot of tattoos, maybe?"

"Gloves?"

"Can't say for sure, but I think I would've noticed if his hands were a lot lighter than his arms. Anyways, a couple cars up is some Jap car. Honda, Toyota, whatever. He jumps in it and starts grinding the starter. 'Cause it ain't starting. My truck does, though. It may look like shit, but the engine's primo. Finally, he manages to fire his up and burns rubber getting the hell away."

"What'd you do?"

The big man paused. "Went to work. What else could I do?"

"That's it?"

"That's it. Got nothing more to say."

Sure you do. The Jetta's still blocking your driveway. Kenmuir persisted. "How about the Jetta?"

A Deadly Game

"What about it?"

"Well, if I'm tracking with you, the Jetta was still in your way."

The big man became silent. Kenmuir had seen this behavior too many times in too many interviews over the years, both as a cop and as a lawyer, not to realize what it meant. The man had more to say, but was struggling to decide whether to say it.

"You said you're a cop. Suit and all means detective, right?"

Kenmuir didn't want to lose this guy. "No, not at all. I'm only *helping* the police. Kinda like a volunteer. I follow up on stuff when they're too busy. Which is most of the time." Kenmuir faked a laugh, being a nonthreatening, congenial guy. "Anyway, I gather you did do something else?"

The big man pulled out a Camel, hesitated, and then offered one to Kenmuir. Pals now. Kenmuir declined, but took out one of his own Marlboros. Keep the camaraderie intact.

The big man exhaled into the sky. "But you know about the law, right?"

"Some of it, yeah. Too many laws for me to keep up with." Another fake laugh.

"Well, let me ask this: if a person has to move a car what's blocking his driveway and, say, that car gets damaged, is that a crime?"

Got it. He was real mad and pushed that Jetta out of the way, sure'n hell. Now that he's calmed down, he's worried I'm going to arrest him for the smashed-in rear fender. Even so, what would the crime be? Maybe malicious mischief, at best. Would he ever be charged? Never. "Don't think so. Not under these circumstances."

"And you don't work for some insurance company?"

"Nope. And I don't intend to talk to one."

The big man nodded. Trust came hard. "Well, what the hell. I went and floored my truck. I tried to avoid the Jetta, but wasn't possible. My bumper—look at it from the front—is heavy duty and raised. No fucking Jetta's going to faze it. When the truck hits the Jetta's right rear quarter panel, it dents the shit out of it and moves the whole car the hell out of my way."

"About a 45° angle?"

"You got it."

Answers that question. "And then . . . ?"

"I take off after the motherfucker, but he's got too much of a head start. Too many quick turns for my truck. I lose him. Bastard."

"Can you describe his car?"

"Sorta. 'Cause it was in my high beams for a little while. It's white, but with a dark left rear fender, like it was a replacement from some other car."

"License plate number?"

The big man laughed genuinely. "You gotta be shitting me. A fucking eagle couldn't have read that license plate in the dark goin' that fast." He exhaled another drag. "But I do remember it had no frame around it. You know, like with the name of the dealer that sold it."

"Gotcha."

The big man snagged the butt of the Camel between the middle finger and thumb of his right hand and flicked it in an arc out onto the scattered tufts of mangy grass that was his front yard. "Am I gonna hear more about this?"

Not at Kenmuir's initiative. Or anyone else's, he suspected. "No guarantees, but I strongly doubt it. And certainly not coming from me."

Thursday morning, April 25, City of Walnut Creek

KENMUIR DILIGENTLY MAINTAINED HIS FRIENDSHIPS from his years with Oakland PD. Partly sentimental (he'd lost too many friends in the past) and partly practical (such friends could come in handy).

Sergeant Milt Prager, now "on line one," was one of those friends. Kenmuir picked up the receiver and, without so much as an hello, said, "What took you so long, Shotgun?" (In fact, Kenmuir had spoken with Prager only Wednesday morning.)

As a young patrolman, Prager had killed two men who'd fired at him as they tried to flee from robbing a liquor store. He'd used his shotgun—and that immediately became his nickname forever. "It took so damn long because, sloppy investigator as you always were, you gave me next to nothing to work with."

"I gave you more than even a marginally competent detective would need. Which means, I gather, that you've run aground and I'll have to do it myself, just like the old days."

"Must be *real* old, because I don't remember any days like that. What I *do* remember is that you didn't give me shit then, any more than now. Which is why, sorry to say, I don't have much to give you."

"No surprise there. But, like I told you yesterday, I don't have much to give. That said, do you have *anything* more at all?"

"Yeah. Sort of. I asked around and the consensus is that your guy's Mark Bellman. Standard dirt-bag who scrounges some menial employment and does some chickenfeed crime, but mainly lives by exploiting welfare agencies. A man of little capabilities, little accomplishments, and little brain."

"You're not listening to the public defenders, Shotgun, which would explain why you've become hardhearted. You have to remember that it's not the criminal's fault. Misunderstood and mistreated, he deserves sympathy, not disdain."

"You know, you're right. I forgot the sympathy part. Damn. I can't tell you how badly I feel ... But he *is* white, has stringy blonde hair, and is covered with tattoos—which comes awfully close to matching your description."

"Address?"

"Last known is 745 Alminar Road, apartment #2E. Still valid? Beats me."

"You run him through DMV?"

Prager paused momentarily. "Oh, man, I never thought of that. What a great idea! DMV! Honest to god, Dave, could you come back and help us out? *Please.*" He shifted his tone and said, "*Of course* I ran him through DMV."

"Don't go all sarcastic with me. You always did need to be reminded about investigative subtleties. And did you thereby learn anything? Like what he's driving?"

"Yes and no. His last official car was an old Dodge Aspen. White, but the registration and license expired long ago. Which is hardly a surprise, since the Bellmans of this world go through unregistered cars like addicts through needles. Good luck finding it. Will you want me to come help you?"

"Fuck you, Shotgun. Next time, I'm calling someone else."

"Fine by me." Dramatic pause. "Oh, but wait . . . There's no one else who'll take a call from you."

"I'll find someone."

"Serious moment, Dave?"

"Sure. What?"

"Does this have to do with someone trying to run down Hank Jackson?"

It was Kenmuir's turn to pause. "What makes you think that?"

"Because the car that got you started on this was the Jetta id'd in the 7-Eleven parking lot by Jackson and one of our officers. Now San Francisco PD's also all over it. And I want us to figure out what's happening, not them. So no bullshit, Dave, if you find out something that bears on it, I want to know. Maybe I wasn't clear enough. *I*—that means *me* personally—want to know. *First* . . . Deal?"

Kenmuir didn't hesitate. He would've done that anyway. In his world, favors get returned. "Deal. No qualifications."

Chapter 6

Friday morning, April 26, City of Oakland

BELLMAN'S ADDRESS WAS THE EXCELSIOR Apartments, a shabby two-story building of indeterminate age—though virtually by definition many years before, as the word *excelsior* had disappeared from the local vocabulary long ago. This neighborhood, like so many others in Oakland, had withered like an untended garden, with tufts of wild grass punctuating cracked sidewalks, mangy and neglected yards, and bars shielding most windows. With young families having migrated to the suburbs and retired couples having been too afraid to stay behind, there seemed to be no residents ready to fight on behalf of the neighborhood, though gangs evidently were ready to fight over it, as was confirmed by "9400" spray-painted on some walls and "NA" on others.

Kenmuir briefly scouted the area and, in the block behind the Excelsior, there it was: not an Aspen, but a 1978 white Datsun 210, covered in grime. A "Jap car," just like the big security guard had said. Its rear license plate had no frame and the primer gray left rear fender certainly could appear dark at night. The odds that the Excelsior was still home to Bellman went up substantially.

Kenmuir expected that Bellman was the social equivalent of fast-food: if you wanted him, all you had to do was walk down the open-air landing until you came to apartment 2E. But you never came to that, because the weathered door after apartment 2D was 2 (four screw holes). Kenmuir presumed they were place-holders for an *E*, so he knocked. The door rattled on its hinges, but no one answered it. So Kenmuir knocked louder.

A high-pitched voice responded irritably. "Hey, you don't have to break down the fuckin' door!" The master of the house was roused. After the door cracked open to the length of a security chain, one dull eye and half of a mouth appeared. "Who the fuck're you?" It was a reasonable question, since a man wearing a coat and tie signaled some sort of official to Bellman and every other resident in this neighborhood.

"Good afternoon. I need to ask some questions about your automobile accident."

Bellman released the chain, fully opened the door, and said, "I don't know shit about any accident." He was unimposing, approximately 5'8" and 160 pounds. A two-day stubble partially concealed the ravages of bygone acne. Most of his hair was tousled and bent; the rest fell down to the neck of a formerly white T-shirt that hung limply above grayish boxers. His forearms were gaudy with nondescript tattoos. *Here we have the Jetta's driver, no question about it.*

"Of course you do, sir. However, there are some aspects of insurance with which we are concerned." *Genius: aspects of insurance, with which. Totally official.*

Bellman affected a tough-guy sneer. "You got a hearing problem? I don't know shit about no accident. You got the wrong guy."

A Deadly Game

"No, our information's very clear. You were driving a Jetta in a parking lot late on Wednesday night, nearly hit a pedestrian, and struck a car. Then you drove away." Kenmuir smiled. Mr. Congeniality. "Remember now?"

"Fuck you." Bellman started to close the door, but ran into Kenmuir's extended foot and knee.

"There were witnesses, Mark." *Dump this Mr. and sir crap.* "The pedestrian and an Oakland police officer saw you." *Unfortunately, they can't identify you, but let's not burden you with distracting details right now.* "Likewise, the guy in the truck where you dumped the Jetta." *Ditto.*

Bellman's expression changed from self-confident to uncertain. He remembered the big dude who shouted at him, but it was too dark and he was too far away to be recognized. Wasn't he? . . . He gently slapped himself on the cheek and said, "Fuck. Did I forget to fuckin' get stolen-car insurance?"

I'll regard that as a confession. "Not *your* insurance, sir. I have a few questions about the car you hit. Won't take long."

"What're you, fuckin' dumb? It was a stolen fuckin' car. You're some insurance dude, so end of story. End of questions. End of answers." Bellman moved more toward the center of the doorway for greater leverage on the door against Kenmuir's leg.

Kenmuir, being a fair guy, had given Bellman a chance to cooperate. On the other hand, he'd never had much patience with Bellman's ilk, so now that chance was gone—which was why Kenmuir grabbed Bellman's T-shirt with both hands, pulled him forward, and then shoved him backward into the apartment.

Bellman stumbled and fell over the coffee table in front of the sofa. Beer cans, not all of which were empty, scattered like aluminum confetti. Kenmuir stepped inside and closed the door behind him, while Bellman scrambled to his feet, dodged the sofa with surprising agility, and ran into the kitchen. If nothing else, Bellman was fast.

Bellman returned with a butcher knife in his right hand. He hunched himself in his version of the posture of a seasoned knife fighter. "Get outta here, motherfucker, or I'll carve your ass."

Kenmuir didn't move. "Put down the knife, Mark, and you don't get hurt. It won't be hard. Like I said, a couple of questions and goodbye."

"Fuck you," Bellman said as he stepped forward, slicing the air between himself and Kenmuir. No one messes with Mark. A formidable guy.

As the waving knife passed from his right hip toward his left hip, Bellman exposed the back of his right hand. Quick as a snake's tongue, Kenmuir's left hand grabbed Bellman's right wrist and twisted it away so the arm straightened. A fraction of a second later, Kenmuir's right palm swept upward, like someone pitching a softball, and struck the underside of Bellman's elbow. The slight grating sound of the dislocating elbow was overwhelmed by Bellman's scream

Kenmuir grabbed the towel that was draped over the arm of the sofa, twirled it into a single strand, and looped it around Bellman's head and over his mouth. He spoke directly into Bellman's ear: "So far, you've got an injured arm. Don't answer my questions and you'll have a broken face. Clear?"

Bellman's reply was lost in the folds of the towel.

"Answer the question. *Is that clear?*"

Bellman vigorously nodded his head. Kenmuir yanked the towel away and said, "There was a black guy in the parking lot. You almost hit him. Were you trying to?"

Bellman gripped his right bicep with his left hand in a futile effort to erase the pain in his elbow. He glanced backward. "Fuck you."

Kenmuir hit the top of Bellman's right shoulder—and a yelp confirmed that Bellman had been reminded how badly his elbow hurt. "Hurts, doesn't it? Now I'll ask again. Were you *trying* to hit the black guy?"

"Yeah. *That* what you want to hear?"

"It's a start. So keep going. Why'd you pick him?"

"I didn't. The guy what hired me did." Bellman partially turned toward Kenmuir. "Look, I'm told to meet someone. I do and he hires me to follow this big fuckin' black Caddy from the Stick the next night. I'm supposed to wait until we come to a stretch of deserted road somewhere and then run the Caddy off the road. It crashes and I keep going. No sweat, I'm thinking. Not hard to surprise someone and run him off the fuckin' road. Easy money and more than I expected.

"Guy tells me to go steal a car and meet him at a closed-down gas station near the Stick. He'll be in a red car. I get a friend to follow me to some bullshit street on the other side of town, near an on-ramp to the Bay Bridge. I drop my car there and my friend then drives me to the Stick's parking lot."

"Good friend."

"Not fucking likely. I had to pay his ass. Nothin's for free, man. Nothin'." Bellman shifted his shoulder. Mistake. He grimaced. "Anyways, there's a game that night. My friend leaves and I wander around, looking for a Jetta."

"Why a Jetta?"

"Easy to get into and easy to steal." He looked superciliously at Kenmuir, as if wondering, *How could you not know that?* "I get to the gas station and the guy's already there."

"Anyone else?"

"Nope. Sittin' all by his lonesome in the red car. Didn't matter, 'cause there weren't no other cars anyhow. I say, 'So what's happenin'?' and the guy says, 'When I point, that's the car you follow.' Then we just sit there. He's in his red fuckin' car and I'm in the Jetta. At fuckin' last the game gets out. Thank god no extra innings. Cars're crawlin' over each other toward the Bayshore or the overland shortcuts. The lot gets empty—except for the sorry sonuvabitch wandering around, trying to remember where he parked his Jetta." Bellman laughed, revealing an ideal training ground for young dentists.

"After maybe an hour, here comes a big fuckin' black Caddy. Red car starts right away and the guy's arm sticks out. Points at the Caddy, as if I couldn't figure that out. Asshole. So I swing in behind it and off we go toward Oakland. Caddy's in no hurry. Doesn't go faster than thirty. Easier than shit to tail, long as you don't get too close.

"Trouble is, there's no deserted roads. I mean, hell, it's almost all freeway. I start to get worried, thinkin' damn, am I gonna have to go all the way to Alameda? Well, fuck, that's exactly what I end up fuckin' doing. Finally, the Caddy pulls into a 7-Eleven. What the fuck's *that* about? I stop by a curb and the Caddy parks at the far end of the lot. Black guy gets out."

Bellman craned his neck toward Kenmuir behind him. "Hey, can you grab me a beer?" He'd been concentrating for too long, evidently.

Kenmuir the valet answered, "Glad to. Soon as you've told me everything."

"Hey, man, it's real hard to keep talking with a dry throat."

"You'll manage."

"Fuck you. So I'm watchin' the black guy go inside the 7-Eleven and all of a sudden the red car pulls up next to me. Where the fuck'd he come from? Beats the shit outta me. Must've been following, like I wasn't gonna do what I was hired to do. Asshole. Through the window he says, 'Wait until the black dude comes out and then run him down.' I say, 'Go fuck yourself. You want to roll over someone, do it in *your* car.' Motherfucker doesn't say shit back. Just points a snub at me. Three feet from my fuckin' face. Looks bigger than the Caddy.

"He says, 'Don't forget I know who you are. Fuck this up and you'll wish the car'd hit *you*.' I figure, better some nigger gets fucked than me."

"Not a stylish term, Mark. Irritates the brothers."

"Yeah, well, fuck them too. The only brother I give a shit about is *me*. So I wait until the black guy comes out . . ." Bellman shook his head in a form of disbelief. "And I still can't fuckin' believe I didn't recognize his ass. Hammerin' Hank Jackson, for chrissake. Anyway, I wait until he's walkin' in the open and then I gun it right at him. And fuckin' miss him. Unfuckingbelievable."

"I need his name."

"Already told you. Hank Jackson."

Serves me right. The troublesome pronoun. "Not him. The person who hired you."

"Fuck if I know."

Kenmuir pulled sharply on Bellman's arm. Bellman yelped. "Jesus, man, I ain't fuckin' lyin'. I seen him those two times, and he wasn't wearing no fuckin' name tag." Bellman rubbed his arm. "Goddamn. That hurts like shit."

Probably doesn't know a name. Wouldn't be a real one anyway. "Okay. No name. So what'd he look like?"

"Some dude, that's all. Blonde hair, lighter than mine. Nice shirt. Gold chain around his neck with some kinda sailboat hanging from it. A pretty boy. What the fuck, man, it was dark. I wasn't like tryin' to memorize his ass, you know."

"Old? Young?"

"Shit, I don' know. Not old as you. Maybe same as me. Maybe younger. Maybe not. Fuck if I know."

"But originally, someone told you to meet him. Who was that? The one who set it up." Bellman's hesitation told Kenmuir he had the answer but didn't want to give it up. "Instead of thinking about what to say, you should be thinking about your shoulder." Kenmuir drummed his fingers on the top of Bellman's shoulder.

Bellman was persuaded. "Name's Chico."

"And where do I find him?"

"Not sure."

More drumming.

"Stay cool, man. Really, I'm not sure." Bellman waved his left hand as if warding off a yellow jacket at a picnic. "He roams around different bars. I've seen him a few times here and there. And *you* don't call *him*. If he wants you, he'll call you or tell someone to have you call him at some number or tell you to meet him somewhere."

"What happened this time?"

"The friend I told you about? The one who drove me to the Stick? He gave me a message. Which is how he knew something was up and was there anything in it for him. Asshole."

Kenmuir took a deep breath and exhaled slowly. "You called this man Chico?"

"No. The message told me when and where to meet him."

"Risky. How does he know if you even got the message?"

"Simple. I either show up or I don't. If I don't, he farms it out to someone else." He shrugged. "Lot of us out there lookin' for work, man."

"Nothing ever changes." Kenmuir nodded his head in disgust. "So where did you meet?"

"Some bar."

"Mark, you're making me work too hard. Have you forgotten what happens when I run out of patience?"

"I'm not fucking with you. It was a bar. I didn't pick it and I don't remember the fucking name. I'd never been there before. It's just up from the corner of 19th and Sawyer. Next to a cigarette store."

"All right. Then what?"

"He's there and he says, 'You want a job driving a car?' I go, 'Sure.' Gives me a piece of paper and a pen. Says, 'Write this down'."

"Because he doesn't want anything in his handwriting."

"Never thought of that. Maybe, 'cause he never, and I mean never, writes anything down. So I do. It's an address and a time. And that's how I met the jerk-off what hired me." Bellman sagged against the couch. The signal was unmistakable. He had nothing left. "That's it, man."

"See, Mark, it wasn't so hard." Kenmuir walked to the door. "You might have someone take a look at that arm. And maybe pick up some bleach for that shirt on the way home."

Bellman gave Kenmuir the finger with his left hand. "Fuck you."

When Kenmuir closed the door behind him, he was unable to hear what Bellman shouted, though he had no doubt about the sentiment.

Chapter 7

Monday morning, April 29, City of Orinda

IN 1937, ALAMEDA AND CONTRA COSTA Counties had been connected by the two bores of the Caldecott Tunnel through the Oakland-Berkeley hills. Whereupon, wildlife headed for higher ground and summer "cabins" in the previously remote east side began to be replaced by more spacious and elegant homes. Even so, nearly half a century later, the City of Orinda barely qualified as a town: a few boutiques, a pricey market with a genuine butcher shop, an ornate movie theater with one screen, no fast-food.

Curving roads and thick foliage preserved a rural illusion. If you wanted the sense of living in the country, but be a mere thirty minutes from San Francisco—and if you had plenty of cash—Orinda was the place for you. As it was for Humphrey "Thumper" Orr, the all-star catcher of the Oakland Athletics.

Orr was 5'10", but seemed shorter due to his tree-stump legs. He supposedly didn't need to squat, but could remain standing because he already was low enough to the ground; he didn't need to buy trousers, but could have cuffs put on Bermuda shorts—or so it was said. However, those stumpy legs could transfer enormous power to a baseball bat at the precise second when the wood met, or "thumped," a waist-high fastball.

Orr had nearly finished what sportswriters were calling his "Awesome April": thirty-three runs batted in, nine home runs, twelve doubles, and a .425 batting average. But today was a reprieve before setting off on a grueling road trip of fourteen games in fifteen days. And the day was perfect: flawless blue skies, zero humidity, temperature in the mid-70s, an occasional cool breeze. Like the Mamas and Papas sang about their Monday, it was all one hoped it could be—even one whose day was to be devoted to completion of the household chores on his wife's to-do list.

The list, by the way, didn't include gardening because, where there were plants, there were bugs. Orr's rule was uncomplicated: don't touch the plants and the bugs won't touch you. His solution was equally uncomplicated: keep paying Carlos the gardener.

By midafternoon, he was tired and hot. He'd sanded a rough spot on the deck, tightened several squeaking planks, and secured a loose gutter. All without so much as grazing a plant. He stood at the edge of his swimming pool and stripped down to his boxer shorts. His wife would object, but she wasn't home and, anyway, his neighbors couldn't see into his backyard.

When he heard the clang of the bolt on the side gate, he saw a young Chicano emerge from around the side of the house. Short and wiry, he wore khaki shorts, a long-sleeved khaki shirt, and a khaki hat. His canvas tool bag, Orr noted with some amusement, was also khaki: *you can see by my outfit that I am a gardener.* He asked, "Where's Carlos?"

"He is not being here. He is hurting his back."

If this guy's got a green card, Orr thought, I'm an astronaut. "You need anything from me?"

"*Nada.* I am being busy." He raised the canvas bag to verify that he was ready to attack plants.

"Well, have at it." Orr turned and dove into the pool. He swam laps until he was cool and then hoisted himself onto the concrete deck. In the summer, the sun could make the surface unbearably hot. Today it was comfortably warm. He lay on his stomach and rested his head on his powerful forearm. As he drifted into a half-sleep, he heard the rhythmic clatter of the hedge clippers behind him. He smiled to himself: *I am being busy.*

He wasn't too insensate not to react instantly to the sting between his shoulder blades. He knew exactly what it was, because it'd happened before. Bug ambush. Bees and wasps sensed his dislike, so they stung him out of spite. He knew the water would soothe the sting, so he began to stand in order to dive back into the pool. Instead, his knees buckled and his legs gave way. He dropped to one knee, strangely groggy and dizzy. When he tilted his powerful neck, he looked up at the blurry face of the gardener.

Despite his khaki costume, the Chicano gardener also hated plants. He'd grown up in a paved world. His yard was the asphalt street in front of his mother's apartment and the asphalt alley behind it. An asphalt playground had surrounded his middle school (he hadn't bothered with the nuisance of high school).

They'd told him the man would be home on Monday and eventually he'd go for a swim. How'd they know? It made no difference. They *always* knew what they knew. "Take this gun and shoot this dart into him. He'll be as helpless as a baby," they'd told him. "Nothing to worry about. Hurt him but don't kill him. What you do is push one of his arms upward until the shoulder dislocates or breaks. Tie his hands behind his back. Then go inside, bust up the house a little, and take what you want. Make it look like a burglary. Simple."

What they *hadn't* told him was the man's name—but he'd recognized him right away. Who in the Bay Area wouldn't? Thumper Orr, for chrissake. He'd almost turned around and walked away. Then he'd thought, *Fuck it. Kinda cool to put the famous Thumper to sleep.*

He stared at the dart-syringe stuck between Orr's shoulder blades. He waited, much as a veterinarian might wait for an injected dog to fall asleep. He felt contempt, spiced with a sense of power . . . Only the simple plan wasn't working.

Orr managed to lift his other knee off the concrete. Now in a catcher's characteristic squat, he began to rise. Gripping his thighs just above the knees, he used the leverage of his arms to push his powerful torso upward an inch at a time. His straining triceps bulged outward. All the while, he glared unblinkingly at the gardener's face and said nothing.

Fuck the plan, thought the Chicano. *Strong fucker. Hurt my ass if he gets on his goddamn feet. Keeps staring at me. Even if he doesn't beat the shit out of me and I somehow do what I'm supposed to, he'll ID me later. Either way, I'm fucked.*

He reached into the canvas bag and pulled out a .32 caliber Walther PPK. He'd fired it many times. He pointed it at Orr's forehead and fired it once more. Most of the sound was muffled by the surrounding trees. It wasn't heard by any neighbors or, if it was, it wasn't remembered later.

Chapter 8

Tuesday afternoon, April 30, City of Oakland

KENMUIR FELT LIKE THE LONE CONTESTANT in an alcoholic scavenger hunt. The prize was Chico, one of the middlemen who litter the margins of crime: arranging things, making sure this guy gets in touch with that guy, all while remaining technically ignorant and legally blameless. Chico would stay close to his established niches, because being available was how he survived. Eventually Kenmuir would find a niche with Chico in it.

Kenmuir's Monday afternoon had begun at the bar at 19th and Sawyer. And a cheery, upscale establishment it was. Dim light, enveloping odor of stale-beer spillage, worn stools, tables with mismatched chairs. No games, no shuffleboard, no darts. You wanna play games? Take a cruise.

The 60-ish bartender had been too weary to be challenging. "Chico? Hard to say. He wanders around. You know 'im? Sure as hell don't look like no customer of his." He tilted his head sideways. "Whatever. Go try the Bottoms Up over on Cypress." Kenmuir had. And then another bar after that, which was how he'd gradually migrated from downtown to Oakland to its outskirts.

Yesterday, he'd been dressed in khakis and a starched long-sleeve shirt, someone who just happened to be in the area and thought he'd stop for a cold one. Unconvincing, he'd realized too late. But not today. He returned to where he left off in the outskirts, now wearing running shoes, Levis and a blue work shirt, a fugitive from the '60s he'd found after rummaging around in his closet. The *coup de grace* was an Oakland A's baseball cap. An unquestionably regular guy. Who'd ever suspect otherwise?

His second stop was the Ca-booze, a bar comprised of three train cars marooned on an abandoned spur. Its gravel parking lot had neither aisles nor stalls; you parked where you wanted to stop. The interior was dark enough when he came in from the sunlight that he paused with his back to the wall. The surroundings were new, but his personal habits were old: there'd be no one beside or behind him until his eyes adjusted.

In more mobile times, the central room of the Ca-booze had been an elegant lounge car; now it was outfitted with a long wooden bar and dark paneling. The car to its left had tables, chairs, and a few booths; the one to its right had a dance floor and band podium. When he could see clearly again, Kenmuir walked to the end of the bar nearest the dance floor, where sure as hell no one would be dancing in the foreseeable future. As soon as he mounted a stool, the bartender appeared. He had no doubt the bartender had been waiting since the moment the front door opened.

"What'll you have?"

Anything but another beer. God, how much do I hate beer? How about a strawberry daiquiri? Right. That'd work. I'd for sure blend right in. One of the boys. Instead: "Got a Miller?"

"Bottle or tap?"

As if it made any difference. "Tap's fine."

As the bartender turned, Kenmuir said, "I'm supposed to meet someone named Chico. He around?" There was one other man at the bar, two at a nearby table and an unknown number in the table-and-chair railroad car.

The bartender spoke over his shoulder. "Not yet. Might be later. Little early for him. Never know for sure." When the bartender returned, he plunked down a foamy mug. "We got a problem I don't know about?"

"Don't think so. But I don't know what you know. Why do you ask?"

The bartender looked questioningly. That was because he had a question. "You a cop? You got the feel of one."

"Nope." *Screw this.* "Used to be, though."

The bartender smiled with some self-satisfaction before he turned and walked away. Over the next couple of hours, the bar gradually filled. The Ca-boozer regulars were rail thin or potbellied. They wore either work shirts with company emblems or soiled T-shirts; no dress shirts, starched or unstarched, for them. Each had a stained, expando-rim baseball cap with a logo: *Readi-Mix Concrete . . . Just Hauler . . . A's*, like Kenmuir's.

Working man costume or not, Kenmuir stood out like someone's wife at a stag party. He simply didn't look like a bar-on-the-way-home-after-work kind of guy. Even so, his isolation at the end of the bar attracted a few disinterested glances, but no comments. When the bartender emptied Kenmuir's ashtray, he said, "Guy you're lookin' for. Chico? Now he's here. Sitting over there." He nodded toward a small, C-shaped booth.

Chico sat facing the open room. On the table was a pack of Lark cigarettes, a Bic lighter, an ashtray, and a clear, sparkling beverage that Kenmuir assumed was tonic or club soda. For Chico, this was a place for business, not recreation. The center of Chico's forehead was pushed in, like a dent in an aluminum can. His overgrown sideburns matched a bushy black moustache that was perched in the middle of his pinched, expressionless face.

Not wanting to be stranded inside the booth, Kenmuir moved up a chair. Chico didn't react. He plainly didn't care if Kenmuir stood or sat. However, once Kenmuir did sit, Chico said, "Been wondering when you'd show up. Got a message from fuckhead Bellman. Said you'd come around."

"And so I have."

"Says you're from some insurance company. That's horseshit, so spare me. Either way, don't matter. Your problem ain't mine."

"I've got no problem. Just need some information. My new friend Mark tells me you have it. Then I'm gone."

Cigarette smoke trickled out of Chico's nose like a struggling steam-engine and filtered through his moustache. "There's all kinds of information, insurance man. Some's for sale and some's not. Some costs more."

"Fair enough. Bellman says you set it up for him to drive a car for someone. I need the name of that someone."

"I did hear he's gotten jammed up behind drivin' some car. If that's what you got in mind, I wouldn't know anything about it."

Kenmuir had questioned dozens of Chicos over the years. He understood how wary they were. *Had* to be, really. "Look, this isn't official. I've got my own reasons—private reasons—for wanting to know."

"Yeah, I'll bet. You look like a cop, you talk like a cop, but *you* say you aren't one. Or so Slinger says." He nodded in the direction of the bartender. "And of course you'd be the first plainclothes type to lie about it. Think I'll pass, thank you very much. Even if I did know anything. Which I don't."

Kenmuir sat back, crossed his legs, and lit a cigarette of his own. Just one fella bullshitting with another. "You read where some asshole tried to run down Hank Jackson? You know, the ballplayer?"

"Don't read much." Chico began drumming his lit cigarette on the side of the ashtray.

"Don't have to. It certainly would've been talked about a lot in this bar. No, you heard. For sure, you heard about it."

"Don't recall. But I'll tell you this, if I did know something—which, again, I damn well don't—I'd wanna keep a very low profile. Heat case. Famous ballplayer. Black guy."

"I can live with that. Wouldn't have to mention your name to the guys I used to work with at OPD, for example."

Chico was able to remain in business by being more valuable outside, on the street, than inside, in a cell. That's why it was often in his best interest to reveal *some* information to the cops or those who could bring them. Like Kenmuir.

Chico used the end of his cigarette to light a new one. "Let's say I'd done someone a favor. Settin' up a driver for 'im. Coulda been any car, if you know what I mean. Coulda driven it anywhere."

"Sure could. I can live with that, too."

"And you can 'cause it's only personal. You no longer bein' a cop and all."

"That's right. Strictly personal."

Chico rubbed his temples with the tips of his fingers. "Well, you wouldn't get the name even if I had it. But I don't, 'cause I never met the ... customer ... before. Didn't belong here any more'n you. Shiny pants, expensive shirt. Hair spray, for chrissake. Says he's lookin' for a guy to drive a car. 'Lotta guys drive cars,' I says. He says, 'Probably won't be the guy's own car.' 'Hey, I says, 'I don't wanna know'."

Chico exhaled a geyser of smoke toward the ceiling. "I see Bellman's buddy. Bellman can drive and he ain't good for much else. I say, 'I can get a message to a guy. You can meet him. What happens after that's up to you. But it'll cost $200.' Customer doesn't argue. Just pulls out two mallards and snaps 'em like some fuckin' card dealer. Real impressive."

"Ever seen hair-spray guy before?"

"Once. At the track. Hangin' around some high rollers. Lightin' cigarettes, laughin' real hard, gettin' drinks. Don't know who he is. Don't know where to find him. Don't want to."

"Got it, Chico. No names. Only one more question. Did he have any kind of chain around his neck?"

Chico's exhale was a sarcastic snort. "No shit. Some gold sailboat hanging from it. Fuckin' necklace on a guy, for chrissake. What's next? Fuckin' earrings?"

Bellman hadn't lied. Sailboat man was local, which meant he could be found. Kenmuir intended to do just that.

Chapter 9

Friday afternoon, May 3, City of Walnut Creek

VISITORS COMMONLY ASKED WHERE the Little House on the Prairie had been. No, that was Walnut *Grove* ... in Minnesota. There'd never been a prairie here, twenty-five miles east of San Francisco. No sod-busters, no buffalo roaming, no cavalry charges. Merely a sleepy town named unimaginatively after a bigger-than-a-stream but smaller-than-a-river that wended through walnut groves. It was better than, say, Walnutland or Walnutville or Santo Walnuto. Now, the walnut groves were long gone. For that matter, so was the creek: like an aged relative, it had been hidden away.

Having been raised in Los Angeles, Kenmuir had refused to commute into another metropolis, beautiful bridges or not. That was why the "Law Office of David A. Kenmuir" was located here, part of a suite shared with three other sole practitioners on the sixth floor of some architect's vision of how a spaceship might look if it landed in the center of town.

Jennifer, the lawyers' shared receptionist, buzzed Kenmuir and said, "It's Mr. Lange. He's such a nice man,"

Kenmuir told Lange, "According to young Jennifer, you're a nice man, roomie."

"Well, I am. Which must be quite a contrast after dealing with you."

"Sadly, you're not in sync with contemporary argot. That's why you misunderstand the true meaning of 'He's a nice man.' It's something girls her age say about father figures. Old men with turkey necks and sparse wisps of hair. In short, granddads."

"Fuck you."

"And the odds of that are the same as you have with Jennifer, old boy. Is that why you called? To fantasize?"

"Nope, tempting though it is." Slight pause. "You free for lunch? Bring me up to date. I'll even come your way."

"When you use the term 'free' in this context, what exactly does it mean?"

"Sorry. I wasn't clear. It means you're free to pay for yourself."

"I understand. Good thing we clarified it, though. No awkwardness later. Say 12:30 at Le Marquis?"

"I wouldn't have expected anywhere else."

When Kenmuir arrived—a few minutes late, as usual—he was surprised to see also Phil Smith, Lange's counterpart with the Oakland A's. A display of thin, Smith could walk through a harp or stand under the shower without getting wet. His face was barely wide enough to accommodate his features: small mouth, tight lips, pinched nose and eyes that almost bumped into each other. A champion quarter miler in high school, the one or two strides he lost in college was the difference between winning and carrying the Gatorade. Simply, "If you ain't the lead dog, the view never changes." Smith concentrated on baseball instead.

Signed by the A's after college as a quick and slick shortstop, he was two years into AA ball when a collision during a routine double play sent his left ankle in about five different directions. That part of his career was over, so he earned his MBA and was hired by the A's front office. He was still in the game, although without a uniform.

At Lange's request, Kenmuir summarized what he'd learned. When he finished, he shrugged and said, "Sorry to say it, but you're right. Someone's pissed off at Jackson."

"Goddamn, I was afraid of that." Lange muttered. "And now it's gotten worse. Much worse."

Kenmuir glanced quizzically between Smith and Lange.

Lange responded to Kenmuir's unspoken question. "You've read about Orr?"

Kenmuir nodded. "Who hasn't? Murdered in his backyard. Apparently a burglary gone bad." He looked at Smith. "I'm real sorry, Phil."

In a high school yearbook, skinny Phil and chunky Humphrey would've been Most Unlikely Couple. The promising player and the promising executive met in the minor leagues and were promoted at about the same time. Each was intimidated by big-city life and big-time baseball. Each helped the other adjust. A friendship became a best friendship.

"Thanks. I just can't believe it." Smith took a deep breath and composed himself before continuing. "Maybe it was a burglary. Maybe not. But the tranquilizer found in his system during the autopsy? *That* makes no sense. He never used drugs. And I mean *never*."

Kenmuir swallowed the last bite of the incomparable *salmon en croute*. "Actually, drugging him might explain a lot. Burglars are thieves. Their job is to steal things. They get in and get out. More to the point, they learn early to avoid occupied residences because that makes it first degree burglary, a major felony which carries a big-time punishment compared to second degree."

"I agree. So you also think he was drugged deliberately?"

Kenmuir held up his hands with the palms facing Smith. "Hold on, Phil. *I* don't think anything. I read the newspaper and speculate like everyone else." He glanced quickly at Lange, as if to say, *what the hell's this about?*

Smith kept going. "But why? And how'd someone pull *that* off? Humph wouldn't have just stood there. He'd have kicked the shit out of the bastard."

Kenmuir said, "I didn't know him, but I imagine you're right. Probably would've put up a hell of a fight—*if* he saw it coming, which he probably didn't." Kenmuir delayed as his plate was taken away. "As for how, wait until his back's turned or he's lying down and zap him with a tranquilizer dart. That's how."

"The autopsy didn't note anything like that."

"You mean the part where the eagle-eyed coroner spots a suspicious pinprick *before* he starts cutting?"

Smith cradled his head in his hands. "I gather that doesn't happen."

"Movies. Paperbacks."

"Tranquilizer gun, for chrissake." Smith shook his head in a combination of disgust and amazement.

Lange asked, "Why do it at all?"

"More speculation? How about kidnapping? He was rich. His megabucks contract was all over the papers. And that's only him. How much you think some doofus would figure the *team* would pay? Very big bucks, that's how much."

"That's just plain dumb."

"That it is. But, if criminals were smart, most wouldn't be criminals. Even so, your average idiot thief doesn't come packing a tranquilizer gun and, maybe more to the point, why go to the trouble of tranquilizing someone if you're just going to shoot him in the head?" Kenmuir put his napkin on the table and scooted back his chair. "No. Something went wrong. Not enough drug was used or not enough got in him. He didn't go down and the bad guy had to make sure that he did." Kenmuir stopped and then restarted. "But what the hell do I know? As I said at the top of the show, it's all speculation."

Smith said, "That's more or less what the police told me, though without the tranquilizer gun part."

"Anyway, we've talked about this," Smith glanced at Lange, "and agree there's a connection. And not just with Jackson. There're also the preseason incidents. Let's not forget Brent Brittain and that hot-shot rookie, Achilles Simon."

Kenmuir held up his hands like a crossing guard. "Slow down, Smitty. There's never been a suggestion of foul play with Brittain. Motorcycles are deathtraps for anyone, famous or not. And that's even when you're not careening down the side of a mountain. Simon? The kid who got his ankle broken?"

Smith nodded and said, "In Tulsa."

"Yeah, Tulsa. Which, thanks to my detailed familiarity with geography, I recall as being in the South. That a couple good ol' boy racist assholes apparently didn't like Simon flashing himself by running around may be disgusting, but it's not exactly shocking. And then what? The bad guy—has to be the *same* bad guy, mind you—in Phoenix and Tulsa moves to the Bay Area where he arranges for sailboat-necklace man to hire Bellman to run down Jackson *and also* hires somebody else to, what, kidnap Orr?" Kenmuir rolled his eyes. "Come on, you guys, it's time to return to regular programming."

"You've got a better explanation?"

"No, I don't. I can't explain the inexplicable. However, I do know that merely because some events overlap doesn't mean there's a pattern. If men in L.A. and New York and Chicago get hurt and they all happen to be whatever ... stockbrokers? ... that doesn't prove that some mastermind's systematically disposing of stockbrokers."

"All-star ballplayers though? *Four* of them? Just luck of the draw?"

"That troubled me at first," Kenmuir admitted, "But, ironically, it's the very number of them that brought me back to reality. In other words, if it were only Jackson and Orr—both in the Bay Area—maybe a coincidence *would* be a stretch. But, when you add in far-flung cities like Phoenix and Tulsa, what else could it be?"

The strained silence was broken by Lange. "Fine, forget about Brittain and Simon. We *still* think that Jackson and Orr aren't flukes. We can't—won't—write them off as a simple coincidence. Not yet, anyway."

Kenmuir lit a cigarette with a commemorative Zippo from his collection: *First Pig Iron. January 1, 1943. Kaiser Steel.*

"Great. By all means talk with the police. They know what they're doing."

"We don't doubt that," Smith said. "At the same time, Detective Woodson, the lead detective, warned us that the chances of solving a homicide decline dramatically after the first three days. It's already past that. They're going to give up at some point."

"Maybe, but it's only been three days and high-profile cases like this get a lot of attention. Don't worry about anyone giving up yet."

Kenmuir saw Lange and Smith flick another glance at each other. "You know, whenever you two do that secret glance bullshit I start hearing warning bells. Now what?"

"Roomie, old pal," Lange began. Kenmuir shook his head and put his hands over his face. "We want you to work with the police on our behalf."

Kenmuir spread his fingers as a kind of futile screen and looked at Lange through them. "One of you is bad enough, but two?" He lowered his hands. "It doesn't matter, anyway. Civilians don't 'work with' the police, as if it were some British mystery on PBS."

"Maybe not, but I think they'd welcome the help. Detective Woodson admits they've got basically nothing."

"Trust me. They won't welcome the help."

"Why not just leave that to us. If we can arrange it, will you do it?"

"*Do* what?"

"Whatever it takes," Smith's voice cracked slightly, "to find out who killed my friend."

Kenmuir was hooked. He knew it and so did they.

Chapter 10

Tuesday afternoon, May 7, City of Martinez

THE CITY OF MARTINEZ, the Contra Costa County seat since 1850, is badly in need of reupholstering. It once thrived as a shipping port on the Sacramento River, but that ended when it was isolated by disrespectful freeways and railroad bridges. Now, the river's still flowing, but commerce isn't. Consequently, when the government offices and agencies shut down for the day, it does too.

When Kenmuir parked in front of the courthouse, it was like pulling up to a house where he'd once lived. On the first three floors were the superior courts and on top was the Office of the District Attorney, the site of his terrific first job, where he learned to be a trial lawyer. So many lessons. So many laughs. He loved the damn building.

He walked two blocks to the city's one high-rise office building. It housed the county departmental offices and was where, by Smith's arrangement, he was to meet Sheriff's Detectives Woodson and Friedman. He didn't recognize their names. He'd been gone too long.

For Kenmuir, the open spaces and cubicles of the Detective Bureau hadn't changed. The names had, but the furnishings were immutable. Metal desks, some gray, some beige, some chocolate; chipped, lopsided metal desk chairs, each canted toward the side of the desk with the telephone; cubicles with cloth partitions festooned with scraps of paper of different sizes and ubiquitous stick-on notes—all surrounded by a loudness that blended into a white noise everyone heard, but no one listened to. In fact, if you wanted everyone's attention, all you needed was silence. After all, good cops reacted only to two sounds: gunfire and no sound at all.

. .

HE WAITED IN THE STARK RECEPTION room until a woman came out of an unlabeled door. She'd evidently volunteered for a fiendish experiment with hair lamination so that, in a battle with a porcupine, the odds would favor her hair. She led Kenmuir with the disinterest of a nurse guiding a patient in an examining room for a barium enema, speaking to no one and no one speaking to her. When she reached Interview Room 3, she stopped so abruptly that he might've bumped into her if he'd been able to keep her pace.

She opened the door, but didn't motion him inside. He stepped inside anyway and turned sideways to face her. He tried to look as puzzled as possible when he asked, "Should I get undressed and sit on the table?" She may or may not have heard him. Instead, she merely closed the door.

The interview room was no lounge. Kenmuir sat on one of two chocolate metal chairs next to a gray metal table that was topped by a nicotine-splotched metal ashtray. When the door opened, the sound of a voice entered first. "Bring another chair, will ya?" A stocky man entered and extended the hand of a gorilla in Kenmuir's direction. It wasn't that the hand was huge; rather, it was extraordinarily hairy.

"I'm Detective Woodson. Cleon. Fucked-up name. I get called Rug. You can figure out why. This here's my partner, Brad Friedman. I'm senior, so he has to fetch chairs and interview the ugly witnesses, fill out forms, and pretty much do whatever I tell him."

Friedman ignored the remarks, passed by Woodson, and also shook hands. In contrast, he was tall, blonde, and the size of a grain silo. Both were decked out in the very finest detective fashion: polyester pants, polyester sport coats, and drip-dry shirts made from the same material as ladies' panties. Woodson's tie might have matched Friedman's coat and Friedman's tie might have matched Woodson's coat. For button-down Kenmuir, both ties would've been useful only as dish towels.

Friedman wore a .38 Special in a holster clipped to his belt by his hip, the sign of a strictly business, no-nonsense detective. Woodson's .45-automatic hung in a shoulder holster—as had Kenmuir's in bygone days—and confirmed a more aggressive, flamboyant style. Woodson slapped a manila folder on the scarred surface of the metal table. "There it is. We got nothin' about nothin'. You might say we've struck out."

Friedman grimaced. "Rug can't help himself. It's been going on since we drew this case."

Kenmuir smiled, but quickly became serious. "Let me make this clear right away, gentlemen . . . Thanks. I know it's a pain to have someone reading over your shoulder."

Woodson waved his hand dismissively. "No sweat, man. The lieutenant already told us he knows you. Ex-DA. Ex-homicide detective."

Kenmuir nodded and said, "Once upon a time, long ago." He immediately changed the subject from his own past to the present investigation. "Look, maybe you could bring me up to date? Start with the scene? Smith took me there this morning."

"Not a whole lot to tell. We were told to drop everything and go. Uniforms and paramedics were already there. Wife and kids at the neighbors. Body by the pool. Back of the head gone. Deader than shit." Friedman rocked in his chair in tacit agreement.

"Tell you the truth, there wasn't much to see. Warm day. Guy's done some yard work. Gets sweaty. Goes for a swim. No struggle, no cuts, no bruises. Someone blasts him in the head and he drops right now."

Kenmuir bit over his lower lip in contemplation. "What d'you mean, some yardwork?"

"There were clippings on the grass next to the hedge. Pretty obvious."

"Gardening stuff around?"

"No. Probably put away. Which is kinda funny, because who puts gardening tools away without picking up the clippings at the same time?"

"Any other clippings? Trash bag? Freshly used tools in the garage?"

Friedman said, "Nothing. Tools were all clean. Couldn't tell if they'd been used or not. Which is doubly funny, because the wife says he enjoyed chores—sort of a Mr. Fixit—but hated yard work. Didn't like bugs and yellow jackets. Can hardly blame him for that. Especially surprised her since the gardener was due soon.

"And him we interviewed. Little old Mexican guy. Been around the neighborhood since Junipero Serra planted the first lawn. Says he was working on yards on the other side of town. Story checks out."

"And the tranquilizer?"

"Nothing but speculation," Woodson admitted. "Big guy like that would've kicked the shit out of most people. Tranquilizer would've put him down."

"Dart gun?"

"Right on, counselor. Also what we're thinking, although that's only among us right now. No evidence, but how the hell else you gonna get it in him?"

Kenmuir gave an exaggerated wince. "It's not private anymore. I'm afraid I speculated out loud about it with Lange and Smith."

"No harm, no foul. We'd probably have done the same if our conversation had gone that way."

"You buy into burglary?"

"No fuckin' way. I mean, it's tempting. Big house, rich guy. But any regular burglar would've split as soon as he found someone home. Especially some strong guy. Besides, a tranquilizer gun—and evidently we all agree on that, proof or not—is way too sophisticated for your garden-variety thief. No pun intended."

"Any grudges?" Kenmuir asked.

"None. Well, maybe the agent he just fired, but he was in Hawaii. And anyway, even the agent says he wasn't fired for personal reasons. Disagreement over free agency tactics. Orr was a free agent after this year. Wife agrees."

"Visitors? Anyone stop by?"

"Not that anyone saw. We talked to the neighbors, but . . . You said you went there?" Kenmuir nodded. "Then you saw for yourself. Typical Orinda. Houses far apart, trees and bushes everywhere. Not an ideal spot for casual observations."

"Mind if I talk to some neighbors on my own?"

"Be our guest. If we missed something and you can find it, great. You got any sense of this?"

"My gut reaction's kidnapping gone wrong."

"Good possibility. Of course, we're long on possibilities and real short on proof."

Kenmuir continued, "Furthermore, I'm not at all comfortable with the clippings. Why all of a sudden get an urge to do a little trimming if he hates yard work? Especially if he knew the gardener was going to take care of it. And he then puts away the clippers—which, mind you, he takes the trouble to wipe clean—but doesn't pick up his mess? Doesn't make much sense."

Woodson shook a Marlboro out of a flip-top box, lit one, and talked as the smoke trickled out of his mouth. "Okay, but if he didn't do the clipping, then who did? And why didn't that guy clean up? Orr was lounging around the pool, but didn't see some stranger walking around the backyard? And doing what, clipping bushes? On the other hand, maybe Orr knew him and stopped to talk before the guy had a chance to rake up. But then how'd the clippers get put away? Hell, maybe the bad guy spent the night in the yard disguised as a bush, for all we know. Nah, the whole thing makes no sense."

Friedman said, "Amen to that. See, Dave, it didn't take you long to catch up. Now there'll be three of us kicking over rocks."

"Well, I'll try to kick some different rocks." He snapped a quick glance at Woodson. "I mean, I sure wouldn't want to throw any curveballs at you."

Woodson laughed. Friedman threw up his arms in mock disgust. "No way I'm dealing with *two* comedians. I'm outta here."

So was Kenmuir, but for a different reason. He could hardly wait to get back in the game . . . officially.

Chapter 11

Wednesday morning, May 8, City of Orinda

A FTER SPENDING NINETY MINUTES repetitively introducing himself to Orr's neighbors as "the A's representative," Kenmuir learned nothing new. What was to be his last house could've been home sweet home for an antebellum cotton king; it made "Tara" look like a miner's cabin. No Scarlett O'Hara answered the door, though: shapeless and homely, she'd likely never caught so much as a whiff of Old Spice in high school. Seeing *her* made Kenmuir want to see *him*.

On the other hand, she'd obviously prevailed in the end, while the former Prom Queen was probably living in a shack, buffeted between six unruly children and a now-beefy football-hero husband. She was as personally gracious as she was physically unattractive. After sensitive, discreet questions about the welfare of the Orr family, she told Kenmuir how "everyone, just everyone" in the neighborhood had discussed where they'd been that day. Only yesterday, for example, she'd learned that her friend Mrs. Ball, who lived on another street, had strolled by with her dog that very afternoon.

That got Kenmuir's attention. None of the voluminous police reports mentioned a Mrs. Ball or any dog walker. Of course, why would they? She wasn't a neighbor.

Would she mind calling Mrs. Ball? She was glad to.

Ten minutes later, Mrs. Ball opened her door and proved Kenmuir wrong about the Prom Queen's grim fate. Mrs. Ball *was* the Prom Queen. She brought glass tumblers of lemonade to a glass patio table shaded by an expansive umbrella. Ripples were subsiding in a kidney-shaped pool, trimmed with mosaic fishes, and explained her wet ponytail. Her golden retriever, Radar, lay at her feet and had nothing to do except look upward at the insides of her tan thighs. Good dog. Happy dog.

Kenmuir didn't believe in instant informality and addressed her as he would a client. She was having none of it. "Please stop calling me Mrs. Ball. My name's Lucy."

He looked at her with exaggerated skepticism. "Right. Mine's Mertz, Fred Mertz. You can call me Fred."

She smiled radiantly. "And you can stop. I've heard them all. It's what happens when Lucille Davidson marries Randall Ball. You've heard that love is blind? It's also deaf." Her laugh was throaty and unself-conscious.

"What about a middle name or a nickname? Some place to hide."

"My middle name is in honor of my grandmother Bertha."

It was his turn to laugh. "Okay. Middle name's out. How about a nickname? Muffy, Pixie, something like that?"

"Never. Besides, nicknames are for men. All my ex-husband's friends call him Slug. It's hateful. I'll suffer along with Lucy." She smiled again. The pride of Pepsodent.

Whatever information might be coming, it couldn't be more valuable than what just dropped like gentle rain from heaven. Ex-husband, as in former husband and no-longer-the-husband. Alas, the lovely Prom Queen was now stranded in a bleak and lonely life, hoping to meet a dashing, witty, and urbane bachelor. Preferably a lawyer. And, as luck would have it . . .

Lucy explained that it was her practice to walk Radar before her two children returned from school. Because her route that day had taken her by the Orrs' house, she was shocked when she learned he'd been killed. She'd wondered how long it'd been after she'd walked by.

"What do you mean, *after*? Why after?"

"Well, because someone else was there when I went by."

"How do you know that?"

"Because a car was there—"

"Gardener's pick-up? Rakes and lawn mower and stuff?" *Slow down, Kenmuir. Don't be a boor. Don't interrupt.*

"No, just a car. Parked by the driveway, kinda beat-up looking. You don't see that much around here, so it stood out. But what really caught my attention were the letters on the license plate: RPB."

Kenmuir cocked his head backward in genuine surprise. "You're kidding. I mean, really? Nobody, but nobody, ever remembers license plates."

"I wouldn't normally, but those are Randy's initials. I thought how irritated he'd be to see his precious initials on some old clunker. Silly, I guess. Do I sound like a real dope?"

"Not at all. We all remember things better if we associate them with something else." *Damn, that could be troublesome: Ken-muir = John Muir = grizzled old hiker. Or Kenmuir = Kenmore = boring home appliance.* "You said old. What about the plates? Were they the old kind, where the numbers came first?"

Her forehead wrinkled. Kenmuir could almost see her memory groping. "I want to say yes. But I'm not positive. I'm sorry."

"No apology needed. What you've got is great. Anything else?"

"Yes, I guess. It was a shade of blue. Not dark. And I think it was an American car. That's all." Flash another smile. "Old and blue and American."

"You tell the police about the car?"

"No. I haven't talked to the police. It never occurred to me." She was obviously alarmed by his question. "Should I?"

"No. Don't worry about it. I'll take it from here."

When Kenmuir left, he gave her a business card. "Please call me if you remember anything else." *And, most importantly, remember my name.*

When she politely said, "It was nice meeting you," he promised himself to make sure it wasn't their last meeting.

If there had been a speed record from Orinda on the southern edge of the county to the Sheriff's office in Martinez on the northern, Kenmuir would've broken it. Compared to his Audi 5000, the 1968 Mustang on the San Francisco streets in *Bullitt* and the 1971 Pontiac Le Mans under the elevated railway in *The French Connection* were just cruisin' along.

The three letters couldn't have electrified Woodson and Friedman more than if they'd been on a winning lottery ticket. They wasted no time taking advantage of the break. "Thanks to you," Friedman bowed in Kenmuir's direction, "we've finally got something to do." It was the kind of neat and methodical project that Friedman loved.

California's license-plate numbering system had changed in April 1980, so there were 1,000 cars from 001RPB through

999RPB. "The new license plates are probably not on an older car, but we can't take the chance. So that'll add a thousand more: 1RPB001 through 1RPB999. We'll be at the mercy of the Department of Motor Vehicles computer, but you gotta believe this case'll get some priority. The list'll have addresses, colors, VINs, makes, and models. Then we pull out every blue car. Some risk, but not much of one since, even if a car gets repainted, it's usually the same color. Helluva lot of cars, helluva long list."

A pile of connected sheets, oversized and unwieldy, would be dropped on a police aide's desk as soon as enough computer time could be begged or bullied from DMV. His task would be to isolate blue and variants of blue.

Friday evening, May 10, City of Oakland

A GRATEFUL PHIL SMITH invited Kenmuir to that night's game between the A's and Mariners at the Oakland Coliseum. Kenmuir felt underdressed without the gloves, parka, and double socks he was used to wearing at Candlestick Park with Lange.

Underrated among the nation's ballparks, the Coliseum had a symmetrical outfield that gave no advantage to either side of the plate. The Oakland hills were the backdrop over the grassy slope in dead center. With the Nimitz Freeway so close that one could throw a ball from the slow lane and hit the stadium, access was easy. The surrounding parking lot was vast enough for the population of Vermont.

Kenmuir and Smith had the open-air owners' box to themselves and chatted idly. After the Mariners took a 6-5 lead and the teams changed sides at the end of the sixth inning, Smith turned to look directly at Kenmuir. No more idle chatter. "What do *you* think happened to Humph?"

Kenmuir flicked his wrists in the equivalence of a shrug. "Beats me. Maybe we'll never know. You'll hate that, but you've got to be ready for it."

"I thought the license number would lead to the killer."

Kenmuir cracked open a particularly large peanut. "Might. Might not. Three letters and a shade of blue aren't a whole helluva lot to go on. Plus the car could've been stolen, so the actual owners will be innocent. Or it's repainted by now and has a different license plate. Or it's clunking around Tijuana with no license at all."

"And you still don't think Orr and Jackson are connected."

"They could be, I suppose. Hard to grab onto that, though. Some scumbag driving a shit car and wielding a tranquilizer gun, as well as a retard like Bellman? That's an improbable pairing. And then what? Some nut case is out there, motivated to set up *both*? Why? Because he's anti-major league baseball in the Bay Area?"

Kenmuir took a swallow of white wine. How he loved the owners' box. "And then he's able to pull it off? That's a neat trick." He put his hand on Smith's shoulder. "Look, you've got to wait. You want answers, and there aren't any yet. Hell, we don't even know enough to ask the right questions, let alone figure out who's the enemy."

"Maybe *that's* the right word. Enemy." Smith returned his attention to the game. Smith's silence lasted only a minute or so. "I guess you'd know about enemies. Larry said you were in Vietnam."

"True."

"From what I've heard, it was a mean place." Like many others, Smith was at once curious about his generation's war and glad he'd never had to find out for himself.

Kenmuir nodded, more to himself than to Smith. "Also true."

"What'd you do?"

"I was part of what you might call a special recon unit."

"What, Green Berets?"

"No, that's Special Forces. I'd never compare us to them, not in training or in function. We were a hybrid. A former First Cavalry Division commanding general had wanted some, I guess you'd say special, troops of his own. So each brigade got two ten-man units that technically didn't exist, but were in fact staffed by seasoned volunteers who were assigned on paper to various other sections of the Division. He was a good ol' boy Virginian so he named them accordingly. The two in my brigade were Jackson and Stuart. Stuart was mine . . .

Chapter 12

Early 1970s, Vietnam, near the Cambodian border

A GUST SUDDENLY BLEW THROUGH THE command bunker, whisking away many of the papers off Captain Bryce Henson's desk and pissing him off as well.

Most debarking junior infantry officers who arrived at Cam Ranh Bay for their initial assignments hid in the latrines to avoid an assignment to the combative First Cavalry Division. Not Henson: when he'd arrived almost a year and a half ago, he'd requested it. He'd been ready for command and commendations—but, instead, he'd been plunked into the vacancy created when brigade commander Colonel Lee Gibson's aide had rotated out the week before. His combat decorations were still waiting.

The wind also ushered in a drenched soldier, shrouded in a bright-green parka with the gold stripe of a second lieutenant in the center of his helmet. His green jungle boots were shiny and the lower lengths of his fatigue pants were not yet bleached by the Southeast Asian sun. Gumby goes to war.

Like an auctioneer looking for the next bid, the lieutenant scanned the soldiers in the bunker, saw the captain's tracks on

Henson's collar, stood at attention, but, being indoors, decided not to salute: "Sir. Lieutenant David Kenmuir, sir. I was ordered to report to Colonel Gibson."

Henson folded his arms across his chest and cocked his head at the man perhaps three years younger than himself. He exaggeratedly looked Kenmuir up and down and then asked, "How long you been in, Lieutenant?"

Kenmuir stared unblinkingly over Henson's head. "Sir, one week, sir."

"Not in-country, mister. In the Army."

"Sir, nearly ten months, sir." Everyone thus learned that the baby lieutenant would be promoted to first lieutenant in two months.

Henson stepped closer. "You think that's long enough to know that you salute when you report in? Do you ... *lieutenant?*"

With his mental salute-or-not-salute debate now resolved, Kenmuir didn't hesitate a millisecond. As if on parade, he snapped his upper arm parallel to the ground, wrist straight, fingers extended and joined. "Sir. Lieutenant David Kenmuir reporting as ordered ... Sir."

Almost on cue, the rickety door at the back of the bunker opened and "full bird" Colonel Gibson stepped out. A tall man with broad shoulders and a narrow waist, he still looked like the wide receiver he'd been for the University of Arkansas, way back when. "Lotta noise out here, people," He turned toward the unknown, but saluting, lieutenant shedding water in the middle of the room.

A Deadly Game

Colonel Gibson glanced at Henson and then at Sergeant Scott. "Who's this?" He flicked his right hand in a perfunctory return salute and said, "You can drop the arm and be at ease, son."

Sergeant Scott handed the colonel a sheet of paper. "It's the new lieutenant, sir."

"Right." Without looking up from the paper, Gibson glanced at Henson: "You and Scottie. My office." He half-smiled at Kenmuir. "You too, Lieutenant. Without the waterfall."

Inside his office, the colonel sat down and spoke to himself as he read the sheet of paper. "I see . . . Good, good." He looked up at Kenmuir, who was standing at "parade rest" in front of his desk; the sergeant and captain sat informally in chairs. "See you went to Stanford. Good school, though not much in football, eh Lieutenant? And Ranger school. Not bad." He turned to Sergeant Scott. "Where should we put this fine young man, Scottie?"

Scott was preempted by Henson: "As we've discussed before, sir, I could use an assistant. Free me up for more significant responsibilities."

Gibson appeared to consider that possibility, but only briefly. "Well, Captain, that time may come but"—he again looked at the sergeant—"didn't Stuart Unit's XO just rotate home?"

"Yessir."

Henson stiffened in his chair. "Sir, may I be heard? About that XO slot?"

"Well, son, you can, but it'll have to be later. For now, this lieutenant's gonna work for Captain Gorman in Stuart. Scottie, have someone get his gear and you take him over there."

Henson's expression was stoic, but his mind was throwing a tantrum. He'd extended his tour to get a combat command, but Colonel Gibson had dodged his every request and kept him trapped behind his goddamn desk—even though a gifted commander of men, which he instinctively knew he was, was supposed to command. A born leader was supposed to lead. His reserves of patience now had been exhausted. So be it: if his job was to assist, then that's exactly what he'd do. He'd "assist" in shifting himself to a combat command. He *had* to see some action.

Almost five months later

CAPTAIN GORMAN'S APPARENTLY accidental death had opened up command of Stuart Unit. At last Henson's patron saint was on the ball. Henson waited one day—enough time not to be pushy, but not enough time to risk any interference—before he lingered in front of Colonel Gibson's desk after the daily administrative briefing.

When Gibson asked, "Something else on your mind, Captain?" Henson remained seated, so as to encourage a collegial attitude. "Yessir, there is. Stuart Unit."

"What about it?"

"I'd like to replace Dan Gorman. I'm the right rank, I'm qualified, and I'm ready." Henson hesitated momentarily. "Frankly, sir, I think I've earned the chance." Even more than Colonel Gibson knew, because it was Henson who'd arranged Gorman's "accident."

Colonel Gibson leaned back in his chair. Instead of replying immediately, he lit a cigarette. He'd anticipated Henson's request and already made his decision. "I appreciate your request, Captain. It's what I'd expect from an officer of your caliber." He exhaled a plume of smoke as he stood up. "Unfortunately, you're too good at what you do here, son."

That wasn't entirely true . . . Gibson *was* mindful that Henson had extended his tour of duty specifically for a combat command, and he deserved consideration for that reason alone. Trouble was, there wasn't much else to consider: His leadership potential was so poor that Gibson doubted anyone would follow him to the latrine, even if they all had dysentery. He was arrogant, self-centered, and disliked by everyone at headquarters, officers and enlisted alike. Indeed, Gibson wasn't aware of Henson having so much as *one* friend.

To lead men in combat, you didn't have to be best man at their weddings. Probably shouldn't be, come to that. They didn't even have to like you, but they sure as hell had to respect you and trust that you'd bring them home. Gibson suspected that the Stuart Unit veterans wouldn't trust Henson to lead them to Saigon on a tour bus with someone else driving.

"We make too good a team, Captain. You're needed more here."

"Which company commander *is* going to get the job? If I may ask."

"Well, I want to keep Stuart's command turmoil at a minimum. Gorman's accident was such a goddamn fluke. Enough's enough. Which is why I've decided to let his XO take over. Stuart's used to him."

In spite of himself, Henson lurched out of his chair. "But Kenmuir's *a lieutenant*! It's a captain's slot, and I'm a captain.

He's not even a career officer . . . " Henson suddenly remembered who and where he was. ". . . sir."

"I know all that, and it's reassuring that you're ready to go if Kenmuir doesn't work out."

Henson left Gibson's office with only one thought: *That lieutenant's not going to get away with this.*

Chapter 13

Saturday morning, May 11, City of Anaheim

FERDINAND "FRISKY" FELLNER WORE LEVIS and a gray T-shirt with a stylized, predatory bird's head underneath the word *Hawkeyes*. The morning was already warm enough to guarantee the sixth day of Southern California's spring heat wave. He wasn't exercising, so his pace was leisurely, more of a shamble than a walk.

Stress would come later. That's how he made his living. He was the closer for the Toronto Blue Jays.

When a baseball team's ahead in the last inning, the closer is summoned to eliminate the opponent's last hitters. He doesn't have the luxury of easing into the game over a few innings, maybe yielding a run or two. Instead, he has to stroll from the bullpen at a moment's notice and immediately throw strikes. Without a quality closer, a team is usually a quality loser. That's why the closer's statistic is called a "save," a victory preserved.

Unlike most closers, Fellner didn't dominate or overwhelm; he prevailed by deception.

He had no aspirin tablets, no rockets, no lasers. Instead, his pitches were like flies in a windstorm, curving, dropping, rising, wobbling. He ignored the center of the plate and only paid attention to its edges.

He loved playing, but he hated the big cities where professional baseball teams were located. Too crowded, too sprawling, too disorderly . . . too everything. "You can take this Iowa boy out of the farm, but you can't take the farm out of the boy," he'd say. Which was why he relaxed—escaped, really—by taking a walk in the very early mornings, after the night people had gone home and before the day people came out.

When the spacious street began to fill with traffic, he left its sidewalks and turned onto those of a peaceful side street of modest apartment buildings, all with stucco exteriors of different pastel colors and most evoking British country estates, like The Beaconsfield or The Devonshire Arms. He smiled at an entrance archway festooned with large "pearls" and hoped the Pearly Gate Apartments wasn't a retirement home.

Eventually, he came to an intersection with an apartment building on each corner and a two-way stop sign. He decided to cross in the through direction. As he neared the limit line for the stop sign to his right, so did a green Chevy Nova. He hesitated and looked to confirm that the car was slowing for the stop sign. It was. Acknowledging the car with a wave of his million-dollar arm, he walked in front of it, about three feet outside the limit line.

The Nova, which had been coasting in second gear, lunged forward as soon as Fellner looked away. Fellner never had a chance: his right leg was struck first by the Nova's bumper and then by its grille, although that would've been visible only in time-lapse photography. However, the angle of the grille did carom Fellner sideways onto the sidewalk, beyond the wheels that otherwise would've driven over him. The minutiae of physics may not have spared his leg, but they did save his life.

According to Fellner's orthopedic surgeon, the pins would allow his femur and tibia to heal "better than normal." His knee was another matter entirely. "Only time will tell. Of course," he added unnecessarily, "your season's over."

Chapter 14

Tuesday morning, May 14, City of Martinez

As the search for the Chevy Nova that hit Fellner was beginning, the search for the mystery car in Thumper Orr's driveway was nearly over.

The police aide had waited impatiently all day Friday waiting for the DMV's computer—undoubtedly a room-sized Sperry-Univac salvaged from *The $64,000 Question* quiz show of 1950s TV—to isolate all California's RPB license plates. Then he spent Monday waiting for a glitch that kept glitching until midafternoon. On Tuesday morning, he'd driven to Sacramento, picked up the printouts while they still were as warm as freshly baked donuts, and returned to the sheriff's office by 11:00 a.m.

He was about as sharp as a bald tire, but he also was very painstaking, very thorough—and *very* slow. Because he read every number—and every color and every owner's name and every registered address—of more than 2,000 license plates before underlining any blue car with his yellow Magic Marker. Shortly before 2:00 p.m., he proudly presented the decorated list to the waiting detectives.

In order to identify the addresses—and presumably the vehicles—located in northern California, Friedman, two other detectives, and Woodson drew an arbitrary midline at Paso

Robles-Visalia. They then began the tedious process of identifying the addressed towns north of that line. By 4:00 p.m., Woodson was sick to death of what seemed to be California's mania for ending the names of all its obscure towns—Requa . . . Zamora . . . Hoopa . . . Pondosa—with an "a." That also was when Arnold Brautsch began one of his periodic, often hour-long strolls through the Detective Bureau.

Officially, Brautsch was a detective in paper crimes, such as forgery and check fraud, although no one could figure out what paper he managed to "detect" by chatting around the office or talking on the phone; unofficially, he was an anachronism, with his Joe Friday flattop and short-sleeve white shirts, and terminally boring. During his daily stroll, he progressively stopped to chat with every detective and every secretary at every desk. It never dawned on him that he might be annoying or, even if it did, he wasn't fazed. He was an equal-opportunity conversationalist.

He eventually meandered to Woodson's desk. "How they hangin', Rug?" He sat next to Woodson's desk in a metal chair with a cushion made from plastic likely synthesized somewhere in Thailand from old crankcase drippings. Picking up the stack of printouts already reviewed and relegated to a corner of Woodson's desk, he began leafing through them, half-heartedly skimming the contents, and asking, "This got to do with Thumper?"

Woodson knew that Arnie was like a bird landing on a limb: sometimes he'd sit contentedly for a while and other times he'd be gone in a moment. One never knew why he came or went, since he had his own sense of timing and was oblivious to anyone else's. So Woodson sighed as a kind of signal that he was too busy to talk. When that proved useless, he said, "Look, Arnie, I'm kinda busy . . . "

Oblivious. "What's with these lists?"

Jesus, Woodson thought, don't do this to me now. Nevertheless, he answered because, for a reason that mystified everyone, Arnie was strangely likeable: "Turns out a blue car was parked at Orr's residence around the time of the killing. Citizen got a partial plate. This is one time when we *did* get lucky. We're trying to track it down. And I'm kinda knee-deep into it here, so I'd better—"

Having stopped listening after the first sentence, Brautsch simply interrupted. "No shit. Whatta lucky break." He fanned a handful of the documents and instinctively discerned the process of reviewing them. Paper crimes, after all. "Now you've gotta go through all the plate numbers to find it? What're these x marks on the side?"

Woodson explained the marks and silently groaned when Brautsch began to thumb through the sheets and read more carefully, all while trading remarks with passersby who playfully asked, "Hey, Arnie, givin' Rug a hand?"

"Documents, *compadre*. That's my life." Brautsch suddenly paused, held a sheet away from his eyes, and then melodramatically brought it closer, like in a cartoon. "Well, I'll be damned. Would you believe it? Here's someone I know." He twirled the sheet in his hand so that Woodson could see the name where he was pointing. "Rafael Sanchez."

Woodson held his hands to his temples. "How 'bout that. Maybe I'll find someone I know when *I* move on—which I've gotta do, man."

Brautsch was unflappable. "You know Sanchez's type. Typical low-life scumbag. Into small-time drugs, running some book, fencing small-potatoes property. Says here that he lives in San Pablo. That's true. Gets called Monica 'cause he's always playing the harmonica. Pretty good, too. Busted him once for kiting checks."

"Doesn't sound like our guy. Long way from bad checks to murder." Woodson didn't look up. *Don't encourage him.*

Brautsch continued, "Nope, you got that right. Wouldn't have the *cojones*. But his cousin would. Raging asshole named Jesus LaPera. Two trips to the joint. Tight with *La Familia*. Nobody fucks with him. How's *he* sound?"

"A lot better. But the car's gotta be blue, and this one isn't."

Giving Woodson a kind of fuck-you look, Brautsch stood up and helicoptered the sheet back onto the desk. "Well, 'azure' sure ain't red, *compadre*." Suddenly, a new tune must've started playing in Brautsch's mind, because he strolled out of Woodson's cubicle as unannounced as he'd arrived.

Woodson reconsidered the sheet Brautsch had tossed onto the desk. No question about it: "azure." But no check mark. On the other hand, azure was one of those colors—like puce, ocher, and vermilion—that no one, least of all Woodson, ever could visualize. So Woodson shouted to the room in general. "Hey, anyone know what the hell color *azure* is?"

He got a variety of shouts back: "Kind of green-ish, I think." "Sorta like gold, maybe?" "Not a color. It's the name of an island." "You ignoramus, that's Azores." "Fuck you."

The dictionary had the last word. It agreed with Brautsch: "light-purplish *blue*."

About an hour later, Woodson called Kenmuir to crow about

azure, Monica Sanchez, and Jesus LaPera. "No doubt about it, Dave, LaPera's a bad motherfucker. May not be our killer, but I sure wouldn't put it past him."

Mentally, Kenmuir was halfway to the door. "At the very least, he's a first-round choice. Think maybe we should chat with the boy?"

There was an odd silence on Woodson's end of the line, like he was calling long distance from Botswana. When he spoke, it wasn't as peppy as before. "We're gonna have a problem with the 'we' part. Officially, you're a civilian. We'll keep you posted, but—"

Kenmuir flared. "That's *bullshit*. Absolute bullshit. I'm not getting left behind." He took a deep breath. "Far be it from me to get self-righteous, but *I'm* the one who found the damn number. I've earned the right to go where it leads."

Back to Botswana. Woodson's silence returned.

Kenmuir continued. "Look, Rug, citizens do ride-alongs all the time. Good public relations. Support the thin blue line and all that. That's what I'll be, your classic ride-along."

"Ride-alongs with *detectives*? When'd that ever happen?"

"A technicality. We'll blaze a new trail in community outreach. Hell, I'll even sit in the back seat."

"Damn, I don't know. The captain'll shit, whether you're an ex-cop or not. Plus we're just about to leave."

"Another technicality. I can be there in twenty. Deal?"

Another pause was followed by, "What the hell. But let's not advertise it. We'll meet you at the Pacheco off-ramp, not here."

"Good man. I'll be easy to recognize. I'll be wearing an azure shirt."

"Fuck you."

Chapter 15

Tuesday afternoon, May 14, City of San Pablo

BECAUSE THE SHERIFF DEPARTMENT'S FORD Crown Victoria was white and had no lettering or emergency equipment, it was considered unmarked. Blend inconspicuously into any neighborhood. Which was nonsense, because no Chicano in any barrio drives a Crown Victoria in *any* color. Carrying three Anglos—wearing ties, no less—it might as well have had "This Is a Police Car" emblazoned on its sides.

That was why Sanchez's neighborhood became eerily deserted as soon as the Crown Victoria began to creep slowly through it. It was like a scene from a post-nuclear disaster movie: no traffic, an abandoned bicycle, an unattended ball, some papers shifting with an occasional breeze.

The house rented by Rafael, aka Monica, Sanchez was of the rectangular, flat-roofed variety common in movies about the temptations and hardships at home during World War II. Lonely and drop-dead-gorgeous wife's husband is slogging it out in Sicily or Saipan, and she's working at the aircraft plant where she meets some 4-F stud who shows very well in a sleeveless undershirt but has the morality of a cobra. One night she has a bit too much to drink at a party and, when he asks if he can come inside, she doesn't say no. That kind of house.

A largely azure Ford Tempo, extensively dented and with much of its original color rubbed or scraped, was parked partially down a driveway consisting of two parallel strips of concrete, each slightly wider than a tire. The Tempo's license plate, oddly pristine in comparison with its abused body, had the letters RPB and three numbers.

Woodson parked so as to block the driveway and thereby made the Ford even more conspicuous. Friedman and he stepped out, and put on their sport coats. They were unconcerned that their handguns were visible, because they knew they couldn't have been more identifiable as cops even if they'd been in full dress uniforms. Woodson held out his hand as if he were directing traffic to stop. In this instance, the traffic was Kenmuir. "We'll check it out, Dave. Give you a shout if it's cool." He tossed the car keys on the passenger seat and said, "You won't need 'em, but there're a shotgun and a .357 in the trunk. Just in case."

Kenmuir didn't want to be left behind, but he'd pushed Woodson far enough already.

The residents had waited in hiding until the white car made its choice. Now they emerged like actors going to their marks at the beginning of a play. Children stood in yards and on sidewalks. Adults lingered on their porches or front steps. All maintained a stationary silence.

With the air conditioner off, Kenmuir could've roasted a chicken inside the Crown Victoria. So he stepped outside for cooler air, but also drifted nonchalantly toward the trunk. An onlooker might not have realized that he was unarmed, but he was acutely aware of it.

Woodson and Friedman stood on opposite sides of the wood-frame screen door that covered the closed front door. It was so loose that, when Woodson knocked on it authoritatively, it banged back at him. A jackhammer at a construction site would've made less noise. Kenmuir jerked in unison with everyone watching from their homes. But there was no response.

Woodson knocked again. Another bang. This time, no one twitched; no one answered, either.

Friedman opened the screen and pounded on the closed front door. A deeper, more resonant noise, but no less loud. Whether it was the vibration or the sound that got attention, a woman's voice squawked something in Spanish. After a moment, a short woman in her late teens, barefoot, wearing short-shorts and a halter top, opened the door. She radiated an attitude of defiance.

Friedman said something. She shrugged and stepped aside, allowing the two detectives to enter. The front door closed, but the weary screen door remained ajar.

Kenmuir slipped the round-headed key into the trunk's lock, turning it so as to spring the lock, although the trunk lid remained closed.

The interior of the house was as quiet as a mausoleum. Whether due to a breeze too insignificant to be noticed or to the gradual effect of gravity on its exhausted springs, the screen door suddenly slammed shut against the wood frame of the front door. Everyone in the neighborhood flinched simultaneously.

It might as well have been a starter's signal—because a series of explosions immediately erupted from inside the house. Someone screamed. More gunshots followed. Kenmuir yanked open the trunk, and grabbed both the holstered .357 and the shotgun.

He ran toward the front door, holding the stock of the shotgun with his left hand and shoving the holstered handgun inside his waistband with his right. By the time he reached the door, he'd pumped a round into the shotgun's breech.

He turned the doorknob and kicked open the front door. There was no reaction or response.

He quickly stepped inside and stood to the left of the doorframe, protecting his back. The barrel of the shotgun tracked wherever he looked in the small living room. What he saw was mayhem.

The teenage girl was curled fetally in a chair in the far corner with her arms wrapped around her head, attempting both to hide and to protect herself. Woodson was seated on the floor, his back against the wall, holding the front of his blood-stained shirt. His eyes were open, but his face was so ghostly white that it was difficult to tell where the collar of his shirt began. Friedman was lying on a skewed couch, almost as if he were taking a brief nap.

Kenmuir heard a noise from the rear of the house. The shooter was running, probably out the back door. Kenmuir passed through the rest of the living room, raced through the tiny kitchen in four strides, struck the back door with his left shoulder, and barged onto a small concrete porch.

The backyard was surprisingly large for such a small house. At its far end was a rickety six-foot wooden fence. Running straight ahead toward it was the Mexican male adult later identified as Jesus LaPera. His long hair flapped against his shirtless back that, like his arms, was covered with tattoos; he held an automatic handgun in his right hand. A few steps before reaching the fence, he glanced backward over his right shoulder.

Seeing Kenmuir, he changed his mind about vaulting the fence. Instead, he extended his left arm to brace himself against it, raised the automatic, and began to turn it toward his unexpected pursuer.

Only ten yards away, Kenmuir didn't break stride. As LaPera's arm was swinging around, he fired the shotgun, jacked another shell into the chamber, and fired again. The first round struck LaPera's right side. The force of the blast hurled him against the fence, erased the inked head of a leopard, and obliterated most of his right lung. LePera ricocheted off the fence almost as if he was eager to greet the shotgun's forthcoming second round. And so he did, when it plowed through the center of his chest.

Kenmuir wasted no more time on LaPera; dead or alive, he wasn't going anywhere. Chambering another round in the shotgun, he ran back into the house. A hasty search of the two bedrooms, their closets, and the bathroom revealed nothing. Kenmuir hurried back to the living room.

He knelt by Woodson. "I'll call for help. You hang in there, man. Don't you go bailing out on me." *This will not happen again. This will not happen again.*

Woodson grimaced and hugged himself, shuddering with a spasm of pain. "Hurts like a motherfucker."

Kenmuir shifted to Friedman. He touched the side of the detective's neck where the carotid pulse should've been. The neck was warm but motionless. When Kenmuir gently brushed Friedman's eyelids, the eyes closed.

Chapter 16

Wednesday morning, May 15, City of Martinez

IN BYGONE DAYS, NURSES IN WHITE uniforms arranged white sheets while doctors in white coats ministered skillfully to patients in white gowns. Bright and clean. Then some nationwide study by a paint manufacturer "proved" that white was sterile and harsh, only suitable for an aged hospital with aged techniques. By contrast, seafoam green was restful and cozy, confirming a high-tech, modern hospital. Luckily, the same manufacturer was able to offer a very good price on vats of seafoam green paint.

Kenmuir walked soundlessly through the open door of Woodson's room in Contra Costa County Hospital. The bandaged detective dozed in a bed tilted so he could comfortably watch the television hanging from the ceiling. A tube disappeared into the bushy hair on his left forearm. A tray with both spongy carrots and carrot-colored Jell-o was on his right.

"Nothing like a quick nap in the middle of the working day."

Woodson didn't open his eyes. "Fuck you, counselor."

"That's good. Using your time to build a more powerful vocabulary." Kenmuir lightly squeezed Woodson's right forearm. "How you doing, Rug?"

"Helluva lot better than Junior. Can't fuckin' believe it." The burly detective looked up. "Funny thing is, we sometimes talked about it. Worried more about me, the way I crash around. Junior, he *always* paid attention and *always* played by the rules. And he ends up buying it. I don't get it." He turned his head away and covered his eyes with his hand. Kenmuir had lived through the same mixture of sorrow and guilt more than once. There was nothing to be said.

Woodson turned back toward Kenmuir. "I got pretty lucky. Took one round in the gut, but somehow it missed everything but the spleen. Hurt like a bastard. All those stories about being gut shot? They're true." Woodson stopped talking as he rocked his head up and down, reflecting on an unspoken thought. Then he asked, "You've been here, haven't you?"

Kenmuir nodded, but quickly changed the subject back to Woodson. "And now? Any better?"

"Comes and goes. Got me on painkillers. The doc says they were mainly concerned about blood loss. Damn near drained myself, I guess. They refilled the tank, and now I lie around, watch TV, and tell the nurses that I'm not quite ready yet."

Kenmuir mimicked Woodson's forced smile. "It's a standard diagnostic technique in many of your better hospitals, my boy. You're lying on some gurney and bleeding like a fresh steak and hurting like a sonofabitch. Beautiful nurse touches your dick. No reaction. Doctor turns to the nurse and says, 'He's hurting.' *That's* the test. All these machines are merely for show."

Woodson chuckled, but stopped abruptly as he tightened his eyes, grimaced, and put his hand on his stomach. Kenmuir said, "If you don't want to talk about it, don't. But what the hell happened? I sure don't know."

"Me neither, it happened so damn fast. Me and Junior barely had time to split apart in the living room. All of a sudden this mean-looking little fuck just sorta appears in the little hallway. He's not there and then he is. I'm looking at him, and he's looking at us, and no one says shit. Then there's a slam. Front door, I guess. Sounded like a bomb."

"Tell me about it. The whole neighborhood jumped."

"So'd the little fucker. Right *now*, he starts firing. Somehow I pull out my weapon and fire back. Too damn late. Don't know what Junior did. I go down, number than shit. Legs don't work and everything gets real quiet. Unbelievable." He took a deep breath and again composed himself. "Where are we now, Dave?"

Kenmuir leaned against the wall on the other side of the bed. "Well, Monica's found some hole and crawled very deeply into it. But he's got nowhere to go. Probably never been more than ten miles from the barrio, so it's only a matter of time before he turns up."

Woodson looked disgusted. "Maybe he can tell us why fucking LePera took us on. Career asshole like that, he'd been rousted 10,000 times. More likely he'd stand there and mouth off about his rights. We didn't even have our weapons out, for chrisssake."

"We're never going to know for sure," Kenmuir said. "My guess? Comes out into the living room. Sees you two, immediately makes you for cops, and figures you know he's good for Orr. What's his choice? Stand there like a good boy and get arrested for murder?" Kenmuir laughed ruefully. "Nah. Better to welcome you to the O.K. Corral."

"That's the truth. But damn, we had nothing on the guy. We weren't even a threat."

"*You* knew that, but *he* didn't. He had to assume that you did. Everything happened real fast for him, too. Maybe he just acted on instinct. Who knows?"

Woodson leaned his head back and closed his eyes momentarily. "At least now we know for sure that he's good for Orr. Don't we?"

"Not positively, but it looks that way. Face it, if he weren't looking at something heavy, he'd just have turned around and assumed the position. He'd been through the drill enough times. Why else go into his quick-draw number?" Kenmuir cocked his head. "Which means, I think, that we've got the *who*, but haven't got a clue about the *why*. And that means it's not over yet. Not for me or your department."

Woodson wiggled his index finger at Kenmuir. "Speaking of whom, what about you? Civilian ride-along and all. Any heat on you?"

"Nah. There'll be a coroner's inquest but it'll end there."

"Says who?"

"Supervising Deputy DA John Trauber. Who, coincidentally, is my best friend."

Woodson smiled. "Fuckin' lawyers."

Kenmuir said his good-bye and promised to visit the next day. He was almost out the door when he heard Woodson's voice behind him. "Hey, Dave." He turned around. "Thanks. You know ... for ... you know."

Kenmuir nodded in acknowledgement, but thought about Danny Franklin, his former partner at Oakland PD. *That's twice I should've been there.*

A Deadly Game

Wednesday afternoon, May 15, City of Walnut Creek

A MESSAGE FROM SMITH WITH Ferdinand Fellner's home telephone number was waiting for Kenmuir when he returned to his office. Kenmuir called right away.

Fellner said, "What happened to Thumper was terrible. I'll help any way I can. But I thought his killer died in a shootout with the police yesterday. At least that's what I thought Mr. Smith said. And that'd make it all over, all done? Wouldn't it?"

"For the most part yes, but some loose ends are bugging us and we're exploring them. Which is why we need to follow up with you. Maybe some further details, something that was overlooked or considered too trivial to mention. Who knows?"

"Ask me whatever you want, but I don't know what a hit-and-run in LA could have to do with Humph. What happened to me was chicken-shit, but not exactly murder."

"You're probably right, but if you don't mind going over it again . . ."

Fellner confirmed the police reports. He joked that his memory must be located in his legs, because he remembered virtually nothing about being hit. He vaguely recalled walking by a green car. Next thing he knew, he was lying down and was traveling real fast with a siren blaring. He assumed he was in an ambulance, but didn't know why. "I'm sorry. I wish I could tell you more. It's strange having a blank in your head."

"Let's go back to the car. You said you remember that it was green. When you first saw it, was it close to you?"

"Yeah. Well, sort of. It was off to my right."

"Stopped for the stop sign?"

"I assume, but I don't remember seeing it stop. In my mind, there's a sort of green blur. That's all."

"Blur? So the car *may* have been moving?"

"Yeah. It's funny you should say that because while I can't say for sure, that's what I keep thinking. That it hadn't stopped yet, I mean."

"Maybe you just figured it would?"

"Possible, but real hard to believe. Generally, I don't trust any drivers, especially in California."

"What about the driver? Could you see him?"

"No. Well . . . A better answer's that I might have *at the time*, but now I can't even remember if the driver was male or female. I've thought about it a lot, and memories do pop back in pieces: sometimes they're mixed up with an accident I was in as a kid, and sometimes they're just weird. Like for instance, I can't shake the feeling that I saw a hand waving me across the street. Probably just my imagination. Damn frustrating, I can tell you."

Kenmuir's left hand squeezed his phone. "*That's* not in any of the police reports, Mr. Fellner. The part about being waved across."

"Doesn't surprise me. I didn't think of it until later, and I couldn't swear to it anyway. To be honest, I wonder if it's just my mind playing tricks on me, trying to find an excuse for my being so damn dumb to cross the street in front of a car. Stupid."

"Just so I get this right: You're not sure, but it's there anyway? The wave."

"That's right. It's a feeling that just keeps nagging me in the back of my mind."

Chapter 17

Thursday afternoon, May 16, City of Martinez

IN THE AFTERMATH OF DETECTIVE FRIEDMAN's death, Doris Day would've been more anonymous in the San Pablo barrio than Monica Sanchez. Not only was he easily recognized—mouth as wide as a slice of melon and black hair pulled straight back from an acne-scared face that looked like the inside of an English muffin—but also a copy of an old booking photograph had been given to every patrolman in the area. It was only a bit more than a day before he was vacuumed up three blocks from his house. He was whisked to the main jail in Martinez so fast that he didn't even have time to warm the patrol car's seat.

Woodson and Friedman's replacements, Detectives Robert Ochoa and Greg Gotz, were informed while Sanchez was en route. In turn, they immediately telephoned Kenmuir who, everyone in the department agreed tacitly, was now as much a part of the Orr investigation as the detectives themselves.

When Sanchez arrived at the jail, he was ushered into an interview room: one metal table, two metal chairs, one locked door. Because he hadn't been formally arrested, he was considered a kind of unofficial guest, much as Kenmuir was an unofficial investigator. Law enforcement sometimes has to be flexible.

When Ochoa, Gotz, and Kenmuir entered after half an hour or so, Sanchez seemed glad for the company. "Where you guys been? I got things to do, places to go." He held out his arms and erupted in a kind of prolonged cough that served as his laugh.

Speaking Spanish, Ochoa asked if Sanchez understood English. Gone were the days when a detective could risk a lawyer's future claim that his Hispanic client had misunderstood the questions.

"Sheet, man, I speek it a leetle bit." Sanchez laughed again but, after scanning the men staring humorlessly at him, he said, "Hey, just kidding. C'mon." He nervously wiped his hands on filthy chinos that had been rubbed too many times in too many places.

Ochoa stonily repeated himself, in Spanish. "Spanish or English?"

Sanchez shrugged. "You speak the language. They don't. English is okay." His cooperative attitude was genuine, since he wanted to distance himself as much as possible from LaPera. He was, as he put it, "a law-providing citizen." Ever since they were boys, he'd been bullied by LaPera and used like a servant, bound by fear rather than friendship. On the other hand, his cousin's vicious reputation had guaranteed that no one ever messed with him.

LaPera had changed after state prison. No less a cold-blooded loner, he now spoke respectfully about fellow *La Familia* members. Sometimes he'd leave with one or more of them and then return a few days later with some money.

"Did he ever ask to use your car?"

"*Ask* to borrow my ride?" Sanchez burst into a spasm of cough-laughter. "Ask? He'd walk up to me and stick out his hand or just shout, 'Gimme the fuckin' keys'." Sanchez smirked, as if the detectives and he shared refinements in common. "Had no manners. Shit, you shoulda' seen him eat. Fuckin' pig."

"Back to the car . . ."

"Yeah. Right. He took it whenever he damn well pleased. I'd leave it short on gas deliberately, so he'd have to buy some. No fuckin' chance. He'd make *me* go buy it with *my* money and then bring it back. Asshole. Check this out . . . Last month we go to see the A's. *His* gas and *his* tickets. No shit. He took *me* someplace. I asked him if it was kinda like a date. A fuckin' joke, for chrissake. Sonofabitch whacked me across the head. Motherfucker." Sanchez reached up and patted hair greasy enough to serve as a Jiffy Lube franchise.

"He says nothin' the whole game. Kept lookin' through some binoculars. Had to be stolen, you think he'd *buy* them? Fuck no. 'What you lookin' at?' I say. He tells me to shut up. Fuck 'im. So I shut up. Halfway through the game, he says, 'Let's go.' Didn't ask if I wanted to go, which I did, matter a' fact, but fucking-a, he just *told* me. Such a raging asshole."

Sanchez paused and patted the front of his shirt, as if it had a pocket, which it didn't. "Any of you spare a smoke? Any kind'll do."

Gotz shook a Kent out of a box, slid a Bic lighter across the table, and asked, "He ever talk about what he was doing? His activities?"

"His 'activities'? You guys crack me up." He lit the cigarette, took a first drag, and clearly loved it. "Like I tol' you already, he was bad. That's what he did. Be bad." He slid the lighter back to Gotz. "He never told me nothin'. Fucker. He said that if I didn't know nothin', then I couldn't snitch him out. Pissed me off. I'm no snitch and, besides that, he'd a' killed me." Yet another cough-laugh. "He did all kinds a' shit. Worked collections for some guy. Never said nothin' to me about it, though I did hear he sliced some guy what didn't pay some money. Cut 'im bad. Usually, he'd go see some guy, and right after that the check's in the mail, *comprende?*"

"Who's the guy?"

"I dunno. Some poor fuck what tried to walk on a debt, I guess. Dumb move when Jesus was around."

"No, not the guy who got cut. The *other* guy, the one who hired him."

"Beats me. That kinda shit goes through Javier. You know Javier?"

Kenmuir looked at Ochoa, whose nod was enough to say, *yeah, we know*. And now they also knew where their next stop would be.

Friday afternoon, May 17, City of Martinez

SEATED IN A SHERIFF'S OFFICE interview room, Javier Hernandez sneered at Kenmuir. "You the *bicho* what killed Jesus. Man, your ass is in some deep shit." Hernandez resembled Guy Williams, the Zorro of mid-1950's television. He was likewise a heartthrob—though, when he came out of the night when the full moon was bright, he wielded a different kind of sword than the masked avenger.

He wore a long-sleeved shirt of light flannel, buttoned only at the wrists and neck. The shirt largely covered a ribbed, wife-beater undershirt. A small cross was tattooed crudely on the webbing between his left thumb and forefinger. A larger tattoo of indiscernible design peeked above the drooping neckline of the undershirt. He sat haughtily in his chair with his folded hands resting on the table in front of him.

"You're talking to me, *chollo*, not him." Ochoa flicked a finger in Kenmuir's direction. "Tell me about you and Jesus La-Pera."

Hernandez shrugged. "What's to tell? Grew up together. Knew him all my life. Until the citizen here," he turned his head in Kenmuir's direction, "murdered him."

Neither Ochoa nor Kenmuir rose to the bait. "Not real interested in your social views, Javier. Talk to me instead about how Jesus made money."

"How should I know? Odd jobs? Not much steady work in my part of town, *jefe*. Tell you what. You come stand on the corner every fuckin' morning."

"Yeah, life's a bitch. Like you or Jesus ever stood on a corner. Or did any honest work."

"That why I'm here, *jefe*? So you can insult a defenseless Mexican boy?" Hernandez wasn't in any personal jeopardy and knew it. In fact, he was enjoying himself.

"We don't give a shit about you, one way or another. We only care about Jesus."

"Why? Jesus is dead."

Ochoa leaned forward across the table. "Let's stop fuckin' around here. We want to know about Jesus getting hired to bust heads."

"Never busted mine."

Ochoa said, "Don't tempt me. You give me a couple names of who hired Jesus and you're outta here, sweet and clean."

"I'm *already* sweet and clean. So how would I know these things, *jefe*?" Hernandez tried to look puzzled. "Don't know for sure, but I think that, what'd you say, 'bustin' heads?' is against the law. An innocent person like me could get hisself arrested behind that."

Ochoa raised his eyebrows in an expression of doubt. "Which is why you need to help us now, *chollo*, because someday you're gonna be arrested, and you'll sure as shit gonna need some help yourself."

"Good advice, *jefe*. I'd like to help you. I really would." Hernandez placed both his hands over his chest in a gesture of earnest sincerity. "And that's exactly what I'm going to do. Right after I talk with my suit."

Ochoa, Gotz, and Kenmuir knew all too well that they had no lawful basis for detaining Hernandez, let alone harassing him. However, they wanted to keep him talking, since a slip of the tongue or even an indirect reference might prove useful. The arrival of a lawyer would end all conversation. Ochoa deflected the reference to a lawyer. "Hey, ease up, Javier. We're just talking. Hell, we're not even talking about *you*."

"And that makes me feel real good, *jefe*. It does. I'll tell that to my suit. Then maybe I talk with you. Or maybe not. *Comprende*?"

Ochoa understood all too well. "And who would your lawyer be?"

"One of your amigos. Name's Mr. Adelman."

Ochoa and Kenmuir glanced at each other. Adelman was a prominent criminal defense lawyer who'd begun as a Contra Costa Deputy District Attorney, but left the office a decade or so before Kenmuir arrived. He was smart, crafty, and thorough.

He also was very expensive. If you had money—or could get it—Adelman was your man.

Ochoa and Kenmuir had the same two thoughts: *This conversation is over, and how the hell can Hernandez afford Adelman?*

After Hernandez left with Gotz, Ochoa and Kenmuir stayed in the interview room. Ochoa slid his pack of Salems back and forth between his two hands. "Adelman's a pain in the ass. Real bastard."

"He can be, but he's tough. More to the point, how can a low-life like Hernandez get enough cash? Let alone be sure enough that Adelman'll come running? Business must be good."

"Not *that* good. And I don't see the Adman trolling the lower tiers. We must be missing something. Think maybe we ought to learn more about what he's been up to lately?"

"That we should," Kenmuir said. "Let me make a call."

There's a symbiosis between criminal defense attorneys and prosecutors. Has to be—because, if every technicality were honored, and every procedure were observed, and every case went to trial, the criminal justice system would grind to a halt in about a week. For that reason alone, both sides needed each other's cooperation, be it administrative accommodation or plea bargaining. The lawyers themselves needed to adjust to the other, because individual adversaries have different peculiarities and preferences, strengths and weaknesses. Consequently, Kenmuir knew that a skillful prosecutor would likely have current insight into Adelman. A prosecutor like John Trauber, whose office was located conveniently in the DA's office on the top floor of the courthouse across the street.

Ten minutes later, Office of the Contra Costa County District Attorney

"Lizard" Trauber had chunked out a bit since the days of Kenmuir's nickname, when he'd silently glided through the Vietnamese jungle. He was conservatively groomed—in his view, only girls and Prince Valiant had hair hanging over their ears—and conservatively dressed in a gray Glen-plaid suit with a teal tie that mimicked the teal accent within the plaid. He'd earned his A.B. and J.D. degrees while Kenmuir was with the Oakland Police Department. That's why he'd been Kenmuir's senior in the DA's office by several years and enjoyed occasionally pulling civilian rank on his former military commander.

Unlike the open bay of the Detective Bureau, the District Attorney's office was designed like an egg carton: two rows of private offices separated by a long hallway, with windows on one side and none on the other. Rank thus was easy to determine: One either had a window or one did not.

Kenmuir read the name on every door as Ochoa and he worked their way back to Trauber's corner office. As soon as he entered, he said, "Jesus, Lizard, is anyone left? I don't recognize *any* names on the doors."

Trauber went behind a spacious desk; a large window was to his left. "Different times, LT. When Phister was doing the hiring, you had to be a proven team player with stability. Married, preferably with children. Ex-military, ideally an officer. Unless, of course, you were a particularly outstanding sergeant like myself. That's long gone. Between retirements and lawyers like you taking their experience into private practice, there's been *beaucoup* turnover. Now, a lot more women—you'd be happy because some are fine looking—and virtually no ex-military. Once upon a time, you were hot shit around here. Now, you'd be just another senior citizen prattling about the good old days."

"Senior citizen?"

"Yessir. Because if I am, you'd be even more so. Check this out. We just hired a new lawyer who's twenty-four. *Twenty-four!* Nobody's that young."

Trauber waited until Kenmuir and Ochoa were seated before he closed the door. He knew Ochoa and Kenmuir weren't in his office for a casual chat, so he got right to it. "All right, what's this about?" He looked at Kenmuir, who briefly summarized the status of the Orr investigation. Like everyone else in law enforcement, Trauber was aware of the LaPera shooting and Kenmuir's actions; unlike everyone else, he'd privately discussed it at length with Kenmuir.

Kenmuir concluded with what they'd learned from Hernandez. "That brought us—and surprisingly, I might add—to Kent Adelman. He still around?"

Trauber answered, "As often as the flu. On the other hand, while they say you can't spend all your time dealing with shit without getting some on you, he somehow manages to stay pretty clean. As defense lawyers go, he's well-regarded by us."

Kenmuir agreed. "My experience, too. I didn't have many cases with him, but he kept his word and didn't lie. Good in court." Kenmuir slid his chair back from the edge of Trauber's desk to cross his legs. "Which brings us to why we're here. In light of Hernandez's confident reference to Adelman, we want to know what's been happening with him lately. Specifically, has he started bottom-feeding for clients? Guys like Hernandez?"

Trauber shrugged. "No way. It's same ol', same ol,' as far as I know. Still one of the go-to lawyers in the county, and it takes high-end dollars to sign him up."

Kenmuir said, "That's what we thought, and it's what puzzles us. Why would Adelman be so accessible, and where'd someone like Hernandez get that kind of money?"

"Hard to say. A lot of money in drugs, so maybe Hernandez is valuable to someone. Or he has a relative or friend who's willing to pick up the tab. Or sometimes a lawyer'll do a favor for a better client. You know, say hello to my little friend, but without the Uzi." Trauber flashed a smile. "Or maybe he took an early withdrawal from his 401(k)?"

Kenmuir rubbed his chin contemplatively. "Right. No doubt Hernandez has one of those. Given how much he's concerned with paying taxes and planning for retirement."

"Exactly." Trauber put his finger on the intercom button on his telephone. "Tell you what. If Adelman *is* his attorney, then he must've appeared with him before. Let's see." Over the intercom, he asked for any files, open or closed, concerning Javier Hernandez. The men chatted for twenty minutes or so before three files arrived in the arms of a short woman in her mid-fifties. She had narrow shoulders and torso, but unusually wide hips. It was as if two halves from two different bodies had been mistakenly connected. On the top was a friendly face, with wide, brown eyes and pink cheeks; the eyes became wider and the cheeks pinker when she saw Kenmuir, who stood up as soon as she came in the room.

"Oh, Mr. Kenmuir—Dave—what a nice surprise."

"Ah, Helen. All of a sudden my little heart sings."

They shared a few reminiscences and some catch-ups. Helen paused before she walked toward the door. "All of us from the old days sure do miss you, Dave."

After she left, Kenmuir looked at Trauber and smiled smugly. "'All still miss you, Dave.' You see, Lizard, you're wrong. The legend *does* live on."

"Did you not hear the 'old days' part, Pops?"

Each man looked at a file and then passed it on. Ochoa spoke first. "Don't know about you lawyers, but from my point of view, only one file matters."

"I agree," Kenmuir said. "Two petty nothings and then the ADW last year, which is when he links up with Adelman. Did a good job for him, too. Assault with a deadly weapon's never easy, and it sure doesn't help when the supposed victim goes south on you. Even better, he managed to steer the case into Judge Simmons' charity ward."

Judge Darryll Simmons was a former Deputy Public Defender appointed to the bench in the first term of Jerry Brown, California's so-called "Governor Moonbeam." Depending on one's perspective, Simmons was commendably or infamously forgiving. For a criminal defendant, an assignment to him could be better than Christmas.

"Still," Trauber said, "nothing special here. It's the kind of case where anyone'd want the Adman. His fee and even bail, mind you, got paid somehow. We'll sure never know how."

Kenmuir exhaled sharply. "Bail's hardly a mystery. Company'll be Liberator."

Trauber looked up. "And how would you know that, oh Great Carnak?"

"You're serious?" Kenmuir looked back and forth between Trauber and Ochoa, both of whom continued to stare. "Sorry, I just assumed ... A few years ago, Adelman became a silent partner—a *very* silent partner, I grant you, but a partner nonetheless—in Liberator Bail Bonds. It's like Hornbeck said in *Inherit the Wind*, 'I may be rancid butter, but I'm on your side of the bread.' That company gives Adelman *both* sides of the bread. No one ever said the criminal business isn't profitable."

"Well I'll be goddamned." Ochoa took a deep breath. "A few years ago, Gotz and I looked into Liberator and some other companies as potential sources of money laundering. Fact is, a lot of bail bonds, especially for drug offenses, are paid in cash. Beat that horse but we got nowhere. Couldn't get enough records, and sure as shit no company would cooperate."

"That's it? Nothing about Liberator in particular?"

"Well, old man Hess owned it for mucho years. When he died, the family sold out to a corporation in New York. That's where Eddie, who now runs it, comes from. Says stuff like, 'Howahyah.' It's like talking to a *Saturday Night Live* skit." Caught up in his story, Ochoa paused suspensefully. "*Here's* the interesting part, though. Eddie's boss works for the New York mother ship. No surprise there, but when we sent out a few feelers into that forbidden zone, the corporate types stonewalled us. And I mean *right now*. We never got a document, an answered question, nothing.

"Pissed us off. We contacted NYPD but, beyond official registrations and such, they don't know much, either. Gave us some names, a lot of whom we already knew, and all mob related. That was the end of the line. I mean, it isn't really, but there's no proof of anything. Not back there. Not out here."

Kenmuir rotated his hands around each other in a keep-it-rolling gesture and said, "Names?"

Ochoa continued, "Well, out west the big boy, literally, is Angelo 'the Whopper' Marini. Evidently he likes the burgers a lot and supposedly can 'whopp' your ass when he gets pissed off. Lives right here, down the road in Blackhawk. Looks like Mr. Clean in the ads, only with hair. Questioned a few times, but never busted despite all the rumors. In any event, he's way too big time for us. The feds can worry about him."

"That's it?"

"No. Marini supposedly has a local, what, assistant? Admin type, not muscle. Name's Jeffrey Pietro McPherson. No one's ever laid a glove on him, either. Not that it makes any difference in figuring out what he does. Looks like a duck, walks like a duck."

Kenmuir wasn't a believer. "Come on. *McPherson*? There hasn't been a gangster from the British Isles since Bugs Moran."

Ochoa quickly disagreed. "Don't let that fool you. The Pietro part's in honor of his maternal grandfather, the late-lamented Pietro 'The Stinger' Marraccini. His daughter married into a socially impeccable, but financially beleaguered, Brahmin family. Like the Jeffersons, movin' on up. Thus was dear Jeff created."

Ochoa supplied a biographical sketch of MacPherson off the top of his head: "He was raised with a passport into two worlds; educated at Exeter, Williams College, and Harvard Business School, he apparently perceived early that money and power were to be found on his mother's side of the family. Granddad arranged for employment; McPherson came with his own ambition and intelligence.

"He started Angel Investments—presumed to be a salute to Angelo Marini—in San Francisco's financial district. After nine years, he shifted it to Walnut Creek. To avoid being as monolithic as Tom Hagen's law practice in *The Godfather*—"I have a special practice. I handle one client"—Angel Investments gathered enough miscellaneous investors to appear accessible, though quite exclusive. MacPherson's cultivated a reputable but low profile. He's visible at the chamber of commerce, attends significant civic events, and gives to select local charities. All very supportive of the community."

Both Kenmuir and Trauber were dazzled. Kenmuir said, "Goddamn impressive, Bobby. No shit."

Trauber: "Ditto."

"Like I said, we try."

Kenmuir summarized: "Fact: LaPera and Bellman both get hired by someone. Though who knows if they're related or only coincidences. LaPera leads to Hernandez who's got the Adman as his attorney. Are we done? No. Because the Adman's not only way out of Hernandez's league, but also has a piece of a bail business owned by a New York corporation that's apparently a subsidiary, though a legitimate one, of organized crime. Or maybe not. But it all might be just a goddamn coincidence." Kenmuir threw his hands in the air. "*Seriously?*"

The three men sat in silence until Ochoa asked, "What's next? Rock a few boats?"

Trauber looked skeptically. "What boats? More to the point, *whose* boats? You and I are law enforcement. We've got to be very careful about messing with the tides."

As usual, Kenmuir wanted to *do* something. "Okay, maybe not a boat, but why not a skiff? Like a chat with McPherson. What about that?"

Ochoa, who never laughed, laughed. "Why didn't I think of that? We'll all stop by for a casual interrogation? Sure. That'll work."

Kenmuir said, "You two can't, I get that. But *I* can. Business type with some discretionary capital, looking for a lucrative investment. We talk for a while. We become pals. Details emerge." Kenmuir looked conspiratorially around the table. "Yeah, maybe it's a long shot. Even very long. But, hey, the Mets won in '69. It's either try for a miracle or do nothing. I pick miracle."

Chapter 18

Friday afternoon, May 17, City of Walnut Creek

Kenmuir called Angel Investments and asked to speak with Mr. MacPherson. As he waited, the telephone played an instrumental, fox-trot version of Little Richard's *Rip It Up*. Preposterous.

"Mr. MacPherson's office. May I help you?"

"Yes. My name's Mr. . . . Little, Richard Little. Mr. MacPherson's been recommended to me. May I speak with him?"

"I'm afraid that's not possible. He's not available at this point in time."

Ah, but is he available at this point in space? "Fine. I'm willing to make an appointment."

"I'm sorry, but Mr. MacPherson's personal calendar's very busy. I'd be happy to schedule an appointment with either of his assistants."

"I prefer to meet with Mr. MacPherson personally. *He* was recommended to me. Not his assistants. I'm sure you understand."

"Well, sir, Mr. MacPherson doesn't meet with new clients until after a preliminary interview with Mr. Mazza or Mr. Scolari."

"Well, the problem is that I'm only here until Wednesday. I hope he'll make an exception in this instance. Tell him that I've been referred by Kent Adelman, who thought that we'd have a good deal in common. Let me give you my number."

Ochoa slid a piece of paper with a telephone number in front of Kenmuir, who repeated the number to the receptionist. "I'm available to meet any time at Mr. MacPherson's convenience Monday or Tuesday."

Kenmuir spent the rest of the afternoon in one of the sheriff's interview rooms, waiting for the private "narc" line to ring. He created a fair facsimile of a gentleman's lounge: one chair acted as a footstool, and the battered metal table was to his right, so both the ashtray and his Diet Pepsi were easily reached. Very relaxing.

He was reading a novel about a former KGB assassin who'd been loaned to the East Germans in order to foil an plot by the Red Chinese to subvert the Politburo, although, as it turned out, that was only a ruse by the Libyans to conceal an Iraqi plan to poison the water supply of Jerusalem at Christmastime, which had been discovered by a Mossad agent who, before being killed, managed to pass the information on to a renegade former CIA operative whose wife had been murdered some years before by the KGB assassin, with whom the CIA operative now had to work in order to save the world from nuclear disaster. All very realistic, Kenmuir had no doubt.

When the telephone rang at 4:30 p.m., it couldn't have been more inconvenient. Kenmuir was a mere twenty pages from the end of the novel, when Danlov (also called Alexei or Ivanovich) and Dirk Henshaw, both armed to the teeth, finally had reached the remote island base where the hostages were being held by the evil former head of the Savak and his cadre of lethal henchmen.

"Hello. Richard Little speaking."

"This is Jeffrey MacPherson's office calling."

Kenmuir leaned back with a satisfied smile.

Tuesday morning, May 21, City of Walnut Creek

IF HE EVER LOST HIS LEASE, Kenmuir decided he'd sooner rent a Winnebago motor home than relocate to MacPherson's office building. Not with a lobby featuring a gigantic metal sculpture that had *"Striving"* engraved on a small brass plate at its base, and that reminded Kenmuir of the sculpture in the middle of the Stanford campus, known irreverently as "The Claw." He didn't like either one. Furthermore, there was no furniture: evidently, any visitor was expected to be going up or out, with no need to sit down.

On the seventh floor, Angel Investments' teenage receptionist led Kenmuir past several secretarial carrels and three offices with interior windows. Presumably, MacPherson wanted to see his employees busily at work. By contrast, the sanctum sanctorum of MacPherson's corner office had no interior windows.

The secretary opened the door and stood with her back against it, so Kenmuir could walk directly toward the man who stood up immediately, almost as if he and the door were connected. MacPherson walked around his desk and extended his hand. "I'm Jeff MacPherson."

Kenmuir had anticipated a menacing Charles Bronson or Robert Mitchum, tough and squinty-eyed. A ruthless and elusive mastermind, who toyed with law enforcement while managing an array of criminal enterprises on behalf of "Whopper" Marini. Instead, MacPherson could've been the receptionist's prom date. He was on the short side of medium height and quite slim. With the exception of an incongruously large nose, his boyish features were as delicate as the hand that shook Kenmuir's, and his face was covered with freckles, as if molded out of a buckwheat pancake.

"Thank you for finding the time to meet with me," Kenmuir said as he sat in the client chair.

MacPherson reseated himself behind his desk. "I'll admit that you've piqued my curiosity, Mr. Little. I've met Mr. Adelman socially. Fundraisers, that sort of thing, but he's not a client."

Kenmuir cautioned himself not to be misled by MacPherson's appearance as Superman's youthful pal, Jimmy Olsen. His nature was more likely the velvet glove and iron fist, etc. "I wouldn't know one way or another. For me, he's merely the source of the recommendation. Does it matter?"

"It might. While I appreciate the implicit flattery in any recommendation, we're not a volume business. Our clientele is rather select. That, I should emphasize, is by design."

"I'd like to think of myself as worthy of such select company."

"Well, you insisted on meeting with me personally, even though I understand you were told that I don't ordinarily do so." MacPherson leaned back in his chair and rested his clasped hands on his stomach, "With all that said, in what sort of investments are you interested?"

A Deadly Game

A substantive conversation was out of the question, since Kenmuir had about as much insight into investment diversity and options as a third grader: get your mom to make some lemonade, grab some cups, and go sit on the corner. Brevity would be the key.

Over the course of the next ten minutes, Kenmuir tried to be a suburban Warren Buffet by parroting as much as he could remember from meetings with his investment adviser over the years. "Frankly, I'm tired of being steered toward the unimaginative. Oil, gas, apartment buildings, that sort of thing. I'd prefer something more exotic, but with profits worthy of the risk. Mr. Adelman suggested that you were aware of opportunities in professional athletics. *That* prospect does appeal to me."

MacPherson's chair didn't so much as vibrate. He was that unfazed. "I'm afraid you've been misled. I'm not much of a sports fan and, if only for that reason, we've never been engaged in that field."

"That's a disappointment. For example, you've undoubtedly read about Humphrey Orr, the A's catcher who was killed recently. I got to thinking, what if I'd taken out some life insurance on him? Or on any other athlete in a high-risk sport. For that matter, it wouldn't even have to be life insurance. It could be anything: arms, legs, whatever."

MacPherson sneered. "Is this some kind of joke? If so, it's in remarkably bad taste. If not, you and I certainly have no future together." He leaned forward in his chair so that his arms rested on his desk. His businesslike expression didn't change, but his large nostrils expanded slightly and his tone became cold. "What *isn't* a joke is your being here at all. You seem to be an educated man, which means you aren't a police officer, although you act like one. A lawyer of some kind, perhaps? Like Mr. Adelman."

"I am. Is that a problem?"

"No, I have nothing against lawyers as long as they know their place and stay there. More to the point, I've worked with many investors over the years. You aren't one. I don't know your reason for going to such lengths to arrange this charade, but my curiosity is satisfied."

"I don't know what . . ."

MacPherson held up his pianist's hand. "This meeting is over." He stood, demonstrating that the meeting truly was over.

Kenmuir didn't stand. He crossed his legs and sat back more comfortably in his chair, deciding to go for broke and see what happened. "It's true, I'm a lawyer. A thug named Jesus LaPera was an enforcer. I'm told he was an enforcer for you. What I want to know is what Thumper Orr ever did to you."

MacPherson dropped his head and closed his eyes for a moment. When he looked up, he said, "How tiresome are the delusions of the police. I may have to endure *them* from time to time, but not *you*, Mr. Little—though I doubt that's your real name." He shifted his eyes toward the office door that had opened soundlessly.

A conservatively dressed man, roughly the same size as the sculpture in the building's lobby, appeared in the doorway. Kenmuir suspected he wasn't an investment advisor.

Kenmuir looked flamboyantly at his wristwatch. "I'd like to chat further, I really would. Sadly, I sense that it's time to go. But we'll see each other again, I'm sure."

In less than fifteen minuites, Kenmuir was in his own office, trying to impose some sense on the jumble of recent events:

- LaPera may not have been a pro, but he was no amateur, either. He had one gun when he shot Orr and ballistics has verified that that he used a different gun to shoot Friedman. No surprise there, since he likely would've dumped the murder weapon immediately. But it also meant he had ready access to other weapons.
- He sure as hell didn't wander spontaneously into Thumper Orr's yard dressed as a gardener.
- No, he was there because he was hired. But by whom?
- And for a specific purpose, one that was served by injection of a large-animal tranquilizer. *What* purpose?
- Sure wasn't murder, that definitely had to be a mistake.

Kenmuir sifted his focus from the ending to the beginning:

- Maybe it was a kidnapping. How much would've been paid for Orr's return?
- Maybe Orr was being punished for something, despite his apparently virtuous life. That would explain LaPera, a professional enforcer. To believe Ochoa, a McPherson had the ability to make suitable arrangements. Maybe research Orr's personal life more thoroughly?
- Maybe just a mistake. LaPera went to the wrong house and confronted the wrong man. Some discreet inquiries about the neighbors and their activities?
- Maybe Orr wasn't the real target. Maybe it was the A's. After all, if someone wanted to damage the team, how better than

to eliminate its biggest star, even if only temporarily? Would the tranquilizer have been used to make Orr so docile that a minor injury could be inflicted?

- Maybe there really *was* a grand conspiracy, just like Lange and Smith thought. But a conspiracy with no pattern whatsoever? *Nah.*
- Are the distributions meaningful? Four stars, with Simon only a rookie, but a highly-touted one. Four from the American League, with only Jackson from the National. Three white and two black. Three from first-rate teams, and two from also-rans. Sites all over the map: Tulsa, Phoenix, Anaheim, Bay Area.
- Simon's mugging was racially motivated, Brittain's was just another motorcycle accident, Fellner's hit-and-run was commonplace. All three, very clear and not at all puzzling. But not Orr: there's no reason, let alone explanation.

This had begun because of Larry Lange and Hank Jackson. Yet he knew virtually nothing about Jackson. It was time to learn about him.

A Deadly Game

Chapter 19

Saturday evening, May 25, City of Walnut Creek

AFTER HIS DIVORCE, KENMUIR HAD INDULGED IN a kind of carnal communism, all for one and one for all. But his playboy script eventually became so refined that he grew tired of it—and himself. Ginny Trauber had set him straight. "You aren't a ladies' man, Dave. You're trying to act like you are, but you aren't. You want *one*. She's out there, but you won't find her by trolling in bars and scoring at the end of parties."

His feast from the sexual sampler of the Bay Area thereupon became more of a series of snacks. Numerous risk-free introductions and referrals came with an implicit certificate of approval and led to sporadic dates of platonic friendship mixed with occasional liaisons of mutual convenience, just enough to stave off acute horniness. After all, he was a bachelor, not a monk.

He hadn't been ready for Lucy Ball. No social context, no endorsement, and no preview. He still wasn't. Wouldn't asking her out be the equivalent of abusing a sales call? "Hi. When we met, you mentioned that your carpets were dirty. I can have them cleaned—and, as long as you're on the phone . . . " Much too tacky. Let it go.

Yet, the more he'd tried to disregard her, the more he didn't want to. So, last Monday, he'd said the hell with it. Nervous as an adolescent, he'd called her: Yes, she remembered him. In fact, she'd read about him after the LaPera shooting . . . Had he been hurt? . . . No, she wasn't leaving town over Memorial Day . . . No, she had no plans for Saturday night . . . Yes, she'd be glad to have dinner with him.

The Brittany Inn was a comfortable anachronism: a suburban dinner house with 1950's elegance in a more sloppy present. Overstuffed, red leather booths; tuxedoed pianist; bar and dining in separate rooms; soft lighting cast by real candles on the tables. A tie wasn't mandatory, but one would've felt slightly underdressed without one.

After their Caesar salads were prepared at tableside, Kenmuir learned that she was from southern California and had gone to Glendale High School (which made sense, since GHS had a regional monopoly on pretty blondes), where she'd been a cheerleader and class secretary. After UCLA, she'd taught American history in high school, while Mr. Ball got his MBA at Cal.

During the main course—petrale sole in a lemon butter sauce for her and venison medallions in a Port reduction for him—they explored what turned out to be a mutual love for history-oriented travel. Both had prowled through many Civil War battlefields.

"If you could only visit one, which would it be?"

Her reply was immediate. "Shiloh, without a doubt. Still enough open space to imagine the battle, but not too much signage to prevent you from seeing it, like the clutter at Gettysburg. I could've spent much more time than Randy the Restless had the patience for. You?"

A Deadly Game

Kenmuir delayed while the waiter poured more of the 1978 Diamond Creek Red Rock Terrace cabernet into each glass. "Shiloh's great. No quarrel. But for me, with an honorable mention for Chancellorsville, I'll take Antietam. It allows the greatest sense of what it was like at the time of the battle. The Dunker church. The sunken road. Even the cornfield's still there."

They declined dessert in favor of her glass of Italian amaro liqueur and his Taylor Fladgate thirty-year tawny port. As they sipped, she talked briefly and unemotionally about her divorce, as if outlining a recipe or summarizing a book. Then came his turn. Not his favorite topic, but other introductory dinners had taught him that it was inevitable. However, divorce was something they had in common, like soldiers who'd been wounded in combat, though in different battles.

He said, "We were married about a year before I went to Vietnam. The man she kissed good-bye was not the same man she hugged when he came home." He chuckled. "It was quite a hug, by the way. She showed up at the airport wearing a raincoat. Maneuvered us over to a corner and flipped open the raincoat. She was wearing *only* the raincoat. 'Welcome home, soldier,' she said."

"I'd never have the nerve to do something like that. What if the coat had come undone?"

"I don't know. I guess she didn't care. I sure didn't. Anyway, it sort of figured. She'd always been a bit wild. Great one for a party, a lot of laughs.

"Though we didn't know it, the future was foretold later that night. After I took a *very* fast shower, she said, 'You relax and I'll get some champagne.' Mistake. I didn't realize how deep-down tired I was. I woke up fifteen hours later." He smiled absently. "In fact, I still wasn't awake, not really. She remained the same, enthusiastic and energetic and full of hopes and dreams. But I'd aged more, physically and emotionally. Then I became a cop, not the lawyer I was supposed to be."

"I thought you *were* a lawyer."

"I am now, but I was a cop first, working goofy hours and hanging around with other cops. Worse, I was sort of withdrawn and not very communicative. Getting mentally reorganized, I guess. It wasn't fair to Mary, who had no high-society lifestyle as the wife of a lawyer and no San Francisco action, but only a house in boring suburbia. Gradually we became less lovers than roommates with common routines, friends, and history. It might've been better if we'd fought a lot. But we didn't. No fireworks. Nothing like that."

"*Something* must have happened."

Yes, "something" happened: what that damn handwritten label referred to merely as "Baby Boy Kenmuir" didn't live. And part of me is still dead along with him. But that doesn't get shared and sure as hell not with a date. Stick with the sanitized version.

"Nothing dramatic. One day she just said she wanted to move to the city. I sure didn't; I loved what's still my house in Walnut Creek. We talked and one thing led to another. For me, it was more of a surrender than a contest. We used the same lawyer: she took what she wanted, and I took the rest. Easy enough. Though she did take some neat stuff, now that I think about it."

Lucy looked at Kenmuir with mock sternness. "Don't get me started on husbands as supposed victims of greedy ex-wives."

Later at her front door, Lucy looked intently into his eyes. She put her right hand against his cheek. He bent forward and kissed her. The kiss wasn't long, more promising than passionate. "I look forward to seeing you again."

"I hope it won't be too long."

He grinned. "Never fear. You have yet to discover how impatient I am."

Chapter 20

Tuesday morning, May 28, City of San Francisco

KENMUIR EASILY UNDERSTOOD WHY JACKSON was a favorite of female fans: Tall and handsome, broad shoulders tapering to a narrow waist and a photogenic smile, he was the paragon of an athlete. If baseball had needed a recruiting poster, Jackson would've been a worthy model.

When Lange said, "Let me introduce Dave Kenmuir," Jackson merely nodded without unfolding his arms. He was unsmiling, sullen, and defiant. He wore Levis and a sport shirt. Damned if he'd dress up for this occasion. Lange had been able to compel attendance, but not congeniality.

Lange moved Kenmuir and Jackson to a private conference room. As soon as he left, Kenmuir asked, "Did Lange tell you why I'm here?"

Jackson turned away from the window and looked hostilely at Kenmuir. "You're the lawyer. You like to talk. You tell me."

Kenmuir briefly reviewed the incident in the parking lot and Lange's worries, but didn't tell Jackson what he'd learned from Bellman or Chico. "Larry thinks you may be in trouble. He wants to help and doesn't want a scandal. If he tried to do something, it'd be 'official.' That's where I come in. I'm unofficial."

"I don't need any help. There's nothing to help with. I told him and I'll tell you. It's private, and it's none of your damn business."

"I have to tell *you*, Hank . . . May I call you Hank?"

Jackson looked up indignantly. "That's what my friends call me. You can call me *Mister* Jackson."

"Not an original line, *Mister* Jackson, but all right." Kenmuir leaned back in his chair. "You and I are starting out on the wrong foot. So let's get squared away. I don't give a shit about you. As far as I'm concerned, you can disappear tomorrow. What I care about is my friend, and *he* cares about you. He wants to help because he's personally worried about *you*. To hell with money. Get it?"

Jackson said nothing.

"Fine. Be an independent, tall-in-the-fucking-saddle kind of a guy. I told Larry I'd meet with you to find out what's going on and see if I could help. But you don't need any help, *Mister* Jackson. Terrific. We're done."

Jackson stood up. "Good. I don't need some white asshole in my face, and I don't need any bullshit help in my personal life. On the field, I do what I'm told. Off the field, I do what I want."

Until then, Kenmuir truly hadn't cared one way or the other about Jackson. However, the "white" reference stabbed him, and his temper reacted: "I apologize. I think you're right. You don't need any help, and you sure as shit don't deserve any. Certainly not from a *white asshole* like me—or Larry. But let me tell you what I held back, and you can help yourself after that."

Kenmuir related what he'd learned from Bellman and Chico. As the story proceeded, Jackson sat down, this time less arrogantly. By the end, he was leaning forward in his chair, his head in his hands.

"Which means you and the brothers can deal with who's trying to hurt you. *Going to* hurt you, by the way—because they will eventually. But, hey, look on the bright side. You'll make some minor leaguer happy as hell because he'll be playing your position when some white asshole cop is trying to identify the maker of the tire tread tattooed over your crushed arms or legs." Kenmuir stood and walked to the door of the conference room. "Good luck, *Mister* Jackson."

Muffled by his hands, Jackson's voice was barely audible. "Hold up, man."

Kenmuir's hand was on the door handle, but he didn't turn it. "You say something?"

"Maybe we ought to talk."

"I've got nothing more to say. *You* want to talk, I'll listen. That's it." Kenmuir walked back toward the conference table and pulled out a chair.

"What I say to you is confidential, right?"

"No way. I'll tell Larry whatever I think he should know. If I eventually have to tell someone else with the club, then I will. I'm *not* your lawyer, and there's no client privilege. However, I won't say anything I don't have to. But what the hell, why should you trust some white asshole?"

"Look, Mr. . . . I'm sorry, I forgot your name . . . That just came out. Couldn't believe I said it. I'm sorry. I really am." Jackson stood up and stepped forward in front of Kenmuir. He extended his hand. Kenmuir looked first at the hand and then upward at Jackson. In turn, he stood and clasped the hand firmly. Jackson placed his left hand on top of the joined white and black hands. "Whatever happens next, I really am sorry."

"Well, I *can* be an asshole and a white asshole at that." Kenmuir offered a conciliatory smile. "Let's hear your side of it."

Jackson told a bizarre story. Several years before, his "baby" brother—also a gifted athlete, but one whose future ended with a broken shoulder in high school—began to bet on sporting events at a place called Nate's. He bet heavily. Sometimes he won big, but mostly he lost. When his gambling debts expanded beyond any hope of repayment, he turned to his wealthy big brother. Jackson did what a loyal big brother is supposed to do and paid the gambling debts.

Unfortunately, what was supposed to be the end became a beginning. Jackson the elder became a private bank to be drawn on, interest free, as need required. And, as the months passed, need required often.

When Jackson finally refused to keep subsidizing his baby brother's bad luck, they argued fiercely. Baby brother yelled, cried, threatened, but Jackson was unmoved. Jackson assumed—naively—that the gambling at Nate's was over. In reality, his brother continued, but didn't reveal his older brother's change of attitude. When the losses inevitably mounted, young Jackson was forced to explain not only that he couldn't pay, but that his brother *wouldn't*.

"You mean to tell me that none of these gambling debts are yours personally?" Kenmuir asked.

"Absolutely. I don't gamble. Frankly, I can't deal with it. When I win, I feel good for about five minutes. When I lose, I'm depressed for days. It's not worth it." He shook his head ruefully. "Obviously, my brother doesn't feel that way. Then, in

A Deadly Game

February, just before I left for spring training, my brother came to my house with two guys. He swears he'd never seen them before. They just showed up at his apartment and told him to take them to my house. That really pissed me off. *My house!*"

Jackson explained that the main guy, unimaginatively named Aces, did all the talking. Aces' logic was simple enough: As baby brother's debts were paid in the past, so should they be paid in the present. Jackson declined. Aces didn't match Chico's description of the pretty boy who'd hired Bellman, but his sidekick did.

Kenmuir asked, "Let me get this straight. Aces and his boy ask you to pay your brother's gambling debts. *Tell* you, really. You refuse. And that's the end of that? All very polite? No threats?"

"Right. And, to tell you the truth, I was kinda surprised. Seen too many movies, I guess. When I said I was done paying, Aces said, 'You sure?' And I said, 'Positive.' He wished me good luck or something like that and they left. I assumed that it was over. They might get a little rough on my brother. But what could I do? It had to stop."

"Aces evidently disagrees."

Jackson shook his head and exhaled in frustration. "Evidently."

. .

Lange was apoplectic when Kenmuir reported back to him. "Jesus. A gambling scandal? What reporters don't know, they'll make up. Believe me, the baby brother part's going to get lost on page seven. League investigation . . . Great. Just great."

Kenmuir said nothing. His friend was blowing off steam and feeling sorry for himself, all at the same time. It'd pass. But

Lange kept it up. "See, I told you so. I *knew* it. Jackson and Orr are connected, surer than shit. And what about the others? Fellner. Simon. Even Brittain, maybe? Damn, I can't believe this is happening." He kept pacing on a carpet that was a testimonial to the description "wear resistant."

"Coincidence is a far cry from connection, roomie. As I said before, they merely all happen to be baseball players. That's it. Think about it." Kenmuir used his right hand to fold back the little finger on his left: "First, Brittain lost control of a high-speed motorcycle and died. No blanks to fill in. Second"—ring finger folded back—"Simon, hardly the same caliber player as Brittain or Fellner by the way, got busted up by some Klan-like assholes. Again, no mystery. Third"—fingers overlooked—"Fellner and Orr. I admit there's something strange with them, but I prosecuted long enough to know that strange things happen all the time."

"It's not that I *want* them to be connected, you know," Lange interrupted.

"Good, because it doesn't make any sense that they are. Especially now that we know that Jackson isn't to blame for anything, and it's just whiplash from his brother. My suggestion? Let's deal with Jackson and leave conspiracies to the novelists."

Lange collapsed into his desk chair. "Can anything be done about Jackson?"

Kenmuir grinned. "Happily for you, I've got a few ideas."

Chapter 21

Wednesday morning, May 29, City of Oakland

Kenmuir remembered Nate's from his days on patrol. It was located in a 1940's neighborhood of clapboard homes spread out south of 98th Street, a mile or so from the Oakland sports complex. Each home was a photocopy of its neighbors: small front yard, but a spacious backyard; three bedrooms and one bathroom; four wooden steps ascending to a wooden porch; detached single-car garage. The residential uniformity had yielded to extensive remodeling over the years: an upper story here, an expansion there, a garage conversion over there; sadly, metal bars had been installed over all first-floor windows.

The garage at 818 Placer Street had become "Nate's" two-chair barber shop long before the space between it and the house had been enclosed to make a recreation room. A tin awning over the front and side of the garage's exterior covered a concrete patio that served as a local gathering place. You could get a haircut, lay off a bet, score a recreational dose of drugs, or learn where frisky companionship might be acquired: a bouillabaisse of social services for locals and visitors alike.

Well over a decade earlier, Kenmuir and Danny Franklin had investigated the kidnapping and rape of a local teenager,

Nate's grandniece. Nate was nearly sixty and openly hostile: "Two white cops gonna give a fucking damn about another black girl gettin' raped?" But their earnestness wore Nate down over time. It wasn't trust, maybe, but it wasn't distrust anymore, either. Later that year, they shared more than a few beers together after the three assailants were sentenced to state prison. Kenmuir hadn't been back since.

When Kenmuir arrived, a group of black men, ranging in age from their early twenties to late forties, was hanging around on the patio, enveloped in a haze of cigarette smoke. Their animated conversation stopped the moment Kenmuir started to walk from his car toward them.

In the abrupt silence, one thought dawned on Kenmuir: *Look, Ma, inn't he dumb? Total number of black males? Eight or so. Total number of white males? Precisely one. Dumb.*

Never an hospitable area for a white guy on an afternoon stroll, the neighborhood hadn't become any more welcoming. This time, however, Kenmuir had no partner. Worse, he had no badge. How bad could it be? He was about to learn.

"Sorry to interrupt, gentlemen." Dave Kenmuir, man of the people. "I'd like to speak with the owner. With Nate. He around?"

A young black, maybe twenty-four years old, stepped forward. "Why you wanna know?"

"Just some business, that's all." Kenmuir noticed the other males had begun slowly to fan out. Maybe not the Rockettes, but a semicircle nonetheless. *Man, you really are dumb.*

"Business? What kind of business? Government business?" The young man kept advancing. "You got some ID? Some metal?"

"Not a cop. Only a businessman." Kenmuir gestured with an open hand. "Hoping I might run into Nate."

"Yeah, well, check this out. You can run the fuck outta here." He glanced around at his buddies. They chuckled and laughed. Funny motherfucker, baby.

"All I want . . ."

"Don't give a fuck. What you *really* want is to get the fuck outta here."

As the introductory remarks were deteriorating from merely unattractive to ugly, an old man stepped out of the barbershop door. His expression was at once stern and alert, his full head of hair was gray and, appropriately, neatly cut. His shoulders were stooped slightly. His gait was a mild shuffle. "Hearin' a lot of damn noise out here. Too much noise, matter a' fact." Nate surveyed and understood the scene in about two milliseconds. He stood by what turned out to be his grandson as he concentrated silently on Kenmuir. He cocked his head and broke into a slight grin. "Well, I'll be goddamned. Long time, detective."

"He's no cop, Papa. Some bullshit businessman."

Nate chuckled softly, as much to himself as anyone else. "Maybe now. You a businessman now, detective?"

"Lawyer."

"Private?"

"Now."

More or less to the group, Nate said, "You all remember me talkin' about the cops what caught the motherfuckers what hurt Charese? This'd be one of 'em." To Kenmuir he said, "Let's go inside. Too damn hot out here."

The family room was dominated by a large-screen television. A Barcalounger on the other side of the room was centered on the television. Nate went directly to it and sat down; obviously, it was "his" chair. He watched as Kenmuir sat on the nearby couch and asked, "Social visit?" Neither trust nor distrust.

"Not really. Sort of old times, though. You still good with secrets?"

Nate merely nodded his head once, affirmatively. Kenmuir decided to tell him—leaving out select details—about Jackson.

Nate waited until Kenmuir finished before he reacted. "Bad story. Know the younger brother. Seen the older brother play a lot. Good ballplayer. I like him." Nate pulled on the lever at the side of his chair to elevate his legs. He pointed at his feet. "Circulation. Old age's fucked up. What's this got to do with me?"

"Nothing personal. Hell, Nate, I didn't even know you were still alive."

"Am, though."

"So I see."

"Wouldn't want my grandson to find hisself in any trouble with the law."

"He won't, this is just for me and that ballplayer you've watched."

"You gonna straighten that out? Nothin' comes back here?"

"Nothing."

Nate pushed the lever in the opposite direction, so he could lower his legs, leaned forward conspiratorially, and spoke softly: "We got a lot of things goin' on, detective. Always have. You know that. But I'm a small fry. God knows how many others do what I do just around here. Collection? Enforcement? I got nothing to do with it."

"I believe that, Nate. But I also know that when someone doesn't pay—someone like Jackson's brother—you've got to account for it somehow."

"True enough. The guy what picks up the money from me, I tell him. What he does, I don' know. Don' want to."

"C'mon, Nate, you've been around too long. You've got to know something. What I need is your help."

Nate paused, hitting his fists together lightly. He was struggling within himself. "I don' snitch. Not my way, but I'm goddamned if I don' owe you. And Danny." He stopped talking for a moment and concentrated on Kenmuir's eyes. "I was real sorry to hear about him." Kenmuir nodded his head once in silent gratitude. Nate pursed his lips and looked down at the floor. When his eyes snapped up, he spoke. "This much I'll say. There's a place called The Oasis in Emeryville. Maybe just a coincidence, but a guy named Aces hangs out there. And he's got a friend what wears a neck chain with a boat hangin' on it."

Wednesday afternoon, May 29, City of Emeryville

LITTLE MORE THAN AN URBAN BUFFER, the small city of Emeryville is a long strip squeezed between Berkeley to the north and Oakland to the south. That strip is bisected by the north-south Nimitz Freeway, which, further south, runs parallel with the MacArthur Freeway, thereby preserving forever the rivalry between the vainglorious general and the stern admiral.

Kenmuir had no problem finding The Oasis amid the many card rooms on Emeryville's main street. Blinking fronds of a palm tree spelled O-a-s-i-s above the naked back of a neon woman with long black hair who was cuddled suggestively around the palm tree. Inside, lamps hung from the ceiling over a dozen or so felt-covered tables, creating an archipelago of bright green islands in the large room. Most of the tables were deserted in the middle of the day, but Kenmuir was more surprised by the number that weren't.

The card players ranged from businessmen in suits to laborers in ball caps. They were bound together by murmured bets, the soft rustle of shuffling cards, and self-consciously passive expressions. They weren't the ones to ask where to find Aces; the bartender was.

The bartender kept shining a glass with a tea towel. "Who's asking?"

"Does it matter?"

The bartender shrugged. "Not to me, but might to you. Just a sec." He walked to an unlabeled door in the back of the room and stuck his head inside. He said something and reclosed the door. After a moment, Tab Hunter or maybe Troy Donohue emerged: longish blonde hair, Sperry Top Sider shoes, crisp and well-creased cotton trousers, lightly-starched sport shirt. Muscular, not bulky, and moving with a cocky swagger that seemed more practiced than natural. A gold sailboat hung from a gold chain around his neck.

Well, well, this would be Chico's turd in a punchbowl.

"Ted here tells me you wanna see Aces. He's busy. You need something?"

"Nope." Kenmuir smiled with false charm. It wasn't the answer the blonde expected.

"What d'ya mean, 'Nope'?"

"Just that. Nope. Don't need anything—other than to see Mr. Aces."

The Adonis stiffened. "Like I said. He's busy. It's me or leave. You don't need trouble, Mister."

"Good point. No one likes a troublemaker. So I'll just make myself comfortable, maybe play some Hearts or Go Fish until he *is* available. How's that?"

Kenmuir saw the man's muscles tighten under his shirt. He decided to back off a bit. In fact, he preferred to avoid a confrontation. With the information he'd accumulated, he would've gone directly to the police—but for Lange's overriding desire for secrecy and fear of publicity. Any arrest with a related investigation concerning Jackson would've been public knowledge in about fifteen minutes.

"Look, I don't have a quarrel with Mr. Aces, and I don't want one with you. I need to talk with him about Hank Jackson. So why not tell him that? I mean, it *is* going to happen, so let's not make a big deal out of it."

Kenmuir didn't expect to reform Aces or his business methods. He only wanted to convince him that Jackson personally was too much trouble, and a police investigation would be worse. Someone else could worry about Aces' behavior. The blonde man stared at Kenmuir momentarily, letting him know how tough he was. He then returned to the darkened door, opened it, and disappeared inside. After a few minutes, he came out and motioned with his hand. When Kenmuir approached him, he said, "I'll have to pat you down."

Kenmuir shook his head. "I'd advise against it. That would pretty well guarantee the trouble we both want to avoid."

Both stood still, waiting for the other to make the first move. The question was *who* would move first. Both knew that eventually one of them would—and thereby eliminate any chance of a quiet resolution.

As it turned out, the door moved first.

The man who appeared was quite a contrast to the handsome blonde. The skin on his face was stretched as taut as a nylon stocking around sunken eyes and over a flattened nose and bony chin. He had a series of thin scars on his left cheek, as if a deck of razor blades once had been shuffled against it. "What's goin' on out here?" His voice sounded like a chain being dragged through a corrugated metal pipe.

Kenmuir stepped sideways around the blonde. "Mr. Aces, I presume. My name's Kenmuir, David Kenmuir. I'm not armed. I only came to talk. That's all, although you might not want to talk out here." Not that they couldn't have. Not a card-playing face had turned in their direction.

Aces took a few seconds to consider the alternatives of now or, implicitly, later. He nodded toward the interior of his office. "All right. We talk."

The large office was outfitted for function, not entertainment. A desk was littered with papers of various colors and sizes, apparently left wherever they'd come to rest after a stiff wind had blown through earlier. A Naugahyde couch patched with duct tape and a couple of wooden chairs served rare guests. Aces sat on one end of the couch and the blonde man, ever vigilant, perched astride the arm on the opposite side. Kenmuir sat on one of the wooden chairs.

"All right," Aces said, "you're here. You wanted to talk, so talk."

Kenmuir leaned back in his chair, casually crossing his legs: his standard portrayal of a nonthreatening, chatty visitor. "Hank

Jackson. Outfielder, San Francisco Giants. Good man. No vices. Has a brother who's no Cincinnati Kid. Loses the occasional bet. In the past, Hank, a family kind of guy, was good enough to pay some of his brother's debts. But no longer. He's out of the banking business."

Aces picked at his fingernails and didn't look directly at Kenmuir. "Brings tears to my fuckin' eyes. What's it got to do with me?"

"This: Jackson's willing to let bygones be bygones. What's over is over. But no more. He wants nothing to do with you. And vice versa. Win or lose, his brother's on his own. Hank would like to be reassured that you and he are of one mind on this topic." Kenmuir could feel his internal temperature starting to rise. *This guy's not gonna agree to anything. It may have to be up to the police, whether Larry likes it or not.*

Aces looked up from his fingernails and glared at Kenmuir through squinted eyes. "Listen up, whoever you are, I don't know what the fuck you're talking about. The guy wins, I pay him. The guy loses, he pays me. If he can't pay it himself, then someone else pays it for him. No more complicated than that. You don't like it? Too fuckin' bad."

Kenmuir replied, "One pays one's debts. I understand that. I even agree with it. What I don't agree with is when your man here arranges for Jackson to be picked off by some lowlife in a car. *That* won't happen again."

Aces leaned forward in the couch. "Who the fuck you think you are? Come in here, *my* place, and accuse me of fuckin' with some nigger ballplayer? Fuck you. And get the fuck outta here." When he stood up, the blonde man bounced off the arm of the couch.

Kenmuir also stood, but slowly. "I was afraid that might be your reaction. Guess you'll do what you want. But whatever that is, it won't be worth the gamble to mess with Mr. Jackson."

Veins pulsed visibly in Aces' pipe-cleaner neck, which had become inflamed with a red rash. He turned to the blonde man. "Bobby, get this asshole the fuck outta here!"

Bobby reached out, intending to grab Kenmuir's arm. He didn't reach quickly enough. The grasping hand was still in motion when its wrist was grabbed. At that moment, Bobby was pain free, but it didn't last long. Kenmuir pulled the wrist forward, and Bobby came with it. As he did, Kenmuir's right knee lashed upward and disappeared into Bobby's crotch. When his testicles were flattened against the knee, Bobby's body contracted, and he bent over, almost as if greeting a Japanese guest.

He never completed the bow though—because Kenmuir's fist smashed into the left side of his jaw, propelling him backward. Semiconscious and nauseated with pain, Bobby collapsed into a corner of the dilapidated couch.

The opening click of Aces' six-inch switchblade knife was loud enough for Kenmuir to hear it over the swoosh of the couch's cushions under Bobby's weight. Kenmuir reacted by instinctively stepping sideways and half-turning away from the sound—but not quite far enough to avoid the slicing arc Aces swung at Kenmuir's side. The blade gashed the underside of Kenmuir's left forearm.

However, as a result of his ferocious lunge, Aces slightly lost his balance. That minor mistake became a calamity when Kenmuir, ignoring the burning streak on his arm, kicked the exposed side of Aces' left knee. The kick came from too great a distance to break the knee, but it propelled Aces backward against the wall.

Before Aces could react, Kenmuir's hand grabbed his hair, twisted his head, and drove his face against the wall. A tooth spun crazily into the air, and blood from his nose erupted onto the wall. Stunned, Aces was vaguely aware of his knife hand being yanked backward and upward. He became more aware when his right shoulder dislocated.

Aces found himself lying on his back with blood running down both sides of his face and his right arm twisted under him. His skeletal chin was tilted upward, trying to flee the tip of the knife being poked by the man kneeling on his chest. For a gambling man, it wasn't an ideal time to bluff.

Kenmuir pushed firmly on the knife at Aces' chin. "You about done?"

Aces didn't move his chin. He merely grunted through lips which might've been sewn shut.

"I'll take that as a yes. Here's the deal . . . You don't go near Hank Jackson. You don't talk to him. You don't go to his house. You don't accept any money from him. He's ceased to exist as far as you're concerned. Am I clear enough about this?"

Responding as much to the knife as the words, Aces snarled affirmatively.

"Very good. This time, I'm going to walk away, and you don't even want to think about next time." Kenmuir walked out of the office and into the card room. *Now* he'd attracted the players' attention. Every face looked back and forth between his bloody arm and the bartender's baseball bat.

Kenmuir looked at the bat and then at Ted the bartender. "Up to you."

The bartender shrugged and shifted his grip unthreateningly to the middle of the bat. "Looks to me like it's all over."

"That it is. You might want to look in on your boss, though. I think Aces has folded."

Wrapping a bar towel around his bleeding forearm, Kenmuir walked outside into the afternoon, mentally diagramming the most efficient route to the emergency room of nearby Alta Bates Hospital.

Chapter 22

Tuesday evening, June 4, City of Walnut Creek

IT WAS NEARLY 7:00 P.M. WHEN KENMUIR migrated to his assigned spot in his office building's underground garage. A few lonely cars were scattered in the cavernous space, waiting for workday stragglers to take them home. Kenmuir was running late as a result of having spent the afternoon in a court-supervised settlement conference with an opposing lawyer whom he suspected had attended a law school where you were taught to draw a picture of a lawyer and, when you could do that, you graduated and were given a framed matchbook cover.

With his coat draped over his left arm, he placed his briefcase on the concrete floor. He turned the key in the door handle, and heard the opening power-locks echo in the silent garage. Next came, "Hey, you . . . Kenmuir."

Two men stepped away from a navy-blue Cadillac limousine several spaces away. One was a Vegas kind of guy with a mass of dark curls flowing over the top two open buttons of his shirt, a kind of hair dickey. The other either had spent much of his life in a weight room or had left his shirt in his dryer's hot cycle for far too long; the veins on his arms looked like a roadmap of Paris.

"No." Kenmuir tried to look unconcerned and casual, but now started moving toward the elevator. "Sorry."

Hair Dickey moved in cadence with Kenmuir. "You're him. Let's not bullshit. The Boss wants to see you. We take you. We bring you back. Simple."

Kenmuir exhaled derisively. "Come on. *The Boss?* You've got to be kidding." His feet were still moving.

"Dead serious."

"I'll bet you are. Tell you what. I'll go upstairs, slip into a black shirt and white tie, and be right back. Couple minutes, max. Then we'll go."

Hair Dickey wasn't amused. "Now, asshole, not later. Let's go." He jabbed his finger in the direction of the limousine behind them. The Nautilus devotee had moved so much closer to the elevator that, in a race for it, Kenmuir would finish second. Running for the garage entrance was a possibility, but not after Hair Dickey said, "Don't bother running. Even if you made it, we'd only show up some other time. Your choice is when, not if." He again pointed to the limousine.

Kenmuir assumed that, if they wanted to hurt him, they wouldn't have approached so casually. Besides, Hair Dickey was right: they could always find him. What could he do, arrange for a different reserved parking spot? That'd fool them for sure. Kenmuir stopped drifting toward the elevator and faced the two men. "Maybe I'll ride up front."

"Maybe you won't. Get in back."

They rode in silence, but without any secrecy. South on I-680, off at Sycamore Valley Road, and straight up to the expensive enclave of Blackhawk, the residential bastion of Contra Costa County's nouveau riche. Flashy, multistory houses on undersized lots with oversized mortgages. Huge rooms, but no money left to furnish them. Sprawling patios and swimming pools only slightly smaller than Lake Erie. Golf course fairways, narrow as driveways, snaking wherever gullies and steep hills had made residential construction unfeasible.

The limousine stopped in front of a set of iron gates that punctuated unusually high terra cotta walls. The gates opened to a long driveway that became a circle in front of an immense house. In the center of the circle a fountain gushed from the bronze helmet of a gigantic Roman veteran from the Punic Wars. Scipio Africanus visits the suburbs.

Once inside the house's foyer, Kenmuir glanced to his left and saw a room maybe the size of the Yukon Territory, and as about as colorful. White velour couches flanked a glass coffee table supported by a striding, miniature polar bear amid white shag wall-to-wall carpeting. The only color was a bunch of purple glass grapes in the middle of the coffee table. "Very tasteful," Kenmuir said to no one but himself. To his right, where Hair Dickey stopped, were twin white doors, almost ceiling height.

Kenmuir suffered a kind of decorative whiplash as soon as he walked through the twin doors. In contrast to the tundra across the hall, this room was some decorator's notion of A Man's Room. All furnishings were in brown suede or brown leather furnishings. Three walls were covered with fish, some big and some small, mounted on suede-covered plaques. The fourth wall displayed portraits of a woman and four children: the woman looked like a bass and the children looked like sturgeon. Kenmuir wondered which wall had been decorated first.

At the far end of the room, a man rose from an enormous, brown leather chair. He uncovered a massive bull's head that was stitched in black against the back of the chair. Zeus would've been proud to have so appeared before Europa. The man's head wasn't much smaller than the bull's. He was in his early fifties and flirted with 300 pounds. Kenmuir had no doubt the mammoth body had strength to match. "Good evening, Mr. Kenmuir. I'm Angelo Marini." His cherubic face displayed a welcoming smile.

My mistake. It really is The Boss. Kenmuir was up close and personal with the reputed head of the mob in the western states, to whom the newspapers and Detective Ochoa referred (but never to his face) as "Whopper." Kenmuir dimly recalled from Sunday school that Daniel had a protecting angel with him in the lion's den. He hoped that his own angel was alert and nearby.

Marini extended a hand the size of a head of lettuce and said, "I'm glad you could find time for our visit."

Kenmuir's hand vanished inside Marini's. "Well, the boys and I were cruising around, found ourselves in the neighborhood, and decided to stop by." When his right hand was emancipated, Kenmuir tapped the face of the watch on his left wrist and said theatrically. "Wow, already time to go."

"In good time, Mr. Kenmuir. All in good time. But first I have a few questions—"

Kenmuir interrupted, "So ask them."

The good-host smile disappeared as quickly as a changed TV channel. "Don't interrupt, Mr. Kenmuir. I realize that you might be . . . irritated, but don't push. A few questions and then back to your office. Don't make more out of it than it is." Marini lowered himself back into the vast space of the bull's-head chair and gestured toward a nearby chair. Kenmuir remained standing for a moment, as if to show that he'd sit when and if he wanted. False independence thus demonstrated, he sat. It also dawned on him that, if he didn't know why he was here, it wouldn't occur to anyone else that he ever had been.

Marini lit a Pall Mall—no wimpy filter for him—and offered one. Kenmuir declined. Say no to something. Truly a fearless guy. Marini sucked a quarter of the length of the cigarette in one drag. Smoke billowed out of his mouth as he said, "Out of nowhere I start hearing about you. You're not there and then you are. I make some inquiries. Small-time lawyer. No offense . . ."

Kenmuir gestured dismissively. Privately, he *was* offended.

"You're no cop because, believe me, I'd know if you were. I like to consider myself well informed about police affairs." Marini actually chuckled. "Then I learn you *were* a cop. Also a prosecutor. You appear to have been restless in your choice of vocation." He took another drag. "I'm told that you're considered a resourceful man with a temper and a bit of a stubborn streak."

Kenmuir held his hands against his chest as if to say *Me?*

"Yes, you." Marini again showed his disarming smile. "And then there was that shooting in west county. Impressive piece of work."

"It wasn't meant to be. I just happened to be there at the time."

"Maybe, but you did something about it—which is more than most would've done."

"Look, I know all this. I lived through it. Can we just get to whatever it is you want from me?"

"All right. Let's. Part is curiosity. I wanted to judge you for myself. Part is wanting to tell you face-to-face that our business interests are clashing."

When Marini took another drag, Kenmuir took advantage of the opening. "I don't have the slightest idea what you're talking about. Hell, I'm not sure I have *any* business interests. Certainly none that would clash with yours. Whatever yours may be."

"Oh, Mr. Kenmuir, I hoped you'd prove less dense. You seem like an intelligent man, but, as they say, appearances can be deceiving."

What the hell? How could I cause any trouble for this big boy? But I have. Sometime, somehow, my travels in the past several weeks bumped into Marini. Where and how badly? "How about a hint? Really, I'm not being dense. I simply have nothing in common with you."

"All right. Let's give you the benefit of the doubt. I realize my business interests are widely scattered. From Los Angeles to, for example, Emeryville."

Whereupon fell the proverbial ton of bricks. Of course. Gambling, bookmaking: all the delights a place like The Oasis offers. When Kenmuir walked in that door, he unwittingly trespassed on Marini's turf. "Now I understand."

"No, you don't. Because, as it happens, you'd already come to my attention through, what should I say? a mutual colleague."

"Somehow I doubt it. Who might that be?"

"His name's Richard Little. About your height and build. Matter of fact, the two of you could be twins."

"Richard Little?"

"Yes. Mr. Little recently sought some financial advice from a local firm, Angel Investments, evidently at the recommendation of Mr. Adelman. Coincidentally, the firm provides a similar service for me."

A Deadly Game

Another ton of bricks. What Ochoa had described as the reputed Marini-MacPherson connection. *How's he know? MacPherson, that prick, must've had me followed.*

"I'm told that Mr. Little solicited some advice from Mr. MacPherson of that firm. Do you know if it was worthwhile?"

"I do—and it wasn't. Mr. MacPherson was unimpressive. Surly manner, weak people skills, as they say." *This isn't going to end well. What doesn't he know? On the other hand, what's left?*

"Strange. I've found him quite delightful and helpful. Maybe it was the subject of your conversation. Why don't you tell me about it?" Marini used an exhale as a dramatic pause. "While you're at it, tell me why Mr. Little lied about his name."

Kenmuir nodded his head negatively. "No can do. As a fellow businessman, you can appreciate the need for confidentiality."

Whatever signal flashed between Marini and his henchmen, Kenmuir missed it. Because a muscular forearm suddenly clamped around his neck and dragged him upward in the chair, arching his shoulders backward. With that prelude, Hair Dickey stepped in front of the chair and drove his fist into Kenmuir's stomach. Partially choked by the crush of the forearm and stunned by the blow, Kenmuir was gasping as his neck was released. Marini didn't uncross his legs or miss a drag on his cigarette. "Don't spar with me, Mr. Kenmuir. You'll lose. While I prefer to avoid the harsher forms of discussion, it's late and I want my questions answered."

Kenmuir leaned back in the chair, breathing laboriously, with his hands over his stomach.

Marini flicked a cigarette ash into the large ashtray to his right. "Like I said, you're a no-name to me. When I heard that someone was killed for shooting cops, I said fine. Then I read that the shooter wasn't another cop, but some piss-ant lawyer. That puzzles me. I ask why some lawyer would be there in the first place. Then that *same* lawyer uses a false name and tries to provoke MacPherson. Still I let it go. Wait and see what happens. What happens is the lawyer plays Wyatt Earp at The Oasis, and now I'm done waiting. You're either some psycho asshole—and I can deal with that—or you've got something eating at you. Which is it?"

He wants to learn from me, but I'm learning from him at the same time. LaPera was connected with MacPherson, no longer any doubt about that. Remotely, maybe, but nonetheless connected. As MacPherson works for Marini, the question's whether LaPera's connected with Marini as well. I keep talking and maybe I learn something about why Orr was killed. Nothing to lose. I hope.

"Just a coincidence. Detective Woodson's a friend of mine. I was around when they were going to interview a sleeze named Jesus LaPera about some stolen car. I went along for old time's sake."

Marini pursed his lips and bobbed his head, as if in agreement. But he didn't agree. "Won't wash. Even if you were just along for the ride, you didn't have to show up later at MacPherson's office. It's not a hard question: Why go see MacPherson?"

Open up a little. If MacPherson truly was an open book, I have to believe he'd be dealing with me one helluva lot differently. No. He's dealing with some blank pages and wants to fill them in. Worth taking a chance. "Information suggested some connection between LaPera and MacPherson. No actual evidence, but good information. The police consider MacPherson's business a front for . . . questionable activities. Allegedly, of course. Presumably you know that, and you surely know more about it than I do." Kenmuir raised his arms. "Not that you're personally involved, needless to say. It's just that you're . . . how did you describe it? Well informed about law enforcement."

"Get on with it."

"Nothing more to get on with. One cop killed and another wounded. They're my friends, so I decided to push it by finding out what I could from MacPherson. Beat doing nothing."

"Still won't wash. I know what the cops think, which is why they've hassled MacPherson and me for years." Marini stabbed a cigarette into the large ashtray. "No, you went for reasons of your own. The cops may have let you and may even have helped you, but you did it because *you* wanted to. I may have to put up with cops because they're cops, but not some lawyer. That clear?"

Again, Kenmuir didn't see whatever signal Marini gave, but he'd been expecting it. All at once, he sensed the movement of the man behind him and, in front of him, saw Hair Dickey's foot slide forward on the dark brown, pseudo-suede carpet. Before the powerful forearm could again envelop his neck from behind, he lunged forward.

Hair Dickey was completely unprepared. With his hands lowered for another blow to Kenmuir's stomach, he was unable to deflect the fist that came up high. Kenmuir's knuckles smashed into the middle of his throat. Instantly paralyzed by his own choking reflex, he was similarly unable to guard against Kenmuir's other fist as it burrowed into *his* stomach. At once breathless and gagging, he knelt on the well-padded carpet.

Kenmuir pirouetted and faced the weight lifter, who'd stumbled in his haste to get around the suddenly empty chair. "Try me, big man."

Two men burst through the double doors as Kenmuir squared off. One came in high and the other, low. They were pointing handguns at Kenmuir, but they were looking at Marini. The room became as motionless as a photograph. Marini looked sideways at Kenmuir. "You about done?"

Kenmuir looked at the unflappable Marini. "Once was enough. Fuck twice." Being summoned like a vassal before an emperor was one thing; being abused by the emperor's servants was quite another.

Marini laughed, seemingly with genuine pleasure. "If that pissed you off, how about getting shot?"

"I've been shot. Just as soon avoid it, but it's your call."

Marini waived his hand in the direction of the two armed men. "Help Dino up. And make sure he stays out of the way." Again, he looked at Kenmuir. "Good enough?"

"Good enough."

If I'm ever going to learn anything about Orr from Marini, this'd be the time. "Like you said, let's cut the crap. You enough of a gambling man to risk talking with me alone? No witnesses?"

Marini chuckled. "I guess I could take that . . . risk."

Kenmuir spoke as soon as they were alone. "You're right. Something *is* eating at me big time. And I admit that I need help. Maybe you can help, maybe you can't. Maybe you won't.

Maybe you're part of my problem. I guess I'll have to take the chance that you're not."

"You really can't just get on with it, can you?"

He had a point, but the introduction was important, if only to Kenmuir. He *was* taking a big chance, and he wanted Marini to know it. "Okay, here goes. Obviously, I didn't see your man MacPherson to discuss soybean futures. I went because he's supposed to be a mover in gambling circles. Gambling's emerging as a theme in what's eating at me." Kenmuir gave Marini every detail first about Jackson and then about the death of Orr. "LaPera wasn't in Orinda to sightsee. No, he was sent there specifically to go to Orr's house. And to hurt him, I think. Not kill him. Either way, there's no doubt LaPera was the one who did it. But someone else was pulling his strings. That brought me to MacPherson—because he's rumored to have used LaPera as an enforcer."

Marini's expression was impenetrable. Other than to flick another ash into the tray, he didn't move.

"I know . . . You've got nothing to say. But that doesn't mean LaPera and MacPherson aren't two cards in the same deck. MacPherson's got money and his businesses—his *real* investments—include gambling. Meanwhile, Jackson's situation is inseparable from gambling. That means Orr's murder probably has something to do with gambling. Q.E.D." He paused. "And I'm now gambling that they aren't connected to you." Kenmuir stopped talking and waved his hand, as if to say, *Your turn.*

"I appreciate the candor." Marini linked his fingers and rested his chin on them. It was like placing a large pink ball on a thick hammock. "Some personal details might help you. I've put on a couple of pounds since I was a kid in Jersey. Back then, I played a lot of baseball. I was pretty good. Not great, but good. The Dodgers, Giants, and Yankees were all in my backyard. Loved the Dodgers. Favorite player was Hodges.

"I've never lost my love of the game. As soon as I came here, I bought A's season tickets. I was around for the great teams: Jackson, Fingers, Rudi, Bando. Later, I cheered for Thumper. Under no circumstances—*no* circumstances—would that wonderful ballplayer have suffered any harm at my hands. Hell, I'd have arranged to protect the son of a bitch if I'd known.

"This much I'll tell you, Kenmuir. If Orr was involved with gambling, I'd have heard. He was not. No one—repeat, *no one*—within my sphere of influence had any reason to do him harm. Why someone else may have, I don't know. You and the police will have to figure that out for yourselves." He lit another Pall Mall. "Mr. Jackson? I'm *very* confident he won't have to worry about his future safety."

"Thank you. That'll make a lot of people happy. But as far as Orr is concerned, I've gone from one dead end to another."

"Yes and no. You've eliminated a possible link between Orr and gambling. And that means I won't expect to encounter you again. Have I made myself plain?"

Kenmuir held up his hands in a gesture of resignation. "Gotcha. I'm to go elsewhere for investment advice."

I'll be careful not to step on your considerable toes, Whopper, but that only means I'll be taking a different route. And I'll decide when I'm done, not you.

Chapter 23

Wednesday morning, June 5, City of Martinez

"BEING A CLERK'S THE SHITS, DAVE. Stuck inside. Fuckin' papers everywhere." Woodson's hairy hand grabbed a stack of papers and crumpled them into a ball. He'd returned to part-time duty. *Desk* duty.

"Why're you rushing anyway? Crime's not going to disappear. I bet it'll still be here in a month." Kenmuir pulled up a chair.

"Tell me about it. Until Junior's replacement gets broken in and I'm unleashed, we're down two detectives. Three homicides in North Richmond and one in West Pittsburg over Memorial Day weekend alone. I gotta get back on the street."

"I understand, but you won't do anybody any good if you don't recover fully. Like it or not, it'll take as long as it takes. Go home and lay up. Get healthy. Commit yourself to a couple of soaps. Master the strategy of buying a vowel."

"Fuck you, counselor." Woodson gave Kenmuir the finger. He'd lost weight and color, but not attitude. "That why you're here? To annoy the infirm?"

"Not entirely. Though that is one reason. Another is to see how you're doing. Which, obviously, is not very well. Also to catch you up on the Orr case."

"*Case?* What case? Ochoa and Gotz have kept me posted. Here, let me summarize it for you: no motive, no suspects, and no weapon. And a dead shooter. Thanks again to you, by the way, but it sure as shit didn't help the investigation." He winced as he shifted position in his desk chair. "I also heard about your cute move on MacPherson. Which, more's the damn pity, netted nothing except some asshole lawyer yelling at the lieutenant about his client's constitutional rights."

"Didn't know that."

"Nothing you could do about it. Besides, the boss knows who MacPherson is. He listened to the foaming lawyer, hung up, and forgot about it."

With melodramatic exaggeration, Kenmuir put his fingers against his forehead. "Oh, yeah, that reminds me. Did I mention where I was last night?" He pretended to start to rise from his chair. "But so what? Why would you care about my glamorous social life?"

Woodson grinned as he nodded his head from side to side. He took a deep breath and slowly exhaled. The long-suffering patient. "Okay, dipshit, I'll play. Where'd you go last night?"

"As you know, I put in a full day. Being no longer on the civil service dole like, say, a semi-retired sheriff's detective. By 1800, you've knocked off and are having a Harvey Wallbanger with the other clerks. Me? I'm still working after—I say again, *after*—the aforementioned full day. Yesterday, instead of returning to my palatial home, I'm invited—some might say kidnapped—and driven to the more humble homestead of Angelo Marini. The Whopper, his very own self."

"Bullshit."

"No shit of any kind. All very true." With his right index finger, Kenmuir drew a cross over his heart.

"Jesus. You've hit the big time. What the fuck's that about?"

Kenmuir lit a cigarette. "Can't be positive. I mean, I heard what he said. And I learned he's got great sources of information, because there wasn't much he didn't already know. Our tiff with LaPera, my hanging out with high rollers in Emeryville. But what truly put me in his high beams was the financial wheeling and dealing with MacPherson. He apparently wondered, who the fuck's this guy and what the fuck's he up to? I doubt he'd have bothered with me otherwise."

"So he shanghais a lawyer he knows is connected with cops? What is he, fucking nuts?!"

"No, he's a shrewd, ruthless son of a bitch who makes damn sure he knows what his functionaries are doing. I think he simply wanted to hear directly why I—as you said, a lawyer who's connected with cops—met with MacPherson at all. And he's also not a bide-my-time kind of guy. No, sir. He's the kind who wants to find out *right now*." Kenmuir took a drag and thought for a moment. "What intrigues me is why MacPherson would've even bothered telling him at all. *If* he told him—because it wouldn't surprise me at all that he has his own informant in MacPherson's office. Beats me."

"Maybe he's worried."

"Because I'm such a threat? Not likely. No, I think he merely wanted to get a handle on what was making me tick and find out what I intended to do next."

"And that was it?"

"Not quite. As long as I was there, I asked him about Orr. Because I'm convinced there's a link between LaPera and MacPherson—just as I'm now convinced there *isn't* one between LaPera and Marini."

"Sounding out Angelo Marini. I'll give you this, you got balls."

"Whatever. However, I will say that he seemed genuinely troubled about Orr. Or maybe more important, he seemed genuinely puzzled. Said he'd never have hurt Orr and, in fact, would've prevented any harm. I believe him about that as well."

"I'll be damned. Hell, I've never even seen the guy. I mean, not that it matters, but what's he like?"

"You'd be surprised. Big-time crime, so he's tough and got a temper. But here's the strange part: He's kinda charming, in an odd way. I liked him."

"What're you going to do now?"

"According to Marini or to me?"

"There's a difference?"

"Oh, yeah. He told me I was done. No reason to rummage around anymore. Certainly not around MacPherson."

"But you disagree?"

"Most definitely. There's still a lot of ground to cover. I just have to watch where I'm stepping."

Chapter 24

Thursday evening, June 6, City of Cleveland

THE CLEVELAND INDIANS HAD RIGHT-HANDER Woodrow "Woody" Whitney and little else. Many believed that Whitney was the most dominating pitcher in the American League. Every five days, he took the mound and suppressed the other team's offense. Every five days, his teammates failed to hit the other team's pitcher. The night before Cleveland may have won, 11-5, but on Woody's nights, the scores would be 1-0 or 2-1, and most often *not* in his favor. Every year, thanks to being stranded in Cleveland, he won a lackluster eleven or twelve games—while simultaneously leading the league in ERA and strikeouts.

Last year, he'd thrown nine innings of overpowering perfection. No hits by the other team. His teammates had banged out ten hits, but scored no runs. The Indians' manager had decided—and was excoriated in the following morning's newspapers for his decision—to let Woody pitch in the bottom of the tenth. The tired pitcher finally gave up a hit. Solo home run. Game over. Another loss: 1-0.

Today had been a rare midweek day off as the weekend's opponent was traveling from the west coast. For Woody, it had meant golf in the morning and lunch at home, followed by a short nap and dinner with friends in the evening. After he and his wife, a former Miss Ohio, said good-bye to their friends, he turned toward their car, but his wife suggested taking a walk. The babysitter was in no hurry with the school year almost over, "so why not take our time?"

The daytime humidity had abated. The streets were nearly deserted as they strolled leisurely by closed shops. She eventually guided him into the alcove of a women's clothing store. It seemed spontaneous, as if something caught her eye. It had—but the day before. A light blue sundress decorated with small daisies was displayed in the window. She asked, "Don't you think that's cute?" Woody had no sense of its cuteness one way or the other, but he recognized a pitch thrown straight down the middle and immediately agreed. She discussed the attributes of the dress: Was it her color? Was the style flattering, or would the pleated front make her look too, well, fat? Was it cut too low? Did the flowers seem too girlish?

Whitney had no answers for these questions, but he'd fielded them before. He merely followed her lead. "I don't think anything could make you look fat, honey. And if it's cut too low, wear it only for me."

They weren't aware that two men had followed them from the restaurant. They likewise weren't aware when the two men arrived soundlessly at the entrance to the alcove. Although it was almost 10 p.m., the men wore sunglasses and had scarves pulled up over their noses, like bandits in a western movie. The taller one held a gun in his right hand and said, in what both Whitney and his wife would describe later as an Hispanic accent, "You. Turn around. Slowly." Whitney and his wife were more startled than frightened. She instinctively recoiled away from the sound. He turned toward it. When she saw the gun, she whimpered, started to cry, and said "Don't hurt us." Whitney said nothing.

The taller man spoke harshly as he stepped further into the alcove: "Gimme your wallets. Now!"

She was terrified and fumbled anxiously with her purse. "Take what you want. Just don't hurt us."

Whitney sidled a half step toward her to partially shield her from what he estimated to be the line of fire. The taller man saw the movement. "You wanna fuckin' die, man? Turn around and put your fuckin' hands on the wall."

He looked over his shoulder at the windows ringing the alcove. "What wall?"

His wife reacted to him before the man could. "Please don't argue. It's not worth it. Give them what they want."

"Listen to the little lady, mister, and no one gets hurt." The tall man flicked the barrel of the gun in her direction. Her hands were trembling and tears were running down her cheeks. She held out her wallet as a sort of offering. The short man snapped it out of her hand.

When Whitney didn't reach for the wallet in his back pocket, the taller man stepped toward his wife and pointed the gun barrel directly at her face. "I fuckin' told you to turn around and put your hands on the wall, motherfucker."

She looked pleadingly at her husband. "Please."

Still saying nothing, Whitney turned around and put his palms against the glass of the store window. As the short man took the wallet from Whitney's back pocket, the other one spoke to the back of Whitney's head: "You shoulda listened to your wife, man."

He raised the gun. It was three feet from the back of Whitney's left hand.

He fired.

The bullet passed through the center of the hand, and splintered several bones a millisecond before the hand was lacerated by being propelled through the shattering glass of the window. The thunderous roar of the discharge echoing in the alcove drowned out her scream of horror and his yell of pain.

The two men ran down the street.

Over the following week, the Cleveland Police Department investigation turned into a chain-reaction. First, one addict sold methamphetamine to a shaggy-haired man in a buckskin vest who happened to be a narc. Looking to trade, the addict told the narc that he might—he wasn't sure, but he *might*—be able to remember something . . . god, what was it? . . . he'd heard about who shot Woody Whitney. So he got his deal.

Second, that information led Cleveland detectives to another hype, insensate and sprawled on a filthy bed in his wretched apartment. Half walked and half dragged to an interrogation room, the hype shrewdly struck a deal of his own—although, much later, the sentencing judge would ignore his insistence that Indians' season tickets were part of the deal—before explaining that he'd been hired by an anonymous stranger specifically to hurt Whitney. Why take such a chance? Because he was told the contract came from "Swampy" Royce and everyone knew you could count on a Swampy contract.

Swampy Royce, a local jack-of-all-trades who bragged about being raised in the swamps of the Florida Everglades, was immediately brought in for questioning. But, unlike the two drug users before him, he wasn't intimidated or brain-dead. He listened to the police accusations with unflappable composure before saying, "I don't know what the hell you're talkin' about. I hired some whacked-out hype to fuck up this Woody Whatever ball player? You're out of your fuckin' minds. Fuckin' crazy."

Swampy lost patience before his interrogators did. "You wanna 'rest me? Do it. But, from what you say, some spic did the shooting. Well, check this out. I'm no spic and I didn't do shit. You got nothin'—except that some asshole's heard my name and's tryin' to burn me so he can cut some walk for himself. Fuck that. It's all bullshit. I want my fuckin' lawyer." He was unimpressed with the detectives' attempts to convince him that a lawyer would only get in the way. "I'll bet that bullshit works sometimes. Not this time. I want my damn lawyer. You got nothin'."

He was right: the police had nothing. He never got his lawyer because he was released instead. The frustrated detectives agreed to put the smug Royce under a microscope. They might have nothin' right now, but they were going to get somethin'.

Chapter 25

Saturday evening, June 15, City of Walnut Creek

THE BALMY EVENING ALLOWED EVERYONE at the party of mainly DAs and ex-DAs, their spouses, and a few dates thrown in for variety to wander freely. Most gathered in the cabana, home for both the bar and the disc player, with satellite conversational groups on the wooden deck or on the slightly roughened concrete surrounding the swimming pool.

Lucy Ball had met too many people too quickly. True, they were friendly and welcoming, but their conversations focused on well-established jokes and shared experiences unfamiliar to her. And she became mildly self-conscious whenever one of the wives made it clear how happy they all were that Kenmuir was "dating again."

Fortunately, she saw that John Trauber, worn down by a combination of too many drinks and too many disjointed conversations, had sidelined himself on one of two Brown & Jordan chairs on the wooden deck. Perfect. Not only was she relieved to be able to join him, but also Kenmuir's repeated glances wouldn't become anxious if she were talking with Trauber or his wife, with whom she'd sat at dinner.

After a few minutes of desultory remarks, Trauber swiveled in his chair and faced Lucy. "So. How you like my main man?" The boldness of too much wine.

"Well, we're just getting to know each other. He's funny and smart and easy to like. We'll see."

"Right on." He laughed and said, "Sorry about the 'right on' part. Have I had maybe nine gallons too much to drink or what? Which is only my klutz way of saying, yes, I hope you will see. But don't get frustrated with him. He's very cautious. Guards himself with a lot of walls."

"Walls?"

"Yep. He's needed them. Any officer in combat has to keep a lot to himself and some distance from his men." It was common knowledge, as Lucy now had learned, that Trauber and Kenmuir served together in Vietnam.

She looked skeptically. "Surely not from you. After all, he does refer to you his best friend."

"And I am. *We* are. However, that came later. When we were civilians and drawn together by circumstances here. But back then, in-country? No way. He was the lieutenant, and I was one of his troops. No, back in those days he relied more on two other guys, his XO and a sergeant E-7."

"Well, neither one of them is his best friend."

"That's right. Because neither can be. They didn't make it back." Trauber knew he became chatty when he was liquored up a bit and feeling relaxed. He also realized that he had to change the subject, because he was in real danger of stepping out of bounds. Long ago, Kenmuir had told him: "We both were there, Lizard, and you have your stories. I can't tell you what to say or what not to say. But leave me out of them."

Trauber was alone in understanding how scarred Kenmuir was by the loss of "his" Stuart Unit and how he'd never forgive himself, regardless of what he or anyone else said.

Trauber shifted to the more neutral territory of Kenmuir's marriage, though it'd be impossible for him ever to be drunk enough to mention the death of Kenmuir's son. If he did, the friendship would end. So, he warned himself, keep it general, common knowledge stuff, like . . . "He's also wary since the divorce. He thinks he took in stride, but he's wrong."

"He said it was very friendly."

"It was. Don't get me wrong, Mary's a sweetheart. My wife and I loved them both. After they split, though, he simply retreated inside. Not consciously maybe, but it was safer there for him, I think."

"Even from you?"

"Oh, yeah. I tend to jump in with both emotional feet. Not LT. He always keeps one foot on dry ground. We're best friends, but we're real different. I'm a local boy. Kind of a screw-up. Killed some time in junior college, joined the Army, went to 'Nam and all that. When we were recovering in the hospital, he encouraged me to return to school when I got back, and I encouraged him to do the same." Trauber grinned. "As usual, I followed his advice, but he didn't follow mine. At least not right away. He was a cop in those days. When his partner got killed, he *really* clammed up. That went on for a couple years. Had to undermine his marriage to some degree, but who knows how much?"

Trauber slowly shook his head. "He's been through some crap. The Nam. His partner. Mary. Other stuff. No wonder he keeps his guard up. Maybe that's why he's flippant so much of the time. Another way of shielding himself." He forced a laugh. "But, hey, what do I know?"

As if responding to a high-pitched warning that only he could hear, Kenmuir suddenly appeared in front of them. He looked at Trauber first and then at Lucy. "You want to be careful about listening to Mr. Heart-on-his-sleeve for too long, Lucy. Very low capacity for firewater." He put his hand on her shoulder. "Get you something? Time to go?"

Lucy shook her head. "No. I'm fine. You're having fun, and I like talking with John."

Kenmuir looked tolerantly at Trauber. "Don't go getting mushy, Lizard. And she doesn't need your version of any true confessions. Not about you and certainly not about me." He winked at Lucy. "Here's a great idea. Talk about anything that leaves me out."

Trauber looked up innocently. "You can count on me, LT."

Kenmuir laughed as he walked away. "Now I feel much better . . . "

Lucy waited until Kenmuir was within the sound of the Stones' *Under My Thumb* and then said, "One of the wives said that only you can refer to Dave as LT, but that everyone can call you Lizard. Why?"

Trauber became serious. "Because Lizard's just a nickname. Anyone can use it. But only a few of us were commanded by the LT. Only we were entitled to call him that. And none of them are here. Or ever will be. Except me."

A Deadly Game

Lucy looked at Trauber. "There's so much more to it than just being good friends, isn't there?"

Fuck it, he thought, *there's no reason she can't know*. "A lot. It goes back to when we were in the 'Nam..."

Chapter 26

Early 1970s, Vietnam, near the Cambodian Border

THE SATURATED JUNGLE PAUSED FOR A MOMENT of silence, exhausted by days of uninterrupted rain. Birds and animals were quiet in their dry havens, unconvinced that the storms had passed. Only the constant sound of dripping persisted. Sitting with his back against the comparatively dry trunk of a tree, Kenmuir twisted his torso to test the stiffness on his right side. The stinging sensation confirmed that last week's wound from the Vietcong's knife hadn't healed in the fifteen minutes since he'd last checked.

He pulled up his shirt and looked at the six-inch slash. "Seen much worse back home from accidents in the kitchen," the doctor had told him. "Biggest worry you've got now is sepsis. Damn climate breeds infection. Throw this powder on it, otherwise, let it breathe."

The red gash was puckered and inflamed, ugly and caked with white powder. Plainly, it didn't like breathing the fetid air any more than the rest of them. Kenmuir, a master of fatal diagnoses, was convinced that some insidious infection was burrowing deeper with every passing moment. Blood poisoning was inevitable and would soon be followed by delirium as his brain degenerated.

"Keep starin' at it, LT, maybe it'll get pissed off and go away." Sergeant First Class Bledsoe stepped out from behind a large fern where he'd added more fluid to the sodden ground. "Mean-lookin' fucker, isn't it? I've had a couple. Take forever to go away."

"Not staring at it, Sar'nt. Performing a field medical evaluation. Something officers are trained to do. Scientific. Much too subtle for the enlisted man."

"Maybe, but if you keep fuckin' with it, the crud's gonna get to it and they'll amputate your ass, that's for damn sure."

"My ass is the least of my worries."

Bledsoe squatted down. "Well, I guess my ass is on my mind. That's because it's what I've been sittin' on for five days now. Are we gonna do something or what?"

"Don't know what to tell you. I was told to go here and wait. 'Be in position' is what the colonel said."

Stuart Unit waited through that night and the next day. At dusk the nearby jungle exploded. About half a mile northwest of their position, the green-black canopy of the jungle glowed with red and orange hues: automatic weapons, mortars, grenades. The glow was traveling in Stuart's direction, and the noise was getting louder.

Kenmuir was on the radio, right now. "Grandstand, this is Shortstop. Over. Read me, Grandstand? Over?" Their call signs had been assigned by Captain Henson, the fanatic baseball fan, and supposedly were so clever that they'd confuse the enemy during radio communications. 'Grandstand' was headquarters.

A Deadly Game

The response to Kenmuir was prompt and militarily correct. "Shortstop, this is Grandstand. Read you loud and clear. Over." Kenmuir recognized Henson's voice. *Where was Major Ruggles?* As XO, Ruggles was supposed to be in command with Colonel Gibson being in Saigon for a few days.

"Grandstand, we've got a lot of action to our northwest. *Beaucoup* automatic and not just AK. Heavier stuff. What's up? Over."

Henson's voice was calm and composed, the unruffled commander under fire. "Minor skirmish, Shortstop. One of their companies bumped into us. Not a big show. Hit-and-run, I expect. Over." After procrastinating so cruelly long, God had decided to pay attention to him and grant his dream. Ruggles had been medevaced last night with appendicitis. Suddenly Henson was in command of the brigade and, hallelujah, was hovering in a helicopter over a potential battle. At last he had the chance to do something spectacular. Maybe a Silver Star. Maybe a deserved promotion to major. And, with a little luck, maybe he'd get to write an obituary for that damnable Lieutenant Kenmuir.

Kenmuir's voice crackled through the radio in response. "Grandstand, company not likely. Repeat: not likely. You're up top. What you see?" Kenmuir heard the sound of the chopper's rotors, so he knew that Henson was flying around somewhere in a helicopter.

Kenmuir stopped talking when his XO, First Lieutenant Colgan, materialized almost magically beside him. Colgan's eyes were rapidly scanning the jungle. "We've got some genuine shit here, Dave. All kinds of movement in front. Worse, it's north to south." The First Cav wouldn't be moving north to south. The North Vietnamese Army would, though.

"Who?"

"Can't tell. No shapes, but the fucking jungle's vibrating. Don't think it's VC. Got to be NVA. And plenty of them. Time to *di-di*. Now," said Colgan.

Kenmuir knew the soft-spoken Midwesterner didn't panic and didn't exaggerate. Back on the radio: "Grandstand, you still with me? Over."

"Right here, Shortstop. Over." Captain Henson, leader of men.

"Listen up, Captain. Not a company. Repeat. Bigger than a company. Over."

"It's Grandstand. Not captain. Over," Henson reprimanded.

"Goddamn it, Henson. Many hostiles coming our way. What're we facing? Over."

Colgan reappeared to answer his question: "*Beaucoup* NVA. Running everywhere. Trying to turn the corner. We gotta get outta here." Like Kenmuir, Colgan knew that Stuart was *on* the corner.

Kenmuir told Colgan, "You and Bledsoe get us gathered up," and then shouted into the radio, "Captain, going to move southwest. I say again, moving southwest. Get clear. Keep you advised. Over."

Henson's reply was immediate. "Shortstop, this is Grandstand. Negative move. Repeat. Negative move. Pick off stragglers at the edge of the NVA company. Stay where you are. That's an order, Lieutenant. Over."

A Deadly Game

As Kenmuir was listening to Henson, he saw that his men had formed a tight semicircle with all weapons pointed toward the jungle. Colgan gave a thumbs-up sign from the far side. They were ready to go. Kenmuir hesitated. They had to leave. Now. But he'd been ordered not to. *Ordered*, goddamn it. Like it or not, Henson *was* a captain and he *was* a lieutenant.

Torn between common sense and discipline, between rebellion and duty, Kenmuir tried one more time. "Henson, you aren't listening, goddamnit. It isn't a company. Repeat. *Not* a company. Where's Ruggles? Over."

"Shortstop, won't tell you again: Use proper call signs. Lead-off's medevaced to Saigon. Appendicitis. I'm in command. Over."

Kenmuir felt a chill even in the heat of his adrenaline. Henson in command. What could be worse? Stuart Unit remained in its defensive semicircle, ready to withdraw from the flashing blurs of human shapes that could be glimpsed occasionally through the thick foliage. No help could be expected from Henson and Kenmuir was out of time. "Almost on us. Got to split. Over."

"Negative, Shortstop. That's a negative. Stay put. Protect the flank. That's an order, Lieutenant. Do you read me? *That's an order!* Over."

Should he disobey a direct order? *Yes.* "Goddamn it, Henson. I'm here. You're not. NVA's everywhere. This is not—repeat, not—some company. Fuck it. We're gone. Over." Kenmuir thrust his arm, with closed first, in the air and pumped it up and down. The sign to move out. At last.

He heard his men instantly yelling, "Move out," in a combination of relief and urgency.

As they were moving, Henson continued shouting into the radio. "Shortstop, you *will* follow my orders. You *will* do what I say. You *will* . . ."

Henson's voice ended when AK-47 rounds shattered the plastic casing of the radio and mangled its interior. Kenmuir spun on his haunches and reflexively sprayed a burst in the direction of the AK-47 fire. He could've sprayed his rounds anywhere, because similar fire was coming from everywhere.

The NVA horde didn't break stride as it overran Stuart's desperate resistance. Kenmuir watched Colgan's soft cap blown off his head and flutter almost playfully into the air. He saw King's chest peppered with so many rounds so quickly that their force kept him standing momentarily after he was already dead. He saw Bledsoe drop to his knees and lean lifelessly against a tree.

Sergeant Trauber was lying on his back, blood soaking the side of his T-shirt, with his head turned to the side because he didn't want to see the grinning NVA soldier who was going kill him. His eyes were clinging to Kenmuir's in an unspoken farewell. Somehow the NVA soldier heard Kenmuir's yell, even in the bedlam around them. He turned his AK-47 toward Kenmuir at the same moment that Kenmuir slammed home a new clip in his M-16. Both fired.

The NVA soldier died when the back of his head splattered over the jungle. Kenmuir himself was struck by AK-47 rounds that pranced upward, first hitting the powdered knife wound which had otherwise been healing nicely, then his right shoulder and finally grazing the side of his jaw under his right ear. Unable to remain kneeling by the ruined radio, he collapsed onto his side.

Ironically, the momentum that doomed Stuart Unit saved Kenmuir and Trauber. As the flanking edge of the regiment, the NVA soldiers were moving so fast that they had no time to stop and confirm their kills. Like the recent storms, they arrived in an intense concentration, unleashed a torrent, and then disappeared, all in less than twenty seconds.

Chapter 27

Saturday afternoon, June 22, City of San Jose

K ENMUIR WAS A DEVOTED COLLECTOR of memorabilia. He thoroughly enjoyed baseball card shows—and comic book shows and stamp shows and political history shows. It was like visiting a museum where, if you liked what you saw, you could buy it: *See that Monet over there? I'll take it. And that Etruscan pot.* Being a poor man's Getty or Hammer was fun.

Originally, the Midsummer Baseball Memorabilia Show had been a hometown buffet of a few local dealers in an hotel ballroom. But baseball cards had become hot commodities, and thousands of dollars were being spent on cardboard memories of old ballplayers. Part-time dealers had multiplied like new fans when a team starts winning; traditional collectors now had to compete with opportunistic investors. The Show had expanded to consume the whole of the city's spacious and brightly-lit convention center with dozens of eight-foot long display tables arranged in multiple rows and aisles between them teeming with customers.

The dealers themselves were as varied as their customers. One had an ebullient greeting for everyone: "Hey, it's the master of disaster . . . Look who's here, the big boss with the hot sauce." Another had an abrasive style probably perfected on some used car lot in the Bronx; haggling with him was like asking a gladiator if he wanted to come out and play. Another was a gracious Southerner with time for everyone, from the all-business adult interested in the expensive 1954 Bowman "error" card of Ted Williams to the a ten-year-old boy who badly wanted the 1982 Topps rookie card of Cal Ripken, but only had a dollar.

Shortly after arriving, Kenmuir and Trauber went their separate ways. One might collect baseball cards with a friend, but true Kit Carsons of cardboard hunted alone. At 2:30 p.m., the two met at a prearranged spot. Trauber had located a number of prospective purchases: a 1961 Yaz and a 1967 Tommy John, incredibly without any rubber band indentations. Delicate negotiations were underway, and couldn't be hurried. They agreed to meet again in an hour.

Kenmuir wandered to a table at a choice corner of a central aisle. It'd been crowded earlier, but now Kenmuir was the lone prospective customer. He was welcomed with undisguised enthusiasm by the proprietor: "Hi there! Good to see you! How can I help you? Looking for something in particular?"

The proprietor surely had been a high school nerd, president of the Protractor Pals or the like, player of a French horn in the band. If one could "see by your outfit that you are a cowboy" on the streets of Laredo, then one could see by his that he was a baseball fan. He was resplendent in the full regalia of the San Francisco Giants: hat, shirt and, unbelievably, pants.

"No, not really," Kenmuir said with startled amusement, "Just looking."

"By all means. Do that. Look all you want. That's the best thing about these shows. Looking. Look at the cards, look at the people. It's great."

"Yes, it is." Kenmuir started to move away. Too effusive.

The bubbly proprietor didn't want him to move away. "What d'you collect?"

Easy answer. "Early 1950s mainly. I like the older stuff." For Kenmuir, no year was better than 1953, with both the oversized, hand-drawn artistry of the Topps set and the vivid, uncluttered photographs of the Bowman set. Today, he'd purchased a magnificent copy of the 1953 Bowman Pee Wee Reese, throwing in midair from the Dodger infield at Ebbets Field, and a 1953 Topps Harvey Haddix.

"I know, I know. They're amazing! It's great. I come here every year."

"Well, I guess it's a fun way to make a living," Kenmuir said inanely.

"Make a living! I'd starve. I just like baseball. Love it. Never played it, though. Wish I had." He shrugged his shoulders in cheerful resignation. "Not coordinated enough, I guess. Never could play any sport. You know how there was always one guy chosen last? I was chosen *after* him." He laughed. Extending his hand, he said, "My name's Howard Peters."

"Dave Kenmuir."

"Glad to meet you, Dave. Nope, not for a living. No way, Jose. I work nearby in Mountain View. How about you?"

"Just another lawyer."

"Sure are a lot of those. Can't live with 'em, can't live without 'em."

"I thought that was women."

"Maybe it's women lawyers," Peters said, laughing again.

As they talked, Kenmuir noticed a sign propped up against the back of the booth. "Congratulations to Howard Peters: Fantasy Champion."

All right, Kenmuir thought, *I'll bite*. "What's a Fantasy Champion, Howard?"

"You've never heard of fantasy baseball?" He reeled back in mock shock, slightly dislodging his ponderous glasses with the sudden movement. "More and more people are playing all over the country. And now my company's even involved. We created a statistics computer program for the office, and then some other people found out so we've sold the program to a lot of statistic services around the country. Nothing big. We don't even market it. We only do it if someone asks. Word of mouth, the best salesman of all."

Kenmuir was starting to like costumed Howard, unself-conscious as a child at Halloween. "What? You invent teams that play against each other?"

"No way. It's the real thing. Every 'owner' has a 'fantasy team' composed of actual players from the real teams. The owner's fantasy team's statistics are a compilation of the individual statistics of real players in real life. Neat, huh?"

"Sounds complicated."

"Nah. First, the team owners pick their players on what's known as draft day. That's the challenging part and the most fun." He laughed. "Then the computer kicks in, arranges the players' statistics, totals them up, and that determines each team's place in the fantasy league's standings. That's why the sign. Last year, my team won. Got a nice trophy, $300, and a fancy sign." He pointed backward. "Not bad. And there you have it, more than you ever wanted to know about fantasy baseball." He bowed slightly, as if to an appreciative audience.

"Well, I'm glad you like it. Too much work for me."

Undaunted, Howard reached into the back pocket of his official Giants pants and handed over a business card. "You may change your mind, because fantasy baseball is becoming super-popular. If you do, give me a call, and I'll try to find an opening for you. Not in our league, though. That bloodbath is confined to the company," he again laughed cheerfully. Before he stepped away, Peters said to Kenmuir, "I hope we get a chance to talk again. I'm here all weekend."

. .

AS TRAUBER DROVE UP I-680 on their way home, Kenmuir and he reviewed the highlights—purchases, impressions, lost opportunities—of the shopping day. Kenmuir eventually mentioned the ebullient dealer in the Giants uniform.

"Saw him," Trauber said. "At the end of the center row. That guy?"

"Could there have been more than one?"

"God, I hope not. You think that's his real job? Baseball card dealer?"

Kenmuir shook his head and slumped a bit in his seat. "As it happens, no. Said he works for some company in Mountain View. Name's Howard Peters."

Trauber turned toward Kenmuir so quickly that the car swerved. The Botts' dots rattled under the tires.

Kenmuir was unfazed. Certainly didn't widen his eyes. "Checking out how wide the lane is?"

"*Some* company? You're hopeless, totally fucking hopeless. The company's called Phosphenes, you idiot." He twitched his head. "God, I'd sure love some shares of that, I can tell you."

Trauber recently had gotten "into" the stock market and overnight had become a self-appointed expert on so-called tech stocks and the Nasdaq.

Kenmuir could be amused or annoyed by Trauber's stock mogul persona, depending on how pedantic he became. "Hopeless seems a bit harsh. I mean, what d'you have, maybe ten shares of Chuckie Cheese?"

"Let me tell you, my provincial friend, Phosphenes is a major software developer and hot property in Silicon Valley. Your pal, Howard Peters, is the owner and a certifiable genius who's rich as Croesus. Very supportive of charity fundraising and a major Giants fan. Just ask your old roomie, Larry." Trauber's sports car jogged around a Volvo whose self-righteous driver was in the fast lane, but at the speed limit, so to hell with anyone else. "Howard Peters with a booth at a baseball card show? Jesus. He could buy out the entire show."

"You *are* putting me on, right?"

"No joke. When you finally buy a newspaper, look up Phosphenes in the Nasdaq. And that's the tip of the iceberg, because most of its stock is personally owned by Peters."

"Here I thought I was doing *him* a favor by sticking around."

"To act the fool is not necessarily to *be* the fool."

"That's profound. Though I guess both are true in this instance."

Trauber smiled. "No argument here."

"Look, I understand that big money's buying into baseball cards. I get that. But some multimillionaire with a booth? That's ridiculous."

"In general, maybe, but not for Peters. Apparently, he's a devoted collector of stuff and not just baseball, either. Has been for years. Hell, he's as much of a packrat as you. Different scale, of course."

Kenmuir glanced sneeringly at Trauber. "Not necessarily. For all you know, I've stashed away many treasures. Big money in private practice, after all. I'm not some Deputy DA hanger-on at the public trough."

"You do realize it's not too late to have the grand jury look into your wanton slaughter of that fine, young Mexican-American boy, Senor LaPera. I could arrange that, you know."

"That's a threat I'll worry about later." Kenmuir turned on the radio and heard the slightest bit of *Sugar Shack* by Jimmy Gilmer and the Fireballs. He immediately turned the radio back off. "Think about this for a moment. *All* baseball players have baseball cards. That includes Orr and the others who've gotten hurt. Could they be tied together by big money baseball-card collecting?"

Trauber shook his head. "No chance. Take out baseball players to affect the value of their baseball cards? What's that? A buck, maybe two? Simon's a rookie and his probably isn't even worth that much. From what precious little you've told me, Jackson's situation didn't even have anything to do with him personally, much less as a baseball player. Brittain was killed in an accident. The key word being 'accident'." Trauber rolled his shoulders, stiff from bending over baseball-card showcases.

Kenmuir said, "Hey. A thought, that's all. That's what inventive minds do. They think."

"Gotcha. A deadly band of elementary school kids is knocking off ballplayers so that, say, Fellner's baseball card will zoom up maybe a couple bucks. Yup, that's inventive."

"You have a better idea?"

"Just about *any* idea'd be better. But, no, I don't. Look, I've agreed with you from the beginning. Coincidence. Bizarre maybe, but no less coincidence. No conspiracy."

Kenmuir silently watched the I-680/I-580 interchange pass by. He fiddled with the air conditioning vent until it blew onto his face. Then he said, "Trouble is that I no longer agree with me. The shooting of Woody Whitney—in his hand, for god's sake—when they already had the cash? Just a coincidence? What're the odds? I'm not saying they are definitely connected, but they *might* be."

"Here we go again. The dog with a bone. So what're you gonna do?"

"Don't know. I'm going to start by learning a helluva lot more about baseball cards as hobby. I mean, just consider today. Thousands of dollars changed hands, I'll bet. For example, how much did you spend?"

Trauber cocked an eyebrow and looked sideways at Kenmuir. "A little more than $300 and please be warned that, if you tell Ginny, you'll be solving your own murder."

"Trust me. I'll be as discreet and close-mouthed as you were with Lucy at that party."

"Wondered when I'd hear about that. She's a nice choice, though, and about damn time."

Kenmuir ignored him and added, "And now I'm also curious about that game Peters was telling me about, fantasy baseball."

"Yeah, I've heard about it. Sounds like fun, actually. A little like buying stocks."

"Stocks? And *I'm* a dog with a bone?" Kenmuir playfully punched Trauber's right shoulder. "I might as well learn about fantasy baseball at the same time. See where it all leads. I mean, hell, I always enjoy a good fantasy."

"And how you going to do that?"

"Don't know. This is all just occurring to me. Maybe I'll give my man Howie a blast. Take on baseball cards and fantasy baseball at the same time."

"Right. You're just gonna call up Howard Peters? Wasn't there a skit about that on Saturday Night Live, just calling up some celebrity?"

"Yes indeed. But Ed Grimley calling Pat Sajac is nothing at all like me and Howard. Besides, why not? Baseball's the guy's passion. Most people make time for their passions. It's like the woman who's so drop-dead gorgeous that she intimidates every man who sees her. She goes out with an ugly guy and people can't believe it. They ask, why him? She answers, 'he asked.' Same thing with Peters. I'll ask. He'll say yes or he'll say no."

"You're dreaming."

"Well, it probably does appear that way to you. That's because you're an intermediate employee in a large organization. You can't possibly understand how we entrepreneurs relate to each other. Commercial vicissitudes, the arcana of venture capital . . ."

Trauber stopped listening and started wondering if Kenmuir could find out if Peters thought it was too late to buy shares of Apple.

Chapter 28

Thursday afternoon, June 27, City of Mountain View

Howard Peters did remember Kenmuir: "The 1950s guy, right? Plaid shirt." He suggested meeting for lunch at a Chinese restaurant near his office. "Can't miss it."

No kidding: a blind man in a cave couldn't have missed the building with its green and red exterior emblazoned with gigantic specimens of Chinese calligraphy. Did they actually say "Smiling Cobra Tires" or "Wilted Blossom Office Supplies"? Irrelevant. Chinese letters *always* meant Chinese restaurant.

Peters was already seated when Kenmuir arrived. A semiprivate booth shielded by a large aquarium and guarded on its sides by two wooden dragons. This version of Peters was business casual. Now missing the Giants baseball cap, his hair was stylishly cut and neatly combed. The rough weave of the baseball shirt was supplanted by a Pima cotton sport shirt of excellent quality. Wire-rim glasses added a professorial look. The turkey had a bit of the peacock in him.

"Thanks for coming to my neck of the woods. Good to see you again," Peters said.

"Thank you for finding time to see me."

Peters grimaced. "Ah. I gather you've been talking with someone. I have enough business lunches, Dave. After you called—and I'm glad you did—I looked forward to this one, precisely because it didn't involve business. I'm still just the geek you met on Saturday." As proof, he laughed like he had that day.

"Fair enough. Besides, computer talk and me? It'd make for a very short or very quiet lunch."

Kenmuir scanned the menu. It had the usual assortment of dishes, all described with the Chinese disdain for plural nouns: Beef with snow pea, Kung Pao chicken with peanut. One pea or one peanut, evidently.

"If you like duck, I can recommend a wonderful dish here." After Kenmuir said that he did, Peters spoke rapidly in Chinese with the hostess. She replied incomprehensibly with what sounded like a question. Peters answered. She nodded and left. Peters returned to the conversation as if nothing unusual had occurred.

During lunch, which turned out to be a whole duck in a sauce flavored with lime, they learned that their paths never should've crossed. In high school Kenmuir was athletic, extroverted, and merely smart. By contrast, Peters was sedentary, socially awkward, and a whiz at math and English. Now, many years later, they discovered what high school would've concealed. Each enjoyed the other's sense of humor, and they shared an enthusiasm for baseball and golf.

Peters confirmed what Kenmuir already suspected: the big money in baseball card collecting was concentrated in the prewar issues: Goudeys, T-205s, T-206s, and the like. Few current cards were expensive. Rather than increase, the values of Orr's and Brittain's cards declined after their deaths.

A Deadly Game

As the lunch plates were cleared, Kenmuir asked about fantasy baseball leagues.

Howard said, "The birth of a future player?"

"No, I'm my own fantasy. Just curious."

"I'm afraid I don't believe that. I've been interviewed before, and you've asked too many questions about collecting for it to be mere curiosity, and now we're shifting to fantasy. No, you have a reason. I think you're a person who almost always has a reason, and that's okay. If I can help, I'm glad to."

Peters explained that the creation of a fantasy baseball league, or "rotisserie league," was no more complicated than getting together ten or twelve like-minded guys. Each "owner" paid his share of a statistic service's cost, plus $300.00, give or take, to "buy" actual major league players. Most of that "buy" money was given to the winner at the end of the season.

He added, "Twenty-three players fill twenty-three mandatory position slots. That way, each team's statistics are generated by the same complement of players. However, identical positions do not mean identical skills. That's where the fun starts." Peters sipped a bit of lukewarm green tea and carried on. "Each player's accumulating statistics are fed weekly into the computer and then grafted from his real-life team onto his fantasy team. The statistics are distributed among a number of agreed categories. Usually four or five in offense, like home runs and RBIs, and the same in pitching, like wins and ERA. The categorical totals are then compared with each other.

"In my league, there are ten categories, twelve teams, and a hundred and forty-four possible points. You try to stack up as many points as you can by gathering the best possible combination of players. A salary cap exists so no single owner can monopolize the dominant players, but has to spread his 'salaries' as effectively and presciently as possible. The goal—and thus the source of fantasy strategy—is to have as balanced a lineup as possible in order to be competitive in all categories.

"Even so, some players are more significant statistically than others. A power hitter like Orr will produce in *three* categories: home runs, RBIs, and runs produced. A closer like Fellner is crucial, since very few major league pitchers get 'saves.' Without a reliable closer or two, a team could be shut out of that entire category.

"On the most glorious day of the year—draft day, kind of a specialized auction—you've got to be careful. If you overspend on offense, say, you'll be on your way to minimal points in pitching, and that'll translate into fifth or sixth place . . . maybe . . . at the end of the season. Because, remember, it's a matter of how one does relatively, not absolutely. For example, if I'm in first place in home runs, I get twelve points whether I have two or twenty more than whoever's in second. So, if I'm thirty home runs behind you and in fifth place, I'll probably never catch you—*but* I might catch the team in third place and thereby pick up two points on you.

"Just like no one player can dominate all categories, so no one category can dominate the teams' relative standings. So you'd better keep close to me in the categories where I'm strong, or I might overtake you in *total* points. And that's what matters: the total, combined points in *all* categories. See what I mean?

"Leagues aren't always the same, because the various rules—like for trading, claiming free agents and reserving injured players—usually are customized to the preferences of the league owners. That's why the organizational computer program, such as the one produced by Phosphenes, has to be adjustable to any league's particular preferences." Peters paused for a thought and then said, "You know, that's not a bad idea. Talk with some computer services. I'll bet they've got a perspective I've never even thought of. In fact, I'll send you a list, and you can call them."

Kenmuir put his head down on the table. "Do you have any idea how confusing this is?"

"It isn't, really. It only sounds that way. It's like teaching someone how to play bridge, say. It's much harder to explain it than to do it. Ditto fantasy baseball. And, if you're baffled now, wait until we get to trading."

"Trading?"

"The lifeblood of the game. After draft day, any owner can trade with another, as long as the twenty-three roster positions remain staffed with eligible players. One might trade for any number of reasons. If his team has abundant RBIs, but few stolen bases, he might trade an RBI producer for a base-stealer. Over time, the team might lose a point in RBIs, but it might simultaneously gain three points in stolen bases. Or, an owner might trade in order to replace a player who's been injured or traded out of the league.

"Best laid plans mean nothing. Here you are, cruising along in good shape and your home run guy or primary pitcher guy runs into a wall. No warning and wham, you're out of business in that category or, worse, maybe more than one category. Nothing can ruin a team faster than losing a key player to an injury. Every week thereafter you get to watch the steady erosion of points in a particular category. Drives you crazy. And you only have three choices: wait for the player to recover, trade for someone else, or say 'The hell with it, I'll wait until next year.' Believe me, I've done all three."

"Question."

"Sure."

"Take a player like Orr. When he was killed, it messed up someone's fantasy league team, right?"

"Big time. Anybody who had him was devastated. He was a fantasy god. Played every day, lots of offense, great stats. In our league, which has players from *both* the American and National Leagues, that's bad enough. But in a league using *only* American League players? Calamity."

"Whitney and Fellner?"

"Both American League, so same answer."

"Simon?"

"A bit different. Though, interestingly, also American League. He's a rookie and was hurt before draft day, so it would depend on whether the league has minor league farm players who can be held over into the new year." Peters rubbed his chin. "Is this helping?"

"It's not a matter of helping or not helping. Right now I'm gathering information. Probably means nothing, but you never know until you know."

"That's cryptic enough."

"That's how lawyers talk. You actually take a course in law school called Cryptic Remarks. It's not something lawyers can risk leaving to chance."

What Kenmuir learned from Peters was provocative. Without a doubt, the "missing" players scrambled the fortunes of fantasy teams across the country. Some teams benefitted, others suffered. Merely a matter of grooming the right dog? Merely good luck or bad luck? Coincidences? Kenmuir didn't know.

Not yet.

Thursday afternoon, June 27, City of Tokyo

TADASHI OKUMOTO, THE CEO of Atashi Industries, had matured during the Americanized economic recovery of Japan after World War II. As the son of a machinist, he'd had neither patrician connections nor advantages. But he was ruthless and a brilliant master of the calculated risk. Thus had he transformed an insignificant manufacturer of agricultural machinery into Atashi Industries' present conglomerate.

One wall of his spacious office was entirely glass and displayed a panorama of downtown Tokyo, thirty-two floors below. Each of the other three walls was paneled in dark wood and held a single painting: an Ito Jakuchu, a Katsushika Hokusai, and a Yorozu Tetsugoro.

His appearance was fastidious and immaculate: his hair was trimmed weekly, his plain navy blue or charcoal gray suits—no frivolous pinstripes for him—were tailored from expensive silk-and-wool fabric, and his brilliant white shirts were custom-made from luxurious Egyptian cotton. His humorless and impenetrable personality was as colorful as the text of a life insurance policy. He had no friends and, if an activity had no business purpose, then it had no purpose at all.

His lone exception was baseball. Everything about it appealed to him: the order, the symmetry, the elaborate statistics, and increasingly the performance of the Ronin, his team in the international fantasy baseball league. And now that had become a source of disharmony. After the Ronin finished second last season, he'd made a few refinements, with particular attention to additional help in strikeouts and steals, and had expected—reasonably, he thought—that first place was virtually assured this year. Instead, the Fates had been unkind. The Ronin had slid to third place and, worse, was closer to fourth than second. Bad *joss*, as the execrable Chinese would say.

Power was the core of his carefully crafted team, because the offensive categories (home runs, RBIs, and runs produced) were what he loved most. But, with the disastrous loss of Orr, his statistical strength was declining faster and faster the more the season wore on. Worse, each statistical slip cost him points in the standings. Something had to be done.

To catch the first-place Walking Wounded, he needed to add a big hitter and maybe a starting pitcher. For that, he'd have to trade part of the future for the present. The eighth-place Gillotines were clearly doomed this year, and its owner P.J. Gill had both kinds of players he needed. He could trade a couple of his very promising, but still raw, youngsters and hope to recapture power statistics now. He'd worry about next year, next year.

Okumoto devoted an hour, a precious hour, to glancing between the several spreadsheets in front of him and the computer screen on his left. His calculations and recalculations finally concluded, he instructed his administrative secretary to place the international call. She acted immediately, knowing that those who delayed in Okumoto's service did not remain long in that service.

A Deadly Game

P.J. Gill was a manufacturer of prefabricated housing and related components. Rare was the mass housing development in the United States that didn't include his company's products. Such a man was accustomed to getting his own way and enjoying the edge in any deal. In short, he was no different from Okumoto.

"Gill-san, I hope you are well."

"Fine, Tadashi, fine. How 'bout you?"

Gill had the distressing American penchant for instant informality. Though they'd never met and had spoken only during the prolonged conference call on draft day, Gill presumed to address Okumoto by his given name. "Have you thought about my proposal, Gill-san?"

"Yes, I have. Anything to distract me from the hum-drum routine of business. You understand." Gill laughed across thousands of miles.

In fact, Okumoto did *not* understand; nothing about business was unwelcome or hum-drum to him. Business was *always* engaging. In fact, he even considered his fantasy league machinations as another form of business, training for the day when he'd own a genuine team of his own, preferably the Seibu Lions in the Pacific League. In the meantime, he had to content himself with fantasy baseball and the likes of P.J. Gill.

"Is it acceptable then?" he asked Gill.

"Not quite. We're close, very close, but we're not quite there. I have my eyes on young Colin Cady. Let's throw him into the mix."

Even the most fluent English-speaking Japanese like Okumoto constantly stumbled over American idioms. The language was like the people themselves: sloppy and undisciplined, giving merely perfunctory observation to rules and order. "I do not understand this 'throw into the mix'."

"Sorry, it's an American expression meaning 'in addition.' In other words, I want Cady to be included in the trade."

Typical American, Okumoto thought. *Always wanting more than what something's worth.* Fortunately, he'd expected Gill not to stray far from type. He was ready, although he pretended otherwise: "I had not considered the need to add another player and thought the proposed trade was fair as presented."

"Well, sorry about that, Tadashi. Eye of the beholder and all that. Look, let's cut to the chase. You got hurt when you lost Orr. Without him, you're going nowhere but down in three categories. You need help if you're going to win, and I can give you that help. Berry's my main man, after all, but it'll cost you. I know I'm out of it this year. What I've got to do is get ready for the future. I need younger, less expensive players I can retain next year. So . . . if you want Berry, we have to figure out a way for me to get this kid Cady."

Okumoto paused, as if considering alternative possibilities. Actually, he'd already spent a good portion of the morning considering those very possibilities. "If that is your requirement, Gill-san, then perhaps you'd consider parting with McCarl as well. He's of no consequence to you, but he'll at least help me in several pitching categories."

Clever bastard, Gill thought. I no more caught him by surprise than if I'd sent him a warning letter in advance. Still, I can live with it. "Done. You want to report the trade, or do you want me to do it?"

"If you'd be so kind, Gill-san."

"Glad to do it, Tadashi. It's been a pleasure doing business with you."

No, it has not. You think that you've done better than me, but you're in eighth place and I'm in third. That is the measure of our skills. With any luck, the next four weeks will validate statistically the wisdom of the trade, and my Ronin should overtake the Walking Wounded for first place.

Chapter 29

Monday evening, July 1, City of Walnut Creek

THE NEXT OF THE STATISTICS SERVICES on Peters' list was "Stats for Bats," in Albany, New York. Kenmuir's call was answered on the first ring with, "Can I help you?"

If so, you'll be the first. "May I speak with Mr. O'Ryan?"

"Oh . . . yeah . . . sure . . . Hang on just a sec? I'm balancing all kinds of stuff." O'Ryan came back after much longer than a sec. "Thanks. You in the market for a stat service?"

"No, actually I'm not. I got your name from Howard Peters."

"Don't know him. Don't think so, anyway."

"You probably don't, but he works for Phosphenes."

"Oh, sure, the computer program company. So you need what?"

"Just some information. Mr. Peters gave me a sort of primer course on fantasy baseball and recommended that I speak with you for more insight. All too complicated for me."

"Nah, it's not all that complicated—not as long as you have a computer. Keep track of all the statistics and sort them out by hand? You couldn't do it even for one league, let alone dozens like I've got. Impossible. Literally couldn't be done. Nope, no computer, no software, no fantasy baseball. It's that simple."

O'Ryan seemed willing to talk, so Kenmuir stayed with him. "Which is where you fit in?"

"Right on. If it can be done on a computer, I do it. Feed in the real-life statistics of major league players. Tell the computer how I want them organized. Push a button and rat-a-tat, the computer arranges them."

"Altogether too mystifying for a Luddite like me."

O'Ryan chuckled. "Good. The more of you, the better for me. I get a seasonal fee and, once a week, you get a readable and well-organized printout of your league's statistics. If you can do that by yourself, I'm out of business."

"How *is* business?"

"Real good, to be honest. Getting bigger all the time. Dozens of leagues, hundreds of owners."

"Expensive?"

"Nah, not really. Figure that a stat service like mine costs somewhere between $70 and maybe a bit more than $100 per owner, depending on the league's statistical requirements. Small potatoes for the individual, but it can mount up for the stat service, even a part-timer like me. Make some extra money, screw around with the computer, talk with people. Do it on weekends, nights. As part-time jobs go, it's the best."

"And you don't know why a particular league's organized the way it is or how it pays out at the end?"

"Nope. Personal choice. But every league I know of divvies up some kind of pot, usually what's left from the entry fees. Say it's $200 a player in a twelve team league. That's $2,400, total. Stat service gets, say, $1,000. That leaves $1,400 for the winner, depending on whether the league pays to second or third place. All kinds of possibilities."

"I understand. As little as a hundred dollars or as much as . . . I don't know . . . a million dollars?"

O'Ryan's sudden silence was deafening. Kenmuir had struck the same chord in a brief conversation with another service. "Mr. O'Ryan? You still there?"

"Yeah, I'm here. You've heard about the million-dollar league?"

"Not directly, but another service alluded to the possibility. I gather it's only a rumor."

"One that's been around for a few years, though."

"Kinda like the hook hanging from the door handle on Lover's Lane. Everyone knows the story, but it's only a story?"

"Hear something long enough, you begin to believe it. And, yeah I've heard about the hook and have always assumed it's just so much urban bullshit—or is it? Maybe it started because it *was* true, it *did* happen. Same with the million-dollar league. I mean, why not?"

Kenmuir pushed. "What've you heard?"

"A collection of rumors. Supposedly, twelve high-rollers have a league where each pays in a million bucks. Which'd make the available payout very near $12 million, because the expenses would be basically the same as a normal league. Of course, it also would depend on whether any runner-up places are paid. I don't know what's harder to imagine: that enough guys would have that kind of money to throw around or that they'd throw it around on a silly game."

"Instead of something sensible and rational like roulette or horses?"

O'Ryan snorted. "I take your point. Just another form of gambling. But it's not, or maybe that's not the way I think of it.

It's a hobby, a way of enjoying baseball by pretending you have a team of your own. Sort of a game within a game. Risking a million dollars wouldn't be fun. I'd be a nervous wreck."

"Me, too. Even so, do you think it's out there?"

"Sounds crazy but, yeah, I do. Different stat services, we sometimes talk. Compare notes, find out what's new. An Atlanta service and I even think we know what league it is."

Kenmuir's mind was racing. "How could you ever figure that out? He has his leagues and you have yours. They'd all be different, right?"

"That's just it. *One* isn't. He and I—and even a third guy, we've recently found out—are servicing the same league. Oh, the *league* names are different, but the *teams* in each league have the same names, same rosters, same stats. Oh, they're the same, all right."

"*One* league. *Three* services? Makes no sense."

"That's what we thought at first. Then we got to thinking. If you can spend such a shit-pot of money, what's a few hundred more for three stat services? Besides, if you've got $12 million or so at stake, you gonna trust it to one service? I sure wouldn't."

"Why trust anyone? Buy their own program and their own computer and do it themselves. Why bother with outsiders at all?"

"We think it's *because* we're outsiders. What do we know? Or care? Just one more league with one more set of stats. Nothing special. They don't know us and we don't know them. A single service could be manipulated. A few mistakes here or there could make for some significant shifts. But not with multiple services."

"Can you tell me the name of the league?"

"No can do. We could be wrong." O'Ryan suddenly exclaimed, "Hah, I just remembered Howard Peters. I actually met him once, when I was selling baseball cards in my former life. Good guy. So I'd like to help, but I gotta draw the line here. It's all speculation, you understand. The other services and I, we don't *know* anything for positive. Why don't *you* tell *me*: Is there really a million-dollar league?"

"I don't know, Mr. O'Ryan." *But I'm going to find out.*

Chapter 30

Tuesday morning, July 9, City of Cleveland

SWAMPY ROYCE SUPPOSEDLY HELD THE HANDLES on a lot of local criminal activity, but the four Cleveland PD detectives on the Whitney Task Force had been unable to get a handle on him. He remained their center of attention but, like a donut, it was a center with nothing in it: a couple of innocuous arrests, no convictions, and plenty of rumors, but no proof.

In addition, they'd interviewed so many of Whitney's friends, neighbors, and even a few enemies, that they now knew more—pro and con—about him than he knew about himself. If they'd been writing a biography, they would've accomplished a lot. But, as they were trying to solve a crime, it'd been a month of frustration, a month of getting nowhere. Worse, it'd been a month of reporting no progress to the chief of detectives, who then reported the same to the chief of police. Like four divers without air tanks, they were feeling greater and greater pressure.

They'd taken to hiding out behind their six-foot high, cloth-covered partitions, a kind of corral where they were free to litter telephone messages, crush coffee cups, and crumple pages from yellow tablets in irritable isolation. Everyone avoided what'd become known as Whitney Corner.

That definitely included Tommy Stevens Jr., a seventeen-year-old police aide who aspired to be a detective himself someday—and who, this morning, poked his head in the entrance between the partitions as reluctantly as a French aristocrat leaning toward the chopping block. The detectives' four desks were arranged in a rectangle, one pair directly facing the other pair. Two detectives were on the telephone and swiveled away from Tommy; the other two were huddled over their desks, one chewing thoughtfully on a pencil eraser and the other resting his head on his folded arms.

Tommy hoped that someone would see him and ask *him* a question. No such luck. Thirty seconds of brooding silence seemed like thirty minutes. Finally, he had no choice. "Excuse me?"

Detective Webster stopped gnawing on the pencil eraser. He snarled over his right shoulder in Tommy's direction. "*What?*"

Tommy, who idolized Webster, was flustered by the brusque tone. "Sorry . . . I'm sorry, Detective Webster." No retreat now. "But I've been reading the Whitney reports as I've been filing them, and I know you guys are trying to get something on Swampy Royce."

"Good for you, Junior. Now you know as much as we do."

"Well, like I say, I was reading reports. And Detective Markwith's says Royce has a girlfriend, a girl named Maryann."

Webster had about as much patience as a groom on his wedding night. "So what? Royce's got a girlfriend. Hell, so do you. She's got no record. We already looked into it." Webster waved his hand, as if at a pesky gnat. "Jesus, Junior."

Now even more embarrassed, Tommy said, "I'm sorry. I should've known that, but I got curious, because I remember her brother from when I first started working here."

A Deadly Game

"Yeah, quite a family, isn't it? Genuine white trash. Come on, if you've got something to say, then say it, for chrissake."

"It just bothers me, I guess. She dropped out of high school last year, and I looked at the picture on her driver's license. She's great looking, so I understand the sex part."

Webster smiled at last. "You do, huh?"

Tommy smiled back, relieved by the break in tension. "Yeah, but Royce is so much older. He's 43!"

"Happens all the time. Besides, we old guys have the charm, technique and stamina that you youngsters lack. If it makes you feel any better, she's a full-fledged adult who can do what she wants with whom she wants, even with old guys. So don't feel too sorry for the lovely Maryann."

"I don't feel sorry for her. Well, maybe I do. Kinda." Tommy hesitated and then said, "Anyway, she's not an adult."

"In the eyes of the law she is."

"How do you figure that? She's the same age as me. Which is one reason why I was interested. She's only seventeen."

"I wish, but no such luck. Markwith ran her, and she's eighteen."

Tommy shook his head. "No, she's not. She was born eighteen *years* ago this month, but her actual eighteenth birthday isn't until *the end of the month*. Right now, today, she's seventeen."

Tommy had Webster's complete attention. "Junior, don't mess with me."

Tommy showed Webster a photocopy of Maryann Williams' driver's license. "See. Here's her birthday. She won't be eighteen for, what, two weeks?"

Webster stared silently at the photocopy. He wrote today's date on a tablet. Above it, he wrote Maryann's birth date. Backward and forward, up and down, he calculated and recalculated her age. Eighteen it wasn't. She was a juvenile. Swampy Royce was shacked up with a *juvenile*!

He shouted at the two detectives who were on the telephones. "We've got the son-of-a-bitch."

After Webster gleefully summarized what Tommy had found, a sheepish Detective Markwith defended himself, though half-heartedly. For a moment, the other detectives were too stunned to speak. Then they weren't: "The man is fuckin' a baby" . . . "I read somewhere that's against the law."

"We may not have stat rape," Webster said, "but we sure as hell have contributing. Who wants to arrest this corrupter of defenseless children?"

"Under the circumstances, I think I'd like that privilege," Markwith said.

"Fine." Webster looked at Detective Agresta. "Gene, you go with him. And for god's sake, don't let Royce ask Einstein here any math questions or we'll lose him."

Markwith grabbed his sport coat. "Fuck you, Web." As he put on his coat, he said, "Thanks, Junior. That's good detective work." Tommy Stevens had never received a finer compliment in his life.

. .

SWAMPY ROYCE'S SECLUDED RESIDENCE was tucked in a grove of trees. Its few rooms were spacious and walls of glass made them seem even more so. The recreation room contained a new Zenith front projection television, a complicated array of audio equipment, and a pool table covered in blue felt.

A Deadly Game

Royce was slumped in his La-Z-Boy, with the back of his head pressed against the head cushion. His eyes were closed, not looking down at Maryann's mane of blonde hair, which was draped partially over his thighs and moving rhythmically. She may very well have been seventeen chronologically, but she was twenty-four physically. Partly for comfort on such a warm day and partly to satisfy Royce's prurience, she wore only the briefest of bikini panties.

When the telephone rang, she looked up from her ministrations. When he said, "Get that, will ya?," she dutifully stood and walked over to the telephone. Her light pink nipples pointed forward haughtily and, as if reinforced with rebar, her breasts hardly moved. "Just a minute, please," she said in a teenage version of sultry as she brought the phone over to Royce.

He answered with his characteristic cheer. "Yeah?"

He was angry when he finally spoke again. "Wait a minute. Wait a fuckin' minute. I don't know what you've heard, but whatever it is, is bullshit. I didn't say shit." He grabbed a small tablet and began to doodle, as he did when he was upset. "I already told ya . . . You ain't listenin' . . . They took me in, asked me a bunch of fuckin' questions, I said shit and they let me go. This was a fuckin' month ago, for chrissake. If they had somethin', they'd have done something about it . . . That's all. No big deal. You think I'm fuckin' stupid?"

Maryann stepped by the side of the desk. She looked quizzically at Royce and mouthed the words, "Anything wrong?" He put his hand over the mouthpiece and told her to get lost. She did, huffily.

Unknown to Royce, the caller simultaneously was giving a thumb's-up to two men parked next to him in a different car. The gesture meant, 'He's there. Go.'

Royce persisted with his protests. "Yeah, I understand. No, no offense ... Really. Everything's good. The fucking cops don't know shit. They'll run around for awhile and it'll fuckin' blow over. Always does. No worry ... Good. Good. Yeah, we'll talk." He slammed down the receiver and walked to the bar. As he was pouring a drink, the two men stopped their rental car near the entrance to his driveway.

The driver got out and opened the trunk. Inside were two suitcases, as one might expect of two businessmen in a rented car. However, instead of shirts, pants, boxers and shaving kit, each suitcase contained an Uzi. The passenger said, "I guess I'll test-fire when we're inside." The driver was silent. For him, a day was perfect if he never heard the sound of a human voice, including his own.

Meanwhile, Royce, still angry, paced around the recreation room and gestured with both hands as he fomented out loud. He ignored the liquid sloshing from his drink. Maryann sat silently in a chair, its leather cool against her naked back. She'd endured these tirades before and had learned when to be quiet.

Royce wandered around the far side of the pool table, past the French doors and windows that overlooked the wooden deck outside. As he paused to take a sip from his drink, the glass in the French doors and one of the windows exploded inward, spraying sharp shards of glass into the room and into him. One fragment, the size of a butcher knife, sliced through the blue felt of the pool table and ricocheted into the cue ball, knocking it into the corner pocket. A scratch.

A Deadly Game

Royce didn't feel the dozens of glass fragments that sliced his shirtless torso and his bare legs. His body had been numbed instantly by what the autopsy would later confirm as sixteen rounds puncturing his chest and right side. That only five of the rounds would've killed him was an anatomic irony he wouldn't have appreciated.

Maryann sat quietly in the leather chair. Her head was tipped forward, as if she were staring at her perfect and still unblemished chest. Two bullets had passed through the chair and into her back, one beyond her left lung and the other, slightly distorted from striking a rib, at the edge of her left ventricle. Neither had exited. The shooters hadn't intended to kill her and, in fact, hadn't known she was in the room.

Holding his Uzi at his side, the passenger looked quickly at Royce, splayed across the two-tone pool table. He'd seen many dead men before. He didn't need to go inside, let alone check for a pulse. "One very dead motherfucker," he said. He turned from the window and walked away with the driver.

A short while later, Detectives Markwith and Agresta, who'd paid no attention to the white sedan or the two businessmen passing them in the opposite direction, rang Royce's doorbell. The elegant residence impressed Markwith. "One thing you gotta say about crime, man. You can do all right."

"That you can, partner, that you can." Agresta again rang the doorbell. "Where the fuck is the Swamper?"

"Dunno. Think maybe he's trying to ignore officers of the law on official business?"

"Swampy? Never happen. As I recall him telling us, he's a model citizen."

Markwith pointed to an exposed aggregate walkway that led to a garden. "Let's go around back. Besides, from what I hear, young Maryann has an aversion to clothes."

Agresta half sang and half whispered, "She was just seven-teen, you kno-ow what I mean . . . "

"Fuck you, Gene."

The walkway curved through a garden that bordered a large patio. As soon as they rounded the corner by the garden, they saw sunlight sparkling off broken glass on a wooden deck two steps above the patio. Each instinctively reached for his handgun as they edged cautiously onto the deck and inched toward the shattered windows. Royce's half-drained body on the pool table required no subtlety of detection. Only the cushions and the far edge of the felt table still showed the color blue. Markwith looked at Agresta. "You want to read him his rights or you want me to?"

"You can while I call it in."

Within an hour, Royce's residence was crawling with detectives, ID technicians, and coroner's representatives. Royce would've been mad as hell.

Webster's concentration was broken by Agresta, who was standing next to Royce's desk. "Hey, Web, better come over here."

Agresta pointed at the doodling on Royce's tablet. "What d'you make of this?"

Amid the swirls and oddly shaped geometric figures had been written the word "Broker." Below that was a telephone number that had been traced over so many times that two of the "4"s might have been "9"s. "Beats me. Bag the whole tablet and take it back to the office. We'll have it dusted and then try the number."

A Deadly Game

Wednesday afternoon, July 10, City of Cleveland

EVERY ORGANIZATION, EVERY BUSINESS, every place where people gather has a grapevine. None is more efficient than a police department's. One minute, no one knows about a killing or a scandal. Five minutes later, everyone knows. For that reason, it was quite possible that Cleveland PD's janitors had more complete details about Swampy and Maryann's deaths sooner than the homicide detectives did.

The grapevine also was the likely explanation for why, the next day, Organized Crime Unit Lieutenant Tyrus Tye asked to see Webster. Tye wasn't Webster's commander, but Webster understood that rank, nonetheless, was rank. Webster promptly reported upstairs.

"Don't see you anymore, Web. Love to have you up here, but Dickhead's so fucked up that he thinks you're worth keeping." Tye's best friend was Lieutenant Dickson, Webster's boss.

"Glad to hear it, sir, but there's too much paperwork up here. I'd die."

"Well, that paperwork—which is called intelligence, by the way—is about to do you a big favor." Tye pulled at the knot of his necktie, granting further freedom to his nineteen-inch neck. Georgia-born Tye had gained the nickname "Bulldog" from his resemblance to the University of Georgia's mascot rather his namesake, sinewy Tyrus Cobb, baseball's famed "Georgia Peach." "Rumor has it that the late-lamented Mr. Royce left a farewell note with the telephone number of his broker. That right?"

Webster was baffled how Tye had snagged that piece of information, which had been held in absolute secrecy by the task force after Agresta had bagged Royce's tablet. Everyone had long suspected that there were no secrets from the Bulldog. Maybe there weren't. Either way, everyone understood that you didn't bullshit the Bulldog. So Webster, he lay low, and said only, "Yessir, it is. It's a puzzle. We've tried the telephone numbers but no stock brokers. No insurance. No real estate. No one even close."

The Bulldog leaned back in his chair. "What do you mean, numbers? Plural."

"Well, technically there was only one number, but Royce had scribbled over it so much that the nines looked like fours, or the fours looked like nines. We listed the variations and tried them all. Not that many, but no luck anyway."

Tye nodded with understanding. "I see. Of course, I don't know who answered, but I'll bet that you got at least one answering machine, right?"

Webster quickly reminded himself about not bullshitting The Bulldog. "You're right. We did get one. So?"

"I'm going to add to your education: It's not broker as in stockbroker or insurance broker. It's *The* Broker, and this boy's a real sweetheart." For the next several minutes, Tye educated Webster about the shadowy figure known as The Broker. No one knew whether it was a man or a committee, but The Broker functioned as a middleman for services that couldn't be obtained through the Yellow Pages. Burglary, assault, robbery, arson. You name it, and The Broker would provide it—for a sizable fee, of course.

The Broker's manner of operation was efficient and neat, just like, say, ordering a fisherman's sweater or a fleece parka from a Lands' End catalogue. An associate of The Broker would give a prospective client a telephone number to leave a message on an answering machine. The message could be retrieved automatically by a telephone call, either from anywhere or even by another answering machine, if one had the appropriate code. The message would be returned through a cut-out number so that any trace would lead to a dead-end. After similarly guarded arrangements for payment, the referring associate would receive a cash commission. As a further precaution, the answering machine was changed periodically so that, even if it were found—as had happened twice, according to Tye—only the client would be exposed and The Broker would remain safe. And The Broker would have no further contact with either that client or his referring associate.

Webster was stunned. "You mean to tell me that Royce was a *paid* contract hit?"

Tye shrugged. "Maybe, but more likely it was a kind of house-cleaning. Royce had his fingers in a lot of pies. He probably was one of The Broker's associates and, if not that, then he would've been an ideal source of local talent to provide whatever 'service' The Broker might've needed."

"I'll be goddamned. Like shooting Whitney?" He stopped himself for a moment to consider the implications. "Someone *paid* to hurt Whitney and The Broker used Royce to hire local muscle? Unbelievable."

"Don't know, but it's a good bet in light of Royce's scribbled note—because, by itself, the shooting's never made sense. Why shoot a guy in a simple holdup for a few bucks, especially when he's not resisting? On the other hand—no pun intended—*if* that was the whole point, then it all of a sudden *does* make sense. It was just business as usual."

Webster hitched a ride on Tye's reasoning. "I'm with you. Which in turn would have to mean that Royce was more than merely a source of referrals, because The Broker otherwise wouldn't have gotten anxious, for whatever reason. No, he must've had closer ties to The Broker and probably way too much knowledge. Not a hard problem to solve: eliminate him and you eliminate whatever threat he represented. That's what you're telling me?"

Tye didn't answer. He smiled as he shrugged.

Webster reached the end. "I'll bet The Broker called Royce to confirm he was home. Royce knows the telephone number by heart and writes it repeatedly. He's nervous. That's why the doodles. Bingo."

Two days later, the Whitney Task Force was disbanded by order of Lieutenant Dickson.

Chapter 31

Thursday morning, July 11, City of Walnut Creek

WOODSON'S TELEPHONE CALL AWAKENED Kenmuir at 8:00 a.m. "Good morning, Starshine. I just got off the phone with Cleveland PD. They finally identified the prick who set up Whitney—but he managed to get himself whacked before they could scoop him up." Woodson summarized what he'd learned from Webster. "He thinks the one number that hit an answering machine could the right one, though."

Kenmuir balanced the telephone on his shoulder and lit a cigarette. "He say what they're gonna do next?"

"Try to trace the answering machine, but they're not optimistic. Maybe sit on it for a while but, like he said, the bad guys know they're coming. They'll be long gone."

"Probably right, but I don't want it to be. This Broker guy could be an opening." Kenmuir inhaled a drag and a thought. "You have the number, by any chance?"

"No, not by chance. By deliberate design, schooled as I am in modern investigative science."

"Though we don't even know if that's the actual number?"

"True. But it's close." Woodson knew what Kenmuir was thinking. "We can't do anything here that Cleveland PD hasn't already done."

When Kenmuir said nothing, Woodson knew what it meant: "You're going to call the damn number, aren't you?"

"Hey, if I'm going to be awake at this barbaric hour, I might as well do something."

Kenmuir dialed the Chicago-area telephone number as soon as Woodson hung up. He expected it would be deactivated but, surprise, it rang four times before a message machine was activated. A nondescript voice said, "Leave a message."

Why not?

"You don't know me, but I was referred to you by a guy named Swampy Royce in Cleveland. He's dead. Does this mean that I have to be referred by someone else? I hope not."

He left his name and office telephone number, and hung up. Also, he assumed that the message would never be returned.

Thursday afternoon, July 11, City of Walnut Creek

Jennifer, the office suite's shapely receptionist, wore a pink sundress with red butterflies in anticipation of what was forecast to be another broiling day. She was unencumbered beneath it. So it was that the suite's four lawyers, all male, paid particularly close attention to that morning's written messages while reading them over her shoulder. Kenmuir felt mildly lecherous, but not enough to abandon his scenic angle.

Jennifer pointed to one message slip and told him "this jerk" had called at least six times since 9:00. "His weird voice is all, like, croaky."

"The jerk have a name?"

"I asked. Will he tell me? No-o-o. And he wouldn't leave a number. All he says is 'I'll call later'. And I go, 'Well, can I take a message?' And he goes, 'No', and hangs up. Jerk."

"Maybe he's just shy. Or nervous."

She leaned back in her chair. The top of her sundress snapped shut as definitively as the jaws of an alligator. "You really think so?"

"No, he's a jerk. Let me know when he calls again."

Fifteen minutes later, she buzzed Kenmuir on the intercom. "It's *him* again."

"Put him through."

He let the phone ring several times before answering. Without greeting, he said, "How can I help you?"

"You've got it wrong, buster. *You* called me." The voice was disguised by a mechanical device that changed both tone and inflection. It was, well, croaky.

"Let's start at the beginning. Who the hell are you?" *Not that I don't know damn well who you are, pal. You're the other end of the answering machine from Cleveland PD.*

"You say some guy named Royce gave you my number? If you got something to say, then say it. You don't, I'm gone."

"No, no. You're right. I called you. I may need your help."

"Help?"

"You know, the kind of help Swampy said you give."

"Don't know what you're talking about."

The line went dead. *Cautious guy. Should be.*

The anonymous caller was back on the line six minutes later. Kenmuir asked, "What was all that about?"

"Nothing. I had another call."

"You bet. You already know I'm not a cop."

"Maybe not, but you're some kind of lawyer. Close enough. You and I won't be doin' any business, Kenmuir. But I'll give you something at no charge. Here it is. You're already in over your head. When that happens, people drown. Keep your head up, lawyer."

"What I . . . " Kenmuir was speaking into a dead line. There would be no return call. He stepped out from behind his desk and wandered around his office as thoughts wandered around his mind, Sherlock Holmes without the opium:

- The anonymous caller was tied to The Broker, if not The Broker himself.
- That meant he had to have arranged Royce's killing in Cleveland. And it also had to mean he was good for Whitney. If those two, then why not the others?
- He's not doing it on his own. His arrangements, but *others* pay for them. He's the bullet, but someone else pulls the trigger.
- Got to involve mucho dollars; The Broker can't come cheap. Cash up front, no easy time-payment plan. And no one would spend that kind of money without a major payday at the end.
- That'd make it all deliberate and not merely coincidental. But why? Something about baseball? Nothing else links them.
- If you know *who*, then *why* shouldn't matter much. But *how* can you figure out *who* if you don't know why? Damn circle.
- Got to be some form of business. Which would mean dispassionate and disconnected, like Tessio in *The Godfather*: "Tell

Michael I always liked him. It was only business." But what could it be about the business side of baseball?

- Manipulate the major league standings? Affect particular teams? Nah. The Indians already were doing badly and depriving them of Whitney only made them worse. Orr was great, but even without him the Oakland A's are challenging for first place. Fellner was the Blue Jays' only closer, but they were never in the championship hunt anyway. No, such a "hurt the team" motivation doesn't seem compelling.

- Baseball team owners are very rich. And very competitive. And *very* egotistical. You're a winner or you're a loser. Some owner is either tired of losing or *really* wants to win? Badly enough to give himself a little help? After all, if *you're* willing to spend millions on a contract for some hotshot hitter or pitcher, why not merely thousands to wipe out the *other guy's* hotshot hitter or pitcher?

- Maybe it's personal. Hurt the owners *themselves*? Maybe you're an owner and you're pissed off at the other owners. Maybe they snubbed you, or didn't treat you as an equal, or got the better of you somehow. You want revenge, but you can't do it directly. So you do the next best thing; you gouge their wallets and their pride at the same time. What the hell, you're rich enough to afford it.

- Forget real life, what about the standings in one of these fantasy leagues? The million-dollar league might be worth it. But does it exist? Or is it a fantasy as well?

- Just a perverse bet? "I'll bet this amount that you can't eliminate Thumper Orr"... Or: "How about double-or-nothing on Woody Whitney?" Some variation on that theme?

• What about no motive at all? A new type of serial killer, one who randomly chooses baseball players. Or maybe *not* random, but somehow perversely connected in a mind as twisted as an old man's toes. Because they're all-stars; because they're country boys; because their baseball cards are offensive somehow? Anything's possible. But the whole point of being a serial killer is to do it yourself, not to hire someone to do it for you. Besides, who ever heard of a *rich* serial killer?

• On the other hand, maybe it's just a bad year for baseball players. Rock 'n' roll singers can have bad years like 1959 and 1973. Likewise movie stars. Why not baseball players?

• Maybe I can't find the answer because there's no answer to be found. Maybe it's a living version of the Analogy Section in the SAT, with that incomprehensible jumble of unrelated details: "Aardvark is to screwdriver as: (a) tangerine is to shotgun, (b) dachshund is to martini, (c) pumpkin pie is to corset, (d) Orr is to Whitney, (e) none of the above. Choose one."

Kenmuir dropped into one of his client chairs. The only thing that made sense was that nothing made sense. Not yet. But it would eventually because, whoever these bastards were, they for damn sure weren't going to get away with it.

As a detective or a deputy DA, he'd always known that he was supposed to be cerebral and emotionally detached. Don't let it become personal. But sometimes, when his impulse to "do justice" intruded, it did.

When he was in the fourth grade, a substitute teacher stuck a strip of masking tape over the mouth of talkative, air-head Demi. She sat in her little chair, sobbing, while tears ran down her cheeks. He stood up, walked across the room, and pulled off the tape. Saying nothing, he then went to the front of the room, stuck the tape on the teacher's desk, and walked directly to the principal's office.

No, he was aware that justice's closest cousin is vengeance and that a sense of righteousness accompanies every punishment. So would it be here.

Behold the pale horse . . . with him riding it.

Chapter 32

Friday afternoon, July 12, City of Oakland

Lange and Smith asked Kenmuir to meet them for lunch at Mirabeau, perched atop the Kaiser Building in Oakland, with a panoramic view of Lake Merritt and the hills of Piedmont, more or less midway between Kenmuir in Walnut Creek and Smith in San Francisco. "Bring us up to date."

It was the kind of businessman's lunch that irritated wives everywhere. "You had that for *lunch*? How nice for you." Three house salads, with raspberry vinaigrette dressing. Veal medallions in champagne cream sauce for Smith. Trout *meuniere* for Lange. Filet of sole *almondine* for Kenmuir. All complemented by a Kistler chardonnay.

Kenmuir's summary was spiced with some turns of the phrase, some drama, some humor. Lange and Smith were current long before coffee arrived and that's when their conversation became inexplicably stilted. As it did, Kenmuir became irritated. Looking at Lange, he asked, "All right, roomie, what's really going on here?" Lange and Smith immediately exchanged sidelong glances. "See, there you two go again. What am I going to be drafted to do this time?"

"Actually, it's the opposite." Lange looked down at the table rather than at Kenmuir. "It's time to stop."

Whatever Kenmuir might have suspected or guessed, it wouldn't have been that. He was rarely at a loss for words, but now he was. He looked repeatedly back and forth between both Lange and Smith, at their downcast eyes and glum expressions. "What's 'stop' supposed to mean?"

The only sound in the silence was the flick of Lange's Bic. He gathered momentum to speak. "Well, we both have bosses. You tell us, we tell them, and now they want this to end." Kenmuir said nothing and hardly blinked. Lange was going to have to continue talking, all on his own.

Instead, Smith rescued him. "Both ballclubs want to put . . . controversy . . . behind them. Move on with the season and create some optimism and excitement. Look to the future rather than perpetuate the past." Smith was rambling and knew it. "You have to admit, it does make sense."

"You bet," Kenmuir said, repeatedly squeezing and unsqueezing the Kistler cork in his left hand. "Great sense. Jackson's problem is solved so to hell with the other three players. Orr's murder—or what'd you call it: his controversy?—technically may be solved, even though no one has the slightest idea why he was targeted. But, hey, it's depressing, and the front office needs optimistic Giants and A's fans to buy tickets. That about sum it up?"

Smith plainly was angered. "Watch out, Dave. You know my feelings about Humph. I just don't have a choice."

Kenmuir felt bad, but only for a moment. At the same time, he was aware that, as employees, they didn't have his independence. But *both* of them? And *both* ball clubs? How much of a fight had they put up? The clubs' positions might be understandable, but that didn't make them tolerable.

The abrupt silence at their table was exaggerated by the neighboring diners at their tables, where conversations sounded as if they were being conducted through bullhorns and where clattering cutlery sounded like dozens of ball bearings being dropped on a tin roof.

Finally, Lange said, "We'll pay for your time up to now, of course."

Kenmuir placed the ice-blue linen napkin on the place in front of him as he stood up. "You can pay for lunch. That'll do."

"Don't be pissed off," Lange said.

"But I am. Though not at the two of you." Kenmuir bobbed his head in a combination of frustration and irritation. "On the other hand, maybe I am. I mean, I'm not sure yet what I think about how *both* of you could let this happen. But if I stay here any longer and keep talking about it . . . " Kenmuir shrugged his shoulders and walked away.

As he was driving home, he did have to admit, if only to himself, that the "cases" truly were stranded. The Contra Costa County Sheriff's Office had nothing but dead ends, too many new felonies and not enough staff; so much for Orr. The Cleveland police were satisfied that the Whitney shooting was solved. The Anaheim police had no objective reason to consider Fellner's accident as anything but a commonplace, though regrettable, hit-and-run. Worst of all, Kenmuir himself no longer had a legitimate basis to be involved in any of it. He'd been fired. Politely, maybe, but no less fired. It was time for an intelligent man, a practical man, to walk away.

That was when he heard Roy Orbison singing *It's Over* on KOFY. Out loud he said, "Maybe for you, Roy. But not for me. No fuckin' way."

Chapter 33

Thursday morning, July 18, City of Walnut Creek

WHEN HIS CELL PHONE CHIRPED, the businessman knew who it had to be. After all, only "Mr. Jones" had the number, and only he had any need to dial it. "Hello. How are you?" The businessman was unfailingly courteous.

The plebian Mr. Jones never reciprocated the courtesy, but always began speaking as if already in the middle of their conversation. "Got your message. Ain't happenin'. We're done."

"I thought so, too. But it hasn't worked out that way. There has to be one more. *Must be* one more."

Jones was unmoved. "You may think so, but I don't. Later's a possibility, maybe, but not now."

The businessman hadn't anticipated any resistance, much less a refusal. He had no time, period, let alone to argue or persuade. He lost his composure. "You can't do that! Timing is critical. If this job isn't done by the end of July, it'll be too late. This is the last one. I promise."

"Promise? Go ahead and promise all you fuckin' want. Like I said, it ain't happenin'."

"Why not? It's no different than the others."

"And that's exactly the fuckin' problem. The others. It's time to back off and wait awhile, let things calm down."

"You don't understand! It has to be *now*. There's too much risk that it'll be too late by August. If we don't act now, do this one more, it could end up being for nothing. *Nothing!*" The businessman heard his voice cracking. *Get hold of yourself. Courage under fire.*

When Jones didn't react, the businessman waited anxiously for him. *Please, please, please,* he prayed.

At last Mr. Jones said, "There'll be a 25% bonus."

The businessman would've paid double it if he'd had to. "Agreed. But just get it done in time."

After Jones' end of the line went dead, the businessman remained seated. He wasn't sure he had the strength to stand, anyway. *So close, so close. Maybe it won't be necessary after all. Maybe a bit of fine-tuning can do the same thing. Devote more attention to my offense and keep that damn Jap off my heels. No, can't take any chances. I'll have to do both.*

From a desk drawer, he pulled an unlabeled file holding a stack of documents, topped by several stapled pages entitled "Week of July 21-28." Leafing through the pages, the businessman lingered longer on some names than others. Finally, his attention centered on Tom Bice. *He's out of it and has to wait for next year. He'll want someone cheap enough to keep next year. Why do I care? Screw next year. All of them can do whatever they want. I'll be gone. My future's now.*

He pushed the intercom button on his telephone.

"Yes, sir."

"Would you please try to get Tom Bice on the telephone for me?"

Within only a few minutes she informed him, "Mr. Bice is on the line."

He smiled into the receiver, ever the collegial co-owner. "Tommy? How're you? ... Good, good. Am I calling at a bad time? ... Good, good. I thought maybe we could discuss a trade."

Friday afternoon, July 19, City of Walnut Creek

WHEN "POISON" COLONNA MET WITH Jeff MacPherson, their meetings were disguised but not secret. To all appearances, they were merely local acquaintances who encountered each other at shops, restaurants, or local sporting events. They did nothing to attract attention and didn't care who saw them.

For example, they patronized the same gym at unpredictable times and not always together. Today, they "coincidentally" enjoyed a relaxing sauna and discussed the businessman's purchase order of yesterday until three other toweled club members entered the sauna. After a brief but collegial chat, they adjourned to the showers and finally to lunch in the club restaurant. That would've made sense to any observer and, anyway, no investigator would've had time to set up a recorder in the dining room.

Colonna tore a slice from a baguette. "One more's too much, too soon. Doesn't sit well with me."

MacPherson rearranged the knife and fork on his placemat. "I understand. You never liked this ... sale ... in the first place. This would hardly make you like it more. However, it's the last from this client, correct?"

"That's what he says, but who knows if he'll want something else later? The fuckin' flake." Colonna immediately lowered his voice in reaction to MacPherson's critical stare, but added, "Well, that's what he is."

Colonna delayed while the waiter—who probably didn't speak much English, regardless—delivered his cheeseburger and MacPherson's Cobb salad. "Look, I was pretty sure what you'd think. So I agreed. Although I can cancel it quicker than shit. What's he gonna do? Sue?" Colonna watched for a sign. He got one when MacPherson merely dipped his head and looked indulgently from under his eyebrows.

Colonna continued, "Okay, so I was right and we don't give it up. But, honest to god, no fuckin' more. We can't keep drawing on this account and I don't care how big the price is." Then he added disgustedly, "And I'm goddamned tired of talkin' in this code shit."

In spite of himself, MacPherson smiled. "I can tell. Safer, though." He folded his salad, mixing ingredients and dressing. "Look, I respect your fear—"

Poison's eyes squinted maliciously. "I'm not afraid of shit."

MacPherson shrugged. "Fine. Your *concern*, then." MacPherson organized a proportionate bite of lettuce, tomato, cheese, and meat. "Still, it's the largest payout we've ever had and that makes it worth some extra risk. Which—and, yes, I do disagree with you—I don't think is all that much. That said, this'll the last. Period. Okay?" He took the bite.

Poison nodded.

MacPherson finished chewing the bite and constructed another. "At the same time, I concur that we should be particularly cautious. So much so, in fact, that I think you should handle this one directly. No middleman. You agree?"

With meat, onion, two slices of tomato and lettuce, Poison had built a cheeseburger perhaps twice as tall as his mouth. He'd managed to cram in another bite, but a mixture of ketchup and mayonnaise oozed out of the bun and onto his hands. "Uuummmm" was the best he could reply to MacPherson's question. After swallowing impressively, he added, "Do you remember that guy with the dog we used a couple of years ago? Big guy. Bigger dog. If I remember right, he's located somewhere in southern California." He immediately stuffed in another megabite.

"Don't remember that, but I do remember the dog."

"Sure would like to see that dog again. You?"

"Me, too. Nothing like a well-trained dog." MacPherson glanced at his watch. "I've got to dash, but I've got one other loose end that needs to be tied off. That'd be our newest friend, the lawyer."

"The one who butts in?"

"The same. First Emeryville, then my office, and now the phone call about Whitney. Maybe worse, he's gotten the Whopper interested in him. Who knows where the hell he's going to end up next?" MacPherson lowered his voice for emphasis. "Plus I simply don't like the cocky son of a bitch."

"Think he oughtta be butted out before he does any real harm?"

"I do."

"How permanently?"

"Don't really care. As long as I don't have to think about him again. Ever."

"Consider him gone."

MacPherson grabbed the tray with the bill. "I've got it." He handed two $20 bills and the tray to the waiter as he walked by. "Anything else to worry about?"

"Nope, no one's got a clue. We're good."

MacPherson stood, shook hands, and left the restaurant. Poison remained. A couple of buddies who'd had lunch together.

Chapter 34

Friday evening, July 26, City of Walnut Creek

A**LL AIR CONDITIONERS WERE TURNED ON.** Any child with a swimming pool immediately became a favorite playmate. Cats and dogs sprawled on their backs in shady spots, looking as if they'd been shot. Husbands coming from work were greeted with, "If you think I'm cooking tonight, you're crazy." Restaurants turned away customers. Backyards were fragrant with mixed odors of briquettes and barbecue sauces. Sex? "Don't be ridiculous." It was hot. Damn hot.

It was still hot at midnight. A slight breeze allowed meager relief. Kenmuir's bedroom windows were open, inviting the breeze inside. The sheet and cover were pushed to the foot of his bed. He wore only a pair of boxer shorts: "I [heart] Syrah." He was propped up on his backrest, reading *A Guide To Rotisserie Baseball* for more details and subtleties than Peters' explanation.

Since his lunch meeting with Peters, he'd tuned in on conversations and encountered a surprising number of people who participated in fantasy baseball leagues. It was like buying a new car: you never noticed any like it before but, once you owned one, the roads seemed to be full of them. Some characterized it as an addiction, others as a fascination. All admitted to pouncing on the box scores as soon as they were available. World

War III had started? President's been assassinated? Bubonic plague's broken out in Contra Costa County? That could wait. What mattered was how "their" players had performed.

If their players' statistics were depressed, then they were too. By contrast, a big day was exhilarating. One friend told him that it was better than sex. Surely that had to be an exaggeration . . . didn't it? At 12:20 a.m., he turned off the light.

When the Five Satins sang *In the Still of the Night*, they were singing about 3:00 a.m. That's when people sleep most soundly, animals are least restless, and birds are silent. Thinking about it later, Kenmuir didn't know why he woke up. A noise registered subconsciously? An instinct honed in Vietnam's sodden jungles? Merely good luck? Whatever it was, it made him squint his eyes at the green iridescence on the digital face of his clock radio: 3:07.

It was then that he heard the sound. A stranger, unfamiliar with the normal creaks and groans of the house, wouldn't have noticed it, but Kenmuir wasn't a stranger in his own house. He heard it—a muffled creak from the hall. He raised his head, though only high enough to flip over the pillow. Like a child verifying that demons really could be sneaking up on him, he listened intently for a repetition of the sound. But there was no sound outside or inside. Groggily satisfied, he lowered his head back onto the cool surface of the pillow.

Then he heard the sound again. Unmistakable. And unmistakably closer.

He painstakingly rolled off the edge of the bed, so that his left foot touched the floor while his torso was still on the bed. Using his arms, he quietly pushed his torso upward. He stood, his left foot on the forest green carpet and his right knee on the edge of the bed. When he lifted his right knee off the edge of the bed, he extended the leg forward as a first step toward the hall.

This is silly. Three o'clock in the goddamn morning and I'm stalking gremlins. Worse, now I've got to pee. His bladder shriveled when he again heard the sound, this time from the hallway. The bedroom door to the hall was open. Living alone, he had no reason to close it. Who needed to be kept out? The door was located near a corner of the room. To one side of it was three feet of wall; to the other side, twelve feet of wall. Against the twelve-foot wall was a tall chest of drawers. Except for the exaggerated glow from the iridescent face of the clock, the bedroom was dark.

Kenmuir knew exactly where he was going. It wouldn't be the first time he'd navigated to and from the bathroom in the dark without serious injury. Though unconvinced that he wasn't indulging his imagination, he took no chances and moved quietly toward the niche where the edge of the chest of drawers met the wall, some four feet from the door. Once he sidled into the niche, he paused momentarily to stop the sound of his own heart beating in his ears.

If he'd been a dog, his ears would've been cocked in the direction of the hallway. But all he heard was silence. A lot of silence.

Then it came again, the muffled creak of the forty-year-old hardwood floor in the hallway. Whatever was wandering around, be it gremlin or garden-variety demon, he wasn't alone. If he needed convincing, he got it when an arm emerged slowly beyond the frame of the open bedroom doorway. The hand at the end of the arm held a .22, the strangely incongruous choice of women and assassins, but a woman's hand wasn't holding it.

Kenmuir knew he'd learn the intruder's intent as soon as he saw his face. If it were masked, the man was a burglar. If it were unmasked, he was a killer—because a killer wouldn't care about being seen, since no memory would survive a .22 round tunneling through his victim's brain.

Then the nose and jaw of a man's face passed beyond the trim of the door. The face was uncovered. The man was a hunter. This was no random selection. The assassin was in *his* bedroom because *he* slept there.

Worse, he had to assume that this gunman was only half the problem. Contract killers tended to work in pairs. If one missed, the other wouldn't; if one encountered resistance, the other would eliminate it. The face in front of him undoubtedly had a companion face nearby. Maybe, but first face first.

The killer's eyes were straining to see in the darkness. If they glanced to the left, they'd see what they were looking for. Instead, they focused on the bed, because *that* was where sleeping victims always were.

The assassin was unconcerned about being too far away to distinguish a sleeping body from rumpled bedclothes. He was a specialist at putting people permanently to sleep; he'd done so many times before. He carefully stepped by the door frame and into the bedroom, watching for any movement on the bed. Movement meant trouble, and he wanted no trouble. No: find the head . . . Put a hole in it . . . Leave.

He didn't watch for—because he had no reason to expect—any movement from his left. Thus, when Kenmuir stepped sideways in front of him, so closely that they almost collided, it was too late for him to react. Kenmuir's left hand locked onto his right wrist, pushing it up and out. He could've fired the gun as many times as he wanted, but would've succeeded only in killing the bedroom ceiling.

A millisecond later, Kenmuir's right hand—curled into a partial fist, so that the middle knuckles stuck out like the edge of a dull cleaver—powered into the assassin's throat. In that instant, the assassin's larynx was shattered and trachea was shut down as effectively as if it were tied in a knot. The assassin dug at his throat in a desperate, but futile, effort to open his crushed windpipe. He sagged in his death spasm, guided by the hand that still gripped his right wrist.

As the assassin's body was falling, a flash of light burst over Kenmuir's left shoulder. The unseen second assassin fired as soon as his partner's falling body had exposed a target, but he only succeeded in over-killing his partner. Kenmuir reacted instantly to the combination of intense light and loud sound.

As Kenmuir heard the second man retreat to the far side of the house, he tore the gun from the hand of the dead assassin, scrambled to his feet and immediately ran to the far end of the hallway. Cordite smoke lingered in the enclosed space. At the end of the hall, he listened for any sound. He couldn't see the front door, but he hadn't heard it open. Besides, he assumed the backup killer wouldn't want to report a complete failure. *No, he's still here, waiting for me to chase him. Better a sloppy kill than no kill at all.*

Kenmuir waited. Silence and darkness returned on the moonless night. The second assassin would wait for Kenmuir to blunder into the line of fire, but he couldn't wait long. Time was on Kenmuir's side. Within two hours or so, dawn would begin to erase the night. The telephone was a possibility, though he assumed his land line had been cut as a routine precaution and his cell was in the bedroom. And, while he knew that he slept alone, the remaining killer might not.

However, Kenmuir was disinclined to wait long. He was inherently impatient and he was mightily pissed off. He wanted to get the son of a bitch . . . So where was he?

Kenmuir figured that he would've run for the most visible cover—and that would be the dining room on the other side of the entrance foyer. What he probably *wouldn't* know was that the master bedroom had an exterior door for access to the back patio. The patio, in turn, had a door into Kenmuir's beloved study—which adjoined the kitchen, which adjoined the dining room.

Kenmuir shouted toward the dining room, "Who the fuck *are* you? Why me?"

Of course, the killer didn't reply. But that wasn't why Kenmuir had shouted. Rather, he'd shouted to let the assassin believe that he was cowering in the shelter of the hall, exactly where the assassin would expect him to be. So he shouted again, "Someone must've heard the shot. The police are on their way." *Oh, yeah. Three in the morning, no telephone.*

Kenmuir reasoned that the assassin, now even shorter on time, would hope that an amateur like Kenmuir would assume all was clear, would come out to verify it, and thus expose himself. Bang. That would be the end of that.

Staying at the edge of the hall where the wooden floor was more secure, Kenmuir stepped over the first assassin's body and quietly opened the bedroom door to the patio. His bare feet made no sound as he ran across the patio to the family room door, which he then edged open just wide enough to slip through sideways. Passing through his study, he stopped at the entry to the kitchen and looked toward the dining room. He could see nothing.

Kenmuir guessed the assassin would station himself near the outside edge of the dining room, partially protected by the wall, with a clear view of the living room and the entry into the hall. *If* so, then Kenmuir had to cross the kitchen in order to reach the doorway behind the assassin.

The kitchen's linoleum, laid over a floor strengthened during one of Mary's home improvement projects, was soundless under Kenmuir's bare feet. *If I slept in the kitchen, I'd be dead now.*

Kenmuir approached the door into the dining room at an angle. When about six feet away from the door, he saw the killer exactly where he'd anticipated, lying down to present the smallest possible target when his target emerged, as expected, from the hall.

Kenmuir pointed the .22 at the assassin's back. "Hey, Hawkeye, leave the gun on the floor and roll over." The startled assassin's head jerked upward. Otherwise, he didn't move. It was as if he'd chosen to ignore both the voice and the person behind him. Kenmuir stepped closer to the door, but kept the edge between him and the assassin. Better some protection than none. "Whatever you got paid, it's not worth dying for. Slide the gun out in front of you and roll over. Do everything *very* slowly."

The man didn't move. No need to. Not yet.

Kenmuir knew what the killer had in mind as surely as if he were thinking out loud: *Be patient and let the target relax with a false sense of control. In fact, the target has no idea what to do next. I'm a professional and he isn't. Citizens don't have the balls to shoot someone in the back. That'll give me an edge when I move.*

When the assassin moved, it was fast. He rolled partially onto his left side and simultaneously swept his right arm and hand in a backward arc toward where the sound of the voice had been behind him. He'd fire at the voice before seeing the speaker, and he wouldn't miss the shocked amateur.

Kenmuir was neither lulled nor bewildered.

Before the assassin's gun hand was halfway through its deadly arc, Kenmuir fired. The .22 bullet hit the assassin above his right kidney and angled upward into his chest. It tumbled and tore through the bottom of his right lung, stopping in the chest cavity. The killer's only reaction was to wince and drop his arm slightly, as if merely jostled by a kick in the back. He made no sound, but again swung his right hand in Kenmuir's direction. Had he not done so, he might've lived.

Kenmuir fired a second time. The bullet entered the assassin's neck an inch below the right side of his jaw. His tongue and the roof of his mouth provided no protection. His head bounced once on the hardwood floor.

Kenmuir retrieved his cell phone from the bedroom and called 911. "Hi, there. Beautiful morning, isn't it? Sorry to bother you, but I've just killed two men who broke into my house. Could you ask an officer to stop by?"

The Walnut Creek Police Department was manned by a skeleton staff that early in the morning. One watch commander (a sergeant), one dispatcher (an elderly woman who was avoiding the loneliness of nights without her recently deceased husband), and one police aide. Cruising the largely deserted streets were six really bored patrol officers. The drunk drivers had managed to get home, and the disturbers of the peace had gone to sleep.

A Deadly Game

Kenmuir's telephone call almost made the dispatcher swallow the end of her headset. She immediately activated the speaker in the watch commander's office. Sergeant Grovenor heard about five words and bolted from his chair, his knee ricocheting painfully off the corner of the desk and spilling the remainder of a brackish cup of coffee. He never broke stride as he rushed for the side door toward his patrol car. Over his shoulder, he shouted at the dispatcher, "On my way. Watch commander in service."

It was a close contest whether the sergeant moved faster than the patrol officers when they heard the dispatcher's announcement of "reported 187." Crime may be crime, but a homicide—Penal Code 187—is the most glamorous: the home run of offenses, the touchdown pass of felonies. Detectives describe their duties offhandedly, like "I work burgs" or "I work narcotics." But a special, deeper tone is reserved for those who say, with steely eyes and taller posture, "I work . . . homicide."

By 3:20 a.m., Kenmuir's street was illuminated by seven sets of flashing emergency lights that rhythmically changed the colors of the bathrobes of the wide-awake neighbors—with the exception of the Learys, who somehow managed to sleep peacefully through the most exciting event to occur on the street since Renee's halter top fell off at the neighborhood Fourth of July barbecue three years earlier.

The last police officer didn't leave until shortly before 9:00 a.m. During his on-site interview, Kenmuir wasn't as candid as he should've been. For the moment, he decided not to contradict the obvious explanation that he was the random victim of two burglars. Didn't know who they were, which was true, or why they picked his house, which wasn't entirely true.

Once the officers left, he spread a couple of towels over the bloody hardwood floor that would have to be stripped and refinished next week. He poured a second Diet Pepsi, lit yet-another cigarette, and walked onto the back patio. He had no doubt that the two men deliberately came to *his* house, to kill *him* specifically; it was no burglary turned sour, no regrettable mistake by two killers who'd stumbled into the wrong house. No, he'd obviously trespassed somewhere during his travels. Was it merely one telephone call to an answering machine? Was it Marini again? Was someone else reacting belatedly to something that happened weeks ago? Whatever it was, he'd put himself into the ballgame, and that someone had decided to take him out. And *that's* what this was about: the ballgame.

He was pretty sure before, but now he was convinced. The accidents to the ballplayers weren't accidental. They *were* part of a plan. They *were* connected. Having poked at the plan, he now was connected with it. Okay. If someone wanted to play with him, then he'd be a player.

He flicked his spent cigarette onto the lawn and walked inside.

Chapter 35

Saturday morning, July 27, City of Anaheim

CALIFORNIA ANGEL PAUL BERRY WAS STANDING in his driveway at about the same time as the Contra Costa County Coroner's van was leaving Kenmuir's driveway nearly 500 miles away in Walnut Creek.

Originally signed as a catcher, Berry hadn't been a very good one—but he'd been an extraordinary hitter. His short, muscular swing uncoiled in the blink of an eye and could smash the head of a bat into an oncoming fastball, curveball, slider, whatever. That meant the Angels had to find another position for him and so they'd plunked him in the unfamiliar and vulnerable position of third base, where he'd felt truly naked.

Gone were the shin guards, cup, chest protector, and face mask that he'd worn as comfortably as a businessman wears a suit. Suddenly, he was left standing in the field with only a glove and a felt hat. It was like sending a tanker from the 2nd Armored "Hell on Wheels" Division into combat sitting on a Tonka truck. Even worse, he never knew when the ball was coming his way. He'd always known as a catcher: give the signal for the next pitch, watch the pitcher wind up and throw. Now, some right-handed hitter would turn on a thigh-high fastball and rocket a grounder down the third-base line at what looked like 800 miles per hour. Instant terror.

The position began to make sense sometime in the middle of his second season. Ground balls seemed to slow down. He learned how to go backward for a fly ball, how to turn the double play, how to charge a bunt, and when to take a relay from the outfield. It'd been less a metamorphosis than a transition. Consequently, he'd been the Angels' starting third baseman for the past six years. True, he had his defensive limitations, but that was considered a fair exchange for his being among the league leaders each season in home runs, runs scored, RBIs, and all other measures of offensive prowess.

Friday night's extra-inning loss to the Red Sox kept him awake until well after midnight, but had no effect on his metabolic clock. Be it a night or a day game, whether he returned home early or late, he awoke at 7:00 a.m. Sleeping late was nice in theory, but he couldn't do it.

At 7:15 a.m., he wandered down his driveway to collect the morning paper. He was wearing a T-shirt, cut-off sweatpants, and a tattered pair of extremely comfortable bedroom slippers. As he bent down to pick up the newspaper, he heard his neighbor's voice.

"Morning, Paul. Just can't wait to read about yourself?"

Berry laughed. Even though Tom Lee, doctor of family medicine, was more the age of Berry's uncles than his contemporaries, the two were close friends. "Morning, Doc, thought I'd bone up on the medical malpractice results. Give us something to talk about." One of Lee's most vocal complaints was how lawyers were ruining the practice of medicine.

"Hey, I was there. You did your part. Two doubles. But you couldn't keep the Red Sox away."

"No kidding. The hell of it is that we really *are* better than that."

"Maybe, but not without some help on the mound. You get to the middle innings and it all falls apart."

"Don't I know . . ."

Later, even Dr. Lee couldn't say from where the Doberman came. "It appeared out of nowhere. One minute we were talking, you know, like we usually do, and the next minute it was there, tearing at him. It was horrible."

The massive Doberman charged at the Angels' third baseman with frightening and single-minded purpose. Its powerful jaws were open. The daggers of its teeth glistened with saliva that sprayed onto its muzzle. Muscles rippled in its shoulders and tendons strained in its neck.

When it was six feet away from Berry's right side, it launched itself into the air. It barreled into Berry's right shoulder and bowled him over like a target in a carnival shooting gallery. The abrasions to his left shoulder and the side of his head from skidding on the driveway asphalt surface were inconsequential compared with the gouges and bites into his right arm and side.

He flailed in a helpless frenzy at the muscular beast whose teeth dug in one place and then another. He rolled and scrambled and kicked, all to no avail. The Doberman was like a cat toying with an injured bird. In the midst of the attack, with its teeth embedded in Berry's right shoulder, the Doberman suddenly froze. Its ears, which had been flattened during the assault, perked upward. Its shiny black head, now stained with red blotches and smears, snapped upward as well. As swiftly as it attacked, so did it lose interest. With its ears still at attention, it turned and sped down the street until it disappeared from sight.

Both men later estimated that the attack lasted several minutes, though it really began and ended in a matter of seconds. Berry's multiple wounds proved more painful than debilitating, more bloody than serious. Even so, the muscular damage incapacitated him until the last week of the season, when he was permitted an occasional appearance as a pinch hitter. His season had ended not on the grass of the Angels' infield but on the asphalt of his own driveway.

Chapter 36

Tuesday morning, July 30, City of Walnut Creek

Kenmuir, Lucy, and several other friends were playing baseball. Lucy was wearing no clothes but, no matter how hard Kenmuir tried to make her turn around, she kept her back toward him. Finally a ball was hit in her direction and she started to turn . . .

Kenmuir's telephone rang, and Lucy vanished from sight.

"What?" Kenmuir barked into the phone.

"Good morning, Mr. Kenmuir, please hold for Mr. Marini."

Kenmuir looked at the face of the clock; it glowed 7:32 a.m.

"Hello, counselor. I hear you pissed off some more people." Marini's voice was alert. Clearly he rose much earlier than Kenmuir.

"That's one way to look at it. I'm surprised it took you so long to find out."

"It didn't. Details did. We should talk. I'll send the limo."

"I'll pass on the limo. Your limo service needs buffing up in the hospitality area. Time?"

"Whenever."

"Great. That's when I'll get there. Whenever."

Kenmuir hung up and rolled onto his side. He tightly squeezed his eyes and tried to return to the turning Lucy, but she was gone.

When Kenmuir arrived at Angelo Marini's mansion at 10:40 a.m., the gates didn't open. Instead, a man only slightly less wide than the gates themselves appeared behind them. He was draped in a garish, bright-pink, Hawaiian-style shirt decorated with hibiscus flowers. Someone evidently had torn down a tent from a Maui wedding reception and put buttons on it. Kenmuir assumed that the tent-shirt covered enough weaponry to equip a platoon. The man's face was expressionless. His attitude seemed to be: *If you have something to say, say it. If not, then what the hell're you doing here?*

Kenmuir leaned outside the car window. "Aloha. I'm here for the celebrity luau."

The big man crossed his hairy arms. It was as if two black sheep had decided to take a nap on his chest. "You'd be the lawyer. Boss said you'd say something smart-ass."

The Incredible Hulk triggered a sensor. The iron gates slowly opened inward. Kenmuir drove up the driveway to the front of Marini's mansion where the bronzed legionnaire still had water pouring over his head. The elaborately carved front door was opened by a petite Oriental woman. Her black hair was cut in a no-nonsense, strictly business style; the lenses of her eyeglasses were thick enough to have once served as headlights for a 1933 Packard. "Good morning, Mr. Kenmuir. Mr. Marini's expecting you."

Kenmuir was led to a tile-covered porch that extended the width of the rear of the residence. It was poised four steps above a terraced lawn that descended to a swimming pool. At the far end of the porch, Marini sat next to a large table shaded by two umbrellas. He rose from his chair—ever the gracious country gentleman—and thrust out his meaty hand while six strides away. "Counselor. Good to see you."

"Likewise you." Kenmuir watched his hand disappear inside Marini's.

When they both were under the shade of the umbrellas, Marini lit a Pall Mall. "I've been keeping an eye on you. Had the feeling we'd bump into each other again. You're a real shit disturber."

"*I'm* the one whose shit got disturbed."

Marini smiled in his disarmingly innocent way. "True. Hired guns, no less."

"You knew them?"

"*Of* them. As I said, I found out some details. One was a lowlife named Tommy Gleese. Dumb as an artichoke. Few years ago he started dabbling in scag and blow. Became unreliable. A junker can go sideways on you at any time. Got by on odd jobs for small players in the Midwest."

"And the other?"

"A guy named Deeker. Real piece of work, that one. Nutso. Never knew what he was going to do next. Once you got around his limitations, though, a damn good shooter. Those two weren't sent just to scare you. They were sent to put you down permanently. Sorry. But that's the way it is."

"Thanks for the solicitude. Do I look for any more visitors?"

"Don't know. For me, you're merely a nuisance. For someone else, you've turned into a major pain, and that kind of attention makes me curious."

"Not your problem."

"Like I told you before, *I'll* decide what's my problem and what's not. And we did agree that you'd stay clear of my business interests."

Kenmuir tried to look puzzled even though he wasn't. He was absolutely sure the two killers came because of his call to The Broker. "And I have. Devotedly."

"Bullshit. Start by telling me what you've been up to. Still trying to find out who killed Orr?"

Kenmuir considered the advantage and disadvantage of opening up again to Marini, especially given that it was at least possible that he actually was the one pulling the strings entangling him. Advantage: Marini had efficient sources of information and presumably was very influential in the hired-killer crowd. Disadvantage: Marini's motives were going to remain secret and undoubtedly differed from Kenmuir's. On the other hand, he was going to do whatever he wanted, regardless of Kenmuir.

"Working on it," Kenmuir answered.

"Tell me everything. From the beginning."

Twenty minutes later, Marini was fully briefed. He'd remained poker-faced—with the notable exception that, when Kenmuir mentioned The Broker, his jaw muscles had tightened perceptibly.

"That's it. You're completely up to speed." Kenmuir lit a Merit. "Any thoughts?"

Marini stood up and stretched. His shadow was nearly as large as the umbrella's. "Most of it I'd already figured out. Everyone and now Berry, all connected to Orr? Reasonable conclusion. I did wonder what you were doing about that. But I didn't know about the, what did you call it, 'fantasy'. . . ? —Kenmuir nodded—baseball league angle. Hell, I've never even heard of that. Fan like me, you'd think I would've." Marini appeared to chew on the inside of his cheek. "Interesting twist. That million dollar league actually exist?"

"Don't know."

"But you're gonna find out?"

"Real soon."

Marini walked to the edge of the porch and leaned against the railing. He stood silently for a few moments, preoccupied with his own thoughts, and then returned. "After that?"

"Not sure yet. I'll keep feeling my way along, I guess. I sure wouldn't mind if someone with, say, resources, was watching out for uninvited guests at Chez Kenmuir."

Marini chuckled. "Resources?"

"Exactly." Kenmuir pushed a bit. "Let me ask you about The Broker. I noticed your reaction when I mentioned him. I gather you didn't know about that morsel."

"No, I didn't. However, you misread me. I've never heard of him."

No, I didn't misread anything. You covered it fast and didn't show much, Whopper, but you showed enough. Whoever or whatever The Broker is, you know something about it. "Far be it from me to push, but I've *got* to believe that I'm being one helluva lot more forthcoming than you are. If nothing else, I need some help in the sleeping peacefully department."

"Again, I've never heard of any . . . what, Broker? At the same time, I'm confident, *very* confident, that no one'll be troubling you further."

In Kenmuir's experience, bad guys and good guys existed in a largely black-and-white world. In high school, the other schools' teams were opponents. In Vietnam, the VC and NVA were the indisputable enemy. As a DA, those who broke the law were caught, prosecuted, and punished. On the other hand, he was beginning to recognize that Marini—a quintessential bad guy by all accounts and reputation—was inserting a distinct shade of gray between the black and the white. Even more incredible, a rapport was developing between them: much less than a friendship, to be sure, but more than a mere acquaintance. Marini had a kind of primeval trustworthiness that Kenmuir respected; lethal but likeable. Amazing.

"Glad to hear that. But you've got to help me find this Broker."

Marini seemed to rise in his chair even though he remained seated. His eyes narrowed and his stare never wavered from Kenmuir's face. "Got to?"

Kenmuir saw this face the first night. The jovial conversationalist was again replaced by *Don* Angelo Marini, a man used to being obeyed and ferocious when crossed. Marini spoke sharply. "First, *you* don't find squat. Second, *you* have already caused enough trouble. Anyone, including this so-called Broker, now realizes that you can take care of yourself and can kick back. Even so, this fight is outside your weight class. Third, I've gone a long way for you—farther than I would for most—because you mean well and because something more is happening than I'm comfortable with. But don't forget what I've already told you. *Don't* fuck with me."

A Deadly Game

Kenmuir looked at Marini's powerful fists, each as large as a cantaloupe, resting motionlessly on the surface of the table. Marini hadn't achieved, and sure as hell didn't maintain, his position by patiently cultivating a consensus through the democratic process. He was there because, as he said, you don't fuck with him.

Kenmuir shrugged compliantly, a relaxed gesture to break the tension. "You'll be relieved to learn that I've decided to accept the persuasive cogency of your argument."

Marini recognized the concession. The fists opened, and he reached for his cigarettes. His eyes opened wider and regained a glint of humor. He shook his head and chuckled. "Persuasive cogency. Kenmuir, you're a genuine kick in the ass."

Kenmuir leaned back in his chair. "Now that I've been sent to my room, what happens next? I'll give you a hint, by the way; I do *not* intend to go home meekly, crawl into bed, and await the advent of the next deadly duo."

"I assume that. However, I suggest you keep your eyes on where you started. This Orr thing. Forget about The Broker. I'm sure that's over. It'll lead you nowhere. Waste of your time."

"I'm to take that on faith?"

"I like that. Faith. That's right." Marini stood up and extended his hand. Evidently, the meeting was over. "Good to see you again, Kenmuir."

"You, too. If you want to know anything more, don't hesitate to call."

Marini laughed out loud. After Kenmuir left, Marini told the Oriental woman to place a telephone call. She did.

Tuesday afternoon, July 30, City of Walnut Creek

AS SOON AS KENMUIR RETURNED to his office, he telephoned FBI Special Agent Neil Roberson, with whom he hadn't spoken in many years. They'd met when Kenmuir, then a detective, had worked with him on a kidnapping case. Contrary to the oft-depicted animosity between the FBI and local police, Kenmuir and Roberson clicked from the beginning. Roberson now was assigned to FBI headquarters in Washington, D.C.

They consumed twenty minutes catching up with each other's lives. Promises were exchanged for future visits. Finally, Kenmuir said, "Neil, this call isn't entirely sentimental. Mainly, but not entirely."

"Really? What a disappointment."

"Yeah, I bet you're shocked, but I'm stuck and need some help. Specifically, I have to find out whatever I can about some asshole called The Broker. Evidently, he's an entrepreneur with Lucky Luciano as a role model. He arranges hits on people."

"Not my area. Organized crime's in another part of the building."

"Didn't know that. Nevertheless, I'm in a bad spot. The hunting of me is not my favorite sport." He summarized Thursday night's events. He told him about the Broker, but didn't mention Marini.

"Jesus Christ, Dave, I thought you'd become a lawyer. No more cops and robbers."

"Me, too. This is probably just a flashback. Which is why you've got to help rescue a simple suburban lawyer."

"Why not ask Cleveland PD? It's their case."

"It is and it isn't. Officially, they're done. Plus, Walnut Creek's not exactly in their jurisdiction. Between too much other crime and not enough leads, what can they do? Anyway, they'd only call you guys. In a burst of efficiency, I'm eliminating the middleman."

"I don't know. There're more turf wars in this building than New York City."

"Well, look, I don't want you to jam yourself up behind this. At the same time, I'm not asking for any secret files. Just who the hell is this guy, and how does he fit into the program? Maybe you could stroll down the hall. Have a Danish and a cup of coffee with Eliot Ness. Few innocent answers to a few innocent questions. No harm, no foul."

"No guarantees. They tense up on me and I'm done."

"Fair enough. However, this is no bullshit newspaper article. Someone's shooting live ammo at me."

"I hear you. I'll see what I can find out."

Chapter 37

Thursday afternoon, August 1, City of Dallas

Mr. and Mrs. Dante Ginetti were among the social pillars of their affluent Dallas suburb. Actually, she was the pillar and he was the platform supporting her. They confirmed the cliché that opposites attract. She was short and either fat or pleasantly plump, depending on how kind one wanted to be. With hips twice as wide as her shoulders, she was good breeding stock, some would say. He was stereotypically tall, dark, and handsome, ideal for crooning a lover's ballad in a Vegas lounge show.

If he had the looks, she had the energy. She was a vivacious and dynamic mainstay of local boards and causes, usually with an agenda in one hand and checkbook in the other. He was a bit quiet and ill at ease, though pleasant and personable when approached. Something more than a trophy husband, something less than an equal partner. Like the other husbands in their crowd, he was a successful businessman. Everyone knew he'd moved there fourteen years ago to take advantage of the Texas construction boom, reportedly after having made a small fortune in real estate "up north."

His Alamo Development Company wasn't a hands-on outfit. It bulldozed nothing, built nothing, marketed nothing. Rather, the company invested in the development efforts of others: a strip-mall in Lubbock, a housing tract in Houston, an apartment complex near San Antonio. The business was prosperous, but not flashy. Its investments were worthy enough, and its books impeccable enough to satisfy any IRS auditor. Something to be proud of.

In reality, he'd moved from New Jersey because someone had to replace Frankie "Snake-Eyes" Martello, who'd died unexpectedly. He knew he'd been chosen because he was reliable and trustworthy, rather than gifted. Dull but dependable. He wouldn't have recognized a real estate development opportunity if a dump truck unloaded one in his backyard. Unlike Bowie and Travis in the original Alamo, he had the benefit of "reinforcements": a savvy banker in New York orchestrated the company's investments, and a seasoned developer in New Jersey evaluated all projects. Ginetti himself didn't fire a financial shot.

But that didn't mean he was idle. Quite to the contrary, he was quite busy. He was The Broker.

He attended to his territory and brokerage without controversy. As a young man he'd realized that the best protection in his world was one's own pants: Keep your dick and your wallet tucked inside them. Pull out either one and start waving it around and you're in trouble. He kept his pants closed and stayed out of trouble.

His behavior and accounts were irreproachable. He shortchanged no one and reported faithfully to his manager. He never deviated from the rules. He knew that fast-and-loose meant fast-and-lost. In four years, he'd be allowed to retire gracefully. His off-shore accounts and investments would let him live then

A Deadly Game

exactly as he did now. He'd be one more retiree in Dallas. Fine with him.

Consequently, he was stunned when he was ordered to drop everything and fly to Oklahoma City. "I got no answers for ya, Dante. They tell me. I'm telling you. No reason, no explanation. Just go."

He worried in the airplane, and he worried in his rented Lincoln Mark IV. He had reason to be worried. You didn't get summoned to a remote location because someone is happy. That happens only when someone, a very powerful someone, is unhappy. Still, he reassured himself, there had to be a reasonable explanation. Didn't there?

The forty miles he drove outside of Oklahoma City seemed like 400. He wanted to arrive quickly; he didn't want to arrive at all . . . He didn't know what he wanted. The meeting place was a farmhouse, and Dante used that welcoming image to deflect his fears: sipping cold lemonade on a shady veranda, munching freshly baked cookies while gazing toward a little creek beyond a white picket fence, a bright golden haze on the meadow.

However, the further he drove, the more deserted and forbidding the landscape became. Flat, dusty, and bleak. Not a car, not a person, not an animal. It made the surface of the moon look like the White House rose garden. He saw the farmhouse from a mile away. The miserable structure wasn't hard to see, sitting in the middle of nowhere. It did have a veranda, although half had collapsed and the other half looked like it was about to. The few remaining pickets hung as loosely as a six-year-old's front teeth. He imagined a prematurely worn woman struggling to nurture some forlorn flowers, pitiful bits of color for a drab landscape. Home, sweet home. *God*, he thought, *how I want to go home.*

He pulled behind the black Cadillac Fleetwood already parked beside the droopy fence. He laughed to himself: a black Cadillac and a black Lincoln parked in front of an abandoned farmhouse in the middle of Dirt Bowl, Oklahoma. Might as well put up a sign: "Closed for Mafia meeting today. Sorry for any inconvenience."

He waited for the cloud of dust to settle before getting out of the car. When he opened the door, the heat seemed to lift the dust from the ground and instantly coat his highly polished Church's shoes. *Bad omen. Dust to dust.* When he reached the top of the remnant of the veranda, the door was opened by a man he recognized generically, but not individually. He might've been looking at himself thirty years earlier. It was the same guarded manner and alert posture of a soldier protecting the safety of one of the organization's bosses, a capo.

Neither man spoke. Ginetti voluntarily spread his legs and lifted his arms away from his side so the bodyguard could pat him down. He carried no weapons, as the bodyguard efficiently confirmed.

"This way," the bodyguard said as he pointed to a room which, in a more refined time, would've been called the parlor. Except for two chairs, the room was unfurnished. Two men were in the parlor; one was seated, and the other stood to his left, a step behind. Despite the heat, the seated man was attired immaculately in what had to be a custom-made charcoal suit with white pinstripes. No off-the-rack garment would've fit him. Everything about him was big: big head, big torso, big hands. Yet, his expression was oddly placid and unmenacing.

A Deadly Game

Ginetti immediately recognized the unmistakable Angelo "Whopper" Marini, who motioned toward the empty chair. It was more a command than an invitation. Ginetti silently cursed himself because, tough as he might want to be, his heart was pounding and his knees were trembling. Ginetti smiled slightly and nodded a muted greeting. Marini's pleasant expression didn't change, but he didn't acknowledge the greeting, either.

With perhaps two New York exceptions, Marini was the man with whom Ginetti least desired a private audience. *Marini came from California just to meet with me. Whatever the reason, I'm fucked.*

Marini allowed Ginetti to sweat, literally and figuratively, for a few moments. Then he said, "I presume you know who I am, Dante."

"Yes, Don Marini, I do. Though I don't believe we've ever met."

"That's correct. We haven't. It may be that this meeting is unnecessary. We'll soon find out."

Marini's emphasis wasn't lost on Ginetti. *Mother of God, I've been listed. But why? What the hell have I done?* "How may I be of service, Don Marini?"

Marini crossed his legs. A friendly chat between colleagues. At the same time, Ginetti knew that neither bodyguard relaxed so much as a tendon.

"You've managed your territory for quite some time, I understand."

Ginetti was sure that Marini knew to the minute how long he'd supervised his territory. "Fourteen years last February."

"A long time. So may I assume that I don't need to review the rules by which you operate?"

"You may." He sounded sarcastic even though didn't mean to.

Marini dropped his eyes and watched his powerful hands smooth the fabric of his trousers over his bulky thighs. When his hands stopped, they were folded over one knee. He looked directly into Ginetti's eyes and spoke with exaggerated calm: "If you use a sarcastic tone of voice with me again, I'll leave this chair and crush your fucking throat. You'll still answer my questions, but you'll have to write your answers. *Capisce*?"

Ginetti's body temperature dropped twenty degrees. "I apologize, Don Marini. I meant no disrespect. I meant only that, yes, I understand the rules."

Marini leaned back. "Good. I'll start over, but I won't do so again. We agree that you have no uncertainty?"

"Yes, sir."

This, Ginetti reminded himself, *is a time for great deference. The big man is agitated about something and I'm damned if I want to see that fabled temper again.*

"And you abide by those rules?"

"Yes, sir, without exception."

"*No* exceptions?"

"No, sir, *no* exceptions."

"Excellent. Bear that in mind as we talk further. I've come here, at great inconvenience I might add, to talk with you about a contract which you sanctioned."

Ginetti's bladder felt swollen to twice its normal size. He'd pay handsomely for access to a urinal. "With respect, Don Marini, you know I cannot discuss contracts with anyone—even you, and I mean *no* offense—except my manager or Don Morelli himself."

A Deadly Game

"You're correct, and I'm not offended. However, Don Morelli knows of my concern with this particular contract and has consented to this meeting. Think about it, Dante. You think you would've been directed to come here, with no warning, unless Don Morelli had agreed?"

"No, I guess not. I didn't think of that."

"And that, Dante, is what this meeting is all about: what you think about and what you don't." Marini took a long drag on his cigarette and exhaled through his mouth and nose. "You a baseball fan, Dante?"

As suddenly as Ginetti's bladder had bloated, it now shriveled. *So that's what this is about. That damn baseball player Whitney. Goddamn Whitney. I didn't like it then, and I don't like it now, but what choice did I have? The contract was fulfilled, as requested. There can't be a problem. But clearly there is.* "Yes. Yes, I am." Ginetti hung onto the general topic like a hat in a high wind: "I'm from Jersey. Yankee fan all my life. I'll see the Rangers now and then, but it's not the same. What I wouldn't give to be back in the House that Ruth . . ." He heard himself babbling nervously.

Marini held up his hand. "We have something in common. That's good. If you follow baseball, then I imagine you know who Woody Whitney is."

I knew it. "Yes, I know who Woody Whitney is, but I . . ."

Again Marini held up his hand. "Tell me about that contract, Dante. Make me understand why—*why!*—you violated one of the cardinal rules of the business. We never, ever, harm celebrities. But *you* did. You tell me why. Walk me through it. From the beginning."

Ginetti took a deep breath. "It was routine: I received the order, and the directions were quite explicit: Whitney was to be hurt, but his life wasn't to be endangered. The injury was to be to his left side. Left hand, left arm, left ankle or left knee. Very explicit about that. Had to be something on the left." Ginetti started talking faster. "I was told he'd be in Cleveland when his team had a day off. That would be the perfect day, because he usually went out with his wife. It was a matter of watching his house and seeing where he went. Very routine."

"So what exactly did you do?"

"I placed the order with a Cleveland asset, a man named Swampy Royce, whom I'd used many times in the past. Very dependable, followed directions, kept his mouth shut, and didn't ask any unnecessary questions."

"And this time?"

"Same as always. Performed well and within the required time."

"No questions about the target or how to do it?"

"No. If he knew who Whitney was, he didn't let on. He asked the usual questions about restrictions. Time, place, or something like that. This time, it was only that it had to be done on a certain day and to the left side. Details were up to him. Just do it. I don't become involved with details unless they're part of the contact."

Marini rubbed his chin. "Let me see if I've got this right: you get an order to cripple one of the most outstanding pitchers in all of baseball, a man whose injury will produce headlines across the country, whose assault will attract the police like flies to shit, and *you*, fully familiar with how much we want to avoid any contact with celebrities, you go ahead and sanction it. Accurate summary?"

Ginetti nodded his head once.

"Did you at least have enough brains to call your manager before you went ahead with this ... this monumental fuckup?" Marini threw his half-smoked cigarette onto the floor and ground it out with a shoe as wide as a tennis racket.

"No, Don Marini, I didn't."

"And so it gets better, doesn't it? Having completely fucked up by having Whitney shot on a public street—in front of his fucking wife, for chrissake—you then figure you can clean up the mess by taking out the shooter, this Swampy Royce character. Does it hurt when you have your head shoved that far up your ass?"

"Don Marini ... "

"You'd better shut the hell up!"

Ginetti knew that this was no time to shut up. If he shut up now, the odds were real good that he'd be shut up permanently. He kept talking. "Don Marini, I did *not* have Royce killed. *That* did not come through me. I knew nothing about it. *Nothing*!"

Marini was unmoved. "So you say. You know that I've already personally spoken with Don Morelli about this. In turn, he told me that you called your manager right away and denied the hit? They don't believe it any more than I do. Such firepower isn't used, outside of the drug assholes, by anyone but us. But no, *you* had nothing to do with it!"

Marini stood up and loomed over Ginetti, who sensed the man behind him take two steps closer. He could almost hear the bullet entering the back of his head. He had to talk faster, say more.

"I swear I had nothing to do with Royce's killing. He was connected to us, but I know he's hands-off without specific approval. And I didn't request any approval because I didn't need approval for something I wasn't going to do." Talking even faster: "For fourteen years I've obeyed the rules. I'm going to retire in a few years. Why would I risk all that? I've got dozens of guys like Royce. If I was gonna take out Royce, you can bet I'd have made less of a mess. I was as surprised as anyone."

Marini paced impatiently throughout Ginetti's frantic speech. The aged floorboards, no longer used to visitors, creaked and popped under Marini's restless weight. "That occurred to me. To your credit, to Don Morelli and your manager, as well. Not your style. Worse, it doesn't make any sense. None. That's what bothers us. A careful guy like you fucks up twice in a matter of days? Twice? I'll tell you one thing for goddamn sure. It'll make sense before I leave here."

Ginetti knew all too well that when someone became a problem, especially someone who doesn't "make sense," the easiest way to solve the problem was to eliminate that someone. He'd arranged it too many times not to know that. If it were about to happen to him, he'd go with his head up and his back straight. But he was damned if he was going to fall for Royce or Whitney. *If Marini's ass is in a sling, it's his own damn fault.*

"Don Marini, I did *not* fuck up. I had nothing to do with Royce. *Nothing.* I admit that I was reluctant to make the arrangements for Whitney, but I did it because, as a practical matter, really, I had no choice."

Marini slammed his fist into his open palm. "I'm sick to fucking death of going around in circles with you. I agree one hundred percent that you had no choice. Because you don't have the authority to take out a public figure *unless* you have your manager's authorization. And you know that—just as I know firsthand that you didn't have it. Because I asked your manager—in Don Morelli's presence, by the way—so there'd be no fucking doubt."

"But, Don Marini . . . I . . . you . . . it wasn't *my manager* who authorized it." Frustrated, angry and scared beyond description, Ginetti started to stand up. Mistake. He didn't reach his full height before both guards withdrew handguns from their shoulder holsters and pointed them at his head. He froze as if he'd been dropped into liquid nitrogen. Very slowly and deliberately, he lowered himself back into his chair, holding both arms away from his sides. "Don Marini, you know that I can be authorized by another Don, regardless of territory, in addition to my manager."

Marini hovered over Ginetti like the personification of doom. He less spoke than growled through his clenched teeth: "You mean to tell me that the Whitney contract was sanctioned by a *Don*!"

Ginetti looked at the mammoth head and the fierce eyes of the ruthless capo. "I don't understand. How . . . Why would you be surprised? It was my clear understanding it was authorized by a Don like you. You . . . "

Ginetti wasn't given the chance to finish the sentence. Marini's open right hand, the size of a ping-pong paddle, slapped the left side of his face and flung him across the room. When Ginetti hit the hardwood floor, he slid a further four feet until the top of his head slammed against the wall. He was dazed when

Marini rolled him over, grabbed him by the front of his coat, and hauled him to his feet. Blood trickled from his cut lip, which was quickly swelling.

Marini again slapped Ginetti. The punctured lip exploded in a spray of blood. He spun down the wall of the room. Ginetti managed to turn over and pull himself into a sitting position against the wall, with his legs stretched out in front of him. His white shirt and tie were stained with the blood now cascading down his chin. He spat blood and saliva onto the floor. Marini grabbed him by the front of his coat and lifted him upward. Ginetti grabbed Marini's wrist and mumbled "Please . . . "

Marini's fury was unrestrained. His guards glanced at each other, silently noting how deadly their boss could be when aroused. "You've got balls, you chickenshit bastard, to try to drag me in on this! *Me*! You dumb fuck, don't you think I know whom I call? When I speak to someone about a contract, you can damn well be sure that I remember. You piece of shit."

Marini pulled Ginetti further upward.

Ginetti muttered through his battered lips. "Not *you* . . . Said *like* you.

Marini held Ginetti against the wall, but didn't hit him again. "Like . . . not like . . . what the fuck's *that* mean?"

Ginetti tried to enunciate. It wasn't easy. "Said *like* you . . . a Don *like you* . . . Not *you*."

Marini let go of Ginetti's jacket, letting him slump back to the floor in a sitting position. He knelt down and glared into Ginetti's face. "You're about out of time. Better make it good."

Ginetti's jaw and lip hurt with each spoken word. "The Salesman . . . my counterpart in Cincinnati . . . called me. Needed an assist. Doesn't happen often, but it happens. Gave me the details, and I recognized the name. Big-deal baseball player. Against the rules, too much heat. I didn't like it and said so, but he assured me it was okay. Authorized by his manager and Don Tullio. That was his exact word, 'authorized'."

Marini shook his head incredulously. "You accepted that? Someone tells you it's okay, so you just go ahead and do it?"

"No. The Salesman isn't just *someone*. He's got the territory just east of mine ... You know all this ... We've helped each other over the years. Like I said, it happens every now and again. I had no reason to doubt him. What's he gonna do? Lie? No fucking way. But I asked again, point blank, 'Don Tullio's sanctioned this?' And he says, 'You got it.' That was good enough for me. I do it."

Marini stood up, but his eyes remained locked on Ginetti's. "If you're jerking me off, you'd better think long and hard, because dying will be easier than staying alive."

"I'm not. Ask The Salesman. He'll tell you."

"And if he doesn't?"

Ginetti's blood chilled. That was possible. If he'd been set up by The Salesman, it was possible. It wasn't as if he had a signed receipt. "Then I guess you'll wonder why I'd make it up. If I'm lying, then why did I make it so easy to trace it back to me. Not much of a secret, was it? Believe me, I'd have left myself a way better out."

Marini straightened his coat and tie. "You can damn well bet I'm going to find out, Dante. If—I say again, *if*—you're on the level, you'll find out that I've got enough class to express my apologies in a proper manner. For now we'll leave it at that."

Ginetti remained seated on the floor as Marini and his two bodyguards left. He was ashamed that his trousers were damp.

Chapter 38

Friday afternoon, August 2, City of Walnut Creek

WHEN KENMUIR RETURNED FROM LUNCH, a telephone message was on his desk: "Mr. Roberson called. Please call before 2:30, your time."

Kenmuir returned the call immediately. "Tell me, Neil, you going to start wearing polyester leisure suits like the boys in Organized Crime?"

"Not likely. Though that might've made it easier. There was some reluctance at first. Everybody's always paranoid around here about something. But once they started talking, I learned a lot. Interesting stuff."

"Do I wait for a formal report?"

"By all means, wait for a formal report. Or you can listen and then forget where you heard what I can tell you right now."

"I think I'll pick . . . Number two."

"Good. It seems that this Broker guy and the others like him—and the answer to your next question is yes, he's not the only one—might as well have been created by the U.S. government, almost like they passed a civil service exam."

Roberson explained that organized crime for decades had maintained an internal system of self-discipline and a peculiar brand of rules enforcement. It took care of itself and, as needed, those competitors who interfered. Meanwhile, official law enforcement left it largely alone, like an unruly child who's permitted to do what he wants in his room so long as he doesn't bother the adults.

Then came the Kefauver Committee and its imitators at the state level. The FBI and various congressional committees started watching constantly. It got so the lowliest functionary couldn't even take a dump without the FBI knowing how many sheets of toilet paper he used. So organized crime reorganized. Mimicking the government, it created its own sub-agencies and local subsidiaries.

"The OC guys actually laughed about it. The new arrangement completely fucked up the FBI. They kept watching, but nothing seemed to be happening. But they were wrong. Everything was still functioning. Operations simply had been splintered and then spread around to an assortment of separate contractors. By the time the FBI figured it out, there were too many places to look, and not enough people to do the looking. Where they'd been able to shine one big light, now they needed ten, twenty. All that made the heat on organized crime start to die down.

"Ironically, the new arrangement provided two unexpected bonuses for organized crime: The contractors became a sort of minor league system that trained, and often weeded out, younger members who wanted to move up. Also, they could more conveniently subcontract with specialists or guys who didn't mesh with the regular crowd.

"And some contactors weren't independent at all. They remained within the general organization, but operated semi-independently in providing a variety of services. They were, in effect, franchises, sort of a 'McCrime.' You got a monopoly in a defined territory, but you had to work off a set menu and had to avoid politicians, cops, entertainers, or others who'd attract too much attention. Drugs sales and trafficking also were *verboten*.

"To guard against any franchisee becoming independently powerful, each was assigned a kind of liaison—called a 'manager'—with the main organization. The manager changed every three years, was determined randomly, and reported to a Don. That way, no permanent alliance could be formed between whoever was running the franchise and his manager. Best of all, if he got busted, it was his ass and not the organization's.

"A few franchisees have been busted over the years. When that happened, there was a gap of a few months until a replacement arrived and continued business as usual. It may not be flawless, but it's damn effective."

"Which, I gather, brings us to The Broker."

"True. That's the code name of one of the franchisees."

"Great. Who's he, and where do I find him?"

"You don't. Neither do I. The OC guys were willing to talk about history and general knowledge, but when it came to the present and specifics, they shut down fast."

"C'mon, Neil. You can't leave me hanging like this. History's great, but I'm being shot at *now*. You must've learned something."

"Sorry, but I could only patch together bits and pieces. For example, The Broker's territory evidently is the upper Midwest, more or less, though he isn't there personally. I get the impression he's somewhere in Texas. Dallas? Houston?"

"Who calls his shots?"

"Well, if I get it, by his manager and the Don over him."

"That, I understand. I meant names."

"They didn't say, and I didn't ask. You've got to keep in mind that I was treading on thin ice here. If I started getting too explicit with questions, they'd wonder why. It was supposed to be a casual chat, not a deposition."

Kenmuir smashed out a cigarette in the astray on his desk. Part anger and part frustration. "And that's it?"

"Not entirely. Apparently there's a gradual changing of the guard under way. For example, the so-called Salesman works somewhere in the Ohio Valley. He's described by OC as young, college educated, might as well be a stockbroker." Roberson laughed. "Or a lawyer, for that matter."

"Fine training for any salesman. What's his name?"

"They didn't say. However, they did allude to the Don over him, some goombah named Tullio, who in turn is very tight with a high mucky-muck in your neck of the woods. Some capo named Marano . . . Mariani . . . something like that."

Kenmuir leaned his executive chair backward and shook his head in disbelief. "Or Marini? *Angelo Marini?*"

"Could be, I guess. Sounds close. Anyway, what's interesting for OC are rumors of a growing, behind-the-scenes clash between the older and younger generations. They think it revolves around a guy named MacPherson, improbably enough. I mean, where's the vowel at the end of that name? They say he's a cold bastard, but smart as hell, and a real comer." Roberson paused distinctly and ended with, "Like I said, bits and pieces."

Quite a provocative collection of bits and pieces. MacPherson again . . . MacPherson arranged for LaPera? Maybe . . . Now he's connected with The Salesman? Maybe . . . And The Salesman runs a territory, like The Broker, but reports to an underling of Marini's? Evidently . . . Could MacPherson be clashing with Marini inside the organization? Maybe . . . Time for another visit with MacPherson? Certainly.

Chapter 39

Wednesday afternoon, August 7, City of Blackhawk

MARINI'S FOREBEARS HAD COME from Terzigno in the shadow of Mt. Vesuvius. For some, that explained his volcanic temper. His anger had smoldered during his brooding return from Oklahoma City. Self-control came hard.

Ginetti understood correctly that The Salesman's manager reported to Sal "the Sap" Tullio. What he didn't realize was that Tullio was subordinate to Marini and, even more, was Marini's boyhood companion. They'd grown up together and joined the organization at the same time. To the extent that Marini trusted anyone, he trusted Tullio.

Marini called Tullio as soon as he returned and summarized, loudly, what he'd learned from Ginetti. "Who do you suppose fucking authorized the contract on Whitney, a fucking all-star and one of the most popular sonsabitches in the whole goddamn Midwest? Who do you suppose *that* brilliant motherfucker was?"

Tullio had known Marini for too many years not to sense the menace in his voice. "Beats me, but I sure as shit know who it *wasn't*."

"Horseshit. The Salesman requested it." Marini shouted, "It didn't occur to you to fucking ask him about it?!"

Tullio gritted his teeth and held his own temper. "Look, Ange, I had nothing *to* ask. I only learned about it *after* it happened. Maybe it seemed like a dumb-fuck thing to do, but it wasn't my call. Ginetti doesn't report to me. Until you started yelling, I had no fuckin' idea that The Salesman . . . that Tony . . . had anything to do with it. Despite whatever's gotten up your ass, I still don't."

"Well, old friend, you don't know the half of it."

"Christ, there's another half?"

"Sure as hell is. According to Ginetti, Tony said that the contract was authorized by none other than you."

It was Tullio's turn to blow. "That's bullshit! You know me better than that. Run a deal behind your fuckin' back and use your own guy to do it? No fuckin' way. I don't have your fuckin' brains, but I ain't fuckin' dumb. And I sure as hell ain't crazy."

"For once I agree with you, Sal. You ain't got my fuckin' brains, you dumb wop."

Although Tullio laughed at Marini's effort to break the tension, he persisted. "Okay, Ange, let's think about it for a minute: What d'we know for sure? For openers, someone's blowin' smoke up our asses. Dante gave the order. He either did it on his own or, like he says, as a courtesy. I gather you don't think he's runnin' his own fuckin' scam."

Marini had chewed on that since Oklahoma. "No, I don't. He's too straight. Everything by the book. He's got no imagination. Hell, that's why he was put there in the first place. Also, if he were going to fuck around, why Tony? It's too easy to check."

The cyclone on Marini's side of the line had blown by. Now it was time for Tullio's own storm. "It's time someone had a chat with the cock-sucking Salesman, I'd say."

A Deadly Game

"I agree. That's your job, not mine."

That was the answer Tullio wanted and the one he knew Marini preferred. "That it is, Ange. I'll take fuckin' care of it."

"Make it fast, Sal."

Tullio's personal relationship with Marini had allowed him to rise higher in the organization than he would've on his own. He knew that, but he also knew that their friendship didn't confer immunity. Marini could charm your socks off, but only so he didn't have to bother removing them before he buried you. He could be utterly merciless.

If he came up with answers, his friendship with Marini would remain intact and life, including his own, would go on. If he didn't, Marini would find answers without him and life still would go on, though quite possibly without him.

He was going to get some answers.

Friday afternoon, August 9, City of Cincinnati

TULLIO DECIDED TO STAGE HIS MEETING with The Salesman as a routine checkup. Appointment in advance. Business as usual. Nothing to worry about. Like many of the younger franchisees, thirty-seven-year-old Anthony Carmel—"Carmelini" had been truncated long ago by parents whose ambitions for their son looked beyond Little Italy—was a graduate of mainstream society. No ethnic enclave, no abbreviated schooling, no head-knocking apprenticeship. His background was no different than any other privileged son of a moneyed father: prep school, Ivy League college, Ivy League MBA.

His battles had been fought in the cafeteria line, not the street. He'd learned how to finesse final exams, not how to bully local officials. His weapons of choice were numbers and words. He was a cultured man who worked for a very lucrative business, not a fraternity. He certainly had no childish nickname from life on the streets, bashing bodies and hanging around the bar or the deli; "The Salesman" came with the job assignment and wasn't personal.

He considered his organizational superiors, like Sal Tullio, as uneducated and lumpish cavemen who had no place in a modern organization. Such relics were a disgrace, from their ignorance of even the most basic business principles to their disgusting table manners, boorish language, and caricature camaraderie with the rest of their *paisan* buddies. As soon as possible, they'd be packed off to Vegas or Arizona or Florida or wherever they went to die. In the meantime, taking orders from the "immigrants" was both galling and exasperating.

He wasn't alone in his thinking. While the dinosaurs, awash in magnums of red wine, were shouting their reminiscences at each other, stuffing their bloated bellies with piles of pasta, and congratulating themselves on how much ass they'd kicked, Carmel and his friends were sipping rare cabernets, discussing potential computer applications, and talking about the future.

It was only a matter of time before they were the governing elite. Unfortunately, that time hadn't yet come. So he had to be cautious and accommodating, especially since he and the others—with the exception of his talented friend Jeff MacPherson, who was oddly unintimidated—were wary about the older generation's tendency to resort to violence when pushed.

When Tullio telephoned the day before to say he'd be "dropping by" on his way to New York, Carmel pretended that he'd be as welcome as his-and-her sinks in a master bathroom. And

A Deadly Game

so it was that Carmel embraced the older man when he arrived and clapped him affectionately on the back. "Don Tullio, good to see you. You're looking well."

Carmel truly would've been baffled by Tullio's private attitude. He assumed that Tullio and his ilk were awed by his education and polish. *As they should be.*

In fact, everything Carmel thought about Tullio, Tullio thought in reverse: *Fucking college wimps. Don't know shit about shit. Think they can find it all in those dickless computers.*

Carmel also was mistaken about Tullio's appreciation of business principles. He understood them very well: when push came to shove, you damn well better be able to shove a helluva lot harder than the other guy. Brains are great, but in the end, it's all about power: I'm stronger than you, so you do what I say. In Tullio's mind, that would be one of today's lessons for the college boy.

"Right. You too, Tony." Tullio motioned toward the sofa and said, "Gotta get off my fuckin' feet. Let's be comfortable."

He sat in one corner of the sofa and Carmel sat in the other. Tullio's bodyguard, a 22-year-old high school dropout from the Bronx, pulled a chair away from the conference table, and sat a discreet distance away.

For the next forty minutes, they discussed the state of The Salesman's recent contracts. What'd been concluded, what was pending, how expenses were comparing with fees. The conversation moved in familiar grooves. Business as usual. During the conversation, Tullio offhandedly alluded to a situation being handled by The Broker. "You do know Dante Ginetti, don't you?"

Carmel couldn't have been more surprised if Tullio had referred to social themes in the novels of Jane Austen. Of course he'd met Ginetti. Tullio should know that, shouldn't he? In all their past meetings, Tullio'd never mentioned another territory. *Why now? What's on his mind?*

"Depends what you mean by *know*. I've met him a couple of times, that's all. Don't really *know* him. He's not part of my crowd." Carmel flinched. "Not *my* crowd, I didn't mean it that way." Carmel heard the defensive tone in his voice and had to regain a casual composure. "Why do you ask?"

Tullio realized that Carmel and Ginetti must've met sometime. Nothing wrong with that, as Carmel should've known. He was momentarily flustered and shouldn't have been. *Got you, you little fuck. Now we'll find out why.* "Nothin'. Just askin'. I've been thinking maybe we need better coordination between territories. If you gotta trade a favor, we don't have no set procedure. But it fuckin' happens. Like, has The Broker ever helped you out?"

Smart and elegant, cultivated and cocky, Carmel nodded at the smiling face of the beast before him. *It can't be, but could this be about Whitney's shooting? Is that why he's here? Is someone pissed? How pissed? Why pissed? Be very careful.* "Sure. We've exchanged courtesies. I've helped him a couple times, and he's helped me." He chuckled self-consciously. "I think I'm ahead, though. Probably helped him more than the other way around."

"Yeah? What about Whitney? Help you with *that* one?"

Carmel didn't know what he'd do first, vomit or pass out. Instead, he opted for screwing The Broker. Every man for himself. "Whitney? The baseball player?"

Tullio nodded matter-of-factly. "Only one I know of."

"No." Carmel acted like he was thinking about it. "No, in fact, I didn't know that was The Broker's contract. Besides, if I'd had anything to do with it, I'd naturally have checked with you first." *What the hell's going on? Jeff explicitly said he'd cover it with Tullio.*

"Naturally."

Carmel couldn't stop. "No . . . Whitney? No. Don't know anything about it."

Tullio shrugged his shoulders. "Then we have a problem."

"Problem? What kind of problem?"

"Well, kid, it goes something like this: The Broker says the assignment came from you. You know what else? That you told him *I* fuckin' authorized it. Ain't that a kick in the ass?"

Carmel's mind raced. *Which way to jump? Tullio's asking questions, so maybe he doesn't know all that much. Shit, maybe I'm worrying too much about me. Maybe it's about The Broker. He can't prove anything. It's his word against mine. Or maybe it's about Jeff. To hell with both of them. I'll play it cool. No way Tullio or any other boss is going to turn off one of the brightest lights in the organization because of some baseball player. I'm too valuable. Hell, I am the future.* "Ginetti's lying. It's a damn lie. He's trying to cover himself. What, my word against his?"

"Don't really matter, 'cause we already know who's telling the truth. What we don't know is why." Tullio stretched his right arm across the back of the sofa, relaxed and unthreatening. The conciliatory old pro. "Hey, I came here. I didn't order you to come to me. This is just talk. So talk to me and I'll get outta here, and we can both get back to makin' money."

I'm being given a way out. The Broker's not dead or I'd have heard. He walked away because he told them what he knew. I'll tell them and I'll walk away. Besides, it wasn't my idea. Me and The Broker, we're just men in the middle. I tell the truth and take my medicine and Tullio reports to whomever . . . Marini? . . . and that'll be that. If it's Jeff, he can take care of himself. "All right . . . Don Tullio." *Time for respect and deference. Dons get off on that.* "I'm sorry if I obfuscated. I was taken by surprise and wasn't thinking straight."

"Hey, it happens." *You're gonna be thinking straight soon enough. College asshole.*

"There's not much to it, really. One night at dinner I was asked to arrange a hit on Whitney. I ask, 'Who's Whitney?' I'm not much of a baseball fan. I didn't worry too much about it because the friend I'm having dinner with, he and I've done some things in the past. No big deal, right?"

It doesn't get any bigger. "Right. No big deal."

"Well, that's all there was to it. I called The Broker and gave him the details. Left it in his hands. *C'est tout.*" Carmel liked to use the occasional French phrase.

Tullio drummed his fingers on the back of the couch. It was the only outward sign of his agitation. "I see. It made sense because you and this 'friend' had done that sort of thing before. Why this time?"

"I owed him. Like I said, he'd done me some favors over the years, and I felt obliged to help him out. I mean, it wasn't like I was dealing with an outsider. I never would've done that." Carmel chuckled as if Tullio were a co-conspirator. "Let's face it. No one else helps us, so we better help ourselves. Don't you agree?"

"Definitely." *I definitely agree that you're a fucking idiot. That's what I agree.* "Who's the friend?"

A Deadly Game

Carmel already anticipated having to give up the name, but didn't want to appear disloyal. "Have to tell you... Don Tullio... I'm a little reluctant. I wouldn't want him to take any heat over this. He's very dedicated to the organization, works hard, and is a good man. Can't we just let that part go?"

Tullio was tempted to laugh out loud and be done with it. *This jerk-off wimp thinks he's been called into the principal's office over some fucking prank. He doesn't want to snitch out his buddy because the boys at Alpha Beta Asshole don't do that sort of thing.* "No can do. We've got to get this whole thing squared away. Who's the other guy?"

"I don't like doing this." Carmel breathed deeply in a final show of discomfort. "But it's Jeff MacPherson."

It was Tullio's turn to be surprised. "MacPherson in California?"

"One and the same. A good man. He and I went to grad school together."

"Christ, you and Little Petey. Quite a team."

"Well, I wouldn't say we're a team. Just two friends trying to do our jobs and attend to business." Carmel smiled ingratiatingly.

"I don't want any mistake about this. *You* set up the contract on Whitney—which was strictly between you and Petey—because *he* asked you to? That about sum it up?"

Makes it sound much more simple than it was. But, in fact ... "Yes, it does."

"Anything else I should know? No loose fuckin' ends, because I'm gonna be pissed if I have to come back."

Carmel all but stood up and cheered when he heard "come back." *No need to come back unless he expects me to still be here. Thank God. I've dodged this bullet.* "No, there's nothing more. Just trying to do a favor for a friend."

Tullio slapped his hands on his knees. "Well, that's it, I think." As he stood up, so did the Bronx high-school dropout. Before he opened the office door, Tullio turned around and faced Carmel. "You know what I can't fuckin' figure out, Tony?"

"What's that?"

"You went to all those fancy schools, and I never got through high school. What I can't figure out is why you're so fucking *dumb.*"

For Anthony Carmel, whiz kid and future Don, too much happened at the same time. He heard Tullio's insult, saw the long nose of a silenced automatic emerge from the bodyguard's coat, and felt a searing pain burrow through his stomach. The pain was brief, but only because he felt nothing at all after the second bullet passed through the middle of his forehead.

Tullio glanced down at Carmel's sprawled body. "We don't beat people up anymore, motherfucker. We just 'obfuscate' their asses."

The two high-school dropouts were laughing as they left Carmel's office.

Friday evening, August 9, City of Blackhawk

TULLIO'S ORAL REPORT HAD BEEN AS POINTED as a stiletto. He'd described what he learned and the consequences. End of conversation.

Marini now leaned back in his padded leather chair and lifted his huge feet onto the gleaming surface of his mahogany desk.

He was surprised he wasn't angrier. He should've been furious, but he wasn't. He was disappointed and even a bit saddened.

Many of Carmel's assumptions had been correct. In Marini's vision of the future, Carmel *was* one of the heirs apparent, those who'd lead the organization into the next century. Marini foresaw that, as the nature of the business was changing, so the organization's style had to change as well. The older Dons wanted the familiar patterns and behaviors to last forever, but they wouldn't. Business in the 1950s wasn't business in the 1980s; and 1980s business wouldn't be business in the 2000s, either. The organization had survived and thrived *because* it found men who could adapt. Men like him and, in the near future, men like Carmel and MacPherson.

Marini and his contemporaries had to be both leaders and mentors, smoothing the passage between the generations. That was one reason why he'd paid special attention to Petey MacPherson. The other reason was sentimental, how pleased Don Marraccini would've been with his grandson's promise and progress, and with how Marini was looking after Petey as he'd once trained, guided, and sometimes disciplined Marini himself. "That's the nature of a family," the old man often had said.

However, Marini admitted to himself, he didn't *like* MacPherson. Oh, there was no doubt that McPherson had intelligence, ambition, and ruthlessness—but he was too arrogant and impatient in their use. If he were going to direct others, he first had to learn to direct himself and realize that men behaved more according to their guts than their brains. In short, a leader of other men had to be respected as well as feared, shrewd as well as smart. Marini wished MacPherson were more like this man Kenmuir.

On the other hand, MacPherson's peers seemed untroubled by his haughty manner. They regularly solicited him for direction and guidance. More's the pity, but perhaps the characteristics, even the assets, of the future were what MacPherson had. However, if not, there were others with more traditional skills who could be groomed instead.

Marini was a patient man, and had time to watch the next generation develop. But he wasn't patient today . . . Little Petey, for god's sake. He didn't even have a franchise. He'd simply gone maverick. Issuing unsanctioned contracts was inexcusable enough—and someone must have paid many thousands for them—but he'd done it for his own profit. Such a man was dangerous. Such a man was intolerable. Such a man was condemned. There was no choice.

MacPherson had to be confronted before he learned about Carmel's death, which would surely be after the weekend. One unreturned telephone call . . . one of what would be many rumors . . . something. That would give him time to plan how to react.

MacPherson was resourceful. Given time, who knew what he'd do? Cut a deal with the Feds? Try to bargain with duplicated or stolen records, hidden somewhere to be released on his death? Threaten through an intermediary after giving some reporter just enough information to be worrisome? He'd do something—*if* he had enough time to assemble his thoughts into some clever package.

Time would be Petey's ally, and he could be permitted no allies. No. He had to be caught off-guard. Marini knew that tomorrow McPheson would be at his weekend home in the wooded hills of the Napa Valley. He could be summoned back, but that would alert him. He'd telephone to ask why it couldn't be dealt with over the telephone. *No, I want our confrontation to be face-to-face. I want to see the bastard's face.*

Tomorrow Marini would drive to the Napa Valley.

Chapter 40

Saturday afternoon, August 10, City of Napa

E VERY GOLFER AND GAMBLER KNOWS it's better to be lucky than good. Kenmuir got lucky several months earlier when a friend had asked him to be his guest at Silverado Country Club's Summer Twilight Shoot-Out tournament. The club, located on the eastern edge of the City of Napa and at the foot of the fabled Silverado Trail, was a gracious setting for members and resort visitors alike. Kenmuir had accepted enthusiastically.

The day began with a 2 p.m. shotgun start on the North Course, followed by cocktails and a barbecue dinner in the picnic grove at 6 p.m. By 8 p.m., some couples migrated to the Mansion for more cocktails and others strolled back to their guest condominiums for a form of dessert. It was time for bachelors to go home.

If Kenmuir hadn't stopped for gas at the Chevron station at the end of Soscol Boulevard, he wouldn't have been standing outside his car, watching the traffic pass by in the faded light, and wouldn't have seen a limousine turn toward the Silverado Trail. He recognized the limousine because he'd ridden in it. It was Marini's.

He'd learned that MacPherson commonly spent the weekend at his retreat somewhere in the Napa Valley hills and suspected that's where Marini was headed. He immediately cleared the pump and followed.

Southbound traffic on the Trail was heavy, as the last wine tasters drove tentatively homeward in the dim light, but northbound traffic was so sparse that Kenmuir struggled to keep a car between him and the limousine. Even when he did, the camouflaging car would turn after a mile or so and make Kenmuir as visible as a bathrobe at a formal dinner.

From a quarter-mile back, Kenmuir saw the limousine turn right at the Angwin turnoff and begin its ascent into the hills. Kenmuir followed. Within a mile, he saw the limousine parked in a turnout where the road veered sharply uphill. He also saw Dino aka Hair Dickey standing in the open and motioning for someone to pull over. Because Kenmuir's was the only car on the road, Kenmuir wasn't puzzled about who was being told to pull over. So he did.

In the turnout, he stopped some distance short of the rear of the limousine. He stepped outside, but remained standing by the open door. He looked at Dino and Dino looked back. Their standoff only needed gunfighter music.

Dino finally walked to Kenmuir. "Not much at tailing someone, are you, hotshot?"

Kenmuir shrugged noncommittally. "Tailing you? Not at all. Merely sampling some of the finer vintages in the area."

"At night? You're all bullshit. Either way, the boss wants to see you."

When Kenmuir reached the limousine, he saw Marini alone in the spacious passenger compartment and Muscular Man behind the wheel. From the interior came a growl, "Get in here, Kenmuir."

After the door closed, Marini said, "Dino picked you out miles back. We gave you plenty of chance to turn away but, no, you stayed on our ass the whole way. What the hell d'you think you're doing?"

Now I know how Nixon felt. Lie or confess? At worst, I'm put in my car and told to get the hell out of here. Maybe good advice. Nah, go with the truth. "Believe it or not, I was getting gas when I saw this boat of yours cruise by. I decided to tag along. All very spontaneous."

Marini shook his head in disgust. "Why do that?"

"Because I think you're on your way to MacPherson's place and, if I follow, I find out where that is. Haven't really thought about what comes after that."

"I told you that MacPherson was my concern, *not* yours."

Kenmuir turned sideways to face Marini. The thickly padded leather seats squeaked beneath him. "True, but circumstances have changed. He sent the two assholes to shoot me in my own house. I know it and by now I assume you do, too. Plus, he's behind Orr's murder and probably what's happened to the other ballplayers. He and I are going to have to come to terms with each other eventually. The immovable object and the unstoppable force. Maybe up here's a possibility, now that I've seen you. Providence or just dumb luck, depending on your point of view."

Marini glared at Kenmuir. "You know goddamn well what my point of view is."

Kenmuir held his hands open as a sign of surrender. "What happens now?"

"If I leave you behind, I don't know where you are. If I take you with me, at least I know what you're doing. Or *not* doing. So you come with me, *but* you do what I say, and you don't argue. Clear?"

"Perfectly."

Now with Kenmuir inside, the limousine made a U-turn, returned to the Silverado Trail, and continued north. About two miles beyond Duckhorn Vineyards, Kenmuir's favorite vintner of merlot, the limousine left the Trail and began to wind upward into the hills overlooking the valley. It was dark by the time they reached the front gate of the fence surrounding MacPherson's estate. When the limousine stopped on the shoulder of the road, Marini said, "This is as far as you go, Kenmuir. From here on, it's between me and him."

Kenmuir shook his head disapprovingly. "I think I'll just tag along. I suspect that what's behind your quarrel is the same as mine. Same end by different routes. Besides, I'm the one who got shot at, not you."

"Don't push it. *This* is how far you go." He stabbed one of his stubby fingers in the direction of the passenger door. "Out. I've got no time for bullshit."

No subtle interpretation of body language was needed to perceive that Marini wasn't in a mood for a clubby discussion of possible alternatives. The alternatives were reduced to one: get out of the car.

Kenmuir got out of the car.

The limousine drove forward a short distance. The driver spoke into an intercom attached to the end of a bent metal post, ironically as if ordering a double Whopper and large fries to go. The radio-activated mechanical gate parted immediately, and the limousine eased forward impatiently, anxious for the gates to open wide enough. Finally, it climbed the slight incline of the driveway. Even after its lights had disappeared over the top of the hill, Kenmuir could hear the gravel surface crackling under the tires.

It was completely dark, with no artificial light visible in any direction. If other residences were nearby, the owners were either not at home or were practicing for an air raid. Precious little light came from the moon and then only enough to see stumps where trees had been cut. The woods were balmy, a few degrees beyond cool, even though the valley floor was quite warm. Kenmuir's light jacket was back there somewhere, in his own car. At least he'd changed into long pants for dinner.

Kenmuir sensed that swarms of hungry bugs had been alerted and now were banding for a nocturnal assault. Their target? The idiot seated on a short stump, wearing only a thin golf shirt that they could easily bite through. Yum.

Kenmuir and the night birds heard the sound of a car door slamming from the direction of MacPherson's house at the same time. The birds flew out of the trees and disappeared into the darkness. Kenmuir couldn't fly, so he remained perched on his stump. "Lucky for us, Video Rangers," he said to himself, "we have our secret decoder watches for emergencies like this." His luminous watch glowed that four minutes had elapsed since the limousine drove out of sight. He badly wanted to be down that driveway.

Then the stillness of the forest was broken again. This time by two shots, not quite blended into one. Handguns, not rifles. Kenmuir had heard such sounds hundreds of times. *It's over. But what's over? And over for whom?*

He backed into the shadows of the trees at the edge of the driveway. Forest shadows meant safety. *What now, hero? I'll wait, but not too long. If the shots were fired by Marini's men, they should be out of there soon. If not, I'll have to mosey on up to the house to ask my buddy MacPherson if I can use his phone to call a cab. Five minutes. I'll wait five minutes.*

Kenmuir found a tree whose limbs drooped over the cyclone fence. He climbed it and edged along a limb until he could drop on the other side of the fence. Four minutes had passed. Close enough.

He moved stealthily amid the pine trees, fifteen or twenty feet from the edge of the driveway. Moonlight filtered through the dense branches, but his puny shadow was devoured by the much larger shadows of trees. No one would expect him to be here. If the limousine appeared, he'd step out and wave it down. If it didn't, he'd do something else. Not sure what, but something.

MacPherson's log "cabin" wasn't that of your average pioneer. It could serve either as a ski mansion in Aspen or as a stockade if hostile savages might someday be marauding in the Napa Valley. The windows of the first floor were ablaze with light; those on the second floor were dark. The wooden, elevated deck in front mimicked the rough-hewn exterior. Landscaping consisted of about a trillion pine needles and the surrounding trees that had survived the clearing of the building pad.

Marini's unoccupied limousine was parked near the steps to the deck. No one was visible and nothing was moving. Kenmuir slanted his route deeper into the woods, zig-zagging from tree trunk to tree trunk, always keeping one between him and the cabin. He moved irregularly, since even an unwary lookout might notice a consistent movement in an otherwise motionless forest.

Approximately a hundred yards from the cabin, he knelt down in order to shrink his silhouette and to eliminate any shadow. He could clearly see the front door and deck. Two shots had been fired. Assuming that someone wasn't practicing with coffee cans, then either MacPherson or Marini was short a soldier . . . or maybe two. On the other hand, why hadn't anyone fired back?

Almost as if on cue, the front door opened, and light flooded the limousine and the deck. The two men who emerged might have been twins: Each was over six feet tall and broad-chested, each was dressed in Levis and a flannel shirt, and held a handgun casually at his side.

They silently answered all of Kenmuir's questions except one: Was Marini still alive?

MacPherson's two men spoke briefly at the bottom of the steps and then parted. One walked out of sight around the far side of the house. The other walked up the driveway in no hurry, the insouciance of a soldier who's been on the same patrol too often. Nothing had ever happened before, so why would it now? Such casualness was understandable, but foolish. It could kill.

Kenmuir could leave as invisibly as he came. It'd be a long walk back to civilization, but he'd endured long walks before. However, to walk away would be to abandon Marini, if he were still alive. He rejected that option consciously, as he already had instinctively: He wouldn't abandon Marini.

The guard sauntered up the driveway; he had no reason to be alarmed. Gravel crunched loudly under his feet as he hummed an unrecognizable tune; his handgun hung loosely beside his right thigh. When he passed Kenmuir's position, he glanced perfunctorily into the unlit depth of the forest. He didn't notice that, three trees deep into the forest, one dark trunk had a slight bulge.

Kenmuir expected that the guard would only go as far as the top of the hill, since he could see from there if the gate were closed. If so, he'd turn around and walk back.

The guard continued trudging toward the top of the small hill. Within the forest shadows, Kenmuir moved behind him. The indistinct rustle of pine needles couldn't be heard over the guard's crunching of gravel. Kenmuir stepped behind a thick tree trunk near the edge of the driveway and disappeared from view.

At the top of the hill, the guard looked toward the gate. He held his arms above his head and stretched, silhouetting the handgun against the moonlit sky. He lowered his arms and lit a cigarette, kicked at the gravel, and let his eyes wander over the valley. He was relaxed and not at all in a hurry. After finishing his cigarette, he strolled down the hill as inattentively as he'd walked up it, again in the middle of the narrow driveway.

He eventually passed by a broad tree trunk no different from dozens of others inside the cyclone fence. Because he didn't look, he didn't see a shadow separate from the trunk and step silently behind him. Kenmuir encircled the front of the guard's neck with his left forearm and grabbed the top of his head with his right hand, digging his fingertips into the man's forehead. A deadly circle was formed when Kenmuir's left hand locked onto the crook of his right elbow. At the instant when the lock was secured, Kenmuir thrust his own legs backward and out.

The weight of Kenmuir's body and the strength of the encircling grip simultaneously pulled the man backward and down. A hinge was created, with the guard's neck as the hinge's junction. The guard's voice and breath were cut off as his throat was squeezed. His cervical spine was bent radically; an inch or two more and it would snap, having stretched almost as far as it could. But Kenmuir wanted to immobilize him, not kill him.

When the guard lost consciousness, Kenmuir stripped him of his belt, rolled him onto his stomach, and used the belt to tightly bind his arms above the elbows. He'd be out for maybe an hour and, when he woke, he'd be able to stand, but not use his arms. Whatever was coming, Kenmuir figured it would be over in far less than an hour, anyway.

Kenmuir dragged the limp body into the forest and laid it on the carpet of pine needles. He tucked the guard's handgun into his own waistband and quickly returned to the shelter of a tree trunk at the driveway's edge. He looked toward the cabin.

The other guard emerged around the near side of the cabin, walking as casually as before. At the front steps, he looked up the driveway for his partner and shook his head in annoyance. His lips moved. Whatever he said, Kenmuir assumed it wasn't a compliment. The exasperated man threw out his arms in disgust and began to trudge up the hill in a walking tantrum so his partner could see exactly how pissed off he was. He looked neither left nor right, because his partner was straight ahead, up the driveway somewhere, doing god-knows-what.

Like his missing partner five minutes earlier, he didn't give Kenmuir's tree trunk a sideways glance. Again Kenmuir emerged from the shadows, but this time he held a stout tree branch. Absolute silence no longer was critical. Kenmuir swung the branch in a vicious arc, an unwittingly excellent imitation of how "Thumper" Orr once had swung at a high fastball. It smashed into the back of the guard's head, and launched him forward. When he landed, his face scraped across two feet of the gravel surface. Now armed with a second handgun, Kenmuir crept toward the cabin, again staying within the tree line.

The cabin's cavernous living room had numerous animal skins serving as throw rugs. Its walls were adorned with bear traps and old wooden skis with primitive bindings, interspersed among heads of elk, caribou, and even a reindeer. The decor evoked a vigorous outdoor lifestyle and visions of hobnobbing with Jim Sublette and Jim Bridger after the day's hunt. As it happened, MacPherson never had stalked any prey—with the exception of when he was eight years old and had fired a barrage of bee-bees from his Daisy rifle at a blue-bellied lizard innocently sunning itself on the trunk of a Douglas fir. No lizard head was mounted on the cabin wall, however.

Three men were poised in front of a two-story fireplace large enough to roast a BMW. Marini sat in an overstuffed armchair; MacPherson and Poison Colonna, each holding a 9mm Beretta, stood in front of him. Marini knew he was as good as dead.

Marini had gambled that MacPherson would be surprised by his arrival, but not alarmed; after all, he'd been a guest many times. Besides, one minute from the gate to the front porch would've given Petey little time to react. It'd been an acceptable risk, if any risk at all.

When the limousine stopped, MacPherson immediately opened the front door. He held his arms outward for a welcoming hug—the convivial host, delighted by the arrival of his cherished friend and mentor. Marini was pleased his strategy had worked: either MacPherson didn't yet know about Carmel or, if he did, he thought his own position was unthreatened. *You cocky bastard. You'll learn plenty soon enough.*

A Deadly Game

Marini raised his arms reciprocally as he mounted the steps to the wooden deck, flanked by his two bodyguards. When they reached the deck Marini moved toward MacPherson for the ritual greeting. As Marini neared MacPherson, a shot exploded from each open window on either side of the front door. Before disappearing into the darkness of the night, the shots were slowed, but not stopped, by the intervening skulls of Dino and Marini's driver, who'd stood stationary because they'd had no one to hug. In an instant, an unharmed Marini found himself standing in front of two corpses.

Once inside, MacPherson sneered at his former boss. "I believe it was you who taught me never to underestimate an opponent. At the risk of a hasty judgment, it sure looks like *you* have." Marini was ushered at gunpoint into the living room and told to sit wherever he wanted. He chose the armchair. "You really expected me to keep waiting?"

"Your time would've come," Marini replied.

"Too much time. Too long to wait. I'd be too tired to do anything except sit at home and give orders."

"You're doing pretty well."

"Hardly. I know the numbers and how much is there. How much is given to your goombahs, whose only qualifications are having hung on long enough. That's a *club*, Angelo, not a corporation."

Marini nodded. "I guess this means you want a raise."

"You're hopeless. You've never gotten it." MacPherson's expression combined frustration and disdain. "I'm better educated, better informed, and better prepared than you. The only thing I'm not is old. It makes no sense. William Pitt was prime minister at twenty-four. Jeb Stuart was a major general at twenty-nine. Why should I just sit around and wait?"

"So you decided to do something about it."

"That's right, and you never even noticed. While you and your pals were bullshitting, I was building something new. It was perfect."

"Not quite. If it had been, I wouldn't be here."

"There is that, isn't there? Carmel didn't have either the imagination or the steel I gave him credit for. His fault, not mine."

"Wrong, Petey. He was *your* man and *you* picked him. That makes it *your* fault." Marini's controlled temper was revealed by his clenched fists. "So smart. Didn't it occur to you why we avoid headlines?"

"Sure it occurred to me. I just came to a different conclusion. You? Do nothing. Don't try anything new. Don't change with the times. That's not my way. Throughout history, great success has followed the young." MacPherson began to gesture and speak less conversationally. It was as if he were on stage, addressing a seminar: "Tonight only: Jeffrey Pietro MacPherson presents *Why I Succeed*."

"I experimented with the occasional—and profitable, I might add—exception. The fee's *much* larger, and the heat eventually dies down. Besides, it's virtually impossible to find an anonymous shooter, let alone one without any motive. The organization was built on calculated risks, and that's part of the problem: You don't have the guts to take calculated risks anymore."

"Why baseball players?"

"Because that's what the customer wanted. You think *I* picked these guys? I don't like fucking baseball. Hell, I don't even like the customer. But he pays the price—a *big* price, by the way, much more than you'd think—to get the job done. Like you're so fond of preaching, business is business."

Marini nonchalantly crossed his legs. "What do you propose to do with me? Is assassinating a Don just another 'calculated risk'?"

"You're learning, Angelo. You'll show up missing. Same with Tullio. That'll raise some eyebrows. Things'll be tense for awhile. They'll look around, but not too hard. Ask some questions, but not too many. Hard though it may be to believe, you've got enemies. Regardless, why would anyone look in my direction? Your devoted acolyte, Little Petey? After all, I gain nothing from your death because I'm too damn young. Organization'll send someone new and he'll depend on me to show him the ropes. Business as usual. The king is dead; long live the king."

MacPherson turned toward Poison. "Find out what's taking those other two so damn long. Make sure that they put the bodies in the trunk. Then we'll take care of Whopper here."

MacPherson noticed the brief frown on Marini's face. "Don't like that, do you, Angelo? It's what everyone calls you behind your back. You've no idea how much you don't know."

Poison asked, "Want me to do him now?"

"No, we'll wait until we get outside."

It was unlikely that Marini had brought a second car, but MacPherson had ordered his two bodyguards to take a look, just in case. Even if the limousine might have carried a fourth man—extremely unlikely as that was—where would the guy be? Sitting on a stump out by the road in the middle of the night?

Neither Poison nor MacPherson saw Kenmuir enter the living room from the vestibule behind their backs. He was thirty feet away. One of the confiscated handguns was in his right hand. The other was stuck in his waistband. "Hello, boys."

MacPherson was a criminal, but Poison was a killer, whose instincts and experience existed for moments like this. Poison was already pivoting in reaction to the sound of the voice before it even registered on MacPherson.

Poison had to turn all the way around to shoot. Kenmuir didn't.

Kenmuir's first shot entered below Poison's right shoulder blade and went through his right ventricle. His second shot penetrated the right side of his neck and severed his trachea. Either shot would've been fatal, though the second would've taken a moment longer. Poison spun crazily, like a drunken gymnast making a hash out of his floor exercise routine. He crashed over a table and slid to a halt on a throw rug, whose folds gathered comfortingly around him.

As Poison was bouncing off the table, Kenmuir swung his handgun in MacPherson's direction. Knowing he couldn't react as swiftly as Poison, MacPherson had sidestepped away from both Kenmuir's voice and Poison's pirouette. He now pointed his Beretta at Marini's temple. At a mere six feet away from the big target, he couldn't miss. He looked in the direction of the mysterious voice, but his gun hand didn't move.

Kenmuir and MacPherson's eyes locked onto each other. If their eyes had been weapons, both would've died instantly. When Kenmuir's right hand tightened slightly, MacPherson said, "Don't do it. I'll blow his head off."

The three men were as rigid as sculptures. Marini sat motionless, aware of MacPherson's weapon, but staring at Kenmuir. Kenmuir, slightly crouched with his right hand cupped in his left hand, pointed his handgun at MacPherson's chest. MacPherson held his right arm stiffly, a straight line from his shoulder to the barrel of the Beretta. Like Marini, he watched Kenmuir.

MacPherson's voice was mixed with as much curiosity as concern. "Just who the fuck *are* you? You're not one of Angelo's boys because I know them. But I know you from somewhere. Where?"

"I'm a disgruntled investor. Tortilla futures. Me and Jesus LaPera."

MacPherson snorted with disgust. "The wise-ass lawyer. I'm not supposed to ever see you again. Guess Poison screwed up."

"Surprise, surprise. I get around. But, unlike the song, you bad guys didn't leave me alone. And now I've gotten around to you."

MacPherson shrugged. "I deduce that you being here means my cavalry won't be coming to rescue me."

"All too true. A couple of hunting accidents."

"What now?"

"That's up to you, but I'm absolutely sure that I can hold out longer than you. You shoot Marini or so much as twitch that gun in my direction and I'll unload this into you." Kenmuir jabbed the handgun's tip in MacPherson's direction. "Put down your gun, and live to fight another day. That's what happens now."

MacPherson chuckled sarcastically. "Not to be pessimistic, but I doubt that Don Marini would endorse your vision of my survival. Right, Angelo?"

Marini's attention remained riveted on Kenmuir. He didn't look at MacPherson or reply to his question. His silence *was* his answer.

For the first time, MacPherson turned his eyes from Kenmuir and toward the side of Marini's head. "Well, Angelo, like I said, it was a calculated risk. It never had anything to do with you personally. Only with what you represented. For someone who prefers violence to intelligence, this should be a happy ending."

MacPherson moved with surprising quickness to bend his arm at the elbow and cock his wrist. When the muzzle of the Beretta stopped next to his right temple, he pulled the trigger.

Marini stood up and stretched, as if arising from a restful nap. He glanced at MacPherson's lifeless body and then stepped over it. He walked across the room and hesitated in front of Kenmuir. He nodded slightly and then, without any change in his expression, he asked, "You mind driving?"

Chapter 41

*Wednesday afternoon, August 14,
City of Mountain View*

Lunch with Howard Peters was much the same as before, except this time Peters spoke French with the proprietor of Le Bistro. The result was a shared beef filet, resting on a fondue of leek with turned vegetables, in a Dubonnet and orange sauce. And a 1978 Ramonet Batard-Montrachet.

Kenmuir had completed his home-study reading about rotisserie baseball leagues. "I think I get it, Howard, but I'm not positive. I wanted to run it by you."

"Watch out. It's a virus, and there's no cure." Peters laughed in his amiable way.

"Yeah, well, here's what I've been thinking. Orr, for example. If I lose him, then based on last year, I'd lose 41 home runs, 123 RBIs, and a good batting average."

"Right."

"And because all the other productive catchers were taken already by other owners, I'd have to replace him with some ho-hum guy with garbage statistics. Which, in turn, means that I'd lose two to three points in each of those offensive categories."

"Right again."

"When that happens, I figure that I'll drop from, say, third place, to fourth or fifth."

"Not sure about that, but you *will* drop. How far depends on who else is on your team."

"Fair enough. Ditto for a player like Whitney with his ton of strikeouts, maybe fifteen to eighteen wins and a solid ERA. Likewise Fellner with saves. And finally Brittain and Berry." Kenmuir continued after the plates were cleared from the table. "But I'm puzzled by Simon. How's he matter one way or the other?"

"Hard to say. Could've stolen a lot of bases. At the same time, you can't forget that whoever owned Barber was overjoyed. No hotshot rookie to replace him. Once Simon got injured, Barber stayed in the lineup and is actually having a whale of a year."

"So it's simple. Whoever had the six players got hurt badly."

Peters shook his head. "That's *too* simple. No one team would've had all of them. They would've been scattered around. More likely two or three teams got hurt, and one or two others got helped. Even then, it would depend on a team's other players. For example, if Fellner's your only closer, you're ruined in saves. But, if you happen to have two closers, losing one might not be all that bad. It just depends. Regardless, *someone* got helped, either because he moved up or because he had the pitcher who took Fellner's place."

As they ate their desserts—the mixed berries in a zabaglione sauce for Peters and the miniature *soufflé framboise* for Kenmuir—Kenmuir summarized what he learned during his conversation with the owner of Stats For Bats. When he alluded to the prospect of a million-dollar league, Peters rejected it out of hand.

Kenmuir disagreed. "I can't prove it, but I think it's out there. Why else have different statistic services, one in Albany and one in Atlanta and, who knows, maybe one somewhere else, unless you're very, very cautious? It can't be that you need more statistics. Rather, it has to be that you can't be dependent on only one. You have to be able to cross-check them so that, if they match, you can be comfortable that the statistics aren't being manipulated."

Peters smoothed the tablecloth in front of him. "Oh, I understand that part. It makes sense. What doesn't make any sense at all is a million-dollar league."

"Why? Given how much money people gamble in Vegas alone, why be surprised that a dozen high rollers have their own high-stakes fantasy league?"

Peters, still unconvinced, merely shrugged in resignation.

"Anyway, let's assume I'm right. Is there a way for us to confirm the presence of duplicate leagues? Like the Stats for Bats owner says he and his stat buddy discovered, but wouldn't identify for me. Could that be done?"

"A bit tricky. Not insurmountable, but tricky." Peters looked up from his coffee. "Can I assume that you're not a very nimble hacker?"

"No. That would be a misassumption. I am generally regarded as the Wozniak of the legal community."

"So you don't need my help?"

Kenmuir looked at Peters with boyish innocence. "Didn't say that. My expertise is computers and *law*. You may be better at computers and *baseball*."

"Probably." Peters grinned. "Couple days okay?"

"Unless you can do it faster."

Wednesday evening, August 14, City of Walnut Creek

IT WAS THE SECOND GAME in the men's over-forty softball league playoffs. Enchantment Lingerie had survived last week's first game by fortune, not finesse. When an error by their opponent had allowed the winning run to score, they moved on to game two.

As usual, Kenmuir arrived late. He quickly slipped off his hard-soled Minnetonka moccasins and put on his Adidas spikes with the distinctive three stripes on each side. Both brands were his footwear of choice since high school, although he would've scoffed at the notion of brand loyalty.

He made sure that his batting glove fit snugly before putting his Wilson "Tommy John" model glove over it. Last, he straightened his fitted New Era hat with the unmistakable, ornate *B* of the Brooklyn Dodgers, a lingering testimonial to the three parts of the baseball world of his youth: Dodger fans, Yankee fans, and everyone else. Its front was creased at the exact height of a baseball card laid sideways inside the sweatband. Accept no substitutes.

He jogged to second base. It was his favorite part of the game, standing on an infield illuminated by lights on a dark night, scraping his metal cleats in the dirt while waiting for a warm-up ground ball. If only for a few moments, he was twelve years old again.

Their opponent was last year's champion, a team that took both itself and the game too seriously. They wore full uniforms with matching shoes, instead of shirts and Levis like all other teams. Worse, they had a weekly practice, rather than simply showing up on game night. They were referred to lovingly throughout the league as "The Assholes" because they were, in fact, assholes. Unfortunately, they also were very good.

The Assholes scored five times, early and quickly. Enchantment Lingerie's own talent waited until the top of the seventh inning. With one out, the score was 5-3, and Enchantment had runners on first and third. Nelson, their catcher, hit a routine ground ball to the second baseman. Even with the much slower pace of softball, it virtually guaranteed a double play and the end of the inning.

The Assholes' second baseman fielded the ball cleanly, approximately midway between the first and second bases. But he had to hesitate lobbing the ball to the shortstop who'd broken late toward second. When the shortstop relayed the ball to first, the throw was accurate but also late. Safe. The runner on third scored. It became 5-4.

Watching from the bench, Trauber said to Kenmuir, "Last year, that doesn't happen."

Without looking away from the field, Kenmuir said, "What's that mean?"

"Don't you remember that hotshot shortstop they had last year? He was damn good. If he's there, there's no hesitation getting to second or rifling a throw to first. Double play and that's the end of it."

Kenmuir cocked his head toward Trauber. "That tall guy with the Howitzer arm?"

"The same."

"Whatever happened to him?"

"Who knows? But if they could hit the rewind button to last year, it'd still be 5-3."

The rewind button. You pull the present shortstop, plunk in the old one, and then what happens? Double play? Maybe . . . Probably. His mind wandered. *Why not remake history? Enough others have. What if the South had won the Civil War? What if Hitler had invaded England instead of Russia? What if none of the ballplayers had been injured? Just say "never mind," like Emily Litella, Gilda Radner's character, and be done with it.*

Kenmuir didn't notice when Enchantment's next hitter flied out to left. Trauber nudged him lightly on the shoulder. "You coming?"

Kenmuir trotted toward second for the top of the eighth inning. As he did, he thought to himself, *Tomorrow I've got to talk with Howard.*

Chapter 42

*Thursday afternoon, August 15,
City of Mountain View*

When Kenmuir arrived, Peters was ebullient. "They're absolutely identical, Dave. I-den-ti-cal."

"I'll be damned."

Peters cocked his head. "If that's true then you're about to be double-damned. I got curious, so I had a member of my staff search among some of the other statistic services, and he found two more. One in St. Louis and one right down the road in San Jose."

"All identical?"

"Except for variant spellings of a few Hispanic names, they're letter for letter."

Kenmuir lapsed into silence for a moment before asking, "Same teams and same rosters. Same stakes?"

"No way to know. Only lists of twelve names, a bunch of statistics, and the current standings."

"Owners?"

"No. Just team names, like the Walking Wounded, Ronin, Gillotines—the misspelling may mean that it's part of someone's name—and so on. For the owners' names, you'd need the registration list. However, these owners might forego surface mailing in favor of posting on the computer, so there might not be any mailing list, anyway."

"Maybe. But, if they're going to the trouble of having different statistic services, then you'd think they'd want some written records."

"Wouldn't have to come from any stat service, though. They could personally print out whatever they wanted from the daily posting. Can't hurt to ask, though." Peters gave Kenmuir the address of By the Numbers, a stat service in San Jose. "If I can do anything else, let me know."

Genuine music to Kenmuir's ears. "Well, now that you mention it . . ."

Peters shook his head in mock disgust, an imitation of Henry II's lament about Thomas Becket: "Who will rid me of this troublesome lawyer?" He took a deep breath and sighed. "*Then* will you tell me what this is really all about?"

"Is that a condition?"

For the first time, Peters' voice betrayed irritation. "No, but it *is* a request. I may not be able to see all the twists and turns, but I'm not blind. Somehow, and in a way I'm coming to understand, your recent obsession with fantasy baseball has to do with the deaths of Orr and Brittain, and the injuries to the others. Will you grant me at least that much?"

Kenmuir hesitated. He didn't want to involve Peters, but his further help was essential. "Yes, I'll grant you that much. And, if you're patient, I'll tell you about it when it's over. But I badly need something from you right now."

Kenmuir told Peters about his "never mind" idea to revise history by restoring Brittain, Fellner, Orr, Simon, Whitney, and Berry to where they'd be in the fantasy league if they hadn't been injured. "We use last year's stats and assume each would've done exactly the same this year."

"Big assumption. However, I see where you're going. That'll give you at least a somewhat accurate sense of what this year's statistics would be. Or maybe should be."

"Better than that, we can compare how each individual fantasy *team* should have performed and learn how those missing players affected the standings. Or if they made no difference."

"That can be done. It'll take some time, even if we get started right away."

"How much time?"

"Weekend's coming. So Monday, maybe Tuesday. That good enough?"

"That fast?"

Peters chuckled. "Of course. With the computer I can do anything. By Tuesday, at the latest, we'll have changed history."

Chapter 43

Monday morning, August 19, City of Denver

IN LESS THAN TWO WEEKS, the call-ups would start arriving from the minor leagues. September was audition month in the major leagues, when rookies and near rookies would demonstrate whether their success in the minor leagues could be transferred to the major leagues. With rosters expanded from 25 to a maximum of 40 players, they'd replace marginal players who hadn't proven themselves during the long season and relieve veterans who now were weary.

Bryce Henson's Walking Wounded was in first place by six points. The second place Ronin was so vulnerable in several categories that it'd likely lose points before gaining them. The Walking Wounded's lead might not be commanding, but it was comfortable. More importantly, Henson knew that statistics after September tended to stabilize due to the shuffle in the major league rosters and the fantasy league standings consequently tended to achieve a kind of equilibrium. He tried not to be cocky, but he was confident.

The final standings were mere six weeks away. Six weeks separated him from nearly $10 million . . . It was his new mantra:

ten million! . . . Then retirement: probably San Diego, maybe Scottsdale . . . Ten million . . . No more snow and a lot of golf . . . A million times ten . . . Screw the bastards who undercut his business. Multimillionaire. No more debt, no taxes and all the leisure time in the world.

The Plan—*his* plan—had worked. He'd found a way. Untraceable and undetectable. Perfect. A plan of genius; it was a shame that he'd be the only one who'd ever know. But *he* did know. Oh, yeah, he knew . . . Ten million.

Okay, technically not $10 million. It'd cost slightly over a million to pull it off, but who wouldn't spend a million to net nine? No one with even half his brains, that's who. He'd spent it, and he'd won. That's what separated a winner like him from the losers: boldness and daring. Hallmarks of a great commander.

Sometimes, he thought about the players. First, Brittain. Then Simon and Orr, Fellner and Whitney and, finally, Berry. After all, he wasn't insensitive or heartless. He truly regretted what had happened to Brittain and Orr. No one was supposed to die. He'd said so in no uncertain terms, so he couldn't be blamed for the incompetence of others. No, his Plan had been flawless; it had been no less so because of others' blunders.

He'd learned in the Army a long time ago that sometimes a few have to be sacrificed in order to achieve a great result. Can't make an omelet without breaking some eggs, as the saying went. Leaders, the great men, made such decisions. He'd think of them all . . . during his retirement.

Nothing stood between him and $10 million. Nothing.

A Deadly Game

Monday morning, August 19, City of Mountain View

KENMUIR AND PETERS SAT IN A spacious conference room, with a wall of windows on one end and an audio-visual complex on the other. In between was a twenty-foot conference table, inlaid with stylized and irregular representations of bursts of light: Phosphenes, like the company name,

Two parallel lines of papers were arranged on the massive table. Peters stood in front of them like a docent ready to begin a tour. "Not exactly reliable with a high degree of scientific precision. I know several professors at Stanford who'd shudder at all the assumptions we've made. But, if we don't have the truth, we're very close."

He motioned in a sweeping gesture toward the two lines of papers. "In the reconstructed model, the first place team, the Walking Wounded, falls to third and very nearly to fourth. The second-place Ronin takes the lead, but the sixth-place Whackers leaps all the way to second."

Kenmuir stared at the sheet that Peters had handed him. "What can I say? I didn't think it would make that much difference. Amazing."

"Frankly, neither did I, but that's because I was thinking in absolute terms, only about the totals. And, as it turned out, the absent players didn't make much of a difference there. But *comparatively?* That was another story.

"In several instances, the amounts were so close that a minor alteration had a major impact. Kinda like a little pebble making big ripples in a pond." Peters shuffled a few sheets of paper. "Here, take a look at home runs. The first-place Walking Wounded—which, by the way, has glided through the season with almost no injuries despite its pessimistic name—has the second-highest home run total: eleven points out of twelve.

"Now we started to have fun. We fed back the presumed home runs of Orr, Brittain, and Berry, and made a partial adjustment for Barber. Voila! The Walking Wounded declined from second place in that category to fourth—which, in turn, meant a drop from eleven points out of twelve to nine. Similarly, when Fellner's saves were added back, the Walking Wounded *and* the Ronin lost a point, but the Whackers gained three. And so on and so on." He pointed triumphantly at the sheets. "You can see for yourself."

"I do see. Why didn't all the teams move proportionately and remain the same in comparison to each other?"

"The answer lies in the comparative distribution of statistics. The Whackers' strength is in hitting, while the Ronin's is pitching. Four of the six injured ballplayers were hitters, and only two were pitchers. Therefore, the missing statistics had roughly twice the impact on the hitting categories as on the pitching categories. You have to feel especially sorry for the Whackers—last year's winner and maybe that's not just coincidental, by the way—because it's almost as if someone gunned directly for it; it'd had Brittain and Orr and lost them both! On the other hand, the Walking Wounded has to cheer. It wouldn't be in first place otherwise." Peters sat down and crossed his arms. "Okay, I've done my part. Do I get to learn what this is all about?"

"Yes, Howard, you do. When it's over, we'll have lunch, and I'll lay it all out. Just bear with me a little longer."

Peters pursed his lips and nodded in understanding. "It's like one of those multipart series where you have to wait for weeks to find out how it ends. I hate them, too. What's next?"

"Like the song says, I'm going to find my way to San Jose."

"San Jose?"

"That's the closest of the statistic services that you told me were monitoring this league. I've got both versions of the numbers, thanks to you. Now I need a few names."

Chapter 44

Thursday evening, August 22, City of San Jose

During the day, Kent Hooke worked as a personnel analyst for Santa Clara County. In the evening, he sequestered himself in the converted guest room above his garage. Perhaps predictably, he lived alone. His statistics service, By the Numbers, was as much a business as a hobby. Half of the room was devoted to computers and ceaseless statistics; the other half was divided between a massive photocopier and a postage machine, separated by a large table stacked with mailing envelopes. When baseball season ended, he shifted to football and then to basketball. Each sport had its own rotisserie leagues. Fantasy had no limit.

Hooke was reluctant to meet with Kenmuir. He preferred the telephone, since his business wasn't set up for guests, and his time in the evening was limited. Why not just ask what you want over the telephone?

Like all salesmen, Kenmuir knew it's too easy to say no over the telephone. Hang up and the unwanted visitor disappears. If Hooke were to be persuaded to reveal names, it'd have to be eye to eye. Hooke relented after Kenmuir mentioned Peters' name.

Hooke could've served as the final exam at a tailoring school: his torso had narrow shoulders and a sunken chest that suddenly expanded into a dirigible stomach, and was supported by whopping thighs. He may have had the physique of a gourd rather than a guard, but no Swiss banker guarded his numbered accounts better than Hooke did "his" fantasy leagues. "Look, I understand that anyone can look up a league on the net. But not the names of the owners who depend on me for confidentiality." Hooke took himself *very* seriously.

"Frankly, Kent, I doubt any of them give a damn. They use cute team names because that's part of the fun. They don't care about anonymity."

"They certainly do. They don't want to be pestered by every Tom, Dick, or Harry who's curious about their teams."

County personnel files have to be awfully safe with this guy. God help you if you want to find out about an employee carpool. "I appreciate your discretion. Really, I do. On the other hand, are fantasy groupies much of a problem? I mean, how many times have you been asked for owners' names?"

"Never," Hooke said proudly. "I think people understand they can be assured of privacy when they subscribe to By the Numbers."

The soft-sell approach brought Kenmuir around the same circle five times in twenty minutes. A change in tactics was overdue. "I hoped to get this information from you informally, Kent. As it happens, I'm not a newspaper reporter, and I'm not doing an article on fantasy leagues. I'm a lawyer." Kenmuir handed a business card to Hooke. "And this particular league is the subject of some serious allegations." *Not quite true, but close enough.*

"A lawyer? You lied to me?"

"Yes, I did. And I regret that. But I did because I hoped I wouldn't have to get you involved."

The overweighted swivel chair creaked as Hooke leaned forward. "What d'you mean *involved*? I'm not *involved* in anything. I provide statistics. That's all."

Kenmuir adopted his serious-lawyer, no-fooling-around look. "I tend to believe you, but it's not that simple. This is a *very* heavy case, with significant allegations of fraud and misrepresentation, to say nothing of the possibility of punitive damages." An allusion to punitive damages, rare as they were, never failed to intimidate non-lawyers. Hooke was no exception.

"*Punitive*!? That's got to be just so much bullshit. I put statistics into a computer and mail the results. What's wrong with that?"

"I don't doubt that you'll be able to prove that, but you know how it is: the mail goes across state lines and that involves federal law. When you add fraud, it becomes complicated." Kenmuir stood up as if to leave. "Look, I won't bother you further. I'll simply subpoena your records, which is what I probably should've done in the first place. Unfortunately, that'll cause some delay in your work here. But no longer than four or five weeks, six at the most."

Hooke had the look of a man trying to eat his first oyster. "Six weeks? It's near the end of the season! I can't be shut down like that. I've got twenty-five leagues!"

Kenmuir sidled toward the door. "That's what I was trying to avoid and why I came personally. Hoped we could work something out, you know, informally. But I respect your decision that confidentiality can't be sacrificed. Not for any reason."

A hardened veteran of civil service infighting, Hooke hadn't survived ugly personnel disputes without being resourceful. "Would anyone have to know where you got the mailing list?"

Kenmuir paused thoughtfully, as if considering such a creative alternative. "Well, now that you mention it, I don't suppose that'd be necessary. I'd have the information I need, and I don't think the other lawyers—or the judge, for that matter—would care where it came from."

He nodded his head in silent agreement with Hooke's inspired suggestion. "No, I don't think I would have to tell anyone ... No ... I can guarantee that you'd never be bothered by me or the case again."

Hooke spun his swivel chair toward the computer. His fingers moved rapidly over the keyboard, and the laser printer hummed into action. Hooke grabbed two pieces of paper that emerged from the printer and handed them over. "There. That's what you want and all I've got."

Kenmuir skimmed the list of unfamiliar names and addresses. Tadashi Okumoto in Tokyo, J.P. Gill in Knoxville. It was the name of the league-leading Walking Wounded, registered in care of a Denver business, where Kenmuir stopped skimming.

The letters in that name seemed to triple in size as they also seemed to tremble: The name was Bryce Henson.

Kenmuir was at once paralyzed and transfixed. *My god. Surely it can't be. How could it be possible? Not* Captain *Henson. It can't be. But it has to be. Doesn't it? How could it not be?*

Chapter 45

Monday morning, August 26, City of Denver

O<small>N FRIDAY, KENMUIR HAD CALLED HENSON'S</small> secretary and introduced himself as Major Ruggles, an old Army buddy. He was going to be in town and hoped to surprise "Captain" Henson. Was he going to be in town on Monday? She'd responded enthusiastically that a surprise reunion was a wonderful idea. "Oh, yes, Mr. Henson will be in the office all day on Monday." Now a fellow conspirator, she confirmed her ability to keep a secret. Even if she couldn't, Kenmuir knew that he wouldn't be alarmed by an unexpected visit from Major Ruggles, the brigade's former XO.

The Monday morning flight from Oakland International Airport reached Denver in a little over two hours. No baggage, a rental car—and in less than an hour later, the receptionist on the twelfth floor of the downtown office building was telling Henson's secretary, "Mr. Ruggles is here."

The secretary was a dowdy woman with a bright smile and a cheerful face. Her hairstyle and clothes were refugees from the early 1970s. "Mr. Ruggles? I'm so glad to meet you."

Kenmuir reciprocated her warm handshake. "Does Bry suspect anything?"

She looked truly astonished. "Oh, no. I haven't said a word. If you knew me better, you'd know how much I love surprises. He'll be surprised, won't he?"

Kenmuir smiled. "I think that's putting it mildly."

She led Kenmuir down an aisle to a corner office. The closed door had no name on the front. "What do you want me to do? Should I announce you?"

"Well, if someone just knocks at the door, what does he usually do?"

"He asks 'what?' or says 'come in' or something like that."

"Good. Let's make it a complete surprise. I'll be the one who knocks. When he says come in, I will." He chuckled, as if enjoying the forthcoming surprise.

"That's a good idea. I'm right down the hall. You be sure to tell me how he reacted."

"I definitely will. Thank you."

Kenmuir felt a pounding in his heart, tension in his arms, and dryness in his mouth. He blamed Henson for what he *did do* to Stuart Unit, but he blamed himself even more for what he *didn't do:* He didn't believe Colgan as soon as he should have . . . He didn't disobey orders, even though they came from Henson . . . He didn't order his men—lead them, really—out soon enough or fast enough. They'd counted on him to save them and he hadn't. As a practical matter, he'd abandoned them. He'd allowed them to die.

Henson had forced Kenmuir into a physical position from which he couldn't escape and thus condemned him to an emotional position from which he couldn't recover, ever. How he hated him for that. He wanted to walk through the door and kill the bastard. That'd be an even better surprise.

A Deadly Game

He waited until the secretary disappeared around the corner before knocking on the door. When a voice on the other side told him to come in, he did. With the exception of hair graying around the edges and Ben Franklin reading glasses, Henson was unchanged. His fatigue uniform was replaced by a starched white shirt and regimental-striped tie. He looked every bit the part of an executive.

Kenmuir wanted Henson to be shocked. Instead, he was merely bewildered. Obviously, some visitor had wandered into the wrong office. "Can I help you?"

Kenmuir shut the door, but didn't respond to the question. He walked halfway toward the desk without detecting a glimmer of recognition. Then he said, "Hello, Captain."

Henson took off his glasses and simultaneously rose from his chair. Suddenly he knew—and now was visibly shocked. "Kenmuir?"

"That's right, Captain. How ya been?"

Henson was completely baffled. Kenmuir cherished the moment. "How . . . what . . . I mean, good to see you. What a surprise."

Kenmuir sat down in one of the client chairs in front of Henson's desk. He made no effort to shake hands. The absence of the ritual gesture of friendship wasn't lost on Henson. He repeatedly shifted his weight from one foot to the other, but kept the desk between him and Kenmuir like the wall of a castle. Ever the gifted tactician.

Kenmuir enjoyed his discomfort. "Sit down, Captain. Relax."

Henson lowered himself tentatively to the edge of his chair. If necessary, he could bolt from it in an instant. He didn't relax.

"You're looking good. Of course, I heard that you and the other guy…"

"Sergeant Trauber."

"… yes, Trauber. That you and he made it after we were overrun."

"*We* weren't overrun, Captain. Only my men and I were. You were upstairs in a chopper, playing general. Roger that, Captain?"

Henson leaned his elbows onto his desk, but stayed on the edge of his chair. "That's crap. Intelligence reported a company. If I thought it was more, I'd have gotten you out of there." Henson squinted and looked as if he'd just had an important insight. "*That's* why you've showed up after all these years? To blame me for what happened in combat?"

Kenmuir deliberately emptied a small wooden container of paper clips on the surface of Henson's desk. He moved the makeshift ashtray to the edge of the desk and lit a cigarette. A conscientious Mormon like Henson loathed smoking, but he said nothing.

"No, though it'd be tempting. Can't tell you how disappointed I was that you didn't stop by when I was in the hospital. Colonel Gibson did—and he told me what you actually were supposed to be doing upstairs. Or, maybe more to the point, *not* supposed to be doing. He also told me about your transfer. Made me real happy."

Henson's face reddened slightly. "I was transferred preparatory to a promotion. Broaden my experience. I earned it."

"Yeah, the colonel told me that's how he dished it up to you. But you can trust me on this one, Captain: you were banished." Kenmuir exhaled a particularly large volume of smoke across

Henson's desk. It rose from the top of the desk like a Scottish mist.

Henson stood up again. "I don't need this. You've clearly got some personal issues and need to blame someone else for your men getting killed. I was sorry then, and I'm sorry now, but it wasn't my fault. Why don't you get the hell out of here and take your grudges with you?"

Kenmuir took another drag on his cigarette. He leaned further back in his chair. He showed no sign of getting the hell out of anywhere.

Henson rested his left hand on top of his telephone. "I don't want to call security, but I will if I have to. I think you'd better leave before this gets messy."

"Messy? What're you going to do, Captain? You aren't up in the air this time. Want to bet that I can be behind that desk before your finger so much as touches the dial?" Kenmuir smashed out his cigarette in the paper-clip container.

Henson's eyes widened. It was hard to say if they betrayed anger or fear. Either way, his left hand moved off the surface of his phone. "You always did get in the way, Kenmuir. Nothing's changed. So say what you've got to say and then leave."

"That I will, Captain, that I will. And I never got in your way. You were just gutless. If someone *did* get in your way, you didn't have the balls to take him on directly. The more I thought about it, lying in that hospital bed, the more it dawned on me how you'd arranged to get rid of people in your sneaky, backstabbing way. Lieutenant Wilson, that poor son-of-a-bitch, reassigned to the Bloody Angle because you thought he was disrespectful. Captain Gorman, dead because some fucked-up private supposedly went berserk all of a sudden? Nah. I don't believe it. You somehow put him up to it so you could get Gorman's command. No way to prove it, but that didn't mean it didn't happen. And I was next, wasn't I . . . Captain?"

Henson feigned a look of boredom. "You're starting to repeat yourself, Lieutenant."

Kenmuir nodded in agreement. "You're right, I am. So how about a change of subject? Let's talk about . . . oh, I don't know, let's just pick a topic at random. How about fantasy baseball?"

Henson reacted as abruptly as if he'd been stabbed with a cattle prod. "Fantasy baseball? What the hell's that?"

"Spare me, Captain. I know all about the Walking Wounded, and the million-dollar league, and what you've done."

Muscles quivered on the side of Henson's jaw. "You're a sick man, Kenmuir, you know that? You need help. Badly. I don't know anything about some, what, fantasy league."

"Sure you do." Kenmuir reached inside his coat and withdrew two sheets of paper that were folded into thirds. He opened and smoothed them, then sailed them across the surface of the desk.

"What's this supposed to be?"

"That's a list of names. You'll recognize them. The owners in a certain fantasy league. You'll note the second-to-last name."

"All right, I play fantasy baseball. So what?"

"Now take a look at these." Kenmuir slid a second set of papers, still folded, across the desk.

Henson didn't bother to look at them. "More lists?"

"In a sense. There're two sets of computer printouts. They show what the league's standings are now and what they would've been without your arranging to eliminate six of the finest players in the American League."

"You've got some kind of proof? Other than your own sad delusions?"

"Oh, yeah. Records of payments and the confession of the guy you hired to do it."

Henson's laugh was somewhere between hysteria and derision. "You don't have shit. And you don't because it doesn't exist. You've nursed so much hatred for me over the years that you've lost touch with reality. I feel sorry for you."

"We'll see."

"No, Lieutenant, it's just like 'Nam. You operate by instinct. You don't plan, you only see what's in front of you. If you had any proof, I'd be talking with the police. Oh, you might be with them because you'd want to see it, but *they* aren't here. You know why?"

Kenmuir lit another cigarette and exhaled the first drag before he spoke. "Why don't you tell me."

"Because any plan of mine—if there really was one—would be perfect. No records and no confessions." He tossed the folded printouts back in Kenmuir's direction. "Here's what I think of your suspicions. Yes, I'm a participant in this league. Yes, my team is the Walking Wounded. And yes, I'm winning—fair and square, no matter what you think. Fortunately, neither I nor anyone else gives a damn what you think."

Yes and no. No, you aren't winning fair and square. Yes, no proof exists anywhere. MacPherson and Poison kept no records except in their own heads, and that filing system's been shut down definitively. Any phone messages have been long since deleted, and you'd have to have been an idiot to pay anything by traceable check.

Kenmuir had come to Denver for two reasons. First, for a form of revenge, inadequate and insufficient though it might be, by making Henson realize that sacrificing Stuart Unit was neither misunderstood nor forgotten. Second, to watch Henson wilt and then be lured into doing something incriminating. However, when he saw the smug captain perched in his neat office, he understood his self-deception and remembered what all prosecutors learn early: spontaneous confessions occur only in television dramas like *Perry Mason*.

Henson was contemptible, but he also was invulnerable. Kenmuir could badger him all day, describe in detail what he'd done, and how he'd done it. But the evidentiary reality was that Henson might have $10 million worth of motive, but he didn't have ten cents worth of means. A businessman in Denver engineer the deaths or wounding of six professional baseball players? How the hell'd he pull *that* off?

Henson was correct. His plan had been perfect. He'd never be prosecuted.

Kenmuir stood up as he smashed a second cigarette into the wooden container. "I wanted to see you, Captain. Now that I have, I'll never see you again."

Kenmuir walked out of the office, leaving the door open.

Chapter 46

Thursday evening, September 12, City of Oakland

When Kenmuir asked to use the A's owners' box, Smith was glad to oblige, if only because the box wasn't in demand for a Thursday night game at the end of the season. Kenmuir invited Marini, who seemed flattered. Kenmuir doubted the big man received many social invitations.

The A's had rebounded from their early season miseries after the loss of Thumper Orr. They compensated for diminished power with pinpoint pitching and speedy opportunism. As pitching and defense restricted the other team to a paltry number of runs scored, the offense put together a few singles, bunts, and stolen bases to score enough to win. Tonight, however, it was apparent by the third inning that this was to be one of those lackluster 2-1 games, where one is treated to neither great hitting nor great pitching. Just another baseball game.

The suburban lawyer and the criminal kingpin, surely the most incongruous pair ever to sit in the owners' box, enjoyed the kind of aimless conversation that men have during ball games. Marini could indulge himself because Kenmuir was neither rival nor sycophant. It was as close as he could come to being merely one of the guys. Kenmuir wondered out loud whether the tragedies of the season made any real difference to the teams themselves.

Marini shelled a few more peanuts from his jumbo bag but answered, "Of course they made a difference. They left a sour taste on the whole season."

"That's not what I mean. The A's were supposed to finish third or fourth, but here they are, close to first even without Orr. The Indians ended up exactly where everyone expected they would, with or without Whitney. The Blue Jays stumbled on this kid Merriam, and Fellner may be out of a job when he does come back. The Mariners moved Joey Alamoggi to first base in Brittain's place and traded for Billy Bonko to play in the outfield. Everything changes and everything remains the same."

"Not for me. Lost my favorite player, Orr." Marini pulverized another peanut shell. "I'm a regular. My own seats, right over there." He pointed vaguely in the direction of third base. "But after Thumper got himself killed, it *wasn't* the same. Kinda lost interest. And that pissed my ass off."

I know it did, Kenmuir thought. *How much, that's the question.*

The score was still 2-1 after two more innings and the fans succumbed to dull disinterest. Marini turned to Kenmuir and said, "You're awfully quiet all of a sudden."

"Sorry, I was thinking about MacPherson."

"Well, don't. We've had guys like him before. Think they can get away with something. They never do. Always ends the same way. Fuck 'em. Can't believe I didn't see it, though. It's a good reminder. Trust no one."

"Lonely way to live, Angelo."

Marini looked back toward the field. "My business, Kenmuir, not yours."

Kenmuir slumped in his chair and draped his legs over the back of the empty seat in front of him. He tilted his head back and exhaled smoke into the cloudless sky. "Speaking of business, what's been the reaction in the, ah, 'investment community' to dear Petey's disappearance?"

Marini kept his eyes toward the field. "Let's just say that, after some initial surprise on the East Coast, his absence has been accommodated."

Kenmuir hesitated before asking his next question, "And your trusty companion? Any reaction to his subtle role in the process?" He *had* to learn if he'd be dislocating vertebra the rest of his life as a result of looking over his shoulder.

"You know how it is with these corporate reorganizations, counselor. Some details always get lost in the shuffle. His name never came up. Once one is satisfied that there's a legitimate reason *why*, there's almost no interest in *how*. Rest assured that you'll hear nothing further on this topic." Marini resumed the crushing of peanuts.

In what had become their trademark style, the A's inconspicuously mounted a rally. There was a single and a steal of second. A sacrifice bunt turned into another single when the third baseman worried more about the runner on second and less about his own fielding. The throw to first was late. One out, two on. A rumble of renewed interest rolled through the awakened small crowd of fans.

"Sixth inning, counselor. I appreciate the invitation and all, but it's long past time that you brought me up to date."

"Up to date?"

"Please. You've been busy. I assume you've found out who hired Petey."

"Yes, but I'll never be able to prove it."

"Let's worry about that later. Go ahead and tell me what you know."

Kenmuir told him. From his discovery of the million-dollar league to Peters' reconstructed statistics, to the list of fantasy league owners, to the confrontation with Henson.

Marini lit a Pall Mall. "You don't like this guy, do you?"

"Would you?"

"No, the fucker's scum. There's more to it than that, though, isn't there?"

"Why do you say that?"

"Your choice of words. Your tone of voice. Look at your hands." Kenmuir self-consciously opened his fists. "I'd like to hear the *whole* story. I gather that it's personal, so you decide. But I'd like to hear it."

After Kenmuir finished, Marini ground out a cigarette in the mound of peanut shells. "Didn't know you'd been in that kind of shit. The war and all. Wrote up your . . . talents . . . to being an ex-cop. Makes more sense now."

Marini lapsed into silence as if watching the end of the A's rally. The runner on third scored on a sacrifice fly before an inning-ending ground out. As the teams exchanged places on the field, Marini glanced in Kenmuir's direction. "You're certain about all this? No bullshit? No lawyer speculations?"

"Oh, I'm sure. I'm the one who talked with him over the radio. I know firsthand what he did in the 'Nam. As for this fantasy thing, he's the one who benefits. If those six players had played like they should have, he'd be a loser."

"Evidently, but that doesn't necessarily mean he's responsible. Could be the luck of the draw. Maybe someone else did it, but didn't get the benefit that he did. Wouldn't be the first plan that backfired."

"He's cagey and he's cocky, but he slipped up in referring to a plan. *His* plan. I heard him loud and clear. Truth be known, I think he meant for me to. Besides, it's what he'd do. Set up someone else and then hide in the background."

"Well, not every crime gets solved, and not every criminal gets caught." Marini laughed. "Hell, here I am. Or so say the local police." As Marini mangled another peanut, his eyes locked on Kenmuir's. He said nothing and, after a moment, returned his attention to the baseball field.

Chapter 47

Wednesday morning, October 9, City of Denver

THE FINAL STANDINGS FOR THE million dollar league, Henson's league, were published on Tuesday. Two of Henson's fellow owners already had telephoned to congratulate him. He was gracious and self-effacing, humbly referring to his good luck and joking that someone had to win. The time for bragging would wait until the annual black-tie dinner in November. As this year's winner, he'd act as host. A check would be handed to him by last year's winner. Ten million dollars.

To one caller he remarked that, next year, he'd probably be the one making the congratulatory telephone call. *Sic transit gloria*, he said. He knew better, though: there'd be no next year. In January or February, he'd send a letter announcing his forced retirement for reasons of health. The reduced financial circumstances of retirement would preclude his continued participation, with reluctance and great regret, etc. As a sort of moral atonement for the bad form of dropping out as a winner, he'd donate $250,000.00 to the pot. Any disgruntled suspicions would be allayed by that grand gesture.

He had much to do. First, discreetly seek a buyer for his company. Among several very promising prospects was, ironically, Atashi Industries. When Okumoto had called in August to discuss a fantasy-league trade, they'd ended up talking about a reality purchase instead. Second, put his home on the market. The sale of such a desirable home was all but guaranteed, according to the real estate broker.

He was as good as gone.

His secretary came into his office carrying a gaily wrapped package tied with red ribbon. "Hand delivered. I took the liberty of removing the outer wrapping. It feels like a jewelry box." She handed him an envelope with the word "Champ" on the front. It held a greeting card with the caricature of a large woman dressed like a Viking, with part of an orchestra silhouetted in front of her. *It Ain't Over 'Til The Fat Lady Sings* was printed inside. Handwritten below those words was a brief message, "Congratulations. The fat lady's sung."

Henson picked up the package. It was large, as if two shoe boxes were placed side by side. He could feel an indentation around the sides like, well, a jewelry box. "Thank you. I think I'll open it later."

He had no intention of waiting. He merely wanted to savor the moment privately. She left and closed the solid-core wooden door soundlessly behind her. She'd been his father's secretary and had taken very good care of them both. He'd miss her. He turned the package over and tore away a corner where the wrapping paper joined. Tissue paper was underneath. He tore a corner of that as well. He was teasing himself.

He saw a highly-polished wooden surface underneath. Cherry or maybe mahogany, he thought. It was a lovely present. He carried the package to the other side of his desk. He pushed his executive chair back and withdrew a pair of scissors from his middle desk drawer. Behind him, the sun broke through the thick layer of clouds that had blanketed Denver all morning. Sunlight suddenly illuminated his office. Because he was standing in front of the panoramic window, his body cast a shadow over the package.

He cut the ribbon and replaced the scissors in the drawer. He was a tidy man. A place for everything and everything in its place. He unfurled the ribbon and tossed it in the wastebasket, then slid his index finger within the folds of the wrapping paper and tore away the tape that held it together. He removed the paper and folded it tightly and compactly. It was the same elaborate and prolonged way he opened Christmas and birthday presents. He loved presents and derived great pleasure from drawing out the suspense. Drove his family crazy.

He wadded the layer of tissue paper and threw it into the wastebasket. Underneath it was a gleaming wooden box with beveled edges. It had no latch or other fastener. It was shaped and fitted like the kind of elegant box that once served to hold a matched set of dueling pistols. It was a beautiful piece of work.

He opened the box. It glided open on unseen hinges, ever so quietly sliding against the velvet edge of its interior lining. He was stunned. The interior was lined in black velvet and contained two rows of three unstained and pristine baseballs. Six small indentations were crafted into the interior lid and six larger indentations into the base. When the box closed, each cushioned indentation surrounded a baseball.

He picked up one of the baseballs. It had a signature written in red ink. Six autographed baseballs. A very thoughtful and fitting gift. He turned the baseball in his hand and looked at the signature. Even without his glasses, he read the name clearly enough: *Humphrey Orr*.

Hurriedly, he grabbed each of the other five baseballs. Like the first, each was signed:

Brent Brittain.
Achilles Simon.
Ferdinand Fellner.
Woodrow Whitney.
Paul Berry.

Under the velvet, the indentations for the six autographed baseballs were formed out of plastique, rather than Styrofoam, foam rubber or cardboard. Plastique is a benign and malleable substance, much like modeling clay—until it's paired with a detonating device. Then it becomes troublesome.

In this instance, the detonator was triggered by pressure—or, more accurately, by the absence of pressure. The box and the detonator within it were designed to accommodate the weight of six baseballs, no more and no less. As long as the detonator was comforted by that weight, the plastique remained harmless. However, when that weight was decreased—by someone, say, picking up one of the baseballs to examine it—the detonator was immediately and irreversibly activated.

The detonator had a slight delay. The designer wanted the box's recipient to have the chance to look at each baseball. After all, what's more disappointing than giving a gift that can't be fully appreciated?

The explosion blinded the recent winner of the million-dollar fantasy league, though he didn't realize it. His body was blown apart in less than an instant and, with the exception of the right foot that remained behind in a highly polished Cole-Haan black wing-tip shoe, hurled out the picture window amid fragments of glass. High above Denver, the sun slipped back behind the cover of the clouds.

Epilogue

In early October, Kenmuir received an envelope containing only a clipping from the *Denver Post*. It reported the death of one of the city's most prominent citizens. An act of terrorism was suspected, though no one could explain why such an uncontroversial businessman would be a terrorist target. Police were baffled.

Later, the deceased man's business was purchased by Atashi Industries, a Japanese company. The price was undisclosed, but was rumored to be much lower than expected, because the business was not nearly as sound or as profitable as it seemed.

By the beginning of the new baseball season in April, the bizarre tragedies of the previous year hadn't been forgotten, but they'd been accommodated. Teams adjusted and commentators commented. All agreed that Fate could be unkind and that Fame was no protection against human suffering.

The Phoenix City Council passed an ordinance banning the use of dirt bikes on Pinnacle Peak. Dirt bikers largely ignore it.

Achilles Simon lost half a stride and his nickname with it. "Blaze" no more, he still ran fast enough to be promoted to the major leagues as a reserve outfielder.

Ferdinand "Frisky" Fellner recovered physically from his leg injuries, but the lingering discomfort affected his pitching rhythm. What had been an uncanny ability to paint the corners turned into a terrifying tendency to get shelled. By midseason he decided to quit. He bought a hardware store in his home town in Iowa. He is, as he always was, a local hero.

Woodrow "Woody" Whitney returned to the Cleveland Indians with a scar on his left hand and a new respect for the dangers of window-shopping. As dominant as ever, he was chosen for that year's All-Star game.

Paul Berry recovered sufficiently to join Whitney on the All-Star team. He's repeatedly asked if his bark is worse than his bite.

The Oakland Athletics wanted to erect a statue in honor of Humphrey "Thumper" Orr. The original design depicted him in the squatted posture of a catcher behind the plate. One irreverent executive thought it looked less like a catcher than someone in a baseball uniform taking a dump. Fearing that the statue might eventually be referred to as "Dumper," the designers changed the posture to one of a batter ready to hit a home run. The statue stands proudly near the entrance of the Oakland Coliseum.

In the midst of her shock and grief following the death of her husband, Mrs. Henson found a plain, unstamped envelope in her mailbox. It contained a cashier's check, drawn on a Panamanian bank and made payable to her alone, for $1 million. "Return of dues" was written in the lower left corner.

The existence of a million-dollar league remains a persistent rumor in fantasy league circles.

Kenmuir and Lucy date regularly and have spent several weekends at Kenmuir's cabin at Lake Tahoe. Both evasively describe their relationship as "mutual," but "not serious."

A Deadly Game

John Trauber talked Kenmuir into co-owning a fantasy league team that they named "Jailbaiters." They regularly argue about strategy: Kenmuir wants to trade with other teams, but Trauber is so emotionally attached to "his" players that he can't bear to part with any of them. The team isn't doing very well. Their entry fee was substantially less than a million dollars.

Kenmuir was Marini's guest at the A's opening game of the new season. Two behemoths wearing very large coats were seated nearby.

Acknowledgments

At different times during the protracted evolution of this novel, I benefitted from the gracious reading and comments of mystery-thriller fan Noel Roberson, old friend Steven Phillip Smith, fellow Army lieutenant Bruce Brittain, and my wife Tessa. I am grateful to all of them.

I would never have finished without the patient and generous counsel of novelist Camille Minichino, who struggled to teach me about the writing of fiction, critiqued my efforts, and unfailingly buoyed my spirits.

At least I did know how to read and write; I knew nothing about the logistics of publishing. I am thus very grateful to Clark Sturgess (Devil Mountain Press), Jackie Pels (Hardscratch Press), and Dave Johnson for their guidance.

That a number of the novel's characters have names the same or reminiscent of some of my friends is intended as a compliment, not a depiction of personality or style.

About the author

G₁ARY M. L₁EPPER, ₁A ₁TRIAL ₁LAWYER, lives in Walnut Creek, California.